Stephanie
You are a
sweet
blessing.

Sweet Rivalry

Jaye Gillespie

Zeph. 3:17

Endorsements

Secrets, heartbreaking memories, and sister rivalries threaten to destroy the beginnings of a fragile relationship between twins long separated by the trauma of their mother's addiction. Forgiveness, unconditional love, and team building might be the answer . . . but dare these sisters risk more hurt to realize their dream of family? Laced with the love of baking—including tantalizing recipes and an exciting, televised baking competition—Terri Gillespie paints a vivid and heartwarming picture of a family broken, but working together, ultimately transformed through their budding and building relationship with the God who loves them most and who inspires their creative spirits. A faith-yielding, faith-building book to swell the heart.

—**Cathy Gohlke**, multi-Christy Award-winning author of *Night Bird Calling*

"With a well woven plot and wonderfully unique characters, *Sweet Rivalry* grabbed my heart from the first page! Terri Gillespie skillfully combines, realistic faith elements, with challenging family dynamics, romance, and a touch of mystery in this moving story about twin sisters who were separated when they were young and reunited in their twenties. Those who enjoy meaningful contemporary stories with heartfelt family themes will love this novel. Well written and highly recommended."

—**Carrie Turansky**, award-winning author of *No Ocean Too Wide* and *No Journey Too Far*

In *Sweet Rivalry*, author Terri Gillespie puts on her chef's hat and mixes up a story with some tantalizing ingredients! A movie-worthy premise—long-separated twin sisters with opposite personalities who share a mutual flair for baking—pairs well with a delightfully twisty-turny plot. Gillespie deftly folds in a strong spiritual thread, laugh-out-loud dialogue, and fabulous characters. As a bonus, descriptions of decadent bakery delights are sprinkled throughout this oh-so-charming book. You'll savor every scrumptious word!

—**Laurel Blount,** award-winning author of *Love Inspired, Lost and Found Faith*

Sweet Rivalry

Terri Gillespie

ELK LAKE PUBLISHING INC

PUBLISHING THE POSITIVE
Plymouth, Massachusetts

Copyright Notice

Library Cataloging Data

Names: Gillespie, Terri (Terri Gillespie)

Sweet Rivalry / Terri Gillespie]

390 p. 23cm × 15cm (9in × 6 in.)

ISBN-13: 978-1-64949-402-3 (paperback) | 978-1-64949-403-0 (trade paperback) | 978-1-64949-404-7 (e-book)

Key Words: Twins; Baking; Family; Relationships; Christian Romance; Salvation; Friendship

Dedication

For those who want to come home.

ADONAI your God is in your midst—a mighty Savior!
He will delight over you with joy.
He will quiet you with His love.
He will dance for joy over you with singing.
Zephaniah 3:17, TLV

Acknowledgments

On a shelf overlooking my desk, there is a sun-bleached, life-size cupcake candle. Ten years ago, when it was given to me by my dear friend, Cathy Gohlke, it looked like the real thing. Dark chocolate-looking cake, topped with pastel pink icing, glitter sprinkles, and a bright red cherry on top.

Cathy gave me the cupcake candle because she loved a story idea I had. *Cupcake Rivalry*, the story of two sisters. There wasn't much to the idea. But she saw its potential and wanted to inspire me.

Thank you, my friend, for believing in the story through the years, even as the candle and my hopes faded. One of the reasons *Sweet Rivalry* is here is because of that cupcake candle sitting on the shelf, as well as your prayers.

Special thanks to my friend Carrie Turansky who has been an inspiration to me for over twenty years. Your beautiful books and your amazing perseverance continue to motivate me. I love our retreats. You teach me so much!

Thanks to Karen Ball, who took an editor's version of a rolling pin and beat and rolled this story into submission. Thanks for loving my story. I don't think I'll ever forget, "Deep POV, Terri."

Thanks to Michelle Lazurek, my agent, who believed in this story within minutes.

Thanks to Deb Haggerty and Cristel Phelps for also believing in this story and helping me make it the best it could be.

Thanks to the *Food Network*. You may have added a few pounds—yeah, a lot of pounds—but your shows helped me give the baking scenes and my fictitious television show authenticity.

Thanks to my husband, Bob, who was patient when meals were the last thing on my mind. And those last few weeks, whew, when showering and dressing somehow were missing from my To-Do lists. Thanks for kissing my greasy head and keeping me encouraged and in prayer.

Thanks to my family—both blood and of the heart.

Thanks to my Heavenly Father—the Creator of the Universe. Thanks for sharing a tiny grain of Your creative spark with me. And, my sweet Messiah, thank You for making it possible to be a redeemed child of Your awesome Father. Love You!

Chapter 1

No.

It can't be.

Sarah switched off the blow-dryer and let it drop to the floor. Trembling fingers increased the volume on her iPad. The acoustics of her bathroom boosted the person speaking. The person with her voice.

Sarah's *own* voice.

But she wasn't speaking. This person—her, but not her—explained how to incorporate fresh strawberries into cupcake batter without making the cake soggy.

Sarah's shaking hands fumbled the iPad. She grabbed it, squatted on the cold tile, and watched again.

Yes. That was *her* face smiling. But not.

This Not-Her had the same half-moon shaped, crystal blue eyes. Same rosebud lips. The petite Sweeting family gumdrop nose ...

The hair was different. Black and chopped short. And she dressed differently. All in black, except for the flour and batter splattered on her apron and clothing.

Sarah looked at the door. *Her* white uniform hung there. Soon, it too would be covered with spatters.

The Not-Her stood before the judges' panel on Sarah's favorite baking program, *Cupcake Rivalry,* tattooed, sinewy arms—another difference—moved a mile-a-millisecond as she explained her cupcakes.

The Not-Her was a … baker? How … ?

Sarah rubbed her forehead and shook her head. Could it … ?

It must be her. It must be Rachel.

"Granny." Her voice faltered. She couldn't gather enough oxygen to push through the word. Her heart beat its way up her throat.

My sister. My twin sister.

Sarah inhaled, then shoved out, "Granny!"

A commercial appeared, she tried fast-forwarding it.

Sluggish, heavy footfalls on the stairs heralded Granny's approach. Sarah stood, then looked down. Right. She needed the iPad. She bent to retrieve it as Granny appeared at the doorway.

Dressed in her Sweet's Bakery uniform, she held onto the doorjamb panting. "For goodness' sake, child. What is all the hollering about?" She dipped an eyebrow. "You're not ready. It's 3:30 and—"

Sarah handed the iPad to her. "Is it—is it her?"

"Who?" Granny gazed at the screen, then narrowed her eyes. "I need my cheaters." She checked her pockets.

"On your head." Sarah untangled Granny's spectacles from her fine silver hair and handed them to her. Trying her best to slow down her breathing—and her hopes.

Granny fumbled her attempts to put on her glasses with one hand. Sarah gnawed her lower lip as she freed her grandmother of the iPad. The readers finally in place, Sarah passed the tablet back and leaned over Granny's shoulder.

"And who am I looking for, sweetie?"

"Hold on. She's a finalist. They're about to announce who is moving to the next round."

The wait was excruciating.

A close-up finally materialized on the screen. "There! Is it Rachel? Is it my sister?"

"Wha—?" Granny covered her mouth with a shaky hand. She squeezed her lids, then opened them. Her eyes fixed on the face. She gasped. "Oh, dear Father in heaven. It's our Rachel."

Sarah's knees went rubbery. After twenty-one years of prayers, searching, hoping—could God be finally answering? She wrapped her arms around herself squeezing the joy out of her pores. "Granny, we have to find them—"

Her grandmother dropped the iPad and fell back against the wall, clutching her left arm.

Sarah froze. "Granny!"

Sweat covered her grandmother's forehead, her face contorted. "Sarah, c-call 911."

Sarah turned toward the echo of a doctor's purposeful stride in the emergency room hallway. Her boyfriend, Drew, stood beside her. She grabbed his arm.

"Geez! You've got me in a death grip, babe."

She released her fingers and fisted them by her side. "Sorry."

The doctor joined them. "Hope Sweeting's family?"

"Yes, I'm her granddaughter, Sarah Sweeting." Sarah gestured toward Drew. "This is my boyfriend, Drew Collar. How is she, doctor?"

"I'm Dr. Simpson. Your grandmother had a myocardial infarction. We need to examine—"

"Isn't an infarction a heart attack? She—examine?" Sarah grasped Drew's arm again. "Surgery? Open-heart surgery?" Her breath came in spurts, and an odd ringing pressed against her ears.

"Take a breath." The doctor led her to one of the brown pleather sofas and sat beside her. "Okay, exhale."

Sarah jittered more than sat.

The doctor continued his instructions. As her breaths deepened, the ear ringing stopped.

"Better now?" He lifted his bushy brows.

She nodded, her cheeks warming as she noticed people—including Drew—watching her. *Go about your business, please.*

"It's too early to tell if surgery is necessary. We're prepping her for a heart catheterization. Once I look inside, we'll better know if we need to perform a bypass, install stents, or if no other measures are needed."

He smiled. "She's stable. We're monitoring her. Those are all good things."

How are those good things? Sarah nodded, then leaned against Drew's shoulder.

Dr. Simpson stood. "Say, is your grandmother the owner of the bakery?"

"Sweet's? Yes."

He smiled. "I love that place." He straightened his posture and cleared his throat. "As soon as I finish the cath, I'll let you know the results."

He looked at his watch. "It's not yet five. The cafeteria isn't open, but there is a vending machine down the hall with a selection of protein bars. Coffee is in the visitors' lounge. You'll need to keep your energy up. It's going to be a long day."

Long day?

"*Five*? The bakery!" Sarah pulled her phone from her denim jacket. "Asher."

She glanced up long enough to say a hasty thanks to the doctor, then strode to the lounge. The sound of Drew's squeaky sneakers followed her.

Normally Granny, Asher, and she began work at four a.m. She turned toward Drew. "Do you think Asher is already there?"

Drew opened his mouth, then shrugged, and shifted his attention to the vending machine.

Of course he was at the bakery. Asher West was like a brother to Sarah and grandson to Granny. She pressed speed dial three.

The first ring hadn't finished when he answered. "Where are you? I've left messages for you and Granny."

Sarah filled him in on Granny's condition—such as they knew.

"I'll call the Prayer Team." Asher sniffed. "As much as I want to be with you and Granny, I'm needed here." He cleared his throat. "Right. I'm needed here." He sighed. "I'll call in Mabel and see if I can get any of the afternoon part-timers. We'll keep things rolling. Don't worry."

He blew his nose. "Could Drew deliver the orders to the restaurants? I can't leave with both you and Granny out."

"I'll ask." Sarah bent toward Drew, who sat looking at his cell and eating a protein bar. "Honey, could you deliver the orders to the—"

Drew shook his head. "I have class. I need to leave."

You're abandoning me?

"You have a class at five in the morning?"

His freckled face reddened. "Right. I suppose I can deliver some." Drew shoved the rest of the bar into his mouth, slipped on his jacket, then gave her a brush of his lips on her cheek.

Watching Drew stroll down the hallway, she chewed her thumbnail. "Drew is leaving now."

Once he disappeared into the elevator, Sarah walked toward the windows at the end of the hall. "Ash, you'll never believe what happened."

"There's more?" He grunted. Probably lifting one of the fifty-pound sacks of flour or sugar.

"This morning, I was watching *Cupcake Rivalry*—"

"Right, the new season began last night."

Sarah leaned against the wall and stared at the dark sky. Stars still twinkled before the dawn chased them away. "Ash, I found Rachel."

"Rachel? Wait. Your *sister*, Rachel?"

Tears coated her face—sobs worked their way up her throat. All the emotions she hadn't begun to process heaved their way now.

Granny.

Her sister was alive.

And finally, the hope of finding her mother.

"Yes." It came out as a whisper. Sarah drew an intake of breath. "It was her. I know it all the way to my toes. We found my sister!"

Chapter 2

Raven Souwer hung up Hollywood Bakery's phone. She finished typing the order for six dozen Dr. Pepper mini cupcakes with Fritos frosting into the point-of-sale workstation. That cupcake had *almost* won her first place on Your Baking Network's *Cupcake Rivalry*. At least they were second.

"Hey, Will, got another order of the DPs. All our fancy training at AI and we're making snack cakes." The chefs at the Arts Institute's internationally recognized pastry program were probably laughing their behinds off. Or disavowing any knowledge of her and Will as graduates.

William Durning held the door and thanked a woman who had picked up a cake for her daughter's birthday. He readjusted the white baker's hat over his man-bun as he walked toward Raven. The only guy she knew who could rock a bun.

"You know what Chef Alexander says—" Will pointed a finger toward the ceiling and clicked his heels together—"'Innovation comes in many forms.'" He slung his arm around her shoulders. "Even cupcakes."

Raven shoved him away laughing. Will was her best friend and the best choice as her partner in the competition.

They had filmed the YBN program months ago, but because the show aired for the first time the previous night, the phones at Hollywood Bakery had been ringing off the wall. Beverly Hills's best bakery—at least Raven thought so. The foot traffic off Rodeo Drive had doubled since placing the big placard outside with hers and Will's photos from the show.

"Another order of DPs—four dozen!" One of the new hires announced.

HB had to hire more employees with the anticipated response. Until today, they hadn't done much. Now their bosses, Elton and Frank, were getting their money's worth.

The bell jingled every few minutes. They'd rung up large and small orders since opening two hours ago. The extra staff were working, but everyone wanted to talk to Raven and Will—the stars.

Raven giggled. *Stars. Yeah, right.*

The phone rang again, and Raven groaned. "Can you—"

Will winked and thumbed the phone. "Holly-weird Bakery, what's your poison?"

Raven snapped a towel toward him. He grabbed it.

"Sorry, ma'am, just kidding around." He chuckled, then frowned. "I—wha—I—"

Whoever was on the other end of the call made it difficult for Will to get in a word. "There's no one by the name of Rachel Sss— Yes. She was on—" He waved Raven over and covered the mic. "This crazy woman thinks your name is Rachel Sweeting. She says your grandmother had a heart attack."

Raven flinched. "Rachel is my name. Or was my name." *Sister? Grandmother?*

Will's chin descended to his neck. "What the—Raven isn't your real name?" He forced the phone toward her. "You need to talk to her. Now."

Raven swallowed around a lump in her throat. Sister? She didn't *have* a sister.

"Raven, take the phone."

She shook her head and backed away. *This is crazy! I'm not talking to some strange—*

Will grabbed her arm and yanked her next to him, then held the phone to her ear.

She elbowed him before speaking. "Hello?"

"Oh, thank You, Jesus," the voice said. "Are you Rachel Raven Sweeting?"

Raven squeezed her eyes shut. "I was."

"I don't understand. Is your mother Elizabeth Anna Sweeting?"

If you could call Lizzy a mother. "Yes. Who is this?"

"Oh, my gosh. Oh, my gosh." Now this woman was hyperventilating. "My name is Sarah Sweeting. We've been looking for you for over twenty years, Rachel."

"Rave," Will whispered. "She's legit. *Look.*" He held his cell toward her. "Her profile pic."

No way she was looking! She pushed his hand away like an offending gnat.

Now the lady switched to crying. "I'm your sister, Rachel. We're twins."

Twins? Raven swayed. Strong arms caught her and from nowhere a chair appeared and her behind landed on it. "You're my sister?"

"Yes! Yes! You see our mother—" The Sarah person talked faster than Will had ever done—even charged up on double espressos.

Her words jumbled together. A high-pitched whine in Raven's ears made it impossible to listen anymore. She raised the phone over her head.

"I got it." Will relieved her of the burden.

Raven leaned forward until her head drooped between her legs. *I can't deal with this.*

"This is William. I—I—You—Slow down, Sis ..."

"H-hang up."

"Arrgh! Lady!"

"Will, please, hang up." *Why is he talking to her?*

He squatted next to her and rubbed her back. "Rave, you're shaking." He stood and stepped away.

"Hey. Hey! Raven's having a hard time dealing—" He huffed. "Take a breath, lady! You just threw my friend's world into a vortex!"

Is this a scam? I can't—

Will. He'll figure this out.

"It's okay. No need to apologize. Now, start from the beginning and speak nice and slow."

An hour later, Raven and Will sat in his BMW, the top down, soaking in the sunshine and beauty of the Pacific Ocean. He had parked at her favorite spot in his parents' gated multi-billion dollar community.

The bluff overlooking the beach with giant boulders rising from the sand like sentries made her feel safe. She took a deep intake of briny, fishy perfection, then exhaled.

Will cleared his throat. "Are you ready to hear what Sarah told me?"

She ran her fingers through her short hair. Below them, seagulls fought over whatever a little girl on the beach fed them. She'd tried, when she was little, to befriend the obnoxious birds. But they only cared for what they could steal from her. Like most everyone she had ever known. Including her mother—

Especially her mother.

Would this person who claimed to be her sister be any different? Did they think they could get money from her because she'd appeared on the baking show? *Ha!*

What about the grandmother? Did she really have a heart attack? *Was* there even a grandmother?

Why couldn't she remember these people?

She glanced at Will. He sat there, one brow elevated, the other scrunched. The look he sometimes gave her because he was too chicken to confront her. "Fine. Whatever. What did she say?"

He sniffed and wiped at something in his eye. "She claims she's your *twin* sister." He rubbed his face then held his chin. "She watched us on *Cupcake Rivalry* and said you look alike except for the hair. You have a grandmother and—get this—she owns a *bakery* in Missouri."

Gooseflesh prickled Raven's arms, then spread to her scalp and down her legs. She rubbed her limbs. "A bakery?"

"Yeah, I had the same reaction when she told me." Will pushed up his sleeves to reveal his prickled tanned skin.

Raven looked away and chewed on her thumbnail. "Is she okay? Is my—the grandmother—okay? She had a heart attack, right?"

Would the woman die before she could ever meet her? It would be just her luck.

Will patted her hand, then held it. "She's stable. They're doing a procedure to see if there's damage to her heart. Sarah says there's a great cardiologist and nurses and lots of prayer."

Raven pulled away and folded her arms against her chest.

She lifted her chin. Another perfect Southern California day. Sparkling blue sky with a few wispy clouds. "Do you think they're legit?"

He gripped the top of his steering wheel and squeezed. "Yeah. I do."

"How did she find me?" Raven picked at dried cake batter on her apron, then flicked the flakes away.

"YBN's website. Our photos and bios are there. She Googled the rest."

Of course.

He leaned forward on the steering wheel and turned to stare at her.

She glowered at him. "What!"

"She wants you to come out to Missouri."

"Impossible." Raven ran her fingers through her hair. Again. And again. And again. Will caught her wrist.

"You need to go, Rave."

She couldn't manage any words.

On the beach, the little girl's mother hefted the child onto her shoulders amidst giggles but left behind a flock of disappointed birds. They hovered a few moments then flew away.

No way.

Even if she wanted to go, there was no way she had the money to fly out there. Even if she had the money, there was no way she wanted to go alone. Besides, she could lose her job. She would *never* leave Hollywood Bakery.

Will tapped her leg.

"What?"

He held up his phone. "Your sister's Facebook profile."

How ... ? On Will's screen was a photo of Raven with long, blonde hair. Except Raven had never had blonde hair—light brown, blue, purple, orange, and now black, but never blonde. She pulled her cell from her apron pocket and found the page.

No denying they looked alike.

This was her sister. Her *twin.*

She scrolled through Sarah's photos. The gooseflesh returned. Photos of Sarah with an older woman who looked like a plumper version of her mother. Was this her grandmother?

It's all true.

Raven turned to Will and opened her mouth. Nothing came out but a squeak.

Will stared at her for a split second. "Yeah, you're going to Minersville." His finger flew through screens on his cell. "And I'm going with you!"

Raven readjusted her overstuffed khaki rucksack on her achy shoulder for the umpteenth time as she and Will made their way to the car rental at Lambert Field.

Meanwhile Will rolled his designer carry-on as he spoke to the car rental folks on his cell. He was dressed like the wealthy, tall, dark, and handsome twenty-something he was. No surprise women turned to gawk at him. He had flashed his brilliant whites at a few who caught his eye, but mainly he focused on Raven.

If anyone made eyes toward her—like she was some cute-whatever—she would do something rude back to them. Good thing her attire kept her unapproachable. Black skinny jeans with black tank and the ancient, oversized black bomber jacket she had found at a garage sale in North Hollywood. Her black boots echoed on the polished tile.

She hesitated. Uh-oh. Would her appearance scare her grandmother into another heart attack? She wasn't exactly cute and huggable. But her appearance would be nothing compared to learning about Lizzy—

Not ready to think about that.

What should she call the woman? Grandmother. Grandma. Granny. Grandmama. Maybe Mrs. Sweeting would suffice.

She shivered. *Can't think about that yet either.*

Focus on walking.

Focus on anything but this *Twilight Zone* episode she was living.

Will. Focus on Will, whose attention was still glued to his phone.

If she invested more than a few minutes of reflection on all Will had done for her in the past few hours, she would puddle onto the airport linoleum. Like all the money he was spending on this trip.

Then there was the look on Elton's and Frank's faces when Will called their bluff when they threatened to fire them both. If she'd been in a laughing mood, the scene would have been hysterical. Once Will reminded their bosses that she and he were hot tickets in the local baking world, and anyone would hire them, they were almost gracious.

"Okay, we got the compact car you insisted on." Will rolled his eyes. "And the trip is over two hours. Our rear ends will pay for your decision."

He eyed the restaurants and shops around. "You wanna grab dinner before we hit the road?"

Raven shook her head. Like anything she ate would remain there long.

"Listen, *I* have to eat. My stomach is gnawing its way to my spinal cord."

Fine. Whatever. I can't pull two syllables together much less tell you what to eat. She shrugged.

"Come on. You haven't said two words since we landed."

Raven exhaled. "Sorry."

"You're in your head again, aren't you?" Will moved next to her and rested his hand on her shoulder. "What are you thinking?"

She chewed her lip. "Nothing that makes sense."

They resumed walking. "You need to talk about it eventually."

"What's *it*, Will?" She lifted her hands and dropped them. "I don't know where to begin. All Lizzy ever said was she once had a mother, but the woman was never supportive. Of course, given that my mother tended to lie to her own advantage, I don't know what to believe."

She stopped walking. "And why didn't Lizzy ever tell me I had a *sister*? A *twin* sister!" She continued her stride. "What kind of person takes one kid and leaves another?" She couldn't fathom it. She wanted to throw something. Hit someone.

"Where is your mother, Rave?" Will reached for her hand.

She waved him away. "Not going there. I said too much already." She sped up her pace. "Didn't you want to get something to eat? How about here?" She pointed to one of the food court restaurants, named Steak 'N Shake. Once they wheeled in, the familiar 50's décor and aromas triggered a craving—

Butterfinger milkshake.

What? Where did one even buy a Butterfinger shake? Raven stared at the menu board. There. In small or regular sizes. But she'd never been to this place.

Had she?

Soon she was sitting at the table, sipping her Butterfinger shake. The peanut buttery chocolate tasted familiar.

Will watched her over the top of his burger—one brow up and the other scrunched.

Whatever, Will. Think what you want. Let me drink my shake.

Would this kind of thing happen here? Childhood memories rise like ghost from a coffin?

She took a deep sip from her shake. Emotion clogged her cold throat.

Did she want to remember her lousy childhood?

Chapter 3

Asher arrived at the hospital after eight. By the time he had cleaned Sweet's kitchen and prepped the new orders, restaurant regulars' orders, and the usual bakery produce, he had worked nearly sixteen hours. As tired as he was, there was no way he would wait any longer to see the woman who was more like his family than his parents.

He stepped into the elevator and pushed the three. The doors performed their snail-like close.

"Hold the door!"

A guy with brown shoulder-length hair ran toward the elevator. Asher fumbled to find the open button and unintentionally pressed the close the door button. *Geez.* "I'm sorry, I hit the—" The doors closed on his apology. But not before the guy cursed.

Asher muttered "sorry" a few more times and prayed for the opportunity to apologize to the stranger face-to-face.

His reflection looked back at him in the mirror-like walls. The long day revealed itself in his tired eyes. He rubbed his face. His usual five o'clock shadow had appeared at three. Normal when the workday began at four in the morning.

Then there was his regular job. He had called his doctoral advisor to let her know he needed a sub for his classes. She wasn't happy, but what could he do?

The elevator dinged and its doors opened. Nothing mattered but Granny.

The cardiac ICU floor's white noise of beeping monitors, hissing oxygen, and the whispers of those providing care made Granny's condition real. He took a deep intake and exhaled.

A few of the nurses nodded toward him. His neighbor, Alma Livingston, motioned to him.

"Asher." She hugged him. "Granny is stable. Sarah will fill you in once she gets back. I made her take a break and get something to eat."

Alma placed her hand on his arm. "Visiting hours are over except for family. But—" she glanced around her. "But that dear woman is as close to family as you'll ever get." She pressed her lips together. "You know what I mean."

Unfortunately, he did.

They walked toward one of the glassed rooms surrounding the nurses' station.

Granny had always been there for him, for all the important moments of his life. From kindergarten to earning his master's in electrical engineering to being baptized, Granny was there. Not his parents. His brilliant, but focused, academic parents.

Granny.

Alma stepped with him through the doorway. There was Granny. Still. So still. Normally, she was a blur of movement.

"The pain medication makes her sleep hard. Talk to her, she'll hear you in her heart." Alma backed out of the room.

Father, help Granny. He stepped toward the bed. Granny's usually perfectly styled hair was mussed. He smoothed the short, fine silver and white hair. She called it her crown of glory.

"I'm here." He took her hand. What could he say? What should he say? "Don't worry about anything. You just need to get well. I—"

Someone gasped. He looked up.

Standing inside the room was Sarah ... no, not Sarah. This Sarah had black hair, cropped short making her blue eyes drill through him.

His heart vaulted. "Rachel?"

She looked at Asher then toward Granny. Her eyes rolled back. He ran toward her as she crumbled to the floor.

Raven awoke to strange faces. A nurse and a guy with dark hair and eyes.

"What happened?" She croaked out.

"You swooned, young lady." The nurse gave her a half-smile. "When was the last time you ate?"

The two of them helped her stand.

"What happened?"

An echo of her voice. Same tone. Same words. Same inflection. But *much* louder. Raven looked over her shoulder.

There she was.

Her sister. Her *twin*.

The face before her twisted into an ugly cry, then a broad beautiful smile, then ugly cry—all in a matter of seconds.

Just like me. Will called it the Bizarro Look. Seeing *her* look on this woman, Raven had to agree with Will's assessment.

Every doubt evaporated. Raven had a sister—a twin.

Her sister ran toward her like a freight train. Raven took a step back. The sister paused and looked at the tall guy next to Raven.

Will walked in. Then another guy followed Will.

Everyone talked. At once.

The nurse shushed them. "All right. Let's take this outside, folks. Ms. Sweeting needs her rest and not all this drama." She extended her arms and herded them into the hallway like Bo Peep.

Raven resisted. She needed to see her newly discovered grandmother. Raven craned her neck over the nurse's shoulder.

The woman lying in the bed reminded her of Lizzy. Same square jaw and surprised brows.

"Now, now—" the nurse-patted Raven's back then turned her toward the hallway— "You can see your grandmother later. She'll be fine."

One last glimpse before she complied. The grandmother laid motionless. She wasn't so sure about the nurse's assessment.

The rest of the group waited for her in a disjointed cluster. She stood next to Will. "Where were you?"

He laid his arm on top of her shoulder. "Sorry. Needed a pit stop."

"I'm sorry, everyone—" the nurse said in a soft voice— "But this won't do. You all need to go on home for now."

"The cafeteria is still open—" the tall guy pointed down the hallway. "We could go down there."

Will humphed and leaned close to Raven. "He's the elevator hog."

This was the guy who shut the elevator door on them? Was Will going to make a scene?

The elevator-hog guy stepped closer to Will.

Raven tugged on Will's jacket. *No, Will, not here.*

"Listen, man, I am sorry. I didn't mean to shut the doors on you. I hit the close button instead of open."

Will folded his arms across his chest. "You couldn't hold the door open with your hand?"

"I—well." The guy's face turned red.

Is he blushing? Do people still blush? On his handsome, rugged face, it was adorable. *Adorable? Did I just call this guy adorable?* Raven's face warmed.

"My name is Asher, and I'm an idiot. Can you forgive me?" Asher extended his hand.

Will gave his snarky smile, which meant he had blown off the offense and was amused. He shook Asher's hand. "I'm Will. And it's all good."

The two of them walked ahead. The third guy looked at Raven and her sister, shrugged, then followed the other two men, his shoes squeaking.

Raven wrapped her arms around her waist. Should she shake her sister's hand? Hug her? Maybe introduce herself.

"I'm your sister, Sarah." She giggled.

Raven nodded. "I—I'm Raven. I don't go by the name *Rachel.*"

Sarah clutched her purse against her chest. "Raven is your middle name."

"Yeah. And I go by a different last name." Raven's belly constricted. "Lizzy—my—our mother changed it."

"Souwer. Like sweet and sour." Sarah chewed her lip. "I remember from the television show."

They stood in awkward silence. Raven could feel a hug bubbling inside Sarah, but no way she was ready for that.

"I guess we should join the guys," Sarah said.

"Yeah."

They walked together, gaits matching.

Raven's breathing increased to match the beat of her heart. This was happening too fast. How was she supposed to handle this weird out-of-body encounter? She wanted to grab Will and get out of there.

Why did he make me come?

The guys had found a table. Only a few people remained in the cafeteria. Will pulled a chair out for her, the scraping echoing in the cavernous room. Raven plopped down like a ragdoll. Her sister, on the other hand, appeared revved up.

Asher introduced Raven and Will to the other guy, Andrew—Drew—Sarah's boyfriend. Raven frowned. She was picking up strange vibes from the dude. He alternated between staring at her and not making eye contact.

She could spot a poser—or danger—a mile away. Will called it her *Rave-dar.* It had saved her life more than a few times.

There was something else, though. Raven glanced at Sarah. Protective. She wanted to protect a sister she'd never known.

Will and the Asher guy decided to grab sodas and chips from the vending machines. Once they left, the table was quiet.

The boyfriend cleared his throat and leaned toward Raven. "So, y'all were on television. Pretty impressive."

Raven shrugged. "We didn't win."

Sarah's eyes lit like a Hollywood premiere. "You may not have won, Rachel—Raven—but the judges said you were a close second." She bounced in her chair. "I would *love* the recipe for the Dr. Pepper cupcakes with Fritos frosting." She turned toward the boyfriend. "Everyone would go nuts over that cupcake. Missourians *love* their Dr. Pepper. It would be a real winner at Sweet's."

Raven smiled. "Sure. I mean, I'll have to ask Will because he created the frosting, but yeah."

Her sister's face radiated something sweet, and—what? Innocent?

The guys returned with refreshments. Asher opened a can of Dr. Pepper. Raven and Sarah exchanged looks then giggled.

Will stopped his diet cola midway to his mouth. "Okay, that was weird."

"Yeah, you'd think they were related." Asher winked at Raven.

They talked about Granny, with Sarah filling everyone in on the prognosis. Which, at this point, was optimistic. The cardiologist had implanted three stents. While the main artery looked good, he said Granny must have been uncomfortable for months.

"What did the doctor say about her returning to work?" Raven picked at a chip in the table's Formica.

Sarah finished chewing a potato chip. "He said maybe in six weeks, she can work a couple days a week. But he wants her to a scale back her schedule from now on."

"What about your finals, Sarah?" The boyfriend wrapped an arm across her shoulders. "She's working on her business degree. This is her last semester."

Sarah exhaled. "I guess I can get an extension. I'll talk with my advisor."

"Hardly seems fair, does it." The boyfriend sat back and crossed his arms. "I mean, your grandmother wouldn't want you to quit. Maybe you could close the bakery temporarily."

"No!"

The same word came from Raven, Sarah, Will, and Asher at the same time.

Will glanced at Raven, then looked at Sarah. "Rave and I know what it takes to run a bakery. We practically run the bakery in LA." He nodded toward Asher. "Asher said he's worked at your place since he was a kid. We can all manage the bakery together, Sarah."

What? Raven stared at her friend. Was he sleep-deprived? Had the Missouri mountain air affected his brain?

Will turned toward her. "Come on, it will be fun." He elbowed her. "It's your family. We have to help."

If I don't want to look like a jerk. "Of course. What time should we arrive?"

Sarah checked her watch. "By four. In about six and a half hours." She folded her hands on the table. "Or any time. You both must be exhausted."

"We're still on Pacific time." Raven gave Will the *we-need-to-go* look. "We should find a hotel and get some sleep."

Raven scooted back her chair and stood.

Asher rose, his muscular frame towering over Raven. "Will, I have an extra bed. It's only a twin, but you're welcome to stay with me at my apartment."

Sarah looked up at Raven with the same blue eyes as her own.

"Raven, can come home with me." Those eyes misted with emotion. "We can have a chance to catch up. It's been a long time."

Raven clenched her fists and sent a pleading look toward Will, but he couldn't take his eyes off her sister.

"You know, Rave, that's a great idea," Will said. "Stay with your sister. Asher, I'll take you up on your kind invitation." Will reached down to gather Raven's purse.

No! I can't afford my own hotel room. When had Will stayed anywhere without a five-star accommodation? With room service.

A few minutes later, it was decided—by whom, Raven wasn't sure. Drew was to drive Sarah back to the grandmother's house then go to his fraternity. Will would drive Raven to the grandmother's house. Asher would meet them at the grandmother's house, then Will could follow him back to his apartment.

All, she had no doubt, so they could watch Raven's reaction to coming home—to a home she didn't even remember.

Once the show was over, they would go on their merry way. Meanwhile, her whole world had exploded into tiny shards, and there was only her to sweep up the mess.

She fought to not grab the keys to the rental and drive back to the airport.

Later, as Will drove behind the boyfriend's vehicle, Raven sulked in the passenger seat. Oh, how she wanted to yell at her now less-than-best friend. Didn't he know she wanted to talk about what was happening to her? With *him*. He was her sanity checker.

Except she was too angry with him now.

"This must be it," Will said.

Raven craned her neck. The headlights revealed a cute Cape Cod painted pale yellow with white trim. Two windows on the first floor had forest green window boxes filled with red geraniums and trailing ivy. The second-floor dormers also had overflowing window boxes. There were shadows of tall trees in the yard.

No memories surfaced—good or bad. Raven exhaled the breath she'd been holding. Perhaps staying the night wouldn't be so bad.

Drew tooted his horn and left Sarah waving at him from the street.

Good.

Raven exited the car and checked for Asher's truck. Where was he?

Will popped the trunk. Raven grunted as she pulled out her rucksack.

"I'll open the door and then help you with the rest of your luggage," Sarah said.

Raven shoved her arms through the straps and adjusted the sack comfortably on her back. "This is all I brought."

"Oh. Okay. Here we go." Sarah led the way to the front door.

The entry door was painted a crayon green—not the yellow-green crayon, the darker one. The prettier one. The door had a rounded top with an intricate iron grill over the glass. Sarah jimmied the key into the lock until the key finally did its job. She reached in to flip on the exterior lights then stepped inside and flipped lights inside.

Raven followed her sister into a small foyer.

Did I live here? Did Lizzy? Raven wiped her sweaty hands on her jeans and tried to regulate her breathing.

"How long have you lived here with your grandmother?" Will asked as if reading Raven's mind.

"All my life." Sarah laid her purse on a comfy-looking couch with large florals printed in reds and blues. "Papa and Granny built this house before mom was born."

"Is—is our grandfather still alive?"

Sarah reached for Raven but stopped. "No. He died in a construction accident before we were born."

More than twenty-four years ago and still Raven's eyes misted. Once again, death had stolen from her.

"Whoa. Look at all the photos!" Will leaned toward the foyer wall beside them.

Raven swiveled to face the wall covered with various shapes and sizes of frames arranged all the way up the honey-oak staircase. It was like a museum with images plastered everywhere.

She couldn't move. Her legs trembled. Where were *her* childhood photos? She had none.

"Rave, is this is you?" Will stood in the living room.

Raven's feet sprouted wings. Sarah joined them in front of a large photo with a beautifully carved wooden frame. Two little girls in floppy, knitted red hats sat on a curb, their feet dangling over a cobblestone street. They were bundled in billowy white sweaters with red plaid dresses, red tights, and red shoes.

One girl with blonde hair looked at the camera smiling, the other with brown hair looked off into the distance. Both snuggled gray teddy bears with matching red sweaters.

"Henry?" Raven touched the bear in photo.

"Who?" Will studied her.

Raven yanked off her rucksack and squatted to unsnap the ties. She rummaged through her clothes and shoes.

There he was.

She lifted the worn gray teddy bear, stitched here and there, naked with missing fur where he had been hugged too hard.

"Henry." She never went anywhere without him.

Sarah gasped and ran upstairs.

Will pointed at the photo. "Is that thing the same bear?"

"He's not a *thing*." She pressed him to her heart. "Henry and I have been through a lot together." *Henry, you're my proof we were here.* She hugged him tighter.

He was one of only a few things she had kept from the period with her mother. All this time she assumed her mother gave her the bear when they moved to California.

Oh, how she'd fantasized over the years that her father gave Henry to her because her father's name was Henry.

"Henry, meet Hank." Sarah descended the stairs, holding out a bear.

Sarah's bear bore more of a resemblance to the stuffed toy in the photo. Gently worn, red sweater still intact— Sarah's teddy hadn't weathered battles like Henry.

Raven stroked Henry's head. She and Henry had survived many battles together.

"Granny bought these for our third birthday."

Will rubbed his arms. "This is getting intense."

The front door opened, and Asher walked in. "Hey." A lock of his black hair fell across his forehead. He swooped it back.

Raven bit her lip then looked away.

"Asher, want to see something eerie?" Will waved him over.

"What?"

Asher joined Will, who explained how the two bears from the photo had just been reunited. Asher proceeded to rub his arms too. He made eye contact with Raven. The compassion flowing toward her was as uncomfortable as it was comforting.

He extended his hand toward her bear and patted its head. "Looks like Henry has stories to tell."

She nodded and swallowed around another glob of emotion.

"Will, my new friend—" Asher laid his arm across Will's shoulder—"I think we need to give these sisters their privacy."

No! Stay! She still wasn't ready for any intimate-type conversations with Sarah.

Once the guys left, Sarah locked up. She turned toward Raven, shrugged, then bit her lip. Just like Raven was biting hers.

Sarah bent to lift the rucksack, but Raven pushed her hand away, "I'll get it."

Sarah stepped back. "Our room is upstairs." She climbed the first step and paused. "Granny's room is on the first floor. We can take a tour later."

Once they reached the second floor, Sarah pointed to two darkened rooms further down the hall. "Granny's office and our bathroom are in between." She entered the room with lights on. "This is my—our room."

The space held two twin beds and was a creamy confection of pastels. The walls were light orange—like an Orange Julius. An overstuffed floral chair was parked in the dormer alcove, a stack of books on a small round table next to it. A desk held an opened laptop, with papers in neat stacks next to it.

From the ruffled pale-yellow curtains over frosted lead diamond inlay windows, to the quilts with stitched peonies, vines, and roses, it was every little girl's dream of the perfect bedroom. At least, it would have been hers had she known it existed back then.

Everything smelled like vanilla.

"This is your bed." Sarah pointed to the bed on the left close to the wall. "I had hoped you would come so there are fresh sheets."

"Thanks." The couch downstairs would have been better, but she was too tired to plead her case. She dropped her sack and purse on the soft yellow rug. The bedspread was too pristine to lay her dirty things on it.

"I mean, this *is* your bed. Granny bought bunk beds for our fourth birthday." Sarah pulled her sweater over her head and opened the closet to hang it up. "She said you begged her for months to buy one."

She pulled the top drawer of a bureau and lifted out a long pink nightgown with puffed long sleeves. "You and Mom left shortly after our third birthday. Granny stored it in the basement hoping you'd be back by our next birthday." Sarah unzipped her jeans then folded them over her dresser. "I found it. Pleaded with her to set it up. She finally gave in."

Sarah slipped her nightgown over her matching pink bra and panties, then removed the bra. "So, it truly is *your* bed." Her face glowed.

She was excited about all this?

Raven just wanted to vomit. "You keep saying *you and Mom*. I didn't *leave*, Sarah. I was kidnapped by our twisted mother and taken away from my home." Raven hadn't realized this heartbreaking truth until the words came out ...

Lizzy robbed her of a normal childhood.

Raven unzipped her jeans, shook off her jacket, then threw them on the floor. She yanked off her boots and threw them on top. She tugged on her T-shirt trying to cover her practical underwear—she had no bra—as she yanked the covers back.

Her breath came in short bursts as she climbed into the bed. She whipped the covers over her body but not before she noticed Sarah gawking at her tattooed arms.

It wasn't like she had full sleeves. She would when she had enough money. Nothing obscene—just flowers and vines, a few quotes about survival. But something in her twin's eyes ...

Raven hid her expression of beauty and art under the covers.

She had no princess nightie to wear. No lacy undergarments. She carried what she owned. Never could tell when everything would be taken away.

Meanwhile, Sarah's tears sent ragged rivers down her cheeks as Raven calmed her breathing and covered her face with her hands. Why was she doing this? Sarah had been nothing but gracious.

She sighed. "I'm sorry. Thank you for your hospitality."

"You're my sister." Sarah's voice was clogged with emotion.

Raven turned and faced the wall. *Not tonight. I can't handle this.* "Good night, Sarah."

Chapter 4

Asher plugged his phone into the charger as Will finally slipped into the spare bed. He had been holding his questions for over an hour while Will was in the bathroom.

"Hey, Will, h-how long have you and Raven been together?"

Will pounded his pillow. No doubt his guest was accustomed to more luxurious accommodations.

Or was he ignoring his question?

"Together?" Will adjusted the sheet and blanket, laid back, then flopped his arms on top.

"Yeah, how long have you been—you know—dating?"

Will laughed. "Are you kidding? We fight all the time. She's like my sister." He lowered his chin and raised his eyebrows. "We're *not* dating."

Did Will even date women? He was so handsome—Hollywood handsome—and dressed very different than folks around these parts and ...

Yeah, none of my business.

Will turned and leaned on his arm. "Ash, I date women."

"Okay. Yeah. Cool." Asher's heartrate accelerated.

"I suppose I could get a crew cut and buy from the Gap. Maybe people wouldn't assume." Will leaned back onto his pillow.

Asher bought from the Gap. He liked their jeans. Rather than take offense, he swallowed and said, "I'm sorry, man.

I promise I have a brain. I'm a few months from my PhD in electrical engineering."

"Impressive." Will yawned. "My parents would love you. They wanted me to give up this baking hobby and get a serious job at their real estate brokerage. Then the three of us would make billions instead of millions." He yawned again and scuffed his face with his hand. "Like we need more money."

"Millions, eh." Asher chuckled. "I guess it's all relative. My parents are far from rich, but plenty disappointed in me. They think my head is filled with fairy tales."

Will's brows squished together.

I suppose now is good as any to lay it out there. "I'm a Christian. They're atheists."

"Got it. So, you love Jesus?" Will nodded.

Asher turned to his side and rested his head in his palm. "Yes. Do you?"

"I'm mildly curious about Him. My parents are atheists. I must admit I investigated the religion thing when I was in high school, just to annoy them. Then I discovered I liked His style. Jesus."

"So, umm." Asher cleared his throat. "How does Raven feel about Him?"

Will snickered. "If you want to watch her go ballistic, ask her. Given what little I know about her childhood, I can understand her thinking the Big Guy doesn't care about her."

Oh no. He'd wondered if that might not happen, given what he knew.

"That bad?"

Will closed his eyes and exhaled. "Like I said, what little I know."

"Yet Sarah just *happens* to see her sister on television. And after over twenty years, they are reunited."

"Cool fluke."

Fluke? No such thing.

Will tried to conceal another yawn. "So, what's up with the girls' father? Is he in the picture at all? I sure didn't see him in any pictures on the walls at their grandmother's house."

Asher swallowed. This wasn't his story to share. "He hasn't been around for a while."

"Figures."

Asher settled further under his covers. Thank goodness Will didn't push the subject any further.

"How about we turn off the lights. Four o'clock is only few hours away."

As the room darkened, Asher's mind kept spinning. Granny, his classes, the bakery ...

And the mysterious, beautiful Raven.

He frowned. Were the Sweeting family secrets about to be revealed? And if so ... were either of the sisters ready to learn the truth?

Chapter 5

Sarah yawned, then took another sip of coffee. She glanced at her watch. Again. Should she wake Rach—no, *Raven*—or give her a few more minutes?

Her sister was sleeping upstairs!

Getting used to her sister's preferred name was easy compared to another reality. *Next, Lord ... Mom.*

Hey, God had answered hers and Granny's prayers about Raven. Why not about Mom?

She exhaled. For as long as she could remember, she and Granny had prayed for her mother and Rachel to return. Even though Granny had turned their mother's room into an office, Sarah kept her own bedroom as it had always been. For when they were reunited.

Yet, Raven didn't demonstrate any excitement over the answered prayers.

Sarah sipped from the chunky, white Sweet's Bakery mug, then rested it on the crystal-creek granite counter of the breakfast island.

Why hadn't her mother ever told Raven about her? Why couldn't Raven remember her? Sure, they were young when her mother left with—no, when she *took* Raven—but Sarah remembered it all. Vividly.

Images floated through her mind ...

Holding hands. Sitting on Granny's lap. Playing outside. Rachel climbing into Sarah's crib each night.

"Hey."

Sarah jumped at the mumbled word and spilled the hot brew on her hand.

Raven grabbed a dishtowel and patted Sarah's hand. "You okay?"

No, I'm not okay. But I want to be okay. Sarah took the towel and wiped the counter.

"Coffee smells good," Raven said.

"The mugs are in the cabinet above the coffeemaker." Sarah finished wiping herself down. "There's half-and-half in the fridge and sugar in the jar."

"I take it black."

Of course. Black clothes. Black coffee. Her twin was nothing if not consistent.

After topping off her own mug and adding a bit more sugar and cream, Sarah headed to the dining room and sat at the table. The island was small and the stools too close together. Raven wouldn't like being crowded.

Raven shuffled over and sat across from her.

Huh. Her twin was wearing her T-shirt, jeans, and socks from the night before. Didn't her sister—

Sarah's heart revved. *Her* sister *was here*. She took a deep breath. Just. Act. Normal.

Oh, and figure a way to ask Raven if she needed more clothes without irritating her.

"How did you sleep?" Sarah's voice squeaked.

Raven scuffed her hand through her short hair causing it to stick up. She still looked gorgeous. "Not so good." She took a sip of her coffee. "You?"

"Same, I guess."

They sat in silence. Awkward, uncomfortable silence.

Would she always have to be the talkative one? And was she the only one who had spent sleepless nights crying because she missed her sister? Her mom?

Apparently so. Neither of them had cared or missed her at all.

Her lips trembled. Her sinuses burned. *Do. Not. Cry!*

"What?" Raven's brows knit together, her eyes squinting.

"Nothing." She would *not* give in to the tears.

"Clearly, it's not nothing."

She had irritated Raven, again.

Raven took a deep breath and blew it through her lips. "Sarah, I know you want more from me. But everything from my past has been crammed into a dark room for years. Everything." She tapped her forehead. "Hopefully, you and your grandmother are somewhere in there. But I'm not ready to open it yet."

When? When will she be ready?

"Are you glad to be here, at all?" Sarah sniffed back evidence of her emotion.

Raven bit her lower lip, then her upper one. "I'm concerned about the grandmother I found out about yesterday. I am freaked out sitting across the table from someone who looks like me. *Exactly* like me. I'm angry Lizz—*our mother*—robbed me of a normal childhood."

"At least she loves you."

"Are you *kidding* me?" Raven stood, knocking the chair over. "You have no idea. You with your frilly curtains and perfect teddy bear."

Every tissue in Sarah's body shook. Why was Raven attacking her? "I'm sorry. I want to understand. I've missed you and my—*our* mother all my life. So many nights, I called your name and cried out for Mom. Every night I questioned why she chose you and not me."

Raven slapped her hands on the table, then leaned forward—nose to her nose. "You. Were. The. Lucky. One." The anger and hardness in Raven's eyes frightened Sarah.

Raven stepped back and shook her head. "You have no idea." She stomped back into the kitchen.

Sarah stood, but her tremors were so bad she nearly crumbled to her knees. Was she going to lose her sister again?

"I'm sorry!" Sarah called out. "Help me understand!"

Raven pressed her hands against the sides of her head, then turned around. Her blue orbs had softened and dampened.

Sarah couldn't slow her heartbeat.

"I'm the one who's sorry." Her arms dropped to her sides. "You've been nothing but kind, and I've been rude and insensitive."

Sarah took a step forward, raising her arms, then stepped back and held her hands behind her back.

If only they could start with a hug. Both of them needed it.

Raven glanced away.

Sarah had to believe God would help her better understand her sister. She would wait.

"Sarah, I'm not the sweet toddler in those photos anymore. I haven't been in a long, long time. I'm—" Two streams of tears rolled down her cheeks. "I'm hanging on by a thread right now. I can't deal with all of this." She rubbed her bare arm under her nose. "But—but I can work. Can we begin there?"

Sarah managed a nod, though her heart tore from her chest.

"Cool." Raven sniffed. "I need a shower and to change my clothes. Do you have a bakery uniform or apron I'm supposed to wear?"

One question answered. Raven did have other clothes. "Sure." Sarah rose from the table and walked toward her sister. She touched her arm. Just a little. "Follow me."

Sarah swept the questions she had into her own dark room. Questions like ... was Raven still in touch with their mother? Could they contact her?

Why did their mother take Raven but leave Sarah behind?

Once again, she would have to wait.

Chapter 6

Raven shivered in the dark parking lot as Sarah unlocked the back door of Sweet's Bakery—her grandmother's bakery.

Say it out loud, Raven. "My grandmother's bakery." She swallowed hard. *I need Will. Now.*

Sarah opened the door and turned on the exterior lights. "In all the commotion, Asher forgot to flip the switch last night." Sarah pointed to the van. "We've had the delivery van for a couple years. It's used, but sure has increased our restaurant and store sales."

The logo on the van was an adorable caricature of their grandmother holding out a plate of cupcakes with pink icing, all on a lime-green background. Sweet's Bakery was written in a curlicue font. Raven smiled as she touched the drawing. *I hope you're feeling better, Grandmother.*

"I had to bully Granny into using her face for the logo." Sarah stood next to Raven—arms folded across her chest.

"It's brilliant."

Sarah's face pinked as her smile rose like a sweet roll. "Thank you. Ready to check out the place?"

Raven followed Sarah, her heart climbing up her throat in anticipation.

She gasped. The bakery kitchen was as spacious as Hollywood Bakery and appeared to be as well-equipped. The black-and-white checked linoleum was perfect—it had a real retro feel.

"The pan washing and storage area is to the left behind this partition." Sarah unbuttoned her coat and hung it on one of the hooks by the door. Raven did the same. "There are lockers for the staff in the basement. I'll show you later." She pointed her thumb to the right.

"Refrigeration and freezer. A small non-food storage area. Oven decks, proof box, and stove further up." She pointed to another partitioned area to the left as she went by. "Our baker's bench and pastry table. Autumn is streusel season, so the area is busy."

Streusel? Raven vaguely remembered making streusel in her lamination class at AI. Did they expect her to make it here?

In the middle of the floor was a stainless table.

"How do you use the table?" Raven ran her finger across the clean surface.

Sarah hugged her stomach. "All-purpose. Staging for the ovens, cake decorating, usual stuff."

Several rolling tray racks were positioned around the floor. The equipment was older, but clean. *I could work here.*
What am I thinking?

Sarah stepped around the last partition. "Bathroom here. Cake boxes on this shelf—there are more in the sales area."

On the wall, across from the shelves, was a large, enclosed box with a metal roll-down door. Raven lifted the gate to the door. Inside were pulleys and a metal shelf. "What's this contraption?"

Sarah laughed. "It's a dumb waiter." She flipped down a large red switch. The metal shelf descended a few inches before she flipped up the switch. "Dry ingredients are in the basement's cold storage. Rather than schlepping them up the stairs, we had this guy installed." She patted the side. "We call it *Wilber.*"

Brilliant! Raven smiled and flipped the green switch. That should make the metal tray return to its position. It did. She flipped the green switch to the *off* position. "Atta boy, Wilber."

The two of them chuckled—identically. The goose bumps stood at attention. She rubbed her arms. *Stop it.*

"Are you cold?"

Raven cleared her throat. "Nah." On the other side of Wilber were stairs. A set going down, another ascending. A second floor? "What's up there?"

Sarah gazed up. "Nothing much. Cobwebs. I had fantasized about an apartment to help bring in extra income."

"Wow." Sarah was more than just a pretty face. Raven pointed her chin toward Sarah. "You have a real business sense about you."

Sarah exhaled. "I'm six hours from my business degree. Want to check out the front sales area?"

Raven stood as Sarah walked away. Why would Sarah slough off a compliment? "Do you even like baking?"

Sarah squinted her eyes and curled one side of her mouth. "Of course. Why? Do I come across like I don't?"

Uh-oh. I'm in trouble again. Raven held up her hands. "Just asking. Show me the sales area."

"Good morning, ladies!" Will entered the kitchen, Asher close behind. Will looked around, his jaw dropped. "Nice. Very nice."

"We were moving on to the front. You want to join us?" Sarah opened the swinging door.

Sarah's jaw tightened.

What did I do now?

"Do you even like baking?"

Nope. No way. Raven's question would *not* wound her again. Just smile, hold the door open, and show off your newly remodeled salesroom.

Will entered first. "Wow! I love this!" He turned around, his eyes large. "This is great!"

She bit back her smile but not the warmth it brought her. This room *had* turned out great. White and pink and lime green, their bakery's colors.

"Tell us how you really feel, Durning," Raven slapped Will on the back and snickered. The bit of warmth faded at Raven's jibe.

Will laid his arm on Raven's shoulders. "You know you're impressed. Don't act like you're not."

She grinned and stepped toward Sarah. "Whoever designed this did a banner job."

"Thanks." Having Raven's respect—even a smidgen—shortened the mounting offense.

"So, give us a tour," Raven said.

"Sarah—" Asher tied on an apron—"I'll start on the bread orders." He reached behind the door then held a clipboard. Leafing through the pages, he looked up. "We have the Olsen birthday and the restaurant streusel orders. You know I can't do the streusel as well as you and Granny."

Right. Streusel prep alone would take most of her morning. Stretching the finicky dough took a special hand. She nodded but let the tired sigh slip as she pushed the door to the store area. "As we come in, the built-ins behind me are where we display our artisan breads and a few of the assembled cake boxes."

"And awards." Will leaned forward to inspect the baking awards Sweet's Bakery had won. "St. Louis, Kansas City, Springfield, and Chicago!" He whistled, then rubbed the hand-milled white columns. "Wow. The craftsmanship on these is amazing."

You're a dependable source of encouragement, aren't you, Will Durning? Sarah cleared her throat.

"It's the Arnold brothers. They are slow, but impeccable." She laid her hand on the whitewashed exposed bricks. The rough texture beneath her palm represented the strength and longevity of this town—and her grandmother.

"When we knocked down the plaster, we found these gorgeous babies." She pointed to the storage underneath the built-ins' counter. Wow, it was really cluttered. When did that happen? Time to reorganize.

"The refrigerated and regular display cases." She waved in the general direction, ready for this tour to end.

Raven followed Will and Sarah silently. Did Raven hate it? Love it? Couldn't care less?

Will walked to the small round table with two chairs. "Is that a table for folks to eat?"

"I wish. No, it's our consult table. I can't decide between moving it to a more private area or keeping it here. There's a lot of traffic in here during the morning and after school." Sarah snuck a look at Raven. Where were the recommendations—or criticism? Her sister remained silent. Staring at the brick floor.

She turned to face Will and Raven. "Then we have the tall refrigeration unit for pick-up orders, and finally the display windows. That's it." She held her breath. Surely Raven would say *something*.

Nope. She just gave a tight smile. Will looked at Raven, his thick brows meeting over the bridge of his nose.

Sarah wouldn't be surprised if she had the same expression on her face.

Will came to stand next to Sarah. "It's a great place. Beautiful." His opened his arms. "A place with heart. I can feel the love."

Okay, Will's sentimental comment would definitely pull some snark from Raven.

"This place does have heart." Raven looked away and sniffed. "Okay. Put us to work."

This place does have heart? That was it? Who *was* this person with whom she had shared a womb? One minute she was rude and even cruel, the next, sweet and amiable.

Her sister was a tough cookie. Was there a soft gooey middle?

Raven paced around the prep table, hands on hips. "I was just trying to help."

She wrapped her arms around her waist and tapped her foot. Will would back her up.

"This is great!" Will carried a tray into the kitchen. "Isn't this great, Ra—Whoa! What bee buzzed up *your* nostrils?"

She grabbed his sleeve and pulled him aside. "She has no idea what she's doing. She *eyeballs* the weights and measurements. How risky can you get?"

"Slow your roll, Rave. This isn't our bakery, it's your grandmother's. And near as I can tell, Sarah has been working here since she was, like, born."

"Argghh. But it's so wrong! Where are the recipes? How can anyone else bake here without recipes?" More to the point, how could *she* bake here?

He lowered his palms a few times. "Not so loud." He tugged her farther from Asher's and Sarah's work areas. *"It's. Not. Your. Place.* Let's follow their instructions and see how it works. Then maybe, just maybe, if she asks, we can make suggestions."

"Whatever." She turned away. *Thanks for your support, Durning.*

Wait a minute.

Raven looked over her shoulder. Will's eyes were fixed on her sister—and what was with that mushy, dopey look on his face? "You *like* her, don't you?"

His focus snapped back to her. "What?"

Her best friend for the last four years blushed. He actually *blushed*. It had to be the Missouri water. Good thing Will's blush was so adorable. She was still going to rib him about it later.

Asher joined them. "We okay here? I have the Miner's Diner order next. One of you want to tackle the sweet dinner rolls for Johnny's SmokeStak?"

"Show me the recipe, I'll do it." Will winked at Raven.

Asher laughed. "Sarah! He wants a recipe."

"It's all about the feel of the dough, guys. You'll get it," Sarah called from the pastry table.

Raven pursed her lips and waggled her fingers. "The *feel* of the dough, William. The feel of the dough."

He gave her a push. "Shut up and grab the sugar."

"Speaking of sugar—" Asher stood on the landing to the basement— "we're low on it. I need to load a new bag on Wilber." He readjusted his hairnet—which hadn't reduced his masculinity one ounce as far as Raven was concerned. "The sun is coming up. Raven, you haven't seen the front of Sweet's. Why don't you check it out before the morning rush."

Will leaned close. "Go. You need to walk off this funk."

"Fine." Was everyone trying to get rid of her? She stormed through the pass-through door yanking off her head covering. Unlocking the door, she swung it open as a gentle tinkle of the bell announced her departure.

Outside, alone on the brick sidewalk, she took a deep breath of crisp, clean air. She looked down Main Street. The sun was indeed rising over the forested and hilly horizon. The tall gaslights flickered, ready for their morning rest.

She drew another breath. She probably should head back.

Nope. Not ready.

She studied the small downtown area of Minersville. Three or four blocks with buildings on both sides. While all the businesses were like one long building, each had unique architectures and fronts. Most were two-stories, but some were three. They looked to be originally constructed of the red bricks so common here, though some of the shops had installed siding or stucco.

The gaslights, spaced every twenty feet or so on the wavy brick sidewalks, resembled sentinels with arms holding planters of colorful flowers. She would love to know the names of those flowers.

Well-maintained Japanese maples were interspersed on the sidewalks. Some leaves were a brilliant red. She loved California's warmer climate, but there was something beautiful about the changing of the seasons.

Okay, back to work. She turned back to Sweet's Bakery. Her mouth quirked. *Sweet,* the opposite of the name Lizzy changed to Souwer.

Unreal.

Had she stepped back in time or maybe onto a quaint movie set? A place where the set designer was asked to create the cutest bakery imaginable?

The entrance of the bakery was sandwiched between two large, boxed display windows. The windows facing the sidewalk had a painted cupcake, and the windows before the entrance door had a few flyers of local events. The windowed door had the Sweet's Bakery logo, like the delivery van, with *Since 1977* added. The proverbial *Closed* sign matched the Sweet's logo.

A lime-green and yellow-stripped awning spanned the front. The brick had been painted a lighter red—almost pink, but it wasn't weird. The column molding and dentals were painted white with green accents.

One of the display windows sported a white picket fence surrounding a scrumptious display of cakes and cupcakes. A few photos floated—via clear thread—above the baked goods. Raven leaned closer. Ah. Candid shots of weddings, birthdays, and various kids chowing on treats.

Cleve—Wait. Is that me and Sarah? Eating cupcakes—pink icing all over our faces, cute pink ribbons in our hair?

She shook herself out of a daze. Come on, don't go soft, Souwer.

Just then the interior lights came on. Sarah must have flipped the switch. Sweet's would open soon. Sure enough, Sarah lifted the window shade and peeked at Raven, then smiled.

No doubt about it. She'd noticed Raven's sappy look.

Raven closed her eyes, her throat clogging. How could she not remember a place like this? At three years old, wouldn't there be *traces* of the memories?

Oh.

Her fingers went to her lips.

Of course. Was *this* why she connected so deeply with baking classes as a kid? How her vague memories made her hungry to learn more about a family skill?

Her arms shivered. Her eyes watered.

If only she could unlock that door to her memories. She had been afraid of them all these years, but ... what if they also contained *good* memories?

No. No way. Taking a chance on finding a few good memories was *not* worth the pain of the bad.

Was it?

One more glimpse, then she straightened her shoulders and walked inside the bakery. The air was steeped in the fragrance of yeast, sugar, cinnamon, ginger, and decades of fresh-baked goods.

Sarah looked up from the cash register. "Are you ready for the Sweet's rush?"

Raven tried to respond but had to swallow back a large lump of emotions. "Sure."

Yes, work. Work would take her mind off these unsettling thoughts. Because the last thing she wanted to do is remember.

Chapter 1

Drew stood at the Alpha Beta Alpha fraternity house's kitchen counter and ate a cold slice of pepperoni pizza. His first class was in ten minutes and then his appointment with the University's Placement Office.

The appointment would bring him one step closer to Untergarten Oil and Chemical's R&D department. Not a lackey sales or engineering job. Real science—research and development. Like Dr. Howard Oscar of Bern, Switzerland. UM alum and inventor of an alternative option for fossil fuel.

He popped a can of cola and chugged it, much like the beer last night after he dropped Sarah off. Too much drama for him at his girlfriend's house. No way he wanted to be there. Besides, he needed to unwind.

The guys were interested in the story about Sarah's sister showing up. They wanted all the details, so he was up late talking. One of the guys suggested Drew try to find Sarah's mother. It would make him look better in Sarah and her grandmother's eyes. Drew could start with a simple Google search and go from there.

A couple of the frat brothers were interested in Raven, since Sarah was off limits. No problem because the guy Raven was with was probably gay. No competition there, right?

He took another bite of the pizza, then threw the rest in the trash.

Maybe he would stop by the bakery and get his free cinnamon bun and coffee from the staff's coffeemaker. Check on Sarah. Show support. He wouldn't tell her anything about trying to find her mother. Yes, a nice surprise.

If Rachel—Raven, whatever—decided to stick around, untangling Sarah from the clutches of rural America would be easier. With her business degree, sweet personality, and beauty, Sarah would do well in Europe—with him.

He had one more ace-in-the-hole to accomplish his objective of moving to Europe. One he had not made use of yet.

His idol, Dr. Howard Oscar, the brilliant scientist, esteemed alum and head of R & D at Untergarten, happened to also be Sarah and Raven's birth father.

Chapter 8

Asher pulled the delivery van door shut, then climbed in and started the engine. The last restaurant order to Johnny's SmokeStak was now delivered—and only forty-five minutes later than usual. Will did a great job with the dinner rolls. They'd turned out fluffy, buttery, and sweet.

He should know. He'd done a quality inspection, with, of course, a generous helping of Granny's homemade apple butter. Granny would be proud.

Granny...

Father, be with her.

He pressed the blinker to turn right into the alley leading to the bakery's back lot. This town needed good news. Everyone was upset by Granny's heart attack. They loved her so much. With good reason.

It was a miracle the sisters were back together. Still, it wasn't his place to share the family's news—as exciting as it was.

Next step was to reunite the sisters with Granny and then with the sisters' mother. If possible. He had the impression the mother was also estranged from Raven these days. The father had been out of the family portrait for decades.

Regardless, this reunion was a blessing.

He punched in the security code to the back door. Once it clicked, he entered the kitchen area. The bakery had officially opened, and he needed to help with customers.

There was Raven, peeking through the swinging door toward the shop area. He cleared his throat. She jumped and stepped back.

"You caught me." She covered her eyes briefly.

Why wasn't Raven with her sister and Will out front?

"Didn't mean to surprise you. Just finished with the deliveries and thought I'd help out front." He took off his leather jacket and hung it by the back door. "You joining us?"

She shuddered. "I'm not ready yet." She wrapped her arms around her tiny waist. "Too many questions."

Asher chuckled. She had no idea. Once the small-town gossips hit the circuit, everyone would know. "Wise decision." He slipped on his apron, crossed the ties in back, then tied them in front. "Let me know if you need anything."

"I noticed a container of coconut milk was about to expire in the fridge. Would Sarah mind if I made a small batch of my vegan fudge and raspberry mini-cupcakes?"

"Whoa." Asher's mouth watered. "I would love to try one or six of those."

Raven grinned. And the room somehow seemed brighter.

He looked away and swallowed. "You know there are several families with kids who have problems with dairy, eggs, gluten—the whole nine yards. They drive all the way to Springfield or St. Louis to buy their birthday cakes. Having that available here would open a new revenue stream for the—"

Ingredients had appeared on the stainless prep table as Asher babbled. Raven now looked at her cell and began weighing and measuring.

Her movements were like a dancer. He could watch her for hours.

She sifted flour with the cocoa powder. "Didn't you say you were helping Sarah and Will?"

"Right." He walked backward toward the swinging door. Someone pushed from the other direction and hit Asher in the rear end. Hard.

"Oh, man! I didn't see you there, Ash!" Will said. "I was checking on Raven to see if she could change her mind and help, but if you're here ..."

Will eyed Raven and raised his brows. Raven shrugged.

"If you need anything, Raven, I'll be right—Yeah, I said that." Asher saluted and followed Will to the shop.

Wow. The place was packed. There were way more people than the usual morning crowd. What had brought the additional mob? There were a lot of college guys.

Oh no. Had Andrew told his fraternity brothers Raven was in town?

He is so cute.

Raven locked in the smaller standard mixer's blade and combined the sugar, vegetable oil, and vanilla extract. Then she poured in the coconut milk and vinegar mixture and beat them together.

"Stay focused, Raven," she muttered. "The last thing you need is to complicate your life even more."

Those chocolate-brown eyes framed in dark curly lashes. The shadow of a beard. Black hair—not from a bottle like hers. She moaned. "Stop it, Raven."

Reducing the speed of the mixer, she spooned in the dry ingredients, then mixed until the batter was a creamy consistency. The scent of chocolate with the fresh tangy fragrance of vinegar and coconut milk was amazing.

She grabbed the forty-eight-count mini-cupcake pan, greased it with coconut oil. There was a pegboard with various sizes of Zeroll disher scoops next to Wilber. She chose the proper size and filled the cupcakes to three-quarters full.

Sarah crashed through the door, leaving behind a cacophony of voices. The name *Rachel* drifted in behind her.

Sarah yanked out her ponytail holder and wrapped it around her wrist. Then growled.

Raven set the scoop down. "What's up?"

"I can't believe this!" She paced, her eyes bulging like a bullfrog. "Drew must have told his fraternity brothers about you, because the whole house is either in the shop or waiting on the sidewalk!"

"What?" *I knew it. The dude is an opportunist.* Raven wanted to throw something. "I'm going to kill him."

"Get in line." Sarah's jaw stretched forward and tensed. "Why would he do something like this?"

Raven moved closer to her sister. Should she try to calm her down? What did Will do when she had a conniption? "Breathe. Just breathe. In through your nose, out through your mouth."

Sarah stared at her, then closed her eyes. She inhaled through her nose and exhaled through her mouth. She bent at her waist, then squatted. A few more breaths, then she sat on the floor, her legs in front of her. "Thanks."

"No problem." *It worked? Who knew?*

Raven walked back to her cupcakes. "I'm making vegan, soy-free, fudge, and raspberry compote cupcakes. Okay?"

Sarah sniffed.

She was crying. *Again.*

"Sure. Great." Her voice peeped. "Sounds delicious."

Raven wanted to believe the sincerity. "Listen, Sarah, you need to have a real sit down with your boyfriend. He seems like a fame hound."

Sarah's back went ramrod straight. "A what?"

"You know, someone who sniffs out famous and successful people and thinks because they hang with them, they'll get noticed. You see a lot of them in Hollywood." Sarah scooped the last bit of batter into the pan, then tapped it on the table to remove air bubbles.

"You're way off base, Raven." Sarah stood and straightened her apron. "You don't even know Drew."

Hmm. Clearly Sarah didn't know her boyfriend, either. Raven opened an oven and placed the pan on the center rack. "I meant no offense."

"He's a good Christian." Sarah pulled her hair back into a ponytail, then walked to the sinks and washed her hands. "This is all a misunderstanding."

"Uh-huh."

"I need to get back out there," Sarah said. "If you're not ready to deal with all the questions, don't come out. I'll take care of it."

She shoved through the door and gave Raven the stink eye before entering the shop area. The Lizzy-stink eye.

Raven fisted her hands and let loose an *arghh*. When would she learn to keep her big trap shut?

Chapter 9

Will admired his first attempt—doubtless his last—to iron his five-hundred-dollar shirt. He hated to put it on and crease it.

"You gonna wear it or frame it?" Asher buttoned his own shirt.

They both chuckled.

"Is this the first time you've ironed?"

Will shrugged. "We have people for that." Will emphasized the *people* with finger quotes.

Asher shook his head. "You're from a different world, buddy." He grabbed a tie, wrapped it around his neck and lifted the collar to tuck it in.

A tie? Men still wore ties? Will tried not to stare. Talk about a different world.

Finished dressing, Asher leaned against the bedroom wall. "How did you and Raven become friends?"

Will slipped his arm into his shirtsleeve. *Still warm.* "We met at AI—the Art Institute—in a basic pastry class. She was brilliant. Mostly self-taught after a few classes at the YMCA. Her foster parents—great folks, she still lives with them—realized she was not only a gifted baker, but passionate." He nodded toward Asher. "Now we know why."

"It's amazing how God wove this thread through her life—like a lifeline."

Huh. Will paused, then continued buttoning his shirt. "That's a different perspective, but it makes sense. She's always told me baking saved her life." Will tucked in his shirt. Did God have anything to do with sending Raven to AI? He shuddered at the bigness of that thought. Was God really that involved in people's lives?

Asher stood, his arms folded across his chest. "Will, just so you know, I don't believe in coincidences. Neither of us know all of Raven's story, and as heartbreaking as it was, she was protected from far worse."

Had God intervened in Raven's life? Maybe it was worth thinking about it. Later.

In any case, he'd keep it to himself. He carried more than one bruise from her punching him for teasing her. She would rip his head off if he brought up anything about *divine intervention.*

"You ready?" Asher nodded toward the hallway.

Time to meet Raven's grandmother. He tried to still the butterflies in his chest. "Ready as I'll ever be."

Chapter 10

Raven slowed her pace so everyone would walk ahead of her. This was it. She was meeting her grandmother. Every muscle in her body had tensed. It was all she could do to take the next step.

Why was she doing this?

She readjusted her shoulder bag containing Henry. Her lips were raw from biting them. Her heart might jump from her chest and sprint back to California rather than face this marvelous, frightening thing about to happen.

Will appeared by her side. Seconds later, Asher was on her other side.

Sarah walked ahead of Raven but abruptly looked over her shoulder.

Raven's gaze locked on hers. Sarah's eyes pooled, and darned if hers didn't do the same.

Sarah disengaged from Drew and extended her hand. Raven grasped it.

Voices and soft laughter came from one of the rooms. A nurse exited the room and skidded to a stop. She was the one who yelled at them the previous night.

"Miss Alma," Sarah said. "Raven, this is a dear friend, Alma Livingston. She's been taking good care of Granny."

"Girls." She placed her hands on theirs. "Gosh, it's so good to see you together again." She smiled, then exchanged her expression for nurse-mode. "Granny is doing well. She may be moved to a regular room soon if she continues doing better. Now—" she zeroed intense green eyes on each of them—all five of them—"No drama."

"Yes, ma'am." Asher practically saluted the woman. "Hey, guys, how about we make our way to the cardiac waiting room."

Raven mouthed a *thank you* toward Asher as the men walked away.

"Your grandmother and I have been chatting." Nurse Livingston gathered the sisters into a huddle. "She knows Rachel is here. Do your best to follow your granny's lead. Whatever she asks or says, keep things light. Are you getting what I'm saying?"

Raven dipped her chin, as did Sarah. Sarah whispered something Raven couldn't hear, then took a step into the room.

Raven lingered at the threshold. Sarah looked back, then guided her into the room.

There was her grandmother. When she'd first laid eyes on her the previous night, it was like seeing an older, plumper version of her mother. Albeit, even with the heart attack, a healthier version.

The grandmother watched her with the same light brown eyes as Lizzy. Tears coated her face. She extended her arms.

"Rachel. My sweet, sweet girl."

Don't correct her. She can call you Rachel. She can call you Herbert, whatever she wants.

Raven released Sarah's hand and ran toward her grandmother. The hug may have looked awkward with all the tubes, but it satisfied the longing she was willing to expose. She sobbed until she had no more tears.

"Sit next to me." Granny released the hug, but not her hand. She stretched toward Sarah. "My dearest, sit next to your sister. I need to see you side-by-side again."

Wow. Grandmother's smile reminded her of Lizzy—well, the mother she had fantasized Lizzy could be. A mother without the cares and burdens of poor choices.

Sarah dragged two chairs over and placed them side-by-side.

"Now, sit and tell me how you two are getting along."

Uh-oh. Should Raven confess things had been tense? That they couldn't be more different than if they were strangers off the street?

Raven looked at Sarah, who gave a near imperceptible head shake.

Right. Keep it to myself.

"We're looking forward to getting to know one another," Sarah said. "Raven made these amazing raspberry cupcakes that the kids *and* their parents loved. Remember young Angus, with the lactose problems? He can eat them, which he did. Three of them."

"Oh my. Three?"

"They were mini-cupcakes." Raven lifted a shoulder. Sarah was making small talk.

Just go along with it.

Grandmother rubbed her chin and chuckled. "I couldn't imagine Marta allowing Angus to overindulge on sweets."

The three of them fell silent. Raven folded her shaky hands in her lap and tried to still her bouncing feet. Grandmother observed her and Sarah. From the look on Grandmother's face… she detected the tension.

"Sarah, honey." Granny extended her hand. Sarah grasped it. "Could you give Rachel and me a few minutes?"

No. Don't leave me alone.

Oh no. The familiar drama of surprise and hurt played out on Sarah's face. What was she hurt about now? Didn't she recognize Raven's panic?

"Of course." Sarah picked up her purse, kissed Granny on the cheek, and stared down at Raven. "Come get me when you're finished."

Raven nodded. Her vocal cords had frozen.

Once Sarah left, Raven worked a smile onto her trembling lips. "I—I brought you something."

"Oh, sweetie, you didn't have to buy me anything."

"I didn't buy it. You did." Raven pulled Henry from her purse and set him next to her grandmother's hand.

Her grandmother lifted the bear and examined him. The frayed seams, which showed Lizzy's repairs over the years of carrying and cuddling.

Raven smiled and patted Henry's head. "I don't remember a red sweater. I'm not sure how it was lost. But he still has his eyes and nose."

"He seems heavier than I remember," Grandmother raised Henry up and down. She smiled. "He looks like he was well loved. Did he meet his brother, Hank?"

"Yes," she whispered. "Hank looks considerably better than Henry. Sarah said you bought our bears for our third birthday."

"Um-humm." The grandmother placed the bear in the crook of her elbow. "We have Henry's sweater packed away somewhere. It was left behind in Sarah's crib."

The sweater isn't lost? Joy bubbled. *Why? It was just a silly toy sweater.*

She didn't care where the happiness came from—Henry would have his sweater after all these years. "Wait. Why was the sweater left in Sarah's crib and not mine?"

The grandmother sighed. "You two couldn't sleep by yourselves. I finally had to move your cribs side-by-side." Laugh lines fanned the corners of her eyes. "Your mother fought me. But I was afraid you would fall."

"I would fall?"

Grandmother chuckled. "You were a real climber. Every night, you and Henry scaled the bars to be with Sarah and Hank."

It sounded like something she would do. She leaned back and folded her arms. Yes, she could see hyper Raven—or Rachel—climbing out of her crib and into her sister's.

The sweet moment shifted into an uncomfortable silence. What should she say—or not say? What might upset the grandmother? Why did she have to stare at her like that?

Grandmother exhaled. "Sweetheart, please don't pretend with me. I have two questions for you. One, are you safe and happy?" She reached for Raven's hand.

"I'm fine. You know. I love my job at Hollywood Bakery. My friend, William—you'll meet him later—is amazing." She shrugged. "Yeah. I'm okay."

"Good. I do want to hear more, but ... sweetheart, where is your mother?"

How was it possible Raven had any more waterworks left in those ducts? She wanted to yank her hand away and run.

"She—" How could she say it? How could she tell this poor woman the truth? What if it gave her another heart attack?

The grandmother closed her eyes. Small streams of tears escaped from beneath her already drenched lashes. "I thought as much. When?"

Thanks, Lizzy. Your legacy of pain continues. "About ten years ago."

Her eyes opened wide. "She left you alone? However did you manage?" She moaned. "Oh, my Lizzy. My poor Lizzy." She sobbed.

Raven sat on the bed and leaned in to hug her grandmother. "I'm so, so sorry."

"Hope, are you all right?" Nurse Livingston stood at the foot of the bed. "Young lady, I asked you not to distress your grandmother."

"Alma—" the grandmother sniffed—"Please, I asked her a question I already knew the answer to. You could help me by handing me the box of tissues." The grandmother ran her fingers through Raven's short-cropped hair. Raven leaned into her caress and kissed her palm.

She glanced at the nurse. "I'm sorry. I shouldn't have said anything." She took the tissues and gave a few to her grandmother.

"Pish-posh," the grandmother said, wiping her nose.

"I was more stressed not knowing for certain."

Nurse Livingston checked her grandmother's vitals and left the room. Raven attempted to return to her chair, but the older woman held her tight.

"How? How did it happen?"

Raven gulped. "Can't we talk about this later?"

"Drugs? An overdose?"

Her brown eyes penetrated Raven's heart. All she could do was nod.

The grandmother released the sigh of someone who had held her breath for a long time.

"I'm sorry. I tried to help her." Raven grabbed a handful of tissues for herself.

"Goodness me, child—" the grandmother blew her nose— "Your mother was supposed to take care of you." She looked toward the ceiling. "Dear sweet Jesus, You told me so many years ago. Help my granddaughter heal from the injury she has had to endure. I surrender my questions to You, Father."

Raven stiffened. Her grandmother may have surrendered her questions to this God, but Raven had a lot she wanted Him to answer for.

"Rachel, please do not say anything yet to Sarah."

Secrets? Not you, too. Raven shook her head. "Why? She's been asking me since I arrived."

"Sarah doesn't know her mother had a drug problem. Lizzy struggled with drugs or alcohol for as long as she was married to your father."

Raven stood. "Wait. She was *married* to my father?"

"You didn't know? Oh, dear." Her grandmother's face paled. She patted her chest as she gasped.

Raven ran for the nurse.

Did she just kill her grandmother?

Sarah was on her fourth tour around the cardiac floor when someone tapped her on the shoulder. Will stood an arm's length from her.

"You okay?" His too-handsome face softened.

She looked away. "I'm fine."

"Yeah. Not believing that." He laid his hand upon her back.

Her arms tingled.

"How about I join you on your next scenic trip? You don't have to say anything. We can just walk."

They took a few steps, and the words just tumbled out. "Granny wanted to talk with Raven alone."

"I figured. Makes sense."

Sarah stalled. "Why?"

"When you saw Raven for the first time, what did you want to do?"

Sarah cleared her throat. Maybe this guy was more than a pretty face.

"You wanted all of us to disappear because you needed to talk with your sister and ask her the questions you've been wanting to ask for a long time?"

She crossed her arms. Twenty years.

"Like, where is our mother?"

"Exactly." Will resumed walking,

How did he understand what she was feeling? What did he know?

Sarah caught up with Will.

"Do *you* know where our mother is?" Sarah wrapped her arms around her waist.

Will turned toward her and gave her a crooked smile. "You look so much like your sister." He pressed his lips together. "I'm sorry. Whenever I try to get Raven to talk about her mother—at all—she clams up or gets angry."

She snorted. Raven had probably been a volatile teenager. In fights. Possibly drugs. Maybe their mother kicked her out of the house because she got into trouble with the law. "They probably had a big fight and Raven left."

"I don't know about that," Will said. "In any case, Raven needs to tell us in her own time."

"I bet she's telling Granny."

"Then you'll know soon."

"Hey, babe. Why aren't you with your grandmother?" Drew stood inches from Sarah, hands on his hips.

Asher joined them. "Is Raven okay? Did something happen?"

Sarah huffed. Why was everyone worried about Raven? "Raven is *fine.*"

She took a breath in through her nose then exhaled through her mouth. She had to calm down if she wanted to visit with Granny. She had always been able to read Sarah better than her Kindle. "Granny wanted to talk with Raven alone. When they're finished, she'll come find me."

"Speak of the devil." Drew pointed.

Raven was walking down the hall, swiping at her eyes and rubbing her nose on her sleeve. Sarah strode toward her. "What's wrong? Is Granny okay?"

"I hope so. That nurse kicked me out. Said your grandmother couldn't have any more visitors." Raven rubbed her eyes again. "I'm sorry, Sarah. I'm sorry, guys."

"You wore her out, didn't you?" Drew narrowed his not-quite green, not-quite brown eyes toward Raven.

Even though Sarah had just thought the same thing, hearing Drew say it, well, it sounded cruel.

"Hold on, Drew." Asher stood between Drew and Raven. "Granny's been praying for over twenty years for her daughter and granddaughter to return, and here is Raven."

Wait—

"I've been waiting too," Sarah muttered.

Everyone turned toward her. Will patted her arm then withdrew his hand.

Sarah fixed her eyes on Raven. "I've been waiting for

you. And Mom too." She jutted out her jaw. *Can't anyone see I'm hurting, too?*

Raven's cheeks reddened. She ran her fingers through her hair. "I can't do this." She turned and ran away.

Will looked at Sarah, grimaced, then mouthed *sorry*. He ran after his friend.

Drew scratched his head. "Your sister seems unstable, if you ask me."

"Drew!" Sarah fought between wanting to defend Raven and agreeing with him. "I need to talk to Miss Alma and see what happened."

She strode ahead, leaving the two guys to catch up. She found Miss Alma at the nurses' station.

"Your grandmother is resting." Alma typed something into the computer, then looked up. Sympathy rested on her face. "If you're wondering if your grandmother's relapse was cause by your sister's visit, you're right."

"See." Drew leaned an elbow against the counter pointing at Sarah.

"No, what I'm saying is having Rachel here after all this time was enough to cause stress. Granny had been talking all day about her arrival. After all she's been through and then to find out—" Nurse Alma's lips looked like someone had zipped them shut.

Alma looked away. Sarah fisted her hands.

"What? Come to find out what?" Sarah leaned over the nurses' counter. "After all who has been through? Granny?"

Alma snapped her gaze toward Sarah, her strawberry blonde bob swinging with the quick motion. "After all your sister has been through. I have said enough. You need to talk to your sister. When your grandmother is ready for visitors, you can see if she's up to talking."

Why all the mystery? Sarah stomped her foot. Why did *everyone* in her life keep secrets from her? "Has this set Granny back? Does she have to stay longer in CICU?"

Alma lifted her brows. "The doctor will decide when he examines her. I've texted him, but he'll be here when he gets here." She stood and walked around the counter to Sarah. "There's no reason you need to hang around. Granny's stable. Go home. Comfort your sister, she was pretty distressed."

She was distressed?

"Let's go." Asher placed his hand on her shoulder. "This has been another long day and we'll need to rise with the roosters again tomorrow."

"Want to grab a bite to eat?" Drew wrapped his arm around her waist and tugged her toward him. "Imo's is still open."

She wasn't hungry, but she didn't want to go home and face Raven alone either. "Sure. Let's go."

Anything to avoid another confrontation.

Chapter 11

"I want to go home." Raven plopped her chin on the wooden table at a weird pizza place, then raised her eyes toward Will. "This is too much. I nearly killed my grandmother, and now my sister hates me."

"Home, home? As in California?" Will spoke around a full mouth.

Raven's phone chimed. She grabbed it and checked. The Gillians. Her once-fosters, now landlords inquiring as to her grandmother's condition.

"Mandie checking in?" Will wiped his face with a wad of flimsy paper napkins as he chewed. Then moaned in delight. *Again.*

"Yeah." Raven typed a quick response.

RAVEN: *Had heart attack. Doing okay right now.*
MANDIE: *Staying longer?*

Was she? Staying longer?

Will lifted a square slice of pizza from the metal circular plate. The pizza's toppings slipped around as he folded the piece and shoved it in his mouth. His eyes rolled as he dabbed his mouth with a new wad of napkins.

"You didn't kill your grandmother, and your sister doesn't hate you. Sarah thinks you're hiding something from her about your mother. Oh, man, you gotta try this."

She leaned back and covered her face with her arms. "Can you stop eating and tell me what to do?"

He reached for another slice. Raven slapped his hand.

"Ow." Will sat back and wiped his face. "Listen, I can't tell you what to do. You know what to do. For the first time in your life there are people—family—who missed you, prayed for you, and want you in their life. Are you willing to throw that away?"

She shrugged. "There's something else. The grandmother wants me to keep the—my—something a secret from Sarah."

"A secret? What secret?"

Raven looked over her shoulder. "I can't say. But all this reminds me of my mother making me the receptacle for all her secrets." She exhaled a shaky breath. "Is she like my mom? Manipulative?"

Will rested his chin in his palm. He said nothing, but he watched her intently.

"You're creeping me out, Durning."

"First of all, you've divulged this much about your mom." He pressed his thumb and index finger together. "Second, I have yet to meet Granny. Third, I look at the people who are closest to her, and they adore her. Fourth, I don't get the sense you adore your mother."

Okay, Durning might be on to something. Raven looked at her hands in her lap. "And fifth?"

He leaned forward and lifted her chin with his greasy finger. "Fifth, I know more about your past than anyone, but, kid, you've got a *lot* of secrets yourself."

She knocked his hand away, then grabbed a clump of napkins to wipe off her chin.

"I know you well enough to know whatever those secrets are, they must be bad. Now you have family who care enough to help you—" He sat straighter, his eyes rounding—"Huh. How about that."

"What?"

Will dipped his chin and waved. She turned and looked behind her. There were Asher, her sister, and Drew.

Great. Was she ready for this?

She bent forward. "What should I say?"

He shoved another large bite into his mouth and shrugged.

Sarah stood next to the table. "Hey, Raven." She laid her hand on Raven's shoulder. Her touch was warm. "I'm sorry. Can you forgive me for chasing you away?"

Raven stood. "You have nothing to be sorry about, Sarah. I am a giant ball of emotion right now. Maybe you and your grandmother would be better off without my drama. I just told Will we should go back to Los Angeles."

"No!" Sarah's lips trembled. "You can't leave me. Us. No." She grabbed Raven and held her tight.

Raven didn't fight the hug—she absorbed it.

Something inside … broke. She wasn't sure what it was, but the embrace comforted her and was reassuring, not claustrophobic.

"And for what it's worth, when she said that, I told her she was crazy," Will muttered between chewing. He grabbed another slice. "This pizza is amazing! It's like—like slimy and sticky, but so good."

The restaurant silenced. Will didn't notice over his groaning and moaning and "so goods."

Several children pointed in Will's direction.

Asher noticed first.

Then Raven saw it. When Will smiled, his teeth were covered in white goo—presumably cheese. He also had several strings of cheese draping from his mouth.

Asher, Raven, and Sarah sniggered. They were struggling to not burst. Finally, the laughter escaped.

"What's so funny?" Will squinted at them. The trio laughed harder until they were leaning against each other.

Raven caught a glimpse of Drew in her peripheral vision.

He was not laughing.

She couldn't have cared less.

Drew slammed his bedroom door. "What is wrong with these people? One second they're blubbering, and the next, they're laughing and acting stupid." He kicked off his shoe, which hit his desk lamp and knocked it over. The other shoe he pushed off more gently.

Would he ever get Sarah to leave this town? Leaving a sick grandmother would be difficult enough, but now her long-lost sister appears, and any minute, their mother could show up.

If only he had more money. He righted his lamp and clicked it on. He would whisk her to California and let Sarah reconnect with her mother—without Raven.

His mother loved Sarah when she came up for a visit. Who wouldn't love such a beautiful, intelligent woman? Sarah's own mother would welcome the sweet and kind daughter into her life.

No such luck. He'd be paying off student loans for years, even with his dream job.

He stood next to his bulletin board. Sarah called it his vision board. He knew God helped those who helped themselves. He had always worked hard.

The corporate brochure of Untergarten Oil and Chemical was tacked open to the photo of researchers—one in particular. Drew had had the slick brochure since getting his bachelors. Untergarten wouldn't hire a measly undergrad, they wanted a PhD, *at least*, in chemical engineering. And in six months he would have his, with a minor in German.

The woman at the Placement Office had him complete Untergarten's online job application this morning. He looked at his watch. Hard to believe it was still today. The days had been long since Mrs. Sweeting's heart attack.

Would Untergarten give him a phone interview?

If he did well, they would fly him out to see the plant and interview with the powers-that-be.

Sarah and he needed to practice his German.

Next to the brochure was a photo of his idol, Howard Shane Oscar. Andrew had copied the guy's senior photo from one of the yearbooks in the library a few months ago. He flicked at the photo. Sarah had his smile.

He couldn't figure out how the whole town knew Oscar was Sarah's father, but Sarah didn't. Professor West—his advisor—was the one who told him. Asher's mom thought Drew should know since he and Sarah were dating.

He pulled off his shirt.

When he questioned Granny about it, she made him promise to not tell Sarah. His frat brother, Lewis, had a brother who was a Minersville cop. His brother said the rest of the town respected Mrs. Sweeting enough to not reveal anything to Sarah.

So, Drew had not told Sarah. Yet.

It was inevitable. He flopped onto his bed. Once he was hired by the Freiburg, Germany, plant he was a short drive to Switzerland where Howard had worked and lived for nineteen years. He had been following Howard on social media and the business social sites for several years now. He knew the man had remarried. He had three kids. Three more kids.

He gazed at a photo of himself and Sarah at last year's St. Patrick's Day festivities. She was so gorgeous. He was the envy of all his frat brothers. It wasn't fair she didn't have a relationship with her mother or father.

His parents weren't the snappiest beans in the garden, but they loved him and thought he could do no wrong.

No ... he wouldn't reveal Howard to Sarah now, but maybe he could do something about reconnecting the mother to her daughters. At least to Sarah.

He yawned.

First thing in the morning, he was working with Professors West and Schmidt on their research project. He pulled off his socks then his jeans. Sometime tomorrow, he would Google Elizabeth Sweeting-Oscar.

He crawled under the covers.

Hold on. Didn't she change her last name? Right. Souwer.

If Raven wouldn't tell Sarah where her mother was, *he* would.

Chapter 12

Raven couldn't sleep, but she was exhausted. Her mind would *not* stop racing.

She wrapped her pillow over her ears to silence Sarah's soft snores. Great. She'd add peaceful sleep to the list of things she envied her beautiful, blonde sister.

Normally, she wasn't resentful or jealous of others who had more than she did. Over the years she had learned those emotions robbed her of the bit of peace she had. She groaned and flopped her arms on the bed. Why wasn't it working now?

So, the grandmother knew Lizzy had died. She even knew she'd overdosed on something.

Why wasn't the grandmother surprised by Lizzy's overdose? She mourned her as though she were a saint. Raven grabbed Henry and held him tight.

Maybe someday I'll mourn her. Maybe ...

I can't deal with this. She pushed Henry away. The moonlight shone on his sad little face. She hugged him again.

Once Raven had come across a big toad on her way to school. It had been badly injured. Wanting to help, she reached toward it, but it flipped and flopped, trying to get away from her.

Right now, her heart flipped and flopped like that injured toad.

She rolled into a ball. The *whys* fought their way through.

Why didn't Lizzy love her enough to stop using? Pow!

Why didn't she protect her from the creeps who beat them both? Pow!

Why did she make her kid do horrible things? Pow!

Anger twisted its thorns with sorrow. Raven held Henry so tight he made a strange crackly noise.

Sarah stirred and mumbled something, then quieted.

She had to get out of here. At least for a walk. She looked at her phone: Two o'clock Missouri time. Midnight for her and Will.

He was responsible for getting her into this mess. So he could just talk her off the cliff of misery.

RAVEN: Come get me. Can't sleep.
Need 2 walk.
Maybe talk.
U owe me. U made me come.

She pushed her phone under her pillow so it wouldn't wake Sarah. The wait was excruciating. Finally, a small vibration. She tugged her cell close.

ASHER: Will snoring. How about me?

Asher? What was he doing answering Will's phone?

ASHER: Sorry. Kept honking.

Right. Will's ringtone was a Bentley's horn. No wonder it woke Asher. She chewed her bottom lip.

RAVEN: OK. Thks.

Her phone vibrated.

ASHER: B there in 10

She jumped out of bed and flung her leather jacket over her tank, then slipped on her jeans before grabbing her boots.

76

In moments, she was at the front door, unlocking the handle. Why didn't they have more security measures? They had no idea what was out there in the world.

She did.

She sat on the front steps, slipped on her boots, and zipped her jacket. Sheesh! It was freezing out here. She stuck her hands in her pockets and hunched her body so less was exposed to the cold.

A vehicle pulled up and flashed its headlights. She ran to the passenger door of Asher's pick-up and opened it. He blew on his hands as she got in. His hair was bed-head adorable.

Yikes. Adorable?

"Sorry, the heater is still warming up." He rubbed his palms together.

"You don't have anything to be sorry about. Thanks for doing this."

Well, she was out of the house and had the opportunity to walk. Even talk. So why couldn't she think of anything to say?

"I thought we could walk the campus. It's well-lit and there's security." He backed up and then put the stick shift in first.

"Sounds good." She sat on her hands as much to warm them as to conceal her nerves.

Once Asher parked in the empty lot, they climbed out. She gasped. The frigid air constricted her breathing. Her nose dripped. She sniffed, then pinched her nostrils together to keep the leak at bay.

She almost jumped back into the truck but stopped. No way was she going to wimp out.

"Hey, wait." Asher ran back to the truck.

What's he doing? Raven wrapped her arms around her shivering body. Asher leaned into the cab, then ran back. He handed her a huge pair of leather gloves and tissues.

"What about you?"

He pulled a glove from each pocket of his jacket and slipped them on.

"Thanks." She slid her hands into the roomy gloves. *Ahh. Much better.*

They walked in silence. And it didn't even feel awkward. How weird was that?

The brisk air calmed her.

Or maybe it was being by his side.

"How long have you known Sarah?" She studied his handsome profile.

"Since we were kids." He paused and chuckled. "I was on my own a lot and wandered into the bakery. Granny gave me a pecan sticky bun and a small carton of milk." He looked down at her with a toothy smile. "She had a kids' table and chairs behind the counter. Sarah and I sat and played Candy Land, eating our sticky buns."

Candy Land? Sticky buns. It was too sweet to believe. But she did. "When did you begin working at the bakery?"

Asher stopped.

She turned to look at him. "What?"

"You don't have to make small talk. I'm fine with you not saying anything or whatever."

Raven waved her arms. "Like crying? Yelling? Revealing my secrets?" Everyone wanted to know about her mother. To know about her life.

Her time in juvie.

Oh. She hadn't thought of her arrests in years.

"Preferably not yelling. Security may haul me in." His cocoa eyes twinkled.

She resumed walking. *Who is this guy?* He was defying her cardinal rule: *Anyone who seems to be too good to be true, isn't.*

Asher caught up to her. Yeah, like any of these holier-than-thou people would want someone like her in their town. Not!

So why did she have a sudden urge to smooth down that hair sticking up behind his head? *No. I have to get out of here.*

Her pace picked up. Her heels stomping on the cold concrete to a rhythm in her brain.

Out of here. Out of here.

She strode forward, then turned around. *Where is the truck?*

He placed his hand on the small of her back. "The truck is this way." Even through her jacket, her skin warmed all the way up her neck and to her cheeks.

She increased her stride to get away from the not-so-terrible sensation. Talk about confusing! Still her body trembled.

"Listen, Wal-Mart is open 24/7, how about we find warmer clothes for you." He spoke louder across the distance she'd put between them.

Why would she want to spend more time with him?

She slowed.

Still, she needed to buy toiletries. Using Sarah's stuff seemed wrong.

She looked over her shoulder toward him. A hunk of dark hair now covered his forehead. He was so darn handsome. And innocent.

Do the guy a favor and keep your distance. Tell him to take you back to the grandmother's house. Now.

She should—

"Sure. Thanks, Asher."

Raven laughed so hard she fell against the mammoth box of big head masks. Asher wore a giant shark head and was humming the theme music of *Jaws* and circling her.

"Stop!" she squealed. "You've got to stop, Asher." She grabbed his arm, then yanked the mask off. "They'll kick us out."

He extended his arms. "There's no one here *but* us."

"Where to next?" He pushed their cart.

The prices were so cheap—as reasonable as the thrift stores—she could indulge in something extra. "Um. I'd like to get a nightgown."

His lips formed an *O*. "How about I check out electronics?"

She chuckled, then relieved him of cart duty. She found several racks of nightgowns, but only had eyes for the long gowns. She ran her hands over them. Some were as soft as a rabbit's underbelly.

There it was. A white gown with a bit of puff at the top of the long sleeves. No pink ribbons like Sarah's, but it had tiny bright red cardinals sitting on budding branches. And it was soft. She rubbed it against her cheek.

Yes, this was the one.

She found Asher then checked out and loaded the cab with her treasures. Her cell's green light flashed. Will had texted her.

WILL: U OK? R U with Ash?
RAVEN: Yes. Shut up and go back to sleep. Talk 2morrow.
WILL: Is 2morrow. Bakery in 30 mins.

"Oh my gosh!" Raven looked at Asher. "It's three-thirty."

He frowned. "Time flies when you're having fun with big heads. I'll get you home in time to freshen up. Let Sarah know I'll be a few minutes late. I can't smell like a pig farmer when I deliver to the restaurants."

Pig farmer? "Thanks for doing this, Asher. It was above and beyond."

He reached over and patted her hand. "It was a blessing for me. I had a good time."

Blessing? When had she ever been a blessing to anyone?

Chapter 13

Sarah drummed her fingers on her coffee mug as she sat at the dining table. She had half a mind to leave. Whoever Raven was with could take her to the bakery—if she was even working at the bakery anymore.

Maybe she already left for California.

Maybe she was beaten up in a ditch.

Her cell rang.

"Raven?"

"No, it's me, Will." How did *he* get her number? Oh, right. They all exchanged numbers last night.

"I thought I'd let you know Rave's with Ash. Not sure where they were, but they're on their way back."

The front door opened. Raven peeked around the door. Seeing Sarah, she grimaced and bit her lower lip.

"She's back. I'll talk to you later, Will."

Raven, her hands full with Wal-Mart bags, lifted them as a wave and shut the door.

"I don't have to ask where *you* were. And Will told me who you were with." *Good grief, I sound like a mother.* Like her mother?

"Sorry. I couldn't sleep." Raven set the bags on the floor. "I tried getting Will, but he wouldn't wake up, so Asher took me for a walk and then to Wal—"

"Why didn't you wake *me*? I would have taken you anywhere you wanted. And Granny is doing better today, in case you wondered." *What am I doing?*

"Whatever, *Mom!*" Raven regathered her bags and stomped up the stairs. The door slammed.

"I'm leaving in fifteen!" It took every effort to not say *with or without you.*

"Fine. Whatever."

Whatever? What*ever?* She *should* just leave. Sarah took her cup to the kitchen, rinsed and placed it in the dishwasher. Leaning against the counter, she took a deep breath and exhaled.

No. She wouldn't leave. How could she?

Would she and her sister *ever* get along?

If Sarah clamped her jaw any tighter, she'd grind a layer of enamel off her teeth. Another busy morning at the bakery with a horde of Drew's fraternity brothers trying to get a look at Raven.

With every swing of the kitchen door, the lug heads strained their unshaven necks to see the mystery woman.

So, what did Raven do? She hid in the back, leaving Sarah to answer unanswerable questions.

At least delectable treats continued to emerge. Apple cinnamon streusel mini muffins and another gluten-free concoction of chocolate and salted caramel buttercream mini-cupcakes today. How on earth did her sister produce these delicacies from whatever ingredients were in the kitchen?

"Dear, are there any more of those delicious chocolate mini-cakes with raspberries from yesterday?" Old Mrs. Hasbro searched the glass cases, leaning on her cane. "Jonni Baker had one and said it was the tastiest thing. And it was healthy too."

Ethel Hasbro had come in every Wednesday for a baked treat for as long as Sarah had been alive. Maybe even as long as the bakery had been open.

"I'm sorry, Mrs. H, we're out. How about your usual cherry-cheese Danish?" Sarah rested her hands on the display case.

Mrs. H always bought one for herself, the other for her giant schnauzer, Handsome. The dog sat obediently on the sidewalk outside.

Which reminded her, she'd forgotten to set the water bowl outside for the occasional pet that accompanied their customers.

Mrs. H. tapped her finger on her chin. "Oh my. I wanted to try one of those tiny cakes."

"They were delicious, but not the best for breakfast, especially for Handsome. Remember the last time you fed him chocolate?"

Mrs. H shrugged a bony shoulder.

Sarah loved this dear woman. "How about Granny's world-famous pecan sticky buns?"

"Make up your mind, lady," one of the college guys grumbled.

"Hey. Dude. Cool it." This from Will, who then went back to helping a customer.

Sarah swallowed. Tension invaded the shop.

"You gonna make me, pretty boy?" Several of the guys moved out of line, toward Will.

Seeing their size, Sarah was sure they were on the football team. And more than capable of crumbling Raven's Hollywood friend like coffeecake.

Will bent over the case and gave the older woman a brilliant smile. "Mrs. Hasbro, my name is William. My friend Raven made these delicious treats fresh a few minutes ago. Want to try one?" Will handed Mrs. H one of the sample apple-streusel mini-muffins. "And we have the crullers on special today. Maybe you'll want to share them with someone special."

Mrs. H popped the muffin into her mouth. "Oh, *my!* Yes, William." She licked her fingers. "Delicious! And I'll take a half-dozen of those crullers with my Danish."

"Pretty boy, I said, 'you gonna *make* me?'" The bulkiest guy had moved next to Mrs. Hasbro. He towered over Will, crossing his arms over his wide chest. "And you forgot your pretty pink bow for your ponytail."

Will huffed. "Yeah, yeah, pretty boy is a pushover. I get it." Will swatted the air, while still focused on Mrs. H. He took his time gathering a half-dozen crullers for her. "You might be interested to know *this* pretty boy has a black belt in karate and is training in *krav maga.*"

He accepted Mrs. H's money and moved to the cash register, then gave her the change.

The old woman patted him on the cheek and winked. "You *are* handsome. And very sweet. Sarah, give my love to your grandmother, and tell her I'm praying." With that, Mrs. H waved and hobbled through the mountain of hulking guys. She paused, then lifted her cane and poked one of the men in the stomach. "Now, you boys behave."

Another of the behemoths opened the door for Mrs. H, his guilt stamped by bright red cheeks.

"Hey—" Sarah leaned toward Will and whispered, *"Are* you a black belt?"

Will ran another customer's credit card and gave a dazzling smile.

Asher, back from his deliveries, pushed another tray of treats from Raven through the swinging door. Ganache-covered cubes of something.

How could someone so hard and brash produce such sweet things?

Asher laid the tray on a counter. A whole gaggle of customers flocked to it. They oohed and aahed and asked the same questions, "What are *these?*" and "Are they free?"

Asher grinned. "They're fudgy, salty, peanut-butter brownies covered in ganache."

Everyone turned toward Sarah. The look of longing on their faces made her chuckle. She nodded toward the tray. "Free samples! One each, please." The last sentence was barely audible above the melee.

Within seconds the tray was empty. A few guys, all of whom were from Alpha, left with more than one brownie bite *and* without purchasing anything.

Sarah stared at Will. His brow raised, he shook his head.

She walked toward the kitchen. Blue eyes peeped through a small opening. Raven made eye contact with her, then retreated.

Oh, no, you don't.

As Sarah entered the kitchen, Raven busied herself with cleaning pans and bowls.

"Everyone loved the brownies. And the other two items you made."

"Um-hum." More clatter from the sink.

Sigh. "We need to talk."

Raven looked over her shoulder, glancing at Sarah through long, curly lashes. Sarah couldn't help smiling. Her twin looked like a child who had stolen the last cookie from the cookie jar.

"Let's sit." Sarah sat on the counter. Raven moved farther down and continued to stand.

"Raven, your desserts are amazing. Creative and luscious. I would love to cost these out to see if they will work for us at the bakery—in this town."

Raven's eyes lit like five decades' worth of birthday candles.

"In the meantime, we need to cut back on the free samples. Folks are eating them and not buying anything."

Raven covered her mouth with her hands. "Oh, no! I am so sorry. Will and I were always a tag team back in LA. I'd bring the samples, and he would upsell."

"Huh." Come to think of it, Will *had* done that a few times, even with Mrs. Hasbro, who *never* bought anything extra. "That's a great idea. It would have been nice to know."

Raven picked at her nails. "Sorry. I forget others don't share a brain like Will and I do."

Sarah hung her head. Did Raven intend her remark to sting? Because it did. Weren't twins were supposed share thoughts and emotions?

Then again, she didn't wake up last night when Raven was so troubled she had to go for a walk. Shouldn't she have known Raven needed her?

Oooo ... my head hurts trying to figure all this out.

"What? What did I say now?"

"Nothing." Sarah pasted on a Sweeting smile. That was always an effective way to hide. "You and William are great together. Like brother and sister."

Raven's posture straightened. Her blue eyes drilled Sarah's.

Maybe she and her twin *did* share part of a brain. She'd sure seen right through that passive aggressive remark. *Great.* Now *Raven kicks into twin-power? When I don't want her to see.*

"Hey, ladies." Asher stuck his head into the kitchen. "We need help out here."

Saved by the ... whatever. Sarah scooted off the counter and followed him out to the shop.

"You okay?" Asher looked down at her.

"Fine. Just fine." *Like I'll ever be fine again.*

Chapter 14

Drew pulled into Sarah's driveway and held his hand over the horn. Normally, he would beep, and she'd run to his car, long blonde hair trailing like silk behind her, happy to see him.

Hmm. Time to step up his game.

Leaving the car running, so it would be toasty warm, he ran to the front door and knocked. No one answered. He tried the handle. Locked. He looked through the door window. The house was dark.

Did they go to the hospital and forget him?

Someone beeped. He turned. Will's white Prius pulled in behind him. Raven jumped out, still in her work clothes, followed by Sarah also in hers.

"Drew, so sorry we're late." Sarah sprinted toward him. She kissed him on the cheek then unlocked the door. "Can we take Raven with us?" Not waiting for his answer, she flew up the stairs. "Asher and Will are meeting us there."

Raven eyed Drew, and he eyed her. If looks could maim, they would both be limping tonight.

"Sure." Best to keep his girlfriend close, and his enemy closer.

Raven made a gagging noise and followed her sister upstairs.

He forced himself to sound positive. "Let's stop at Lion's Choice for a roast beef sandwich." Maybe he should turn off his ignition. He didn't want to waste gas.

"Oh, sweetie." Sarah called down to him. "We were late because Will took the four of us to Lion's Choice. Will and Raven have never had their roast beef, so I suggested it on the way home. I'm so sorry. We should have asked you to meet us there."

Seriously? You didn't think to invite me? I mean, I'm just your boyfriend! "I'm starving."

Sarah ran downstairs and laid her hand on his shoulder, then proceeded to the kitchen. "Let me fix you a sandwich." She opened the fridge. "Oh, we have pizza from the other night. You can warm it in the microwave."

He could warm it? "I don't know how to use yours." He sniffed, letting her know what he thought of that idea. "It's different than the one at the house."

"Good grief!" Raven shouted from somewhere. "What *are* you, two years old?"

Sarah spoke up. "Ours *is* different than the one they have at the fraternity." She placed a few slices on a plate, then punched in the time. She opened a drawer, pulled out a fork, and placed it on the breakfast counter. "It'll be ready in no time."

He sniffed again. "Any napkins?"

"Right there, on the counter." She pointed to the napkin holder, then grabbed a couple, folded them into an isosceles triangle—the way he liked—then ran past him. "We'll be ready to go in ten minutes."

"No rush." He tried to modulate his tone to nonchalant.

After moving the fork on top of the napkins, he made himself comfortable on the island stool. As the microwave hummed, he tapped his fingers on the granite. The timer dinged. He waited, craning his neck toward the hallway.

I guess she didn't hear the ding from upstairs. Better let her know it's time to retrieve my dinner ...

No. Wait. It would be more thoughtful if he retrieved his own meal. Even though they were so rude and forgot him when *they* went to dinner.

"Hot. Hot. Hot." He puffed as he pulled the steaming plate from the microwave and dropped it on the granite. He shook his fingers and blew on them.

The cheese was like molten lava. But once it cooled, he had to admit it tasted good. After he finished, he looked up.

Raven. Again. She leaned against the doorframe watching him.

Those eyes, so similar but so different from Sarah's, were like refracted lasers. His stomach churned.

He wiped his face with the napkins. He was *not* giving in to her intimidation. Raven was as tiny as Sarah. He could take her down.

Her brows knit together. She stood erect, jaw tight. He stood, arms by his side, but his hands fisted. *Yeah, that's right, lady. I can take you down.*

"All ready." Sarah appeared next to her sister. She looked at Raven, then him. "Is everything okay?"

"Peachy." His Georgia accent reappeared. "Just peachy."

But not for long.

Chapter 15

Hope Sweeting fluffed her hair. She sighed. At least she was out of Cardiac ICU and in a regular room.

"Are you up for visitors?" Sarah's sweet face leaned into her room. "All of us are here."

"Yes, my lovelies. Oh my, yes!"

Drew followed Sarah. Then Rachel and Asher. Then a handsome young man she didn't recognize. He carried a beautiful floral arrangement. If she wasn't mistaken, they were orchids.

"Hi, Mrs. Sweeting." The young man spoke as he placed the flowers on the windowsill next to her other bouquets. "Wondering who I am?" He moved closer to her bed. "My name is William Durning—my friends call me Will. And I'm Raven's best friend."

Raven? Her Rachel was using her middle name? Elizabeth had always wanted to call a child that—ever since she'd read Edgar Allen Poe in junior high.

"I'm sorry, Granny—" Sarah placed her hand on Will's shoulder. "Will didn't know we always called her Rachel."

Will's stricken face moved Hope to compassion. "Sweet boy, a rose by any other name smells as sweet. And thank you for the beautiful flowers. Are they orchids?" She extended her hand toward him. He took it with both his and warmed hers.

You can tell a lot about a person by their hands.

"Please, everyone, sit." At last, a nice long visit.

There were only three chairs, so Sarah and Drew sat next to each other. Asher pulled the last chair toward Rachel.

Dear Asher, he was such a gentleman.

He and Will found room on the sill and sat among the flowers.

She laid her hand on her heart and sighed.

"How is the bakery?"

Sarah and Rachel smiled at each other and then at Asher and Will.

Hope chuckled. "You four look like kittens who found the creamery."

"Are you sure you're up to talking about business?" Rachel—Raven—asked, concern darkening those crystal-blue eyes.

"Fiddle-faddle, the bakery and all my customers are family."

The four of them talked at once. Finishing each other's sentences. As near as Hope could gather, Will was also a baker and had fit right in with Sarah and Asher. Although he looked more like a movie star.

Her Sarah's eyes certainly sparkled. Was it over baking ... or Will? Hope sighed. "Isn't this all so wonderful?"

Sarah reached for Hope's hand. "Now we have to pray harder for Mom to return."

Hope tried to hide her gasp. She glanced toward Rachel, who looked at the floor. What could she say? "It's all in our heavenly Father's hands."

So, Sarah hadn't yet discovered the horrible secret Rachel and she shared. She needed to tell Sarah. Soon. But not here. Not like this.

Hope's glance moved to Drew. His stare drilled into her. Was he reading the secret in her heart? Hope looked away. She had never fully trusted Drew—even though he attended church with them.

Her fingers kneaded her blanket. Yes, she would reveal the tragic news of Lizzy's death. But she would never reveal it was due to drugs.

Never.

Drew opened his laptop and pulled up Google. Something wasn't right. And he was getting to the bottom of it. Those looks passing between Raven and Mrs. Sweeting?

Suspect, at best.

Were they keeping secrets from his Sarah? Not if he could do anything about it.

Hours later, he had a stack of screenshots and news articles. He shut the computer and rubbed his scalp. *Poor Sarah.*

Elizabeth Sweeting-Oscar—aka Lizzy Souwer—had died of crack overdose. Ten. Years. Ago.

How could he tell Sarah?

He stood and paced the small patch of linoleum.

Why would Sarah's grandmother and sister keep this from Sarah? It didn't make sense. According to several articles, Raven was the one who found her mother in the crack house and called 911.

There had been a feature story about her in the local newspaper out west because of Raven. She had been an A student despite living in squalor.

Who knew how involved Raven was in all the drugs? She may have been a user too. Or sold them. She might even still be using.

He shook his head. No, probably not.

His teeth gritted. But maybe ...

Get real. How could she be an *A* student and be an addict? Maybe she sold drugs? He should check for criminal records.

Raven looked guilty of *something*.

He lifted his cell from his holder. Two o'clock in the morning—too early to call Sarah. Besides, his interview with Untergarten was in an hour. He had to prepare and change clothes. He needed to be focused on his future. His and Sarah's.

She'd suggested the black tie. He grabbed his shaving kit and toiletries and headed for the showers down the hall.

He needed to do what he could to make sure the way Sarah's mother died didn't go public. Untergarten would only do a background check on *him*. Right? He wasn't married to Sarah, yet. He had the ring. But ...

No. He should be fine.

"Guten Morgen, Frau Müller. Es freut mich, Sie kennen zu lernen." He practiced as he gathered his shirt and tie. He could wear his jeans since the screen only showed him from the waist up.

His German instructor, Mr. Schmidt was specific about how to address the personnel manager. He had made Drew practice. "Good morning, Ms. Müller. It's a pleasure to meet you." And he insisted Drew used the proper inflection, so his Southern-American accent was erased.

"The first impression, *Herr Collar,* will help them overlook any small mistakes later," Professor Schmidt had said.

Drew turned on the bathroom light and shut the door. He couldn't afford any mistakes. This job meant everything to him.

Nothing—and no one—would stand in his way.

Chapter 16

Sarah sat on the living room couch and watched for Drew through the front window. She curled her blonde strands behind her ear as she struggled to settle her thoughts.

Not like Raven had been forthcoming about their mother, but since that visit at the hospital, Sarah sensed Granny hid something from her too.

Today at the bakery, Raven was overly kind and accommodating. Sarah felt like the kid who was about to be told her puppy had been run over.

Drew pulled into the driveway and tooted the horn. She grabbed her jacket and purse. "Drew's here. I'll see you later."

Raven stepped away from the kitchen. "See you."

Sarah lifted her glass of champagne and clinked Drew's glass. "To a great phone interview and on to St. Louis for interview number two. Cheers."

"Cheers." He took a long sip, then held the flute.

Sarah took a tiny sip, the bubbles burning her nose, then set the glass down. "So, is there a possibility you could be hired at the St. Louis plant during the interview?"

"We'll see." He finished his glass and poured another one. "I suppose I could start there and then put in for a transfer further down the line."

Transfer? To where?

His brows scrunched. "What's with the face? You don't want me to have my dream job?"

What? She grasped his hand. "No, no. Not at all. I want you to be happy, Drew. It's—now that my sister is back in my life, I would hate to be so far away. When—if—we get married."

He sneered. "Like you two have been getting along so great."

Wow. She pulled her hand from his and placed both in her lap. "Drew."

He took another drink—more like a swig. "You don't know, Sarah. Your sister isn't all she claims to be."

She twisted her napkin under the table. What was wrong with him tonight? "What do you mean?"

"I *mean* she's lying to you. And I suspect, your grandmother is too." He squinted, and Sarah shivered. His countenance was positively ... menacing.

Was he getting drunk? Where was the kind Christian man she'd known for years?

"Listen." Light returned to his hazel eyes. "I don't like anyone treating you badly." He took another sip. "I hadn't wanted to tell you this until later. We have important decisions to talk about. But it's probably best to get this out of the way first."

He reached toward her and opened his hand. She paused, then placed hers in his.

"I have some difficult news." He placed his other hand on top of hers.

Her breath hitched.

"Sarah, your mother is dead."

Something roared in her ears.

"No. No, she's not. Why would you say such a thing?" She yanked her hand from his grip. *He's not making sense.*

"I'm sorry. She's been dead for ten years."

She covered her ears. "Stop saying she's dead!"

It couldn't be true. Raven was back. They could be a family again.

"No!" She stood, knocking her chair sideways.

"Babe, you're making a scene." He came behind her to right the chair and get her to sit.

She pulled away. "Did Raven *know?* Did she know all this time?" She grabbed his shirt.

He wrenched her hands away. "She was the one who found your mother and called 911." Drew sat Sarah back on her chair.

Found her? Found Mom dead?

"I don't understand. How could she not tell me?" Sarah pounded the table.

Drew grabbed her hand, then handed her his champagne. "Here, drink this."

She shoved it away. Raven knew? She was there?

She hid this from me? Why?

"I need to get out of here." She snatched her purse from the floor and ran for the exit.

No, God! Mom can't be dead.

"How did she die?" Sarah leaned against the passenger window.

Drew said nothing. She turned and watched him squirm, his hands tightening on the steering wheel.

Right. She bit her lip. "Drugs?"

His surprised expression was all the answer she needed. "How did—"

"Kids. Whispers and looks from adults while growing up." She ran her hands through her hair, then rubbed her temples.

How could you do this, God? All those prayers ... and she was dead all this time!

"Why wouldn't Granny tell me my mother had a drug problem? I could have prayed more. I could have—" *God! God! God!* She pounded the passenger window.

She sobbed.

She screamed.

Drew pulled into the driveway as bile rose in her throat.

Her childhood home represented love and safety and *truth*. Now, she knew. All was deception and lies.

She grabbed the door handle and shoved opened the door, but her seatbelt restrained her. She yanked and pulled to release it. It wouldn't budge. She let loose another scream.

Drew reached over and unclicked her belt.

She strode toward the house. The front door opened. There stood Raven. Raven who *lied* to her.

"Why didn't you tell me? How could you not tell me our mother *died!*" Her fingers itched to grabbed Raven and shake her.

Raven cried out. Her eyes ignited. She ran toward Sarah—then past her.

"You *jerk!*"

What? What was she doing?

Raven ran to where Drew stood, by the open car door, and shoved him. Hard. He tried to brace himself with the side mirror but missed and fell, chin-first, against the mirror. Then he hit the ground with a grunt.

Before Sarah could even react, Drew glared up at Raven, his face a mask of shock and hatred. "What the—? Are you *crazy?*"

Sarah covered her mouth. Move! Stop them! But she couldn't. She couldn't budge.

Raven stood over Andrew, her fist raised.

No! Sarah broke free of whatever had held her and ran to her twin. She laid her hands over Raven's tightened fists. "It's okay, Raven. Go inside. I'll be right there."

Raven's breath came in spurts. Her eyes connected with Sarah's, and her hands relaxed. She blinked, then looked at Drew. "I-I'm so sorry." She covered her mouth, then sprinted to the house.

Sarah extended her hand to Drew. He elbowed it away. "Your sister is certifiable." He stood and brushed himself off. "I'm calling the police." He pulled his phone from his belt.

"Please, Drew." She placed her palm over his cell. "She was upset. She thought she had to protect me." She *was* protecting her, wasn't she?

"I don't care. She *hit* me." He sniffed.

Are you whining? Raven is half your size. Sarah tried not to laugh.

"She didn't hit you. She pushed you, but you fell against the mirror." She examined the spot where the mirror had made contact. It was red, but no blood. "It was an accident."

"Caused by *her!*" Drew slapped her hand away.

Sarah gasped and stepped back. *He hit me?*

He didn't mean it. "It doesn't look too bad. You'll have a nasty bruise. You were more surprised than hurt."

He grimaced and turned away. "She shoved me hard."

"She weighs less than I do—maybe a hundred pounds tops."

He glared at her.

Come on, Drew. Why are you acting like this?

"Let me go inside and get an ice pack," she said.

He slammed the passenger door, then walked to the driver's side. "I may not call the police, but I *will* call my lawyer. She's not getting away with this."

Lawyer? He had a lawyer? "Please, don't do anything rash."

"Rash, she says." With that, Drew climbed into his car, slammed the door, then peeled out of the driveway.

Would he call the police? Hire a lawyer and sue her sister?

She stood alone in the cold.

My mother is dead.

Sarah went inside and locked the front door.

"Is he calling the cops?"

Sarah jumped. Raven sat on the floor in the darkened living room.

"Honestly, I don't know." Sarah joined her.

Raven groaned.

"What were you *thinking?*"

Raven rubbed her face with her hands. "I made oatmeal cookies with dark chocolate chips, raisins, and pecans. Want some?"

Actually, she *could* use a cookie right now. Maybe a dozen. She sure didn't want to think about the craziness that just happened.

After a half dozen cookies, they sat back on the stools and wiped the milk and crumbs from their faces. Almost in perfect rhythm.

They hadn't spoken a word, just sighed at another of Raven's treats.

Sarah wiped her hands on a napkin, then swiveled her stool toward Raven. "That was an impressive push." She placed her elbow on the counter and rested her chin on her fingers.

Raven shrugged. "You asked me earlier what I was thinking. I was thinking Drew hurt you, bad. I was thinking our grandmother wanted to tell you about our mother in her own way."

There it was. Her new reality.

Their mother was gone. How was she supposed to deal with this?

"When? When was she planning to tell me?"

Raven mirrored Sarah's posture. They stared at each other.

Raven's eyes filled. "I don't know," she whispered. "I wanted to tell you right then, with her. She told me not to and to not—"

"To not tell me Mom died of a drug overdose."

"How—"

Sarah rubbed her face with her hands. "You know, I was thirteen when I suspected drugs might have been involved in Mom leav—kidnapping you." There. The words she had kept hidden away were finally free. "But I figured something as significant as that ... well, you would have told me. Or Granny. *Somebody* would have said something."

Raven squeezed Sarah's hand, then released it. "I wanted to. It was eating me up inside." She took a sip of milk. "Sarah, does our grandmother typically not tell the truth?"

"No! She has always been the sweetest, most caring person ever. Everyone in town loves her."

"Right. But she kept our mother's drug problem a secret."

True. "I guess she was trying to protect me."

"So, how was it you guessed—you know, about Lizzy?"

Sarah gave a humorless laugh. "This is a small town. Growing up, kids from school sometimes said cruel things about our mother. You know, the mean girls."

"Didn't you ask Granny about it?" Raven took another cookie and broke it in two, then set it down.

"I may have when I was younger. But, I don't think so. Maybe I didn't want it to be true, so I didn't pursue it. You know what I mean?"

Raven nodded.

Raven's questions were helping Sarah begin to make sense of this new disturbing reality. Her breathing had calmed.

"What about you? How did you live with Mom's drug problem?"

Raven looked away. "You survive. I've moved on." Raven jumped off the stool and began cleaning up.

That was it? "I moved on"? So, her sister wasn't ready.

There was so much more Sarah wanted to talk about. Needed to know. Nevertheless, this night was a breakthrough between them.

It had gone from her worst day to a real beginning in their relationship. All because the truth was revealed.

Now, if she could convince Drew to not call the police.

Chapter 17

Scarface slapped Raven again. The pain was like a hundred wasps stinging her at once. Raven looked at her mother. Begging her with her eyes to help her, but there was only the dead fog of drugs.

"I said, where is the package? Get it and deliver it, now." *He lifted his meaty hand.*

"I don't know *where it is. It's time for school." Raven held her homework. The essay she had written about her favorite day. She had written it in the tattered notebook she stole from a Dollar Store.*

Whack! Raven crumbled to the floor. She saw his heavy boot just before it—

"Raven!"

Someone grabbed her. Shook her. She tried to punch and fight them off.

"Ouch! Raven, it's *me*. Wake up!"

Raven opened her eyes. The bedroom light blinded her. Her arms were held down by her sister. "Sarah?"

"There you are. You had quite a nightmare."

A nightmare? It was a nightmare. He wasn't here.

Yet her body still shook—her nightgown was soaked in perspiration.

Her new gown, with the tiny red cardinals.

No. She'd left that violence behind, in her past. How could she let it intrude on her new life? A geyser of pain erupted, and she sobbed in her sister's arms.

"Here's Henry." Sarah placed him into Raven's arms, then wrapped her own arms around them both.

Sarah began humming and rocking her. Raven allowed herself to relax in her sister's comfort, then frowned. What—?

A distant memory nudged at her.

Rocking. In a chair? Whose arms?

A woman's arms.

She smelled like cinnamon.

Raven tried to concentrate, to see her face. Was it her mother?

The face came into view.

Grandmother. Granny! Singing to her.

For once, Raven didn't push a memory away. She settled into it.

And slept.

Raven scuffed into the sunny kitchen. She had overslept. Sarah must have gone on to the bakery.

A note lay on the counter next to a small glass ladybug. The whimsical thing made her smile.

Good morning. I didn't want to wake you. There's orange juice in the fridge and a few hard-boiled eggs. The coffee is ready to brew, press the button. Call me if you want to come to the bakery. Or take a break. I have my last midterm at ten, so if I'm not available, one of the guys will fetch you. Someday, I hope you will trust me enough to share your pain. That's what sisters are for.

Love you,
Sarah.

Eight o'clock already. She would eat, then shower and be ready before Sarah left for her class.

Raven reread the note several times as the coffee brewed. Each time she came to *that's what sisters are for,* she choked up.

A tiny bud of something grew in her.

In the quiet of this house where she had lived so long ago, there was hope. Was she truly home?

Tears fell freely. No one to see and hover offering comfort she didn't want. Just feelings she could feel.

She poured a cup of coffee. Could she stay here? Live here?

Impossible.

What about her job in LA? What about her best and only friend? There was no way *he* would want to live in a small Missouri town. How had he lasted this long? He didn't need a job, but he loved the work. And he loved Beverly Hills.

And then there was Granny. Could she trust her? Or was she self-serving and deceitful like Lizzy? But even though Sarah knew now that Granny had lied all these years, her sister still believed Granny to be a good person.

Sarah should know, right?

She was one of the purest souls Raven had ever encountered.

She was certain Sarah would want to confront Granny tonight. She sipped her coffee.

Would Drew be there?

She rolled her eyes.

He hadn't called the police, or she would have had a different morning. But this wasn't over. He would get even somehow, some way. She knew his type.

All too well.

Her cell rang. A California area code, but no name, and she didn't recognize the number. She let the call go to voicemail. It might be another bakery interested in her since the airing of the show. She had received several calls like that.

The show had changed her life. Only not in the way she'd imagined.

Well, time to clean up.

She tidied the kitchen and headed for the showers. She would need to do laundry after they visited Granny. Or maybe Asher and she could take another midnight run to Walmart.

Her cheeks warmed. He was like no other guy she'd ever met.

She climbed the stairs and entered the bathroom. As she undressed, she looked at herself in the bathroom mirror. Her tattoos, brow and navel piercings, scars, and short hair didn't fit the all-American girl someone like Asher would want.

She shook herself. So what?

She belonged in the impersonal world of Los Angeles. Not a quaint, small, Missouri town. She didn't belong here.

No matter how much she wanted to.

Chapter 18

Asher dropped in on his parents at the Chemical Engineering department before his next appointment.

"Good morning, Mother. Father." He kissed his mother's cheek and shook his father's hand.

"Son." His father focused on the file in his hand. "What can I do for you?"

"Oh, Arlin. Asher doesn't need a reason to visit us."

"I wanted to check in. I've been busy helping the Sweetings since Granny had the heart attack."

"Um-hmm." His father lifted one of the papers in the file. He stopped and turned his attention to Asher. "What about your research project with Professor Sparlin? You haven't neglected your *real* work, have you?"

"Yes, Asher." His mother touched Asher's arm. "You shouldn't neglect your research. If you want to teach here, a doctorate is necessary."

"Don't worry, I spoke with my advisor on Monday, and I have an appointment with her." He looked at his watch. "In fifteen minutes."

A sound from the doorway caught their attention, "Professor West."

"Yes?" Both his parents responded. In unison.

Asher's mother gasped. "Dear me, Andrew, what happened to you?"

Asher looked over his shoulder. Whoa! He grabbed Drew's shoulder and looked at the large bruise on his chin and jaw. "What happened, buddy?"

"Nothing. I ran into a door." He narrowed his eyes as though communicating a hidden message. "Professor West, I know my advisory appointment is next Monday, but can you spare a few minutes? I wanted to review my findings with you and relay my good news about Untergarten."

"Certainly, Andrew," Asher's mother said. "Asher, come by any time. And don't neglect your work, dear."

His mother and Drew entered her office and closed the door.

He was about to say goodbye to his father, but he had already shut his office door.

"Hey." Drew peeked from Asher's mother's office and motioned to Asher.

What was this about? Asher stepped toward him. "What's up?"

"Listen, I didn't run into a door."

"Figured as much."

"It was Raven. She *punched* me." Drew's whispered words were so intense he spit on Asher.

He stepped back, as much from the accusation as Drew's spittle.

"Mr. Collar, you're wasting your advisory time." Asher's mother tapped her desk.

Drew closed the door.

Asher stared. *Raven? Punched Drew?* No way a petite woman could hit a six-foot man. Not unless she was standing on a ladder!

Still ...

Raven wasn't at the bakery early this morning when Asher arrived. All Sarah had said was her sister had had a rough night. A rough night ... hitting Drew? Did Sarah know?

Stop. Better to not make assumptions. He'd have to get both sides of the story. The truth was generally somewhere inbetween.

He glanced at his watch. Oops. The Electrical Engineering Department was across campus. If he wanted to make his appointment, he'd better hurry. The mystery of Raven's altercation with Andrew Collar would just have to wait.

As he sprinted, the image of tiny Raven leveling the athletic Drew made him chuckle the whole way there.

It wasn't funny. He shouldn't laugh.

He grinned.

Who was he kidding?

It was hilarious!

Until a few minutes ago, Will and Mabel Abel—Will laughed every time he said her name—were the only hands on deck for another busy morning. And folks were a bit surly without Raven's creative free samples.

Sarah had carried her sweet personality to school to take her midterm.

He rang up another sale.

Raven had walked the mile and a half to the bakery and arrived as Sarah left. While Raven's pastry creations were great, he could use an extra pair of hands.

Asher walked through the swinging door, tying an apron around his waist.

Thank you.

"Ash."

He dipped his chin, his customary smile missing. "Sorry to leave you so long without help."

Will thanked the customer paying for a special order of two-dozen donuts and two-dozen Danish for their women's Bible study.

"Mrs. Johnson—" Asher stepped around the counter and grabbed the large boxes. "Let me carry those to your car."

"Why, thank you, Asher." She cooed. "Keith wasn't available to pick up the refreshments this week."

"And how is Pastor?"

The two chatted as they exited.

Right. *Johnson*. Asher said his pastor's name was Keith Johnson.

Will helped the next customer pick out cookies for a men's Bible study. Folks around here sure studied the Bible a lot. Or maybe they liked cookies and pastries.

The chatter in the bakery went silent. All eyes focused behind him. He twisted around. Raven stood there, holding a tray of goodies, looking for all the world like a fawn trapped in high beams. Her bottom lip tight between her teeth, she nodded.

Wow. She was allowing strangers here to see her. Even knowing they wouldn't think of her as a brilliant pastry chef, but as Granny's long-lost granddaughter and Sarah's twin sister.

He couldn't be prouder.

"Looks like we have another new delight, folks. What do you have for the citizens of Minersville?" Will gave a flourish of his hand.

"I have four-dozen samples of stout chocolate mini-cupcakes." She set the tray on the counter next to the cash register.

He laid his arm across her shoulders and gave her a squeeze. Her small frame shook like his mother's Chihuahua on bath day. "Folks, our Raven—whom you might also know as Sarah's twin sister, Rachel—has made her famous beer cupcakes."

The flock of interested customers moved toward her. Will almost stopped them, but Raven gave a slight shake of her head.

Silently, one by one, they approached her, whispering "Welcome" and "God bless you." Several reached across the counter and hugged her. Touched her hand.

Many said they had prayed for her and her mother.

All spoke with such reverence and awe.

Will couldn't speak around the lump in his throat. *What is this?* He watched as his rough and tough friend accepted the sweet reception.

Good grief. He was crying. He wiped the stream of tears with his arm, then ran another credit card. People had purchased boxes of donuts, muffins, cupcakes, bread, cookies, cakes, pies, and anything else Raven said was tasty.

No one spoke above a whisper—it was like they were in church.

Of course. That's what it was. Something holy.

After Mabel waited on the last customer, Will looked around the bakery. Only a few baked items were left, and it was hours before closing.

Asher and Sarah walked in just then. He saw the reality register on their faces—the cases were empty.

"What happened?" Sarah stretched out her arms and spun around. "We're *sold out?*"

"Pretty much." Will couldn't stop the grin. Which was good, because he didn't want to.

Mabel Abel removed her apron and folded it over her arm. "This was one of the best days I've ever had at Sweet's. If it's okay with you kids, I'll head home early. I can't wait to tell Walter!" Her smile was so wide it rattled her dangling donut earrings.

Will high-fived her. "Way to go, Mabes!" She giggled, then walked through the kitchen.

"How?" Sarah rubbed her arm.

Will pointed at Raven. She shrugged, then shifted her gaze to Asher.

Oh. Will's heart skipped.

His best friend liked Asher?

He looked at Asher. *And* he *likes* her.

Hmm. This day was getting even more interesting.

Well. Since Raven wasn't forthcoming with the chain of events leading to the empty display cases, he'd have to fill in the gaps. "How this happened was your sister made her grand entrance. A hush came over the crowd and they pulled out their wallets and cleaned the place out!"

Silence.

Okay, so maybe his elucidation was lackluster. Perhaps he should have blown a trumpet. "What, guys? Is this a bad thing?"

"No, it's great." Sarah was not convincing. She placed her fingertips against her lips and walked to an empty case.

Nope, not convincing at all.

Raven wrapped her arms around her waist. "What did I do wrong? I thought you'd be happy I made an appearance."

"It's okay," Sarah said. "I'm being silly. This is great."

Raven reached toward her. "What, Sarah? Please, what did I do?"

Will watched his friend. The realization hit him. But not for his friend.

Sarah stared at the brick floor. "I wanted to be the one to introduce you to the town. To our customers." The sorrow on her face was profound. "I missed the moment. Again."

Raven's face crumbled and she ran out the front door. Will took a step to follow, but Asher beat him and followed her.

Sarah stood, sobbing. He didn't even hesitate. Will pulled her into a hug. She laid her head below his heart— she fit perfectly. Her trust warmed him like nothing ever had. Her hair smelled of sunshine and roses.

"You want to let go of my *girlfriend!*"

A hand grabbed Will's shoulder and jerked him back. Drew.

Instinctively, Will stepped in front of Sarah, knocking Drew's hand away while protecting Sarah from her boyfriend's sudden fists.

"Stop it, Drew!" Sarah backed away. "Will was only comforting me."

"Yeah, I bet."

The front door opened. Raven ran toward Sarah, taking up a position between her and Drew, her own fists up and ready. "Stay away from my sister."

Drew backed away.

Will didn't blame him. It was like being faced by a tiny but fierce wild cat.

Drew narrowed his eyes. "You're lucky I didn't call the police last night. You make one move toward me, and I'll make an exception about not hitting a woman."

"Yeah, Drew." Asher came to stand in front Raven, his hands on his hips. "There's no chance of you doing that here or anywhere else."

"*Stop* it! *All* of you!" Sarah rushed to Drew's side and linked her arm through his. "This is a misunderstanding. Ganging up on Drew isn't helping, and it's wrong."

Will closed his eyes for a moment. *Oh, Sarah, open your eyes.*

Sarah tugged her boyfriend toward the door. "Asher, please close up. I'll see you all at the hospital. It might do us good to remember Granny needs us—*all* of us." She and Drew turned and left.

Will stood looking at the others. Yup, their jaw were dropped too. "*What* just happened?" His heart raced faster than his sports car.

One moment Sarah was in his arms ... the next, she was gone.

Chapter 19

"I need to walk." Raven pulled her jacket off the coat hook next to the bakery's back door and slipped it on.

Sarah was upset. Obviously.

The last thing Raven wanted to do was hurt her sister. Not when they'd been getting along better.

Hadn't they?

Raven huffed. *I don't get this relationship thing. At all.*

Will stood, watching her like he was a tomcat and she the mouse.

"Do you want company for your walk?" Asher hung his apron and pulled on his Pea coat. "Or is this a don't-bother-me time?"

Will stilled stared at her, his green eyes penetrating hers. *Wait. Is he angry with me?*

Breathe. Relax. "I need you both. Apparently, I'm missing or misunderstanding everyone's physical cues. I can't tell if someone's angry with me or what." She flopped her arms by her side. "I like relationships simple and non-emotional."

Will snorted and turned away.

"What, Will?" Why was he so angry?

"You know what?" Asher opened the door. *"You two* need to talk. Everything here is locked up. All you need to do is punch in the code." He waved before exiting.

Raven walked to the pan cabinet and sat on top. Will leaned against the fridge, his countenance rigid.

"Will, are you angry with me?"

He looked down for a moment, then back at her. "You know I couldn't love you more than if you were my own sister, right?"

"I guess so."

He huffed. "See, that's your problem."

"My problem? What are you talking about?" She grabbed the closest thing and threw it toward him. He moved before a pie tin hit his chest.

"You threw a pan at me!" He shook his head. "It's a good thing I love you, because being your friend is *not* easy."

Her heart and stomach sank to her toes. She swallowed back the urge to run. He was right. Why would anyone want to be friends with her? She was a mess.

"Don't do it."

She picked at a freckle on her arm. "Don't do what?"

"Don't crawl back into your dark hole of depression. Don't ghost on me."

"I'm not." She turned from his probing eyes.

"Do you even care you have a sister? A grandmother?"

Tears flooded her eyes. "Yes!"

He walked toward her, then laid his hands on her shoulders. "Let's begin there." He lowered his forehead onto hers. "You've been through a lot in your life. It manifests from time to time in ways you don't even recognize. For the first time in your life, you have real family. Whether you stay here or go back to California, you *have* them."

"I don't want you to leave." She sniffed, but it didn't make a difference.

He pulled her into a hug, and she let him. "Who knows? I might want to hang around this small hamlet. Show them real style."

They chuckled together.

"But Rave, be careful with Drew. He's not someone to mess with. His agenda for our Sarah isn't good. But if you continue to poke him and ridicule him or—"

Go ahead. Say it. "Shove him."

He lifted his head. "What? You *hit* him? You gave him the giant bruise?"

Had he lost his mind? "No! I pushed him and he lost his balance, then hit his chin on the car side mirror." Raven tried to hide her smirk. Given Will's warning, it was nothing to smile about.

"Are you sure you didn't punch him?"

"You don't believe me?" Raven watched Will's face. His expressive brows raised. He *didn't* believe her. "Will, I didn't hit him."

He looked away for a moment. "Fine." He sat on the cabinet and pulled her next to him. "Tell me the details."

She did so, fighting the anger again that she'd felt last night. Drew was such a—

"Jerk! He told her without you or Granny there to console her?" He lowered his head and ran his hands through his thick hair, unloosening his ponytail.

"Worse. He told her Lizzy overdosed."

Will's head shot up. "She overdosed? You never told me your mom was on drugs."

She shrugged, but her trembling lips put the lie to her nonchalance. "I found her. Called 911. But it was—it was too late."

"Oh, man. I am so sorry. How old were you?"

"Just turned fourteen." She'd spent her first night in juvie after they took her away. They didn't know what to do with her. Didn't know if she was involved. It hadn't helped that, when the social worker tried getting her a counselor to "help deal with her grief," she threw a chair at the poor woman.

Will kept muttering, "Oh, man."

And *this* was why Raven didn't like talking about this stuff. It freaked people out. They didn't know what to say or do—or they tried to fix her. *Which is impossible.*

"I don't want to mess things up with Sarah, Will. She's one of the kindest souls I've ever met."

His eyes took on a dreamy, little-boy look. "She is."

Raven punched his arm. "You like her."

"Ouch." He rubbed the spot where she hit him. "Raven, stop. You don't know your own strength."

What a wimp. She was about to punch him again, when she stopped. She frowned. "How often do I, you know, smack you?"

Still stroking his arm, his brows knit together. "A lot. Did you see the welt on Andrew's jaw? I have had varying degrees of bruising on my arms and back from your good natured or angry strikes."

Her heart pounded. How could she not have realized that? "I didn't hit Drew," she whispered.

Why *would* Will believe her? She abused him, her best friend. How was she any different than her mother or any of her mother's other boyfriends and dealers?

And I'm not on drugs.

"Will, I am so sorry. You've been nothing but a good friend to me, and I have treated you like my personal punching bag. Literally." Was it possible to feel worse than she did right now? She hoped not. "Why would you stick around?"

He chuckled. "It's the chocolate-covered peanut-butter balls." He laid his palms on his knees. "Listen, this may sound like religious mumbo-jumbo, but I knew you were different. It was like God pulled back a curtain to let me see who you were. Inside. Deep inside. Like I had to dig deep."

Oooo, how she wanted to punch his arm again, but instead she sat on her hands. "Okay. I get your point."

"Good. Now, let's go find your sister and see if you can make amends."

Music welcomed Raven as she entered the house. It wasn't a song she recognized, but it was pleasant. Sarah sang a few lines, then stopped, then began again. Raven didn't want to disturb her—she seemed peaceful.

Then Sarah's phone rang. The music stopped—and even from this distance, Raven could tell Sarah was distressed.

She ran upstairs and into their bedroom.

"Is she okay?" Sarah asked whoever was on the other end of the phone.

Sarah noticed Raven and grabbed her arm. She whispered, "Granny had another heart attack."

No. Raven's legs trembled.

"Okay. We'll be right up there." She paused to listen. "I don't care. We're coming up."

Raven nodded. No one could tell them they couldn't see their grandmother. Or at least be there.

"Thanks for letting us know." Sarah disconnected the call, then bent over and groaned. "It was a small infarction. But they moved her back to CICU. Just to be safe."

"Let's go. You and me. No one else." Raven reached for Sarah's hand. "Please."

Sarah nodded. She stared at Raven, searching her eyes.

Raven wanted to give her sister whatever she was looking for.

"I'm sorry."

"I'm so sorry."

They spoke at the same time. Then giggled.

Raven squeezed her sister's hand. "You have nothing to apologize for. I was way off-base shoving Drew and then acting aggressive toward him this afternoon."

"Why did you do it?"

Oh, boy. How to avoid calling Drew a poser and opportunist? She had no doubt he would make Sarah's life miserable if she moved in with him or, God forbid, married him. Should she tell Sarah she had enough experience with these types to recognize one at fifty paces?

No. Just stick to the facts Sarah understood. "Drew shouldn't have told you about Lizzy—Mom."

Sarah nodded. "Granny should have."

"Exactly. He should have waited until Granny could break it to you."

"No, I mean, Granny should have told me as soon as you told her."

Raven released her grasp. "Sarah, what could I do? She is our grandmother. A grandmother I just discovered. She begged me to not say anything, especially about the overdose."

"I know. And I know why she did it. To protect me." She sighed. "Let's head to the hospital. See how she's doing. We can talk more in the car. Or we can talk about something else—like perhaps ..." She winked. "... your crush on Asher?"

Raven contemplated chucking Henry at her.

Great, I do have a violent streak.

Sarah grabbed Henry and fake-bopped Raven over the head.

"Oops, don't want to give you a shiner." Sarah chuckled. She raised and lowered the bear a few times, then hesitated. "Henry gain weight?"

"Funny." Raven snatched him back and laid him on her pillow.

How could her sister read her so well?

Did Asher see it too?

Sarah backed out of the hospital parking space. Their visit with Granny was nonexistent, but Miss Alma let them stand by the open door and watch her sleep. And they caught the doctor before he left for the night.

"Cautiously optimistic," he said. Granny could move back to a regular room soon.

Yes, it was good we came.

Raven fiddled with the door handle.

"You want to talk about what you're thinking?"

She looked at Sarah and chortled. "I have about a dozen lines of thought surging through my head. Which one would you like to talk about?"

"Pick one."

"Do you know anything about our father?"

Sarah blew air through her lips. "I hadn't expected that question. I had planned to ask *you* eventually."

"I don't know much. Lizzy called him *The Donor.*" Raven made quotation marks with her fingers.

That was disgusting. How would Sarah erase that thought? "Ew."

"Yeah, great thing to tell a kid. I didn't know what it meant until I was older." Raven folded her hands in her lap. "Do you know anything?"

"I know he signed over his parental rights to Granny." Sarah squeezed the steering wheel. Another rejection. *Have I no value, God?* "Should we ask her about him?"

Raven shrugged. "Not now, but eventually, yeah. Can you remember anything?"

Conjuring up this memory wouldn't be fun for Sarah, but Raven needed to know. "I was four or five when he left. I don't remember much of what he looked like. Except he was handsome. I thought he looked like a prince." She swallowed and fought to not feel the pain she was about to share.

"I remember he gave me a white stuffed polar bear—the one on my bookshelf." She'd clearly gotten the better end of the deal staying with her grandmother in a small town surrounded by people who loved her, but her parents *both* abandoned her. Both made a conscious effort to ditch her.

God? I'm having a tough time believing You really love me. Especially with evidence like this.

"I remember standing on the couch looking out the living room window and watching him drive away." Pounding on the window, crying for him.

"Oh." Raven laid her hand on Sarah's arm. "Maybe we shouldn't talk about this yet."

Sarah glanced down at her sister's hand. "I don't know. There seems to be a whole room full of stuff I've locked away that I need to deal with."

Raven withdrew her hand and chuckled. "Me too. It's the size of the Banc of California Stadium."

I suppose that's pretty big.

"We're a mess, aren't we?" Sarah laughed.

"It's nice to know we're a mess together." Raven smiled. "Do you think he's remarried? Has more children?"

Huh. Another family? Great. Another opportunity for rejection.

"I don't know."

"You know, we could have siblings. Half-brothers and sisters." Raven bounced in her seat.

Well, this was new. Raven hadn't been this excited even when they met. Why would she care about the children of a father who never cared about them?

"Is he still in town?"

"No. The last scuttlebutt was he had moved somewhere in Europe." She exhaled. "Which I'm not supposed to know."

"Hmm. Apparently polite society has as many secrets as the drug world. What's up with that?" Raven rested her elbow on the door.

Sarah had never looked at it that way.

"Maybe it's all about protection." Sarah turned into their subdivision.

"Protection?"

"I don't know. We either protect those we love, or we protect ourselves." She pulled into their driveway and put the car into park.

"Yeah. Speaking of protection." Raven shifted in her seat to face Sarah. "I pushed Drew because he hurt you."

"Raven, he wasn't trying to cause me harm. All he did was tell me something he thought I needed to hear."

"I know you believe he was helping you, but he's not who you think he is, Sarah."

Sarah's back stiffened. Why was Raven doing this? They were getting along. Connecting. Why did she have to start in on Drew again? "You haven't known him for a week and you've judged him this way?"

Sarah turned off the engine, unbuckled her seatbelt, and opened the car door. "Stop, Raven. Stop."

Raven followed her into the house. "Maybe I'm wrong. The last thing I want to do is hurt you."

Sarah turned. There was no denying the vulnerability on her sister's face. *I can't let you talk that way about Drew.* "Can we agree to disagree?"

Raven sloughed off her coat and hung it on the coat rack. "Fine. Just so you know, I'm watching him."

Sarah chuckled. "If you can promise to not hit him again, you can watch him all you want."

"Pushed him!" Raven huffed. "No promises. I reserve the right to protect my loved ones."

Okay. At least it was a peaceable agreement. More or less. "Any of those oatmeal cookies left?"

Wait. Loved ones?

Now, to get Drew on the same page.

Chapter 20

Will lifted the metal tray from Imo's counter and was assaulted—in a good way—with smoky BBQ flavor. He resisted grabbing a piece as he carried it to the table. Could someone get addicted to this pizza? Was there like an *Imo's Anonymous?*

Setting the pie down, Will grabbed a slice as he sat. "Hey, I Googled the mystery cheese you said was on this. It's called *Provel.* What is Provel?"

"Brother, the less you know, the better." Asher scooped up a slice. His eyes bulged. "Wait! Oh, man. Forgot to thank the Lord." He lowered his chin and made conversation with the Almighty. Simple. Short. Comfortable.

It wouldn't surprise Will if God responded—or joined them in a slice.

"Dig in, buddy," Asher said.

He lifted one piece and took a bite.

"Hot! Hot!" Will filled his cheeks with air and rolled the bite around in his mouth, then chewed. The sweet, smoky, and tangy taste hit all the right notes on his supposedly sophisticated palate. *Okay then.*

"Was I right?" Asher waggled his eyebrows.

"God bless Missouri." Will shoved in another slice. "Forget California cuisine, give me comfort food." Will raised his giant Dr. Pepper cup. "Is this comfort food?"

Ash laughed so hard he spurt his Mountain Dew. "You are a hoot. And I needed this." He wiped his face with his napkin.

"Confused by Raven?"

He shrugged. "I also had a rough meeting with my advisor. The first draft of my dissertation is overdue."

"Ouch."

"Yeah. Then hearing from Drew about the incident between him and Raven. *Then* Granny's second heart attack and Sarah asking that I not come to the hospital."

That last one must have really hurt Asher, for sure.

A comfortable silence encircled them as they scarfed down their dinner. Will had never been content in the quiet. It was too ... lonely.

A Malibu mansion might seem like a dream home, but it was a cold and solitary setting for his childhood. Not a home.

He chewed another slice.

He would never want to trade his dysfunctional upbringing for Raven's, but watching Sarah in her environment demonstrated to him life could be different—filled with warmth and purpose.

Will put his slice back on the tray.

"Ash ..." Was he really going to ask this? Yes, he was. "When did you know God was real?"

Asher wiped his mouth and swallowed. "Wow. Didn't expect that."

"You don't have to answer if it's too personal." Will's heart raced. Here was a guy who really seemed to know God.

"Not at all." Ash looked toward the ceiling. "Remember when I told you about wandering into the bakery when I was a kid?"

Will nodded and held his breath.

"Even as a kid, I realized there was something more in life. At first, it was finding that someone cared about me. Granny asked me about school. Congratulated me on good grades. At home, all I got was the obligatory 'Challenge yourself, son.'"

Asher and he were similar in more ways than Will thought.

"I couldn't wait to go to the bakery after school. I belonged there. My parents were brilliant, but I knew at an early age their love came with conditions. They love me and want the best for me—according to their terms." Ash leaned forward his brown eyes glowed. Something Will had seen more than once in his new friend—and with Sarah.

"As young as Sarah was when we first met, she talked about Jesus like he was her best friend. I half-expected him to step through the kitchen door and join us as we played Candy Land." He sipped his soda.

"So, you knew—"

"I knew I wanted whatever brought them such peace, no matter where they were. Even in a bakery."

Will wanted that peace. "Raven needs that peace."

Asher gave Will a knowing smile. "My friend, we all need it."

"Some of Raven's chaotic past has spilled into her well-ordered present. Like her hitting Andrew—or shoving Andrew."

Asher nodded. "What she did seemed over-the-top to me, until Sarah told me what Drew had done."

"Yeah, not cool."

Will wanted to ask Asher more about his faith, but he didn't know which direction to take his questions. Instead, he picked up another slice.

"Great pizza, huh?"

Asher chuckled and wiped the provel-goo off his teeth.

They finished the last of the pizza, then groaned and leaned back, holding their stomachs. "We may live to regret this meal, Ash."

"Ready to head home?"

"Maybe we should walk home and get rid of this bulk?"

They both laughed as they ambled to the truck.

Will had to ask himself, *when was the last time he had gone out on a Friday night and returned sober? Like never.* Could he get used to this?

Chapter 21

Raven waited in bed while Sarah finished brushing her teeth.

Their drive home from the hospital had ended amicably. Raven had suggested an oatmeal cookie snack. That was when the conversation took a wrong turn.

She tucked Henry under her arm. Sarah's bear, Hank, sat on the nightstand between them.

Had she misjudged Drew? People had criticized her all her life. Wrongly accusing Drew was the last thing she wanted to do. Sarah seemed to like this guy.

Raven didn't read love, but then what did she know? She'd never been in love.

Sarah walked into the room and turned off the overhead light. She shuffled her way to the bed and crawled under the covers. "Good night."

Uh-oh. She doesn't want to talk.

"Can I ask you a question?"

Her sister drew in a breath, then exhaled. "Sure."

"How did you and Drew meet?"

Sarah turned to her side to face Raven. The moonlight hit her face. She glowed like an angel. "We met at the bakery." She smiled and smoothed her blanket. "He was picking up a bunch of donuts for his fraternity. Granny didn't like him at first." Sarah looked away.

Hmm.

"He won her over after he started attending our church and Sunday school. He even serves as usher once a month."

Doesn't mean anything. "Is he from here?"

"No. He's from Georgia, a small town called Cartersville." She yawned.

"When does he graduate? Does he have a job? Will he move back to Georgia?" This wasn't good. Would Sarah leave Minersville? Leave Granny?

"Whoa. What's with the third-degree, Raven?"

"Are you seriously considering marrying this guy?" Raven's body tensed. Her breath came in short spurts. Her heart revved like a racecar.

"We're done."

"No, I want to know. Are you abandoning Granny? Are you moving to Georgia? Or anywhere other than here?" Raven sat up and moved her feet to the floor. "He's—he's taking you away."

"I can't talk with you when you're like this."

Raven's hands shook. Her body broke out in a sweat. Her heart sped up until she thought it would jump from her chest. "I—I can't—" She couldn't catch her breath.

"Raven?" Sarah pushed back her covers.

"N—n. I need—" Raven stood but fell back onto her bed. What was wrong with her?

Sarah knelt beside her. "Breathe, Raven. Breathe in through your nose. Good. Now exhale through your mouth."

As Sarah stroked her head, Raven focused on the sound of her sister's voice—her words. Somehow it penetrated the wall of anxiety.

Sarah patted Raven's back. "Oh, your gown is soaked. Let's change you into something fresh."

Raven let a sob escape. "This is the only one I have."

Sarah hugged her. "I have plenty. You can pick any one you want."

Later, snuggled into her bed, wearing one of Sarah's rosebud gowns with pink ribbons around the sleeves, Raven closed her eyes.

She'd been having these attacks since grade school.

When she moved in with her fosters, the Gillians, she had a terrible one. They took her to the hospital, where a doctor gave her a diagnosis.

Panic Attacks.

She hadn't had one in years. So why now?

She watched Sarah sleeping. Her shiny blonde hair framed her head like a lace fan.

Being there was wonderful. Being there also brought up stuff from her terrible past.

I'm losing control.

Maybe she should go back.

No.

She needed to be there for Granny. Especially if Sarah left—no, she couldn't think about that now.

God, are You there?

What was she doing? When had He ever been there for her?

She was so damaged, how could He ever want anything to do with her? How could *anyone* want anything to do with her?

"Mrs. Sweeting, you okay?"

Hope turned her head toward the nurse changing her IV.

She'd awoken from a horrible nightmare. Lizzy was calling out to her, begging for her help. Little Rachel had fallen down a deep hole. No matter how Hope tried, she couldn't get to them. Each step put her farther away. It was useless.

"I'm fine, nurse. Just a bad dream."

The nurse patted Hope's shoulder and finished the IV.

"Is Alma here?"

"Did I hear my name?" Alma peeked around the curtain. Still in her coat, her sweet face and smile did much to assuage the demons of guilt and regret.

"I'll let you two chat." The nurse left and drew the curtain closed.

Alma took off her coat and laid it across one of the chairs. She sat on the bed and held Hope's hand. "Abba wanted me to come to work early tonight. Apparently, He wanted me to see *you*. What is troubling you, my friend?"

Thank You, Father.

Hope sighed. She was finally ready to lay down the burdens she'd carried for too long. "Secrets. Too many secrets."

"Lizzy wanted to call her Raven from the beginning. I had insisted she be named Rachel. Two strong women of God, Sarah and Rachel." Hope wiped away more streams of tears. "My daughter, however, wasn't interested in emulating these women. She wasn't interested in anything of real value. She wanted nothing from me, except my money."

Hope grasped the thin blanket with her hands. "What does this old woman have to offer anyone anymore? I failed with my own daughter!"

"Your granddaughters are women now." Alma patted Hope's hands gently until she released the coverlet. "They both need you. Therefore, you need to do everything the doctor recommends so you can go home and be there for them."

"Where do I begin?"

"You can begin by letting go of all these secrets. Elizabeth's drug problem, her death, her overdose. Tell Sarah. Mourn the loss of her mother and your daughter with her."

The grief surfaced again. Her heart ached. Was she having another heart attack? She sobbed in Alma's arms. "My Lizzy. My poor daughter." No. It wasn't a heart attack. Her heart was breaking and would never be the same.

She sobbed until there were no more tears.

Alma stood and straightened her uniform. "I'm sorry, Hope. I have to begin my shift." She poured a cup of water and put in a straw. "I'll come back during my break. If you're awake, we'll pray. In the meantime, you need to hydrate and rest."

"I can't thank you enough." She held Alma's hand and squeezed it. "I was ready to give up."

"You can't. I have seen enough in this hospital to know Raven has deep wounds only Jesus can heal. Does she know Him?"

"I don't believe so."

"Then we have a lot of praying to do, Granny." Alma smiled and gave her the cup of water.

Yes, I need to get stronger. My girls need me.

Hope closed her eyes. *And I need them.*

Chapter 22

Asher watched the sisters. They hadn't said more than three words to each other since he returned from the double-portion deliveries.

Will lifted his chin toward the back door. Asher and he went outside.

"Did something happen after I left?" Asher leaned against the delivery truck.

Will whistled. "They were fine until Drew arrived." He kicked at the dumpster. "The guy was all lovey-dovey and asked Sarah to go with him for his interview on Monday in St. Louis."

Right, if Sarah and Drew get married, she will move. Away from Granny.

And it was only a matter of time before Raven and Will went back to California.

Something pierced Asher's heart. He reached up and rubbed the center of his chest.

"Ash, are you thinking what I'm thinking? What if they get married? They could be moving to—"

"Germany."

Will's jaw dropped and eyes widened. "Germany?"

Great. I did it again. Forgive me, Lord.

"Drew is interviewing with Untergarten Oil and Chemical. They have a branch in St. Louis, but the main office is in Freiburg, Germany. He's been talking for a couple years about working there."

Will paced the parking lot, running his hand through his hair. "Germany? This will kill Raven. She was beginning to open her heart. Oh, man."

"What about Granny? Her whole life has been this bakery and Sarah. With her health and Sarah—Granny may have to sell the bakery." Asher's family was breaking apart.

"No." Will pointed at Asher. "I'll buy Sweet's before anyone else tries to take it. Raven and I will run the place until Granny is strong enough, then we can run it together."

"Raven—do you think she'll want to stay?"

Will stopped, then shook his head. "Boy, you do have it bad."

Asher's face heated. This conversation was getting carried away. "Listen, Drew may not get the job. He wants a position in R&D, the alternative-fuel division, and those positions don't come easy." Asher shoved his hands in his pockets. The chill was getting to him.

"Right. So, maybe he won't get the job." Will stopped pacing and wrapped his arms around his chest. "But he *will* get a job eventually. Are the two of them serious?"

How would he know? He wouldn't know love if it kicked him in the gut.

"Ash?"

"I guess so. At least, Drew seems serious."

The door opened. Sarah stepped out, then stepped back. "It's freezing. What are you guys doing out here without coats?"

Will muttered something.

"What do you need, Sarah?" Asher rubbed his arms.

"Are you finished with deliveries? I need to use the van to run to Phelps Distributors."

"I'll do it," Asher said.

"No. I need to get out of here." She rolled her eyes.

"I'll take her. She'll need help with the heavier stuff." Will lifted his brows. Apparently, he was saying something between the lines.

Asher snickered. And Will said *he* had it bad.

Will increased his speed to merge onto Interstate 44. Sarah hadn't said much since they left the bakery. She rested her chin in her palm as she looked out the passenger window.

"So, you're going to St. Louis on Monday?"

Sarah shrugged. "I don't know. I shouldn't." She tucked her hair behind her ear, then turned toward him. "I don't know what to do. Granny is still in ICU. Raven is upset with me for even thinking about it."

Will swallowed around a mound of guilt. Hadn't he had the same reaction? "Sarah, what do *you* want?"

"I guess I need to—"

"No, not what you think others want. What do *you* want out of life? What would you do if you could do anything you wanted?"

Sarah bit her lower lip. Her full, rosebud lip. Will refocused on the road.

She blinked. "No one has ever asked me."

He glanced at her. "Aren't you taking business classes?"

"I thought it might help with the bakery." She moved her leg to sit on it. "No, that's not exactly true. I like the business part. Exploring ideas for expansion. Granny said she doesn't want to expand."

This is interesting. "How do you want to expand?"

"Oh." Her hands became animated. "I have one dream, in particular. You know the shop next door that's for sale? I want to buy it and add on a small diner. Only breakfast and lunch. Fresh breads for sandwiches, and I love making soups. Fancy desserts—like Raven makes."

Will listened as Sarah launched into her ideas. She'd thought about this a lot. From décor to menus to the type of silverware she would use. Her dream was more than a fantasy, it was a plan.

Drat! He'd been so caught up in what she was saying he missed the exit. He took the next exit and turned around before she even noticed.

They laughed as he followed the revised GPS directions.

"Sorry," she said. "Can you tell I've been thinking about this a lot?"

He pushed the turn signal. "Don't apologize. I love your passion, and it's a viable idea."

Silence.

When he glimpsed at her, she studied him. He swallowed. *She's so beautiful.*

"Will?"

"Yeah?"

"Doesn't it seem like we've known each other a long time?"

He swallowed again. "Yeah."

"You have arrived," the GPS said.

The guy who always had a quip and clever line was tongue-tied.

He had it *so* bad.

The trip back to Minersville was subdued. Will's efforts to keep the momentum for Sarah's dream failed. She spent her time looking out the passenger window. While the mountain scenery was beautiful, he wanted to rescue her from whatever thoughts had shut her down.

"Thanks for getting the almond flour and coconut oil," he said. "Raven can do wonders with those, especially for the gluten-free recipes."

"Umm-hmm."

"What is your decision about Monday?" He had no right asking, but he had a whole truckload of worry about her and Drew that had moved to front and center in his mind.

She sighed. "I was thinking about that."

Gooseflesh prickled his arm. "You don't have to tell me."

She stretched her arms forward, like a kitten in the sunshine. "I must confess, my first thought was I shouldn't leave Granny to go off on a date with Drew, but—"

"You didn't like Raven telling you what to do?"

She chuckled. "Am I that readable?"

He shrugged. "You and your sister are more alike than you realize."

"Possibly." She lifted her bottled water from the console's cup holder and took a sip. Then lifted his. "You thirsty?"

"Parched."

She handed him his opened bottle. He fumbled and spilt some over her hand and in his lap. *Smooth, Will. Smooth.*

"Oh! I'm so sorry. Do you want to pull over?"

He looked down. "Yeah. There's a puddle on the seat."

"Pull over, we can dig into the bundle of dishtowels."

He pulled onto the shoulder and clicked on his hazards. Watching for a break in the traffic, he exited the van and walked to the back. Sarah had already reached the back, opened the door, and ripped open the plastic wrapping around the towels. She grabbed several and handed them toward him.

Not *to* him, because she had averted her gaze. "I'll wipe the seat." Grabbing a few more, she walked back to the front.

It was just water. What was the big—

He looked down.

Perfect. It looked like he had wet his pants.

He did the best he could, then threw the soaked towels in the back and shut the door. By the time he climbed into the cab, his seat was dry, and Sarah sat there, eyes twinkling, her hand covering her mouth.

He started the engine. "Get it over with."

She howled. "I'm so sorry. It's not funny."

Turning on the left turn signal, he waited for a line of cars to pass then sped up to merge onto the highway. "Oh, it's funny. But you better watch your back." He joined her in laughter.

Somehow in the levity of this moment, Will knew his embarrassment would someday be a funny memory they could share.

Would there be a future where that happened?

Or would Sarah leave with his memories *and* heart?

Well, it must happen in America. Not that Raven had ever heard of the custom. Sweet's Bakery was closed on Sundays. Too bad her internal clock hadn't recognized the fact.

Awake, dressed, and nowhere to go.

She wandered the living room with her third cup of coffee. It was too early to call anyone to take her to the hospital.

Their visit with Granny the previous night was taut with unsaid words.

When would Granny do the right thing and tell Sarah? When would Sarah tell Granny she already knew? When would Sarah tell Granny she was going to St. Louis with Drew?

When did I become everyone's dumping ground for secrets?

She scuffed her hair and turned around, stepped toward the kitchen, then stopped—

Sarah's Bible sat on the counter.

She gulped her coffee. "Ah! Hot!"

Since their return from the hospital, she and Sarah had been entombed in silence. As stubborn as they both were, who knew how long it would last.

Sarah going with Drew to St. Louis was a bad idea.

Why couldn't her sister see what Drew was? And, if they moved to St. Louis or Georgia, or anywhere other than a commutable radius to the bakery, Sarah would be abandoning Granny.

Abandoning *her.*

Raven's stomach clenched—her heart beat out of synch.

God? Are You there?

She gasped. No question now—there was something in the water.

Fine.

"Here's the deal, God." Raven jabbed a finger toward the Bible. "You don't owe me anything, but I know You love Granny and Sarah. They're good people. I want to call Your attention to the fact that this is not a good thing. Her going to St. Louis with him—Drew. You may know him as Andrew Collar.

"It's a big mistake. Going will change her life, and not for the better. Granny *needs* her."

Raven collapsed against the kitchen wall. Her lips quivered. Her sinuses burned.

"*I* need Sarah, God. Please, don't take her away from me. Not now."

She rubbed under her nose. Trying to catch her breath, she walked around the kitchen.

This isn't about Drew, is it?

Was this her fear of Sarah being taken from her—like her mother had taken her from Sarah and Granny?

"God, for every good thing they have brought into my life—stuff like a sense of belonging—my anxiety has kicked into overload. Because, what if I lose it all again?"

Would God take it all away again?

Whatever. She dropped her mug into the sink with a clatter.

Oh, yeah, He could. He'd done it to her before. And worse.

She stepped to the window, pressed her forehead against the cold glass, and stared into darkness.

Best to not count on anything.

A spark of light flashed like a lightning bug.

Tiny, all but lost between the trees. Gradually, the pinprick grew and along with it, colors.

She held her breath and watched the most colorful sunrise she had ever seen.

The vista before her revealed itself in simple grandeur. Rolling hills. Trees. The pines mingled with the autumn-colored trees beginning to shed their leaves.

The morning light uncovered the backyard's largest tree. A hulking branch had a thick rope with a tire attached. Did she and her sister swing together on that tire?

Did Sarah think about Lizzy and me while on the swing? Pray for us?

Why did God only give Granny and Sarah a fifty-percent miracle? Only a sullen sister, who made people uncomfortable. And why now, after all these years?

Raven backed away from the window. This whole house was steeped in a history she didn't know. A past she craved and needed. The holes in her heart could be filled in this place. She knew it.

But not without her sister. Maybe Granny too.

As sweet and compassionate as Sarah was, they shared one heck of a stubborn streak. The rigid jaw and razor-sharp glare she saw on her sister was a mirror image to her own.

She chuckled.

So, deal with Sarah the way I want to be dealt with. The way Will helped her see the rare times she was wrong. The way the Gillians had helped her care about life again.

She had to do something.

Sarah couldn't go with Drew to St. Louis. Raven clutched her heart. Drew could steal her sister away.

That wasn't going to happen—she'd do whatever she could to prevent her sister from making a big mistake.

Thank You, Lord. Will is coming to church.

Asher finished buttoning his shirt and tucked it in.

This wasn't Will's first time at a church. He said he'd attended a large church for a few weeks when he was a teenager.

Asher walked into his tiny kitchen and poured a cup of coffee, then sat at the small dinette. He brought the cup to his lips and stopped.

Father, we're not a fancy congregation with all the bells and whistles of a mega church with lots of money. What we do have is an amazing pastor who loves You and Your Word. I pray that Will senses Your presence, and he knows You love him and have a plan for him. In His name—in Jesus's name—I lift this day to you. Amen.

"That coffee smells good." Will stood next to the coffeemaker.

Asher didn't know much about men's fashion, but he had no doubt Will was wearing the latest—and probably most expensive—pants, shirt, and jacket he'd ever seen. Although it wouldn't keep him warm. "You look sharp."

He lifted the edges of the jacket. "Too much?"

"Nah. Bring the style, brother." He sipped his strong brew.

"Maybe I should change. The last thing I want is to look like a foreigner."

Asher chuckled. "Too late, buddy. Own it." He stood. "I thought we could stop at the IHOP for breakfast. Have to get there before the Baptists or the place fills up."

Will laughed.

Was that a trace of nervousness? Nervous was okay.

This was serious after all.

Chapter 23

If only Star Trek translators were real.

Asher's pastor has asked everyone to offer the *hand of fellowship*. What the heck was that? Asher had taken off toward the back of the church, so he'd be zero help.

A huge dude wearing tattered overalls covering an equally tattered shirt shoved a beefy hand toward Will.

"God bless ya." The guy pumped Will's arm, nearly yanking it from its socket. And ... was that the faint aroma of manure?

He held his breath. "You too."

The next man was less enthusiastic and aromatic but repeated the same sentiment.

Ah. So, *hand of fellowship* meant *shake someone's hand*. Seemed anti-climactic.

Was *God bless you* synonymous with *nice to meet you*?

Asher returned to his seat. "Sorry. Had to check on a friend."

Ash's pastor—Keith Johnson—walked toward the pulpit and everyone quieted. The pastor was a short, balding guy in his forties. He looked nothing like the polished California pastors he'd seen.

"Let us pray."

Will meant to pay attention to Pastor Keith's prayer, but he spotted Sarah two rows up.

He sighed. She looked really nice, beautiful. Drew was stuck to her like Gorilla glue. As if sensing Will's observance,

Drew put his arm around Sarah's shoulder and whispered something in her ear. She nodded and smiled.

Why am I here? To torture myself?

After the prayer, everyone sat. The preacher asked the congregation to look up someone named Titus. *Who is Titus?*

Asher pulled what Will assumed were loaner Bibles from the pew rack and found the verses the pastor was talking about. Titus, the third chapter.

His wandering eyes caught Sarah and Drew, their heads together.

Ack! Will took a deep breath and exhaled.

Why am I here?

He looked around. Would he even fit in a place like this?

Asher glanced at Will and smiled.

He was there because he was ready to learn more. If Asher and Sarah were examples of what it meant to have a relationship with God, then it was worth exploring. Worth learning how to live like they did—although he didn't know if that was possible.

It was living like they knew it was all true.

"It's not about what you do," Pastor Johnson said.

What? Uh-oh.

"In Titus 3:5-7, Paul talks about those good deeds we do, that they have nothing to do with being redeemed. It's Jesus's mercy. So, we're justified by his grace, not by anything we do."

Pastor stepped away from the lectern. "It's not by us following the letter of the law perfectly. Which we can't do, by the way."

People in the pews chuckled. Someone said, "That's right."

Okay, so why do good things?

"So, should we just forget about obeying the law? Of course not. In Roman's 3:31, Paul warns that having faith doesn't mean we nullify the law. In fact, we're supposed to uphold it. But remember, what *we* do doesn't allow us to spend an eternity in the presence of our heavenly Father. It's what *Jesus* did. When Jesus cried out, 'It is finished,' it really was. For us. For all time."

Will's arms prickled. The pastor looked to the ceiling. Will wasn't sure why, but a lot of the Christians did that—looked up as though getting some heavenly signal.

The pastor strode back to the pulpit.

"Our Father loved us so much, he was willing to sacrifice his own Son. It begins and ends with love. How many of you would do anything for someone you love?"

Hands went up throughout the congregation. Including Sarah's and Drew's.

"How many would give your life for someone?"

Fewer hands.

Will sat on his hands.

"Here's the clincher, my friends. Jesus did this *before* we loved him. He did it because he loved his Father so much. And his Father loved us enough to ask Jesus to sacrifice himself."

What kind of love is this? Will had never known this type of love. Did God really feel that way about him?

He laid his hand across his chest. If his heart beat any harder, it might tear through his six-hundred-dollar shirt.

Can Asher see my heart bouncing around in my chest?

"We don't earn God's love by following the Law. He already loves us. Because we love him, because we're grateful to him and Jesus, we want to do what's important to him. This is why we commit to living a biblical life."

Commitment because of gratitude and love? Could Will love God enough to satisfy him?

"Can we ever love him enough?"

Is this guy reading my mind? Will shifted in his seat. It was either that or jump up and run.

Someone whispered, "Not enough."

Will leaned forward, elbows on his knees.

"No, we'll never love our Heavenly Father enough. But it begins with *wanting* to love him enough and knowing why. Knowing the cost. When we make that commitment, my friends, the real adventure begins."

Will couldn't breathe. He closed his eyes and lowered his head. *God, I want to love you enough. You want to be my Father? I don't even know what all of this means.*

Large blobs of tears fell onto his Italian trousers. He didn't care.

If you can see all my sins, then I figure you know who I am. I want to be a good person, but I guess more than anything I want to be your kid. What do I do? How do I do this?

The only sounds in the congregation were a few coughs. Awe tensed his muscles. Was God in the room? *If I lift my head, will God be there?*

"My friends, for those of you who want to begin the adventure, it will be one of the simplest and most difficult prayers you'll ever say. If you are sensing now is the time to commit your heart to our Father, that now is the time to acknowledge how our sins have driven us from him, then do it. And then acknowledge and thank Jesus for his willing act of sacrifice. Rejoice that no grave could hold him! You can speak these words to yourself or out loud. 'Father, I have sinned.'"

Will mouthed the words, but they shouted in his heart.

"'I don't want to be far from you, I want to be your child.'"

A few whispers scattered like pebbles around him. He swallowed and took a shaky breath. He breathed out, "I want to be your child."

"'Thank you for sending your Son, Jesus to die for my sins. This Jesus who is Lord and rose from the dead. I'm ready for my new life. Amen.'"

He repeated the rest to himself. His trousers were soaked, like yesterday while driving with Sarah. His nose was nasty too—and he didn't care.

Like a balloon floating to the heavens, he was free.

But from what?

He didn't know, and he didn't care.

Tissues appeared in front of his face. He looked to the right and thanked Asher.

Asher moved his face until Will could see him—his friend's smile was on high beams.

"My friends, if anyone here said this prayer for the first time," the pastor said, "be sure and tell someone. If you don't know anyone here, come up and tell me. We have a Bible for you and reading materials to explain what happened."

Will chuckled. *Yeah.* There was a lot of explaining someone needed to do. Now, he just wanted to savor this feeling of freedom—of peace—for as long as he could.

God loved him.

The congregation sang another song and then stood as Pastor Johnson gave a benediction. Overalls-dude pounded Will on the back. "God bless ya, buddy."

Will blew his nose and thanked him. The greeting meant more than Will could express.

"Will, did you just become my brother?" Ash laid his arm across Will's shoulder.

Brother?

If they were both God's children, then Will supposed they *were* brothers. He choked up again. "Yeah. I think I did."

Will was positively glowing. Sarah could see it even from across the fellowship hall. What hap—?

Oh!

Her heart skipped. How wonderful!

She made her way toward him when she ran into Miss Alma.

"Sarah, sweetie—" Alma hugged her—"Your grandmother was doing better as I finished my shift. Are you and your sister planning to visit her this afternoon?"

"Yes, we are."

Drew appeared at her side holding a cup of coffee and one of Sweet's mini pastries.

"Miss Alma," he said as he chewed. "Here's a question. I have an interview in St. Louis tomorrow, and I thought it would be fun to bring Sarah along. Is Granny okay enough for Sarah to be gone for *one* day?"

Sarah's stomach rolled. She'd already decided she wasn't going.

Nurse Alma eyed Drew, then shifted her gaze toward Sarah. "Medically, she should be fine."

"Excellent." He focused on Sarah. "See? I told you she'd be okay. Besides, your sister can step up to the plate for once."

"Drew!" Sarah's face heated. Where was her Southern gentleman?

"All righty then. I need to go home for shut-eye before my shift tonight." Alma shook Drew's hand. "I'll pray for God's will for your interview tomorrow." She hugged Sarah again. "If you decide to go, enjoy your time in the city."

Sarah glanced at Will and Asher. They were deep in conversation with Pastor Keith and his wife. She didn't want to interrupt.

It was so good to see that Will came to church today and that he stayed for fellowship. Neither he nor Raven had seemed interested in God. Would Will tell Raven he was at church today?

"How about we go," Drew said. "I need to get ready for our trip tomorrow."

She looked once more toward Will.

"Sure." So ... she was going to St. Louis.

She was *not* looking forward to Raven's reaction to that.

Raven sat in Granny's home office between mountains of photo albums. She had discovered two huge boxes marked *photos* on the closet floor.

She'd also found her mother's old sewing machine. Lizzy's name had been painted with flowers and curlicues. Whatever medium she used had chipped.

Raven had memories of the things her mother had fashioned by hand when she was a kid. Kerchief tops, rag dolls. Lizzy mended stuff they unearthed from dumpster diving and trash picking. She'd even mended Henry more than a few times—whether he needed it or not.

These photos gave her a better glimpse into her mother's childhood. Trips to Six Flags. Birthday parties. Graduations. Formal Dances.

How could Lizzy throw this life away?

She'd have given anything to have had half the childhood Lizzy did.

As she perused album after album, the perfect childhood continued for one of Lizzy's twins—Sarah. Trips to Six Flags. Birthday parties. Graduations. Formal Dances.

She grabbed a long, narrow, green album decorated with hand-drawn blocks and stars and hearts—and the words, *Private! Mine!* She ran her fingers over the indentations where a determined pen drew the graphics and warning.

This is Lizzy's personal photobook.

She hugged it to her chest. Were there secrets she would uncover? She inhaled deeply and exhaled. Was she ready to learn any more of Lizzy's secrets?

Raven opened the cover gently. Each page was comprised of three acetate sleeves with photos.

In the first set of photos, Lizzy looked to be in her mid-teens. Waist-length shiny blonde hair like Sarah's.

Raven touched the young, beautiful face. "What happened to you?"

Photos of Lizzy with friends canoeing down a river. Splashing one another with their paddles. At a picnic.

Raven flipped through a few pages of various outdoor activities when she came to a photo with Lizzy and a guy.

Her mother stood next to a handsome man dressed in a weird suit with shamrocks. Lizzy was in a white formal with sparkly green shamrocks. They both wore shiny emerald paper tuxedo hats. Her hair was piled on top of her head, curls dangling. She was like a beautiful, delicate China doll. Fresh. Young. Innocent.

Raven pulled the photo from its plastic sleeve and turned it over. Lizzy's handwriting had written, *Howie and me. St. Patrick's Day Dance.*

Based on the date, Raven figured Lizzy was seventeen. The guy looked several years older, maybe twenty, twenty-one.

Wait a minute ... Lizzy was eighteen when she had Sarah and her.

Was this their *father?*

Raven returned the picture to the album, then turned back a few pages and reexamined the scenes. The Howie-guy was in a lot of the photos. It wasn't until the St. Patrick's event that they were together like a couple.

This Lizzy looked like a young woman in love. Howie, like a man in love. What had happened between them?

She turned the next page. The sleeves were empty.

The next page, the top two sleeves were also missing photos. Then the bottom sleeve. Lizzy. Her countenance dour. Clearly, she was with child.

Rather, *children.*

Elizabeth Sweeting stood on the front step of this very house dressed in a pretty, flowy long yellow dress. Alone. Her jaw rigid.

Raven pulled the photo from the sleeve and turned it over. *Wedding Day.*

Granny was telling the truth. Her parents had *married.* All her life she had been called the ugly names of a child born out of wedlock. Knowing this shouldn't have mattered, but somehow it did.

Raven shoved the photo into its holder and slammed the cover.

How was she supposed to deal with all this? Seeing the face of her father. Knowing her parents were married. Knowing he deserted his own children.

Why hadn't he tried to find Raven? Rescue her? What about Sarah? At least Sarah was worth keeping.

Had Granny had something to do with him going away?

Raven's hands shook as she took a sip of her now-cold coffee.

The front door opened. Raven froze.

"I'm home," Sarah called out.

Raven relaxed. "Hey! I'm upstairs in Granny's office."

Sarah ran up, then took in the mess. "You found the photos, I see."

Raven shrugged. Would her sister be annoyed, or fine? Raven never knew.

"Let me change clothes and I'll join you," Sarah said as she took off her coat.

"Sure. I made tuna salad sandwiches for us." Which reminded her, she had almost used the last of the eggs, mayo, bread, and tuna. "We need to go grocery shopping."

"Okay." Sarah disappeared down the hallway. "We'll go to Walmart after visiting Granny."

Something was on her sister's mind. Where were those twin powers Sarah talked about?

Raven's cell chimed. She searched and found it under one of the piles of albums. A text from Will.

Will: Can we talk?

Will had turned his phone off all day. Or he let the battery die, again.

Raven: Now?

A happy face emoji. Since when did Will use happy face emojis?

She sent back a roll-the-eyes emoji.

Will: P/U 10?
Raven: K.

Raven stood, her knees creaking. Sarah walked into the office wearing an oversized flannel shirt with black leggings, her hair in a ponytail. "Did you say there were sandwiches?"

"Um, yeah." Raven held up her phone. "Will texted. He wants to talk with me."

Sarah's eyes lit up. "Cool."

"You know something I should be aware of?"

Sarah smiled, then swiped her mouth to wipe the grin away.

Whatever.

Maybe Will could run her by the Walmart. This thing he wanted to tell her, he could tell her there.

"You went where?" Raven was about to punch Will's arm but thought better of it when he flinched.

"You heard me. I went to church with Ash." Will turned left into the Walmart parking lot.

There really *was* something in the water. Will at church. Her talking to God. What did this all mean?

"I'd say it was no big deal, but it is." He parked and turned to her. "There are too many coincidences for them to be coincidences. It's like we were guided here."

Raven shook her head, then unclicked her seatbelt. The last thing she wanted was to agree with him. Or admit to balancing on the edge of crying all day long.

"I need to go shopping." Raven opened the door and stepped out. Picking up staples should curtail the longing for her to find out more.

Will stood on the other side of the vehicle. With his sunglasses and the breeze ruffling his hair, he looked like an ad in a men's fashion magazine. A couple shouts from girls in a passing truck further confirmed the thought.

"Come on, pretty boy," Raven slammed the car door, "let's go."

Will followed her toward the store entrance. "You might be able to fool everyone else, Rave. I know you're dying to ask me questions. You're too stubborn to admit it."

Raven jerked a cart from the shopping cart train. She pushed it into the store and went to the produce section. If all Will had wanted to do was annoy and frustrate her then she could have stayed home and eaten her tuna sandwich.

"Raven, you're my best friend. This is important. Something happened to me."

What was she doing? She stopped and looked at him. He had shoved his sunglasses onto his head, which revealed his green eyes that—

They exuded something she had never seen before. "What? What happened?"

He looked around and lifted his arms and let them drop. "I guess this is as good a place as any." He pushed the cart for her. "At that church? I think God was there."

God was there? "Hmm." She gripped the side of the buggy letting him guide their direction.

"His love was palpable." Will picked up a bag of apples and laid them in the cart without checking them first. "Some of this I can't explain yet. Maybe I should have waited to tell you until I could. It's just for the first time, I believe my life means something to Someone bigger than me, bigger than anyone."

What am I supposed to do with this? She kicked the wheels of the cart.

"You know it's hard for me to hear this. Where was he when *I* needed a big God? When drug dealers kicked me in the gut?"

Will stopped. "I've thought a lot about you. About how unfair most of your childhood was. But, Raven, you're here *now*. And maybe we have to look at the amazing things happening to you now."

Easy for him to say. "How can I trust in *any* God who ripped me away from my family and made me live with a crackhead mother."

"Your mom was the one who kidnapped you, not God."

Raven fisted her hands. "Don't you think I know that? But if this God you *felt*," she made finger quotes, "is so great and powerful and wonderful, couldn't he have ... *shouldn't* he have stopped her?"

Was she really doing this? Having an argument with Will about God in the middle of the produce section of Walmart?

Will laid his hand on hers. "I don't pretend to understand how all this works. I only know what I experienced. Freedom. And the first person I thought of was you. I wanted you to have this amazing thing too." He lowered his head and sighed. "It's naïve of me to think I could fully describe this encounter." He took a few steps.

Her friend had had a magnificent incident, and the first person he wanted to share it with was her? "I'm sorry, Will."

He stood still. His expressive brows lifted.

She shrugged. "I know this is significant to you, and as usual I'm making it about me."

His eyebrows almost reached his hairline.

"Shut up." Raven didn't want him to get all schmaltzy with her. "Anyway. Tell me what happened."

By the time the cart was nearly filled with various food stuffs, most of which she had no idea if Sarah needed, Will had shared his experience.

They walked in silence down the paper-products aisle. She grabbed a box of tissues and tucked them under her arm, because she might need them with what she about to say next.

"Thank you for telling me. Truthfully, I don't know how to respond." She swallowed. "Mostly because you and I haven't spent much of our friendship talking deep stuff."

He gave her a crooked smile. "Yeah."

"And this is like ocean-deep stuff."

He nodded.

"I've been thinking about things I haven't thought about since I was a frightened kid hiding from the crazy people in my mom's life."

Will gave her the pity look she hated.

She turned away. "Coming here, meeting Granny and Sarah and Asher has shown me how much I lost when Lizzy took me."

"You don't have to lose—"

Raven stretched her arm behind her toward Will. She couldn't look at him or she'd never finish what she needed to get out. "I'm afraid, Will. I'm afraid Drew will take Sarah away—away from her family and a life ..." She didn't know how to finish.

"It's like he's kidnapping her."

She spun toward him. The waterworks started. She fumbled with the tissue box and managed to split it apart, losing half the contents. "Great."

Will took the box and grabbed a handful and gave them to her. "I wish I knew how to help you." He dropped the tissues into the cart, then bent over to pick up those that had fallen to the floor. "I have my own issues with Drew and how he treats Sarah."

Raven watched her friend wrestle cleaning up the mess she had made. She squatted beside him and helped. "You like my sister."

"That's beside the point." He straightened and cleared his throat. "I can't go there. I don't have control over Sarah or Drew or any of their actions." He took a deep breath and let it go. "It's too big for me, but I believe this Person—this God—is big enough to sort through it all and give me peace."

Raven stood next to Will. Who was this person talking to her? Will claimed he didn't have the answers, but somehow ...

It seemed he did.

Hope woke with a start and looked around her hospital room. She rubbed her eyes and sighed. She should be grateful she was out of ICU, but it was hard to not feel bitter about not being in her own bed. Wearing her own clothes. Having some privacy. Being with her granddaughters.

"Granny?" Rachel peeked around the door. "Up to a visit?"

Hope scooted her behind into a sitting position. "Of course, sweet girl. Is Sarah with you?"

Rachel stood just inside the room. She looked like Lizzy when she had a lot on her mind.

"No, sorry. Sarah will be here later, but I brought my best friend, Will. Is it okay for him to come in?"

"Of course."

Will entered with an armful of flowers. "Hi, Mrs. Sweeting." His face was radiant.

"Dear boy, you don't have to keep bringing me flowers. And, please, call me Granny." His bright white smile was so charming.

Once the flowers found a home on the windowsill and the two settled, the room crackled with anticipation. Rachel—Raven—sat on her hands, her feet dangling like a little girl. "What's on your heart, dear one?"

She shrugged and looked away.

Hope's stomach dropped. Was she planning to leave? Go back to California? Her heart monitor picked up speed.

"I'm concerned about Sarah."

Such emotion in those whispered word. "What concerns you?"

"She's going with Drew to St. Louis for his job interview. If she goes, I'm afraid something bad will happen."

Will raised his eyebrows and grimaced. Hope dipped her chin and focused on him. "Will, do you have any thoughts on this?"

His face colored. "I'm here to support my friend."

"That's not an answer, young man."

He cleared his throat. "I've known Raven long enough to know when she gets these *feelings,* there's usually just cause. She doesn't trust Drew, and she's worried about her sister."

Warmth covered Hope's heart. Raven was concerned for her sister. She couldn't help smiling. There appeared to be tensions between the sisters, but at least some were based in concern and perhaps ... love?

"Come here and sit beside me, sweet girl." Hope patted the bed.

Raven tucked her small frame next to Hope and laid her head on Hope's chest. Hope wrapped her arms around Raven's thin shoulders. Her granddaughter sniffed, then took a swipe at her nose.

"Sarah is a good girl. She's also a praying girl. If she gets any direction from God to not go, she won't go."

"What about my mother? Did she pray?" Raven lifted her head. Her eyeliner was smudged. Hope swallowed around a great ball of emotion.

Will stood and left the room.

If only Hope could give her granddaughter a pretty story. But it would be a lie and Raven knew too well who Lizzy was.

Hope exhaled. She moved her hands to hold Raven's beautiful face. "It wasn't all your mother's fault. Lizzy was a handful and confused. Instead of trying to figure out how to find her help, I hid the problem. I kept trying to shove her into what I thought she should be."

The tears covered both their faces.

"I'm sorry you suffered for my mistakes."

Raven tucked herself against Hope's body. She sniffed. "Lizzy was good at getting whatever she wanted. Including with me. She was a master manipulator." Raven lifted her head. "I guess I'm scared about Sarah leaving you. What happens when she gets married?"

"Up until my heart attacks, I figured I'd manage," Hope bit her lip. "Sarah would have inherited the bakery should anything happen to me. I've had several offers to buy the bakery. Well, the building, not the bakery. It seems downtown Minersville is now prime real estate."

Was she talking about this? Out loud? "The money was good, but it would break my heart if Sweet's didn't exist anymore."

Raven sat up. She leveled an intense scowl. "You *can't* sell Sweet's."

"No way." Will reappeared in the room.

Hope smiled. The boy must have been standing there this whole time—eavesdropping.

"Will is right. Otherwise, all this town will have is grocery-store bakeries. You still use old-fashioned methods of baking and unique recipes, not the same recipe with modifications for everything. Our bakery in Hollywood seldom varied their dough recipes."

"The varied recipes *Raven* created." Will smiled like a proud brother.

Raven stood and walked toward her friend. She transferred her penetrating stare to him. They stood having a conversation Hope couldn't hear, because they didn't say a word.

Finally, Will nodded. "Raven and I might—what am I saying! I love it here! For the first time in my life, I'm wanted and needed. If you'll have me, Mrs. Sweeting, I would be honored to work for you."

Raven beamed. Years of pain and sorrow seemed to melt away from her beautiful face. "Me too."

Oh! Was this happening? God was giving her a gift she never expected or deserved. Until recently she had always thought Sarah would inherit the bakery and continue the Sweet's legacy. She thought her dream had died when Drew set his sights on Sarah.

She didn't want to lose having Sarah in her life each and every day. Even so, having these two talented kids working with her was a miracle. She realized she hadn't responded to them. Their eager looks began to fade.

"Here's the thing, kids." Hope forced a sober expression on her face but couldn't hold it. "Will, you will need to call me *Granny* if you plan to work with Raven and me." She opened her arms to embrace these amazing young people. They made short work entering that embrace.

Now she had to find the money in the budget for two more staff, then tell Sarah there were two more partners at Sweet's Bakery. Somehow, she wasn't confident about Sarah's reaction.

"Can I join the hug?" Sarah stood in the doorway, hugging herself, a look of insecurity on her face that Hope hadn't seen in years.

Hope opened her arms wider. "Of course."

It seemed she would be telling Sarah about her decision sooner than she thought.

Chapter 24

Sarah lifted her foot off the gas pedal. She was speeding again.

Every time she thought about her conversation with Granny the previous night, it fueled her lead foot. *Maybe I'm not in the best frame of mind to be driving.*

Drew's clunker wasn't working, naturally, so she was drafted as chauffer because he needed *to concentrate on preparing for his interview.* Or so he'd said. She gripped the steering wheel until her hands ached.

Think of something else. Like ...

Will's handsome face popped into her mind. His wide smile. His kind emerald eyes. His ability to recognize her worth in ways no one ever had.

He would find the time to talk with her.

Will would look at things with humor and the composure of the unbiased. He'd let her work out this malaise of rejection she carried these days. Then again, part of her funky mood was because of him. Granny wanted Will and Raven to be part owners of Sweet's.

Granny had never offered *her* partnership.

She pressed fingers against her temple, then reached over to turn on the radio. Drew nudged her hand away his pen. "Sorry, babe. I won't be able to concentrate."

She huffed. "Drew, I need to talk."

He patted her arm. "We'll have time to talk after the interview. Can't you save whatever is bugging you until then?"

Bugging her?

The car sped to eighty. She lifted her foot and waited until the car slowed to the legal limit of seventy. If she didn't get control of herself, they might end up in an accident or jail—at the least, get an expensive ticket.

Okay, God. You know I'm angry. And hurt. And—oh great— jealous. How could Granny do this to me? I've always been there for her. I didn't leave—to go off to exotic places.

Raven's dewy eyes appeared in her mind. "I didn't leave, Sarah. I was taken from my family."

Her thoughts always landed there. Her mother had kidnapped her sister and run away. The whys of her choosing Raven over Sarah shouldn't matter, should they? From the meager information Raven was willing to share, her childhood was—horrid.

Yet it did matter. Was Granny choosing Raven over her, like her ...?

Couldn't *someone* take her side? For once?

"Sarah!" Drew grabbed her arm. "You missed our exit!"

She swerved onto the shoulder, then righted the car. How had she missed the signage for the major interchange of I-44 and I-270? "I'll take the next exit and circle around. We'll be fine."

He shook his head and went back to studying his confounded materials. She wanted to knock them from his hands and make him pay attention to her.

Breathe, Sarah. You're not Raven. You don't do things like that.

She exited the highway and drove the overpass to get on I-44 going west. The next exit took her to I-270 north. A few more exits to Creve Coeur, then their destination, Untergarten. Her cell rang in her purse.

"Drew, could you see who's calling? It might be the hospital."

He looked up from his papers, brows tugged together. "Where's your phone?"

"In my purse on the backseat."

He reached over his shoulder, then repositioned himself to lean around. After a few grunts, he flopped back into his seat. "I can't reach it. It stopped ringing. You can call them back when you drop me off."

Great. Now she could add worry to the simmering brew.

Once they arrived at their destination, she'd call whomever back. She prayed for protection for anyone she knew, including her and Drew, then tried to focus on driving.

Wait. Did she drive past Untergarten? She turned around and attempted again—all the while Drew reminded her, he was *almost* late.

Once she parked, he jumped from the car and sprinted to the glass office building. Finally able to retrieve her cell, she checked her calls.

Will. He left a message. She played it immediately.

"Hey, Sarah." Will's voice could melt chocolate. "I know you're on your way to Drew's big interview. Everyone is fine. Granny and the bakery are fine."

You mean *your* bakery.

"Calling to check on you." He paused. "Sarah, I may be off-base, but when Granny announced the good news about Raven and me, I—I—" He exhaled. "I noticed the brave front you put on."

She gasped.

Will chuckled. "You and Rave are more alike than you realize."

What difference does it make, now?

"If you don't want us part of the business, please let us know. I can't speak for Rave—and maybe you'll be okay with your sister joining you as partner—but I don't want to intrude in any way."

Wait a minute. He thinks I'm already a partner in the bakery?

"I'm falling in love. I love this tiny town and its people and this bakery."

Gooseflesh appeared on her arms and warmed her cheeks.

"Call me when you get a few moments. Talk with you soon."

Sarah hit redial, her heart beating in staccato. The cell rang. She glanced at her watch. Ten. The morning rush should be finishing. His voice mail came on. At the beep, she debated whether to hang up or leave a message.

"Yes. Will. Sorry I missed your call. I was driving." *Lame, Sarah.* "Drew is in his interview. I mean, he went in. Anyway. I appreciate you checking to see how I am. I guess I should never play poker with you." She laughed, then hiccupped.

Oh no. Here come the tears. "I'll talk to you later." She squeaked the last word, then disconnected the call.

She rested her forehead on the steering wheel and let the tears come.

Will brought the last tray of chocolate-chip-oatmeal-raisin-pecan cookies from the kitchen.

Were there enough? Probably not, given how quickly the other six trays went this morning.

Bible studies were like *the* place to be around there. Which reminded him, Asher had invited him to a men's meeting at the church. The pastor guy had asked if Will wanted to be *discipled*, whatever that was, even though he wasn't a member of their church.

He slipped in the tray and slid the glass door close.

"Hey, your cell rang a couple of times," Raven said as she handed a box to a customer and thanked them. She nodded toward the back worktable. "By the time I found it, whoever called was leaving a message."

Sarah. He knew it was her. And he had missed her.

"Okay. Thanks." He tried to sound nonchalant, but Raven's smirk told him he hadn't fooled her.

"Say hi to my sister."

He grabbed the phone and scrolled down his recent calls. Sarah had called, as had Hollywood Bakery and his parents. "Hollywood called."

Raven wrapped her arms around her waist and bit her top lip.

He leaned back against the table, grateful the bakery was empty. "Are you ready to give them notice?"

She shrugged. "I guess so. I mean last night we were all gung-ho, but in the light of day—I mean—this is big."

"Are you having second thoughts?" Will's stomach dove to his white work shoes.

She shrugged again. "What do you want to do?"

Will swallowed. "I want to stay here. Work here. Live here."

Raven now chewed her bottom lip.

"But if you don't stay, Raven, then I won't. It would be too weird."

"Great. I don't need to take on your future too." She flung her arms in the air and paced.

"Whoa, dude. You okay?"

She yanked off her hairnet to run her hands through her hair. "I don't know. This is like a major commitment."

"Yeah?" Will didn't get it. Raven now had a real family that loved her. Were welcoming her with open arms—literally. She could be part of something genuine. Important. "Are you scared?"

She stopped. "Aren't you? What if we ruin her business? What if we blow Granny's retirement or something? And she loses the bakery? Or her house!"

"Whoa." He placed his hands on her shoulders. "Look at me. As long as I'm alive, and even after, it will *ne—ver* happen."

"How can you be so certain?" Her sky-blue eyes looked up with such vulnerability. His friend was changing before his eyes.

The front door jingled. A mom and her two toddlers entered.

Raven wiped at her eyes, slipped her net on, and stepped toward the front counter. "Good morning. May I help you?"

She was in customer-service mode. They would finish this conversation later. They had to.

"Oh, dear," the mother said. "Is this all you have left of the chocolate-chip-oatmeal-raisin-pecan cookies? I'll need to take every one of them for our women's Bible study."

Raven looked at Will.

"Go for it, ma'am," Will said. "I'll whip up another six dozen for the rest of the Bible study folks."

As Will walked through the swinging door, he slipped the phone into his apron pocket. Three calls to return. Two he wasn't looking forward to.

One, he couldn't wait to return.

Sarah nibbled on a chocolate croissant. It had been over an hour since Drew left for his interview. Was this a good sign?

She had never interviewed for a job—had never needed to. If things continued between them, she would need to learn how. Minersville wasn't where her boyfriend wanted to stake permanent residency.

If she and Drew were serious enough for marriage, then she was leaving Minersville. Leaving Granny. Leaving Raven.

After over twenty years of praying for Raven—and her mother's—return, she was leaving her sister behind?

Can't think about this.

Drew might not be that serious. He might not get the job.

She took another crumb-size bite of her pastry. There was a small strip mall a block from Untergarten, where she had found a treasure—a French bakery and coffee shop. Raven would love this place.

She kept checking her phone, as if doing so would get Will—er, *Drew* to call any faster. And Will hadn't called back either. Why?

It shouldn't upset her. They were just friends. He was busy.

Truth be told, since Raven and Will had arrived at Sweet's, business had grown and was running smoother than it ever had. When Sarah reviewed the past week's receipts, sales had increased close to thirty percent.

Perhaps it was the novelty of the long-lost sister returning. The news brought curiosity seekers. Or maybe Raven and Will were better at the business and baking. A lump formed in her throat. She would not cry in this *patisserie.*

Her cell rang. Drew.

She gave the shop workers a wave, then went outside and answered the video call. "How did it go?"

"Only amazing! They all but offered me a position in St. Louis on the spot."

Oh. "Wonderful." She worked to pump up her enthusiasm. For as long as she had known him, this had been his dream company. She really should research to learn more about them.

"I had planned on taking us out to dinner, but the director and her assistant wanted to treat us to dinner tonight at Brasserie by Niche. It's a French restaurant." He inspected her. "You need to buy something nicer. This is your interview, too, Sarah. We have to be on pointe."

Drew's words came out so fast it was hard to take in everything he said.

"I'm at the car. Where are you?"

She ran down the sidewalk. "I'm on my way. I was at the cutest French bakery."

"French bakery? And we're dining at a French restaurant? Must be God." He continued talking about the interview and how impressed they were and how Untergarten, the director said, would be lucky to have him. He barely took a breath.

When she arrived, she hugged him. "Oh, I'm so proud of you!"

He held her at arm's length. "Babe. Whoa. You're all sweaty." He looked over his shoulder toward Untergarten's building. "You need a shower and a better outfit."

I need a shower?

The interview was important to him—he didn't mean to embarrass her.

"We'll figure it out." She molded a sincere smile onto her face.

"How about we check out one of the malls and you can freshen up in the ladies' room." He checked his watch. "We have more than enough time. Nothing to worry about, babe."

She wasn't the one who was worried.

He kissed her lightly on the cheek then focused on his cell. "There's an outlet mall, thirty minutes from here. Daphne said to meet her back here at seven. They'll have the company limo take us to the restaurant."

"Daphne?"

His cheeks flushed. "Oh, Daphne Lugar, the St. Louis branch director. Her assistant, Erik somebody will be coming as well. You'll love them." He opened the passenger side of the car. "And they'll love you, babe."

Things were moving as fast as Drew was talking. Both made her queasy.

She opened the driver's side door, slowly. When would they have quiet time for her? When could she share what happened with Granny? Was she supposed to squeeze it in between all his plans and good news?

"Ready for the adventure of a lifetime? This is the beginning, babe." Drew was like a kid at Six Flags amusement park. There was just one problem.

Sarah was not excited or amused.

Chapter 25

Asher wiped the stainless table. He had twenty minutes until his first class, then he was due at the lab to work with his advisor, Professor Sparlin. The professor had been gracious with his absence the past week.

"You still here?" Will entered the kitchen carrying several empty trays. Another high-volume day—and it was only Monday. "I thought you'd left for school."

"I'm about to." He shot the dishrag over Will's head into the soaker sink. *Nothing but net!* "Did you ever connect with Sarah?"

Will shrugged a shoulder. "She's busy sightseeing. You know, celebrating."

If Will were any gloomier, his chin would drag on the floor. "Coming tonight to Bible study?" Maybe getting into the Word and learning more about his heavenly Father would prioritize his thinking. Give him perspective. At least distract him.

"I wouldn't miss it, buddy." Will's smile didn't reach his eyes.

Asher grabbed his coat. "I'll see you at the apartment?"

"You bet." Will dumped the trays into the soapy water and began washing them. He turned. "I'm visiting Granny after work. I'll text you if I'm running late."

"You're going to the hospital?" Raven brought another empty tray. "We sold the last of the Dr. Pepper cupcakes."

She dipped the serving tray into the sink and placed her hand on Will's shoulder. "Can I come with you?"

Will nodded. "Can I have a few minutes alone with her?"

Raven's hand slipped away. She turned and went back into the shop area.

Asher had his shoulder against the door. Ready to go. He needed to go. "You two okay?"

"We're fine. Get to class." Will kept his back to Asher as he continued to clean pans.

What was his friend hiding? "Will?"

"Granny asked Raven and me to become partners."

Asher strode to Will and pounded his back. "Great!" Will grimaced. "Not great?"

Will grabbed one of the towels hanging over the sink and dried his hands then turned around. "Oh, it's great. I love the idea. Especially since asking Jesus to guide my life. This was a major answer to my prayer to find a place I could call home."

"What's the problem?"

Will lifted his chin toward the shop.

Raven. Asher leaned against the pan cabinet. "Does Raven not want to stay?" Even as he said it, Asher's stomach crashed.

"Deep down, she does," Will whispered. "She wants it more than anything. She's just afraid she'll fail Granny. Then, there's the Sarah issue."

Asher shifted his stance and watched the door. Was Will about to discuss Sarah or Drew?

Will nodded. "Have I said too much?"

He smiled. "I have to get to class, but while I'm doing differential calculus, I'll be praying."

"I appreciate the prayer more than you know." Will extended his hand.

Asher leaned over and gave him a brotherly hug, then headed outside.

All the way to the university he battled the images of different scenarios about Raven and Sarah until finally he prayed out loud, "Father, my mind is not at rest in You. I am letting go of all my imaginations. Jesus, You take them. Please help me focus on my responsibilities. Thank You."

By the time he parked in the electrical engineering lot, the images had disappeared, and differential equations danced in his head.

During the unexpected lull, Raven explored Granny's ancient recipe binders in the basement office. Someone had typed them. The pages were worn and brittle from batter spatters of every color—blue, white, and pink. Some had coffee rings, most had handwritten adaptations. She ran her hand over them and smiled.

The history these sheets held.

She could makeover the blueberry muffin recipe. Granny had taken a simple recipe and added a crumb topping. Sounded good. But how could she make it decadent?

Shoving her pencil behind her ear, she circled the linoleum.

Begin with blueberries.

She loved blueberry pancakes. Blueberries in savory dishes. Blueberries on cheesecake. *Oh.* She stopped. Blueberry muffins with cheesecake centers. *Yes!*

She ran upstairs. The exhilaration of creating something unexpected and new grew inside her as she put together the pieces to the recipe puzzle. She grabbed a paper towel and yanked her pencil from behind her ear and began jotting down the new recipe.

Wait a minute ... didn't Will come into the kitchen and ask her something? She waved the thought away while placing the mini cheesecake into half of the blueberry cake batter. Apologies could be made later—or might not be necessary once he sampled her new creation.

As the final cupcakes baked, she envisioned a lighter cream-cheese frosting using less cheese and adding a touch of sour cream. The timer jingled. She ran to the oven and tapped the muffins. Perfect. She moved them into the blast chiller, then put the finishing touches on the frosting.

Pulling the baked cupcakes from the chiller, she piped and thick-swirled them, then added a few fresh blueberries. Wasn't there fresh mint in the fridge?

She tucked one leaf between two blueberries as though it had grown there. She fought the urge to sprinkle a few grains of double-refined sugar. It would be too sweet.

She stood back and examined the wee one. Adorable! Placing the cupcake into her palm she hefted it. *Hmm, somewhat heavy. Maybe make the cheesecake portion smaller?*

Time to sample. She took a bite, careful to get a fresh berry, frosting, cake, and cheesecake into her mouth.

Oh. My. Goodness.

The lightness of the muffin, the decadence of the cheesecake, and the freshness of the berries did wonders to her taste buds. The delicate balance was achieved.

She popped the rest into her mouth, grabbed another cupcake, then ran through the swinging door. "Taste this, Will!" A few crumbs flew from her mouth, stuffed as it was with cake.

Will turned, his arms deep inside one of the display cabinets, he retrieved a red-velvet layer cake. "Let me get this cake boxed."

She chewed her giant bite further before she noticed a well-dressed woman who stared at Raven, eyes wide.

"I'm sorry." Raven swallowed and lifted the uneaten cupcake. "I created a new cupcake."

"How exciting. People say you're a genius with all sorts of confections." The woman clutched the shoulder strap to her leather briefcase and walked closer. "What is it? What are you calling it?"

"It's—I don't know what to call it. It's a blueberry cupcake with a mini-cheesecake inside."

"How about Blueberry Surprise?" She offered.

"I like it," Raven said. "You want to try a sample?" She handed the cupcake to her.

"Can I eat it now?"

Will and Raven answered together, "Yes!"

She took a dainty bite, which only included the frosting and top layer of the cake. Still, the look of delight on her face was worth every ounce, cup, and teaspoon Raven measured to find the right flavors.

The woman undressed the cupcake, then took a larger bite and chewed awkwardly, using her pinky to remove a bit of frosting from the top of her lip.

"You've got a glob of frosting on your face too." Will whispered to Raven. She wiped her face with her apron.

The woman groaned and moaned. She kept chewing as she examined the cupcake. "I changed my mind, call it Blueberry Decadence. I'll take a dozen of these. No. I'll take however many you have!"

"We can sell you a dozen," Will said. "With the cream cheese inside and in the frosting, it will be the perfect complement to your red-velvet cake for your guests."

The woman had taken another mouthful and shook her head. "The cupcakes are for me. The guests can have the cake." She chewed then paused. "No offense to the cake."

They all laughed.

The woman extended her hand to Raven. "My name is Sally Phelps. I own the bank down the street."

Phelps Bank? Raven wiped her hand on her apron and shook Sally's hand. "It's a pleasure to meet you. My name is Raven."

Sally smiled. "The pleasure is all mine, believe me." She finished the cupcake and did a little dance.

As Will rang up Sally's order—which was substantial, given he charged her twice the price of a regular cupcake—

Raven and Sally chatted about the importance of introducing young women to more businesswomen role models.

"Raven, I am president of the Young Women Entrepreneurs. We have a monthly meeting at the university. I would love to have you speak. It's a small group, maybe fifty or so, but there are a lot of young women thinking about their futures. You could make a difference in their lives."

Speak? Fifty is small?

"She would be amazing. Can she get back with you?"

Sally lifted her brows. "Of course."

Will packed Sally's order into one of the large white paper bags with sturdy handles that he'd picked up at the distributor—and paid for himself—although Will would never tell anyone.

"May I assist you?"

Sally smiled at him. "I'm only a few doors down. And with this bag, I'll manage fine. Thanks for the offer." He opened the door for her. She thanked him again, then paused at the doorway. "Raven, consider my invitation. You have a lot to share with the world. Not simply remarkable sweets."

Once they were alone, Raven squealed. "The president of a bank loved my cupcakes and believes I can help other young women."

"All those bad things you went through could help others."

She stared at him, then turned away. *I wouldn't go that far. I can talk about baking. Don't ask me to talk about my horrible, messed up life.* "I guess I better clean the mess I made before the after-school crowd arrives." She pushed the door to the kitchen.

"Rave, are you going to accept Sally's invitation?"

She looked over her shoulder. She knew what he was really asking: *"Are you going to accept Granny's offer and stay?"*

Was something—or *Someone*—showing her it might all work out? She swallowed and looked at the floor. She had been fooled into thinking things would work out before.

"I'll think about it."

Hope waved goodbye to the purple-haired young woman. *What a sweet and talented girl. And she loved Jesus.*

Several of the beauty-school students often visited and offered to beautify the patients.

Hope opened the drawer in her bed-side tray and looked in the built in mirror. A shampoo, trim, and blow dry was just the thing she had needed.

The young woman had tattoos like Rachel. Even though Hope didn't approve of tattoos, she had no doubt this girl loved Jesus. *What a great time of fellowship.*

"Hi, Granny," Raven and Will entered her room. "Wow! You look great." Raven wiggled her brows.

Hope patted her hair then opened her arms for a group hug.

Once the chitchat finished, Will sat in one of the chairs, but Raven stood. "Will wanted to talk with you privately."

"Is everything okay?"

"Everything is fine." Will reached out to pat her hand. "I'll text you when I'm finished, Rave."

"Sure." Raven nodded then left.

"What is on your mind, young man?" She couldn't help the nervous flutter. A quick glance at the heart monitor—everything was fine.

He leaned forward, resting his elbows on his knees. "I may be off-base here, and if I am, please tell me so." He lowered his head, then raised it. "I am concerned for Sarah."

"Sarah?" Hope expected him to discuss Raven. "Why?"

"Last night, when you made the announcement to Sarah about Raven and me being partners, she seemed unhappy."

Really? "I didn't notice. Are you sure?"

He nodded.

"She seemed happy for you both." Hope had already called her lawyer today to have him bring the paperwork. Was she premature?

"This may be overstepping my boundaries, but does Sarah *know* she's in your will to inherit Sweet's?"

"Of course, she—" Hope paused. *Well ... wait a minute.* "I first changed the will from Arthur, my late husband, to Lizzy. A year or so after Lizzy left with Raven, I made the girls the heirs. Twelve years ago—oh, my ..."

Hope covered her mouth with her hands. *How could I?*

Will leaned forward. "What is it, Mrs. Sweeting? Should I call the nurse?"

"No, dear boy, no." She held his hand. "Twelve years ago, I changed my will to Sarah as sole heir."

"Sarah would be happy to know that."

Hope closed her eyes. *Father, please forgive me. I gave up hope. I didn't believe you would return my granddaughter.*

"I'm sorry, Mrs. Sweeting," Will knelt next to the bed and held her hand. "I didn't want to upset you."

She patted his hand, then grabbed a tissue and dabbed at her eyes. "You didn't upset me, dear boy. Raven's return has rattled a few bones in this old girl's closet." She sniffed. "Why didn't Sarah *say* something? It hurts my heart that she thinks I would exclude her—for any reason."

Will kissed Granny's hand. "Sounds like an easy repair." He returned to his chair. "And as honored as I am with your offer, it's not right. You only met me—"

"Raven clearly loves and trusts you."

Will smiled and sighed. "She's my best friend, and I would do anything for her. Which is why, if she stays and accepts your offer, I will stay. I don't have to be a partner in the bakery."

Hope's mind bounded back and forth between the *if she stays* and his noble rejection of her offer. "Is Raven having second thoughts?"

Will opened his mouth to speak, then closed it. He pressed his lips together, then opened them. "I can't say what Raven is thinking. It's a conversation you two should have. And I may be forcing her to have a discussion before she's ready."

Hope studied him. Something happened to Will. He had changed since the first time she met him. "Will? Do you know Jesus?"

Will's eyes lit the room. "Yes. Well, I'm working on it."

Hope chuckled. "Honey, we'll all be working on it for the rest of our lives. It's great to know we'll be working together." She opened her arms for another hug. This time as big sister to her younger brother.

Maybe more like her grandson. If he stayed.

Raven read the text from Will. She left the small lounge.

The fifteen minutes alone playing Word Cookies had not distracted her enough. Should she accept Granny's invitation? Could she be satisfied living in a sleepy small town?

"Raven?" Asher exited the elevator.

"Hey." She pocketed her cell.

"Are you leaving?"

Raven shook her head. "Will kicked me out of Granny's room." She smiled. "They're speaking privately."

"Everything okay?"

They walked toward Granny's room. "I think so. We both have a decision to make."

"I see."

Had Will confided in Asher about her so-called fear? "Did Will tell you anything?"

"Only about the offer, which is brilliant. You both would be perfect for Sweet's."

Perfect? Her cheeks warmed. "Thanks."

They entered the room to Will and Granny laughing. Asher grinned. "Can we get in on the party?"

Granny welcomed them. Whatever Will discussed had had a positive effect—on them both.

They visited together as though she and Will had been part of their lives forever. Will shared a sample of Raven's newest creation and told Granny about the bank president's invitation.

Granny beamed.

Asher shared about a breakthrough in the EE lab.

Granny beamed.

Raven stared at Will. He hadn't revealed much about his day. Had her drama eclipsed her friend again? Maybe he wouldn't want to live in a small town where she blew up everything and he had to clean after her.

Will talked about a few of the customers. He knew their names and their kids' names. As he spoke, his face softened, his smile widened.

Granny asked him about several of her favorite customers, and he knew them.

Asher leaned toward Raven. "You okay? You're pretty quiet."

She gazed at his kind eyes. "I loved hearing Will recap the day. I get lost in the creative part. Sometimes I forget why I do what I do. It's about giving people a delicious experience. Memories. Will never forgets. He delights in it. It feeds him."

"What are you two whispering about over there?" Granny eyed them.

Raven repeated what she told Asher.

Will stood and walked to Raven. "That might be the nicest thing you've ever said to me." He wrapped his arm around her shoulder. She lightly punched him in the ribs.

"I hope not. I wouldn't be much of a friend if that were true."

Will gave her a noogie. She pushed him away, laughing.

"Okay, children. Settle down." Granny didn't bother to hide her chuckle.

Asher checked his watch. "Will, if we're going to make the men's meeting, we need to hit the road."

Will nodded, gathered his jacket, then nodded to Raven. "I'm riding with Ash. You can take my car back to Granny's house. Okay?"

Men's meeting? What was that? She had a mental picture of men with painted chests, chanting. "Sure."

They hugged her and Granny goodbye. When Will gave her their usual side-hug, she whispered, "What kind of *men's* meeting?"

He smiled and shrugged.

Oh, we'll be talking, buddy.

"Come, sit by me, sweetheart." Granny patted her bed.

What were Asher and Will up to? No worries. Will could never keep a secret from Raven.

She *would* get to the bottom of this.

Chapter 26

Brasserie by Niche was beautiful and elegant and intimidating. Sarah clutched the fine linen napkin in her lap because it kept slipping off the slick fabric of her new spring dress. Cute but not sensible, given the draft blowing directly on her.

One of many discomforts she'd endured during their meal. Not the least of which was the conversation had been in German, in which Daphne and Erik were both fluent. Drew had held his own, but she understood only a few words here and there.

She may as well have been a piece of furniture.

Nevertheless, she smiled and nodded and held Drew's hand when he offered it to her, from time to time.

Daphne was gorgeous. Tall, blonde, dressed in a dark burgundy business suit. *I bet she's warm.* Simple gold jewelry—a linked chain around her neck and wrist. No doubt expensive.

But no wedding band.

Erik, Daphne's assistant, also tall and blond and handsome, sat ramrod-straight next to Daphne. With their perfect posture, their chins were flawlessly perpendicular to their shoulders. Making them appear that much taller.

Perhaps the restaurant could provide a booster seat for Sarah.

The server placed the *café au lait* next to her. The others drank their brandy. She would have enjoyed a sip or two, but she was, after all, the designated driver for the next two plus hours.

She stifled a yawn as she sipped her coffee, which was strong and delicious.

The server reappeared holding a tray with a champagne bottle and four flutes. He popped the cork and made a great show of pouring the sparkling liquid.

She tried reminding Drew with a series of raised brows that she wouldn't be able to imbibe. But he ignored her and accepted a glass from the waiter for her.

Drew leaned toward her. She could smell the brandy on his breath. "Come on, let's celebrate. Look there's barely a mouthful."

He lifted his glass, as did Erik and Daphne. "To a bright and successful future," Drew toasted, then sipped.

Sarah brought the glass to her lips but kept them closed. Something bumped against them.

Part of the cork?

She examined her glass. Something sparkling caught the chandelier lighting. She grabbed her fork and retrieved it from the bottom.

A ring?

Drew knelt on the carpet next to her. He took the ring from her. "Sarah Hope Sweeting, will you marry me?"

The whole restaurant silenced. Sarah's heart beat against the filmy dress, her cheeks heated.

Should she? Everyone looked at her. Waiting.

You've imagined this moment since you were a kid? Why are you hesitating?

She glanced at Daphne. Did the woman just look at her watch?

"Yes," she whispered. She cleared her throat and spoke louder. "Yes."

Restaurant patrons and staff cheered and clapped. Drew kissed her hard, lifting her from the chair, he squeezed the air from her.

I'm getting married?

Sarah yawned. Again.

Next to her in the car Drew snored, his face pressed against the passenger window. A few minutes after merging onto the interstate, he was out like a used bulb.

She was getting married!

It was too dark to see her engagement ring—only its silhouette.

Drew said it had belonged to his grandmother. A vintage, white gold setting with pavé diamonds surrounding a sweet round diamond in the center.

For the first half hour of the drive, she replayed Drew's proposal. Extraordinary. A ring in a champagne glass. Like something out of the movies.

But having Daphne and Erik witness the proposal, then shake hands with them afterward, made the ordeal—

Ordeal? No, the *event* more like a business deal than a romantic celebration.

She shrugged. Perhaps one day they could laugh about his business-deal proposal. Especially if Drew got the job.

How soon would he get the position?

Come on, Drew. Wake up. I need to talk! She pounded her hand on the steering wheel.

It was after midnight, or she'd call Granny.

She would love to talk to her sister, but Raven wouldn't be happy for her. At all. She dreaded even telling her.

Asher? No. Will might be there and—

And what?

Her cheeks warmed. She rubbed a sweaty palm on her dress. *Fine.* She would think on her own. She needed to process the whole evening, and there was at least another hour of driving.

She was getting married. If Drew secured the Untergarten position, they would move to St. Louis.

Move.

Away from Minersville.

Away from Granny.

Away from Raven.

Sarah's mouth dried. She grabbed the half-full bottled water. Unscrewing the cap, she tilted the bottle and took a big gulp. She squeezed too tight and managed to dribble liquid on her chin and down her front. Wiping her chin with her forearm, she replaced the empty bottle in her cup holder.

The image of Will spilling water into his lap appeared in her mind. The two of them laughing so hard they couldn't catch their breath.

No. Now was not the time to think of Will. She squirmed in the driver's seat.

St. Louis was a great city. She loved the stores, museums, the zoo, the shows, baseball and hockey games. City life would be exciting. Always something to do. Better job opportunities for a business major. She could even get her MBA at one of the two most prestigious universities in the nation.

And it was only a few hours' drive from Granny. Raven would love St. Louis. They could all visit. She exhaled. Right. Moving would be an adventure.

She and Drew were young. They could travel and see all sorts of wonderful places.

What about the bakery?

She clutched the steering wheel. Was she abandoning her grandmother? Her sister?

My dream?

But hadn't Granny already given Sweet's to Raven and Will? Left her out of the picture altogether? The tears she had pushed aside earlier now made their entrance with a vengeance.

God? Did You want *me out of the way so Raven could replace me*

Sobs overtook her. Her vision clouded with a flood of tears. She had better get off the road or she would have no future. Neither would Drew.

The exit sign for Eureka was ahead. She veered onto the off-ramp. To the right was an all-night gas station and Denny's. She pulled up to a pump and sat sobbing as silently as possible, her hands covering her mouth. If she continued like this she might explode.

The gas meter read half empty. She could make it home, but she needed the cool night air on her skin. Opening the car door, she stepped out. The brisk air and her wet top made her shiver. She reached in the back for her jacket and purse.

After inserting her debit card, she selected her gas and let the pump do its job.

The sobs had dissipated—but not the tears or sense of rejection. Would she ever be enough?

She rubbed her hand under her nose. Why couldn't she be happy? This was supposed to be one of a woman's best life moments. But did she deserve to be happy when her granny was in the hospital?

She looked up. "God? Are You listening?"

The only responses were the crickets and highway traffic. She hadn't expected an answer. But she did need her heavenly Father's love right now, otherwise she would begin the litany of sorrows from her past that would take her deeper into her disappointment.

Why wasn't Drew awake to help her pray through this?

She placed her behind against her car and pushed until it rocked. She peeked through the window. *Nope, still sleeping.* Another shake. His head rolled back, his mouth opened.

Good grief. Wake up!

She rocked faster. His head fell forward, then shot up. He turned and looked around. He muttered as he opened the passenger door.

"Wha—Where are we?" He rubbed his eyes and coughed.

Sarah finished pumping the gas and put on the cap. "We're in Eureka. I needed a break." She sniffed.

He stretched and yawned. "I've got a morning class. I need to rest." He rubbed the start of a beard. "What time is it?"

"Around one. I'm getting a cup of coffee. Join me?"

"Can we get it to go?"

She huffed. "Fine. As long as you don't go back to sleep."

"Whoa. What are *you* upset about? I thought you would be happy. The interview went great. I asked you to marry me." He shoved his hands into his pants' pocket.

"I'm sorry. Remember I wanted to talk with you about something Granny said. But then you proposed and fell asleep. Now it's all jumbled in my brain."

"Right. Sorry. I forgot." He put his arm around her waist, then yawned. "Let's get coffee. I'm still buzzed. I need to get the alcohol out of my system before class."

Once they were back on the road, Sarah recapped Granny's announcement. How deeply it affected her. Even now, a specter of rejection hovered over her.

She glanced at Drew. He leaned one elbow on a bended knee looking at her. "I don't see the problem, babe. Maybe God was preparing you to leave the bakery. You know, God's timing and all."

Having Drew say it made the idea more logical. "I guess so. It's sad. My sister is back, we're a family again, and I'll be moving away."

Drew grunted. "You two aren't getting along. Maybe you both could use some distance. I sure—" He looked at Sarah. "What!"

Maybe Drew wasn't the right person to talk with. He couldn't be impartial where Raven was concerned. What he said didn't sound like God's voice—more like his own hurt and agenda.

Why hadn't she made the connection that dating Drew could mean marriage and moving away from her grandmother?

I need to get alone and listen for God's voice—not mine, not Drew's, not Raven's.

"Are you mad at me now?" He folded his arms across his chest.

"No." *Sort of.* "I guess I need to know God's will in all this."

"Let me know when He tells you." His tone reduced the temperature in the car.

She shivered.

He turned away from her. "I need to get some shut-eye. Wake me when you get to the frat."

I am engaged, and I'm miserable, Lord. Is this the way it's supposed to be?

Raven sipped her coffee, keeping an eye on the clock. Sometime in the wee hours of the morning, Sarah had crawled into bed.

Raven didn't let on she was awake. Or rouse her sister when the alarm went off.

Then there was the sniffing. Sarah had done a lot of snuffles before she finally drifted off. Did her sister have a cold?

Huh. Bet she was crying.

Was it wrong to hope it was the latter and her tears were caused by Drew?

She drained her coffee. After a night of her own tossing and turning, she could use another cup, but—

Another cup of coffee ...

Wait! What if Sweet's installed a coffee urn or espresso maker at the bakery? What if they added a breakfast bar with stools, then people could drink their coffee and eat a few breakfast treats? She rinsed her cup and upturned it in the sink.

Will would love this idea. It could increase revenue for Granny.

She grabbed her coat and listened for any signs of Sarah waking. Silence. Good thing she had Will's car.

When she arrived at Sweet's, Asher and Will were opening the back door.

Hardly out of the car, she called out to them. "Guys, I have a great idea!"

The brainstorm tumbled out like a bag of apples as the others entered the kitchen. Asher nodded and Will smiled.

"I love it," the two said in unison.

Will looked at Asher. "Should we check with Granny? See if we have it in the budget to invest?"

"Sarah handles the business. We begin there," Asher said.

"Oh. Okay." Raven tried not to sound deflated. Somehow, she'd thought they would go pick up a coffee machine today. Of course, it made sense to go to Sarah first. *Rats, I should have woken her.*

"I have to get started on the bread making, guys. Will, you want to help?" Asher pulled one of the flour bags by the worktable.

"Sure." Will grabbed his apron.

"Can you pull the dough I started last night?" Asher grunted as he lifted the flour.

While the guys worked on the bread, she grabbed the day's menu of orders, pastries, and baked goods. She wanted to add the blueberry cheesecake cupcakes she made yesterday. There were a lot of decorated cake orders. She inspected the refrigerated case's inventory of pre-baked cakes.

She had plenty of layer cakes, but she needed to prepare two chocolate full-sheet cakes and one white half-sheet cake.

If Sarah was too sick to work, they'd be in trouble, timewise. Raven shoved her pen behind her ear. "Asher, is Mabel scheduled to work today?"

He looked up, elbows deep in dough. "Not on Tuesdays. She works Fridays and Saturdays, sometimes Thursdays. Why?"

"I've got a half-dozen decorated birthday layer cakes and three decorated sheet cakes to make today. And we don't have any sheets prepared." She looked at her list again. "Oh, wait. One of the sheets is a gluten free." Didn't look like she could add the Blueberry Decadence to the list after all.

"Mabel can help with baking, but she's not a decorator. Did you check the freezer for any sheets?"

Will waved a floured hand. "You know I can knock out the decorated cakes. When are they scheduled for pick up?"

She sent a grateful smile to him. Will was an artist when it came to cake decorating. She flipped through the clipboard and found the individual cake orders. "The earliest pick-up is ten. A retirement party for one of the professors. Yikes, it's a *full*-sheet."

She went to the freezer and looked inside, then exhaled. "We have enough of the regular cakes, I only have to make the gluten-free."

"We'll get it done. Don't worry." Asher slapped a large wad of dough on the table, then began kneading. His muscles bulged through his T-shirt.

Raven forced her gaze to the clipboard.

Hers and Will's training had primarily been pastry, not bread. She'd never been interested in pursuing the discipline. Good thing Will seemed interested. Without Granny, because of her health, or Asher, because he would be a brilliant professor, it was essential for Asher to train Will.

Back in California, smaller bakeries had discontinued artisan breads because it either took expensive machinery or major muscles. Keeping these breads on the menu made them unique.

Even after working a week with her sister, she wasn't sure what Sarah's passions were. Her sister could handle anything, but what did she *want* to do?

As Raven prepared her ingredients for the gluten-free cake, she paused.

Hey, look at her. She was thinking like a manager. Perhaps even like an owner. A smiled formed on her face.

She hummed a melody she didn't recognize.

Was she saying yes to Granny's offer?

Sarah arrived at Sweet's in time for the rush mob. She washed her hands and tied her apron around her waist, then backed through the swinging door into the shop. Raven and Will were swamped. Asher was either still delivering or had gone on to class. She grabbed two plastic gloves and looked at the lighted number box.

"Twenty-seven."

A woman she didn't recognize gave Sarah the numbered ticket. "Goodness, this place is hopping."

"Yes. Sorry for the wait. What can I get you?" Sarah's sinuses were beating against her head like a timpani. She sniffed.

"Everything here looks delicious. What would you recommend for a romantic breakfast for two?" The woman's eyes sparkled as if she knew the secrets to a happy relationship.

Not now. No more tears. "I'm not sure I'm the best person to advise you—" Oh, did she say that out loud? "Sorry. The cheese Danish stollen with cherry or apple topping—it's both sweet and creamy-savory."

The lady stared at Sarah for a few seconds. "Are you all right?"

Was she?

Let's see, I'm engaged and can't tell anyone because my sister hates my boyfriend, and my grandmother is in the hospital. Will walked by. *Then, there's this guy I'm not sure about.*

She turned her head and sneezed.

And I'm getting a cold.

"I'm *great.*" She said it too loudly. "I'm fantastic. I got engaged last night."

Every head in the shop turned toward her. Several of the regulars flocked to her and began reaching over the tall display counter, asking to see her ring. Which meant she had to take off the plastic glove.

They ooed and ahhed accordingly. It warmed her frazzled heart.

Somewhat.

The two people she *wanted* to notice stood like statues, their mouths drooping. Raven and Will looked at each other, then snapped from their trances. Will gave a tightlipped smile and wave. Raven looked away and swiped at the counter.

Once things calmed down, Sarah finished the lady's romantic-breakfast order and called for the next number.

The last of the rush crowd carried their treasures out the door. Sarah's stomach was in knots. She was about to reap a harvest of disapproval from her sister. As for Will? Who knew what he'd say?

He answered that quick enough. "Interesting morning."

"I need to finish decorating cakes." Raven yanked an empty tray from the display case opposite Sarah, making a clatter.

"I said I would do those," Will said.

"Nope." Raven pointed a glare at him that would pierce a hole through concrete. "You can hang here and help Sarah." She kicked the swinging door and disappeared into the kitchen.

Sarah didn't have to be Raven's twin to know what her sister was thinking.

Will shrugged and grabbed the broom. He walked toward Sarah. His green eyes warm, he leaned forward and lightly kissed her cheek. "Congratulations, Sarah. God bless you and Drew." He gazed at her as though searching for something, then moved to the front of the store and began sweeping.

She touched her cheek. Why did she feel like she had run over his kitten?

Her cell rang. She pulled it from her apron pocket. Granny.

"Hey," she said. "Everything okay?"

"Audrey Carmichael called." Granny's speech was clipped, "She said you announced you're engaged."

Sarah slapped her forehead. "I'm sorry, Granny. It slipped out. I wanted to call you last night, but it was too late, and then I overslept and came straight to work."

"It's okay, sweetheart." Granny's tone had softened. "I can't wait to hear all about it. What time are you and Drew coming to see me?"

"I'll find out and let you know."

"I'll be here." She chuckled.

They said their goodbyes and disconnected. Sarah sneezed three times, doing her best to stay clear of anything edible. She snatched a towel and the disinfectant spray and did damage control. And sneezed again.

"God bless you," Will said. "Are you getting sick?"

"No. I can't be." She finished wiping down, then pulled more empty trays from the display case. She hesitated.

"Do you want me to take those into the kitchen?" Will leaned on the broom, a crooked smile on his handsome face.

"No. Time to face the firing squad." She squared her shoulders and entered the kitchen.

Raven sat on the floor by the sinks, weeping. She looked up, her eyes and face red.

Sarah took a step toward her sister. Raven held up her palm. "May I have a few moments?" She grasped the edge of the sink and pulled herself up.

"Sure. I'll be in the shop." Sarah set the trays on the worktable and stepped out, hands shaking. Another onslaught of tears waited.

Her cell rang. Drew.

"Hey, babe." Drew's chipper attitude grated her insides. "How's my future wife?"

She wailed and ran for the front door.

"What in the world! Are you okay?"

She partially covered her face with her free hand and strode down the sidewalk past Elmer's Butchery and Miner's Micro-Brewery, then toward the university. Would she walk the two miles to the chem lab where Drew was? The weather was nice enough. She had enough adrenaline.

No, she only needed space. "Just a minute, Drew," she said through a sob.

A horn honked. Someone yelled from the car, "Congratulations, Sarah!"

She waved. *Maybe the walk was a bad idea.* "Granny wants to see us tonight. Someone told her about our engagement before we could."

"I guess so. Listen, babe. The reason I called is I have great news. I didn't want to tell you yesterday because I was afraid it wouldn't work out, but Daphne interviewed me for the Germany home office. She was impressed and has recommended they fly me out to—are you ready for this? *Germany!* I have an interview on Monday! In less than a week, I'll be talking to the big wigs of Untergarten for my dream job!"

Germany? "Are you saying you want to move to Germany if they offer you a job?"

"Of course! Germany is where all the cutting-edge research is on alternative fuels. I would be crazy to not move there."

Sarah struggled to breathe. "Why is this the first I've heard about this?"

Another honk. More congratulations. She waved without looking.

"Sarah, why in the world would I learn German if I wasn't planning to get a job in Germany?"

Could he stop saying Germany? "I figured you'd travel to G—there from time to time because it's the home office. Knowing the language would make communicating easier when you travel." She swallowed. "Why didn't you tell me?"

"I told you, Sarah. Listen, you'll love Germany. Switzerland is only a few hours from the plant. Think of the Alps. Bavaria. France. It will be amazing."

She couldn't think at all. Her brain had imploded.

Another honk accompanied by congratulations. She didn't bother to wave. "I have to get back to work."

"Sure, babe. I'll pick you up, and we'll get dinner and see your grandmother. You'll see, it's like I said last night, God knew what he was doing finding your sister and bringing her home. She can take care of your grandmother and the bakery."

Sarah moaned, then sneezed—three times.

Then one more.

Chapter 21

Will locked the bakery as Raven waited for him in the car.

He never wanted to go through another day like today. Part of him wanted to pack his designer luggage and go back to LaLa Land and his former shallow life. He could have his pick of hundreds of women there who would love to be Mrs. William Durning.

He opened the driver's side door and dropped into the seat. Raven rested her head against her window and stared out into space.

Who was he kidding? He couldn't go back to that life. He loved Jesus, and Jesus loved him. He wanted to learn more about living biblically like Bud, the Bible study leader, had said last night.

He clicked his seatbelt, then started the car. Yep. He'd stay and hang with guys named Bud. He chuckled.

"What?" Raven didn't move a muscle.

"Nothing. I could use pizza, how about you?" Will's cell rang. *Asher.* "Hi. How was *your* day?"

Asher chortled. "Boring compared to yours. Is it true?"

Will sighed. "Rave and I are headed to Imo's. Want to join us?"

"I'm a block away. I'll grab a table."

Will pocketed his cell, then pulled out onto Main Street. "Ash is meeting us there."

"Um-hum. You and he are getting pretty tight." She swiveled her head enough to look at him.

"He's a good guy. I've never had a friend like him."

"I have." She poked him in the ribs. "They're nice to have."

As they entered Imo's, Asher waved. He had saved a table toward the back. The dinner crowd filled the place. Ash gave a side hug to Raven and a brotherly pound-the-back hug to Will.

"Is a hamburger pizza okay for you, Rave?" Will asked.

"I can't eat. Just a lemonade."

Asher and Will went to the counter and stood in line.

"She doesn't look happy."

Will looked over his shoulder toward his friend. She rested her chin on her hand and stared out the window. "She's taking Sarah's engagement pretty hard."

"How are you taking it?" Ash squeezed his shoulder.

"Wondering why my heart feels like it has been yanked from my chest. Otherwise, fine and dandy."

They placed their orders, got their drinks, and went back to the table. The overall mood was more like a wake than dinner. Someone's cell played *Pure Imagination* from Willy Wonka.

Raven reached into her jacket and looked at her cell. Her brows crinkled. "Hello?"

It didn't take long for her eyes to widen and her brows to lift. Her side of the conversation consisted of yeses, uh-huhs, and thank yous.

Raven's hand went to her chest. "I'll let you know. Thank you for thinking of me."

She disconnected the call, then laid her phone on the table.

Will grabbed her hand. "Who was that?"

Asher's name was called. "Don't say anything until I get back!" He pointed a finger at Raven then moved it until it touched her nose. She smiled.

Both Will and Raven bounced their legs and drummed their fingers on the table.

Asher plunked the pizza down. "Okay, give us the scoop."

Raven took a nibble. She looked at Will, eyes the size of the pizza pan, then took another bite. "This is scrumptious."

"Raven!" The guys said at the same time.

She wiped her fingers and took a sip of her lemonade. "It was the producer from Your Baking Network, remember her?"

Will thought hard. "Sunny someone?"

"Sunny Lofgren. They're putting together a new show. One of the contestants had to drop out and they want me on the first episode." She bounced in her seat. "They want to start filming in a week. Can you *believe* this?"

Asher squeezed her hand. "You will be amazing. I mean, you *are* accepting the offer, aren't you?"

Will got a weird rabid-butterfly thing in his gut. What if this lured Raven back to California?

She chewed her lip. "I don't know. With everything going on here, it's not a good idea to leave. Still, I am honored they remembered me." Raven finished her slice and wiped her fingers. "What do you think, Will?"

"Do you *want* to go back there?" *Back to the chaos and temptations?* Fame. Better job opportunities.

Raven's countenance dropped. "What do you mean? I'm not talking about moving back to LA, I'm talking about being part of this new show."

He crushed his napkins. His heart flopped, then flipped.

"It's not a good idea right now." Will picked up a slice, then put it down, staring at the table.

"Maybe not, but since when are you my boss?"

He palmed his face. "Sorry. I can't take another discussion about change." He tugged on her fingertips. "I'm sorry. It is a cool offer. I'll pray for you."

She pulled back her chin. "'Pray for me.' That was condescending."

Oh, great. "I didn't mean—I—"

All he wanted was peace and pizza. Instead, Raven and he had dragged the chaos along as another guest.

The rest of the meal was tense. Not what Will wanted. Raven wanted to process the YBN offer with him, but he just couldn't. They all needed to get used to Sarah's engagement and its ramifications.

The dread and stress curdled the gooey pizza in his stomach.

Drew pulled into Imo's parking lot, his taste buds craving cheese and meat. Sarah laid her hand on his arm. His engagement ring looked beautiful on her long, slender fingers.

"Can we eat somewhere else?"

What? He stared at her. "Why? You were the one who wanted pizza."

She nodded toward a truck and small compact. *Oh.* "The gangs all here, I see." He backed the car out. "Where to?"

"East Meets West?"

He gave an exaggerated sigh. "Fine."

After a hearty meal, which he only enjoyed because he forced himself, they headed to the hospital. From what Sarah said, her unceremonious announcement at the bakery had made its way to her grandmother. He had called his parents that morning. Since he had asked for the ring over the summer break, he let them know it was official.

They parked and entered the lobby holding hands. Sarah pressed the elevator button. A few seconds later the doors opened. Raven, Will, and Asher stood there.

Sarah withdrew her hand.

Oh, no, you don't. Drew retrieved it and locked his fingers tight.

"Hey, guys. Congratulations." Asher hugged Sarah and shook Drew's hand.

Will extended his hand toward Drew. "I already congratulated Sarah. Best wishes to you. You are a—a blessed man."

"I know." *And you need to stay away from my girl.*

Raven and Sarah hugged, then Raven turned her head, swiped at her eyes, and sniffed.

Oh, please. You'd think Sarah was dying! Not that she was much better. She'd been snuffling and sneezing all evening.

Maybe the sisters were both sick.

Raven leaned in like she was about to hug him, then straightened and stuck out her hand. "Congrats."

I bet that hurt. But hey, he'd won. He could afford to be gracious. He leaned forward and kissed her on the cheek. "Thanks."

She grimaced and took a step back.

Whatever. The sooner they moved to Germany, the better. A hand-sanitizer dispenser stood next to the elevator. He availed himself of a big glob.

"Granny is excited to see you two. Have a great evening." Will put his arm around Raven's shoulders and the three of them walked away, looking like someone had died.

"How cheerful."

Sarah followed him into the elevator and pressed the four. "Do we have to tell Granny about the possibility of us moving?"

"To Germany? Why? Don't you want to get married, Sarah?" He folded his arms across his chest.

Why was she acting this way? Drew was offering her an incredible life. Most girls would be chomping at the bit to live in Europe!

She rested her hand on his arm. Even in the poor lighting, her engagement ring sparkled. "I'm getting used to the idea. Besides, you don't know if you have the job, yet."

He shook away her hand. What was she saying? "You don't think I can get this job? You don't think I'm good enough?" He ran his palm over his hair.

She slid her arms around his waist. "You deserve the job. I want you to be happy. If this is your dream, then it's my dream too. I've never lived outside Minersville. I'm being silly." She laid her head against his bicep.

He rested his chin on the top of her soft hair. "I understand. And we can wait to tell your grandmother about Germany." He moved his arms around her. "Too bad you can't come along for the interview. Then you could explore the area. And we could go to Switzerland to see your—"

Oops!

The doors opened, which was fortunate because he almost spilled the frank and beans about finding her father.

He couldn't spoil the surprise. It would be the perfect wedding gift.

Chapter 28

Asher dropped his keys on the entry table while Will hung his jacket on the coatrack. Asher eyed his friend. "Are you sure you don't want to talk with Raven? Go for a walk. She needs to talk out a lot of stuff."

Will looked at him. "I need to think. Maybe try the praying thing. Every good thing I thought we had is disintegrating. Has it simply run its course, and Rave and I need to move on? Or does it mean I need to move on? I don't know."

"*You* want to go for a walk?"

Will chuckled. "Sounds like I need one." He reached toward Asher and laid a hand on his shoulder. "Raven is hurting right now. She's confused and rootless—like I was. Still am, sometimes. She needs a real Father—our Father. I have no idea how to get her to a place where she'll understand. She may not listen, but if you let her talk, it might help her."

Asher's heart pounded. Was he up to the challenge—the responsibility? "I'll call and ask her. If our Father," Asher smiled at his new brother in Jesus, "opens the door, I'll step through and do the best I can."

"Good enough."

The two prayed. For Sarah and Drew and Raven.

Will headed to the bedroom.

"Okay, Dad, it's in Your hands." Asher sent another quick prayer, then punched in Raven's number. First ring—

"Hey, Asher."

Wow. She sounded raw. "Need a walk?"

She sighed. "All I do is burden you with my garbage."

"A garbage man is a worthy profession," he said.

She sighed. "Why are you doing this?"

His heart skipped. He wasn't sure. Or was he? "I guess—I don't know. Maybe it's because I remember having questions. Granny helped me a lot until I—"

"Until you found Je—sus?" She dragged out the syllables. "Are you trying to convert me like you did Will?"

Wow. Convert? That was harsh. "You know your friend better than I do. Do you honestly believe I could make him do anything he didn't want to do? Could I make *you* do anything you didn't want to do?"

A long pause ensued. He pressed his lips together. *Lord*?

She growled. "You're right. It hurt my feelings when he didn't tell me he was going through all this ... this metamorphosis."

Asher laughed. "You make him sound like an alien."

"Don't laugh, he is like an alien." She chuckled. "It's what I love about him." Another pause. "I'd like to take our walk."

Despite his offer to pick her up, she wanted to drive separately. He arrived at the university's EE lot first and waited outside his truck.

He shivered in his heavy down coat. All she had was the beat-up leather jacket—she'd freeze.

She parked next to his truck. He opened the door for her. She looked up and smiled, those blue eyes engaging his heart once again.

"It's cold. I've got an extra jacket in the truck."

She stood and hugged herself. "Thanks."

Once she slipped his puffy, blue, down coat on and zipped it, she stood before him looking like the Michelin man. Her arms floated above her missing waist. Not fashionable, but it would keep her warm.

She giggled. "Call me Veruca Salt." She puffed out her cheeks and waddled ahead of him. "Just don't play Willy Wonka and blow me up like a blueberry."

They laughed, hard. Raven bent trying to catch her breath and nearly tumbled forward. He grabbed what would have been her waist to keep her from falling. She straightened and placed her hands on his arms. "Thanks. I needed a good laugh."

"I aim to please, ma'am. How about we walk?"

They strolled in silence, except the occasional sniff from Raven. Asher prayed as he thought, not wanting to say anything until she was ready. It was nice just being together.

The sniffing increased. He pulled a handkerchief from his back pocket. He had read somewhere when he was a kid that a gentleman should always carry a handkerchief. He tried to most of the time. In the years since he began doing it, he had given them away to dozens of people— mostly children.

He shook the handkerchief out and handed it to her. She looked at it, then lifted her expressive brow.

"It's a handkerchief." He pointed to her nose.

She took it, her hand dwarfed by the coat sleeve. *She's so cute.*

She turned away from him and blew her nose, then handed the hankie back.

He grinned. "Keep it."

She stared at it, then folded it carefully and tucked the handkerchief inside her sleeve. "Thanks." She continued walking. "Were you a Boy Scout or something?"

"Nah. My parents labeled it as a sexist organization. Which was a shame. A lot of my friends from school were scouts, and they were always doing fun stuff."

Raven nodded. "I always wanted to be a Brownie, but, you know ..."

He didn't. Maybe Raven would trust him enough one day to share her story.

They reached the university's library. He'd always loved the modern architecture. The giant windows with steel and wood. Since the library was open until midnight, the lights were a beacon in the darkness.

"Want to sit in the library? It's a lot warmer."

"No. Thanks." She patted her roundness. "I'm nice and toasty. We could sit on one of those benches."

Once they sat, Raven bounced her feet, then noticed what she was doing and stopped. "My thoughts are all over the place. I don't know where to begin."

"What has you most emotional?"

She looked at him. "I guess it's Sarah. I can't get rid of the feeling that Drew is not a good person—at least for her."

"I've known Drew for a few years. He's focused on his goals and future. That's not a bad thing."

"I guess." Her feet bounced again. "He was out of line when he told Sarah about our mother's death. Granny or I should have told her."

Asher nodded. He agreed. Over the last few days, Asher had wrestled with Drew's motive for that. Was it intentional or merely insensitivity?

"Am I crazy to think it was wrong?"

Okay, now he was on the spot. He had to be honest. "I don't think you're crazy."

"Thank you. I know you don't like talking about other people. Having come from a gossip-loving town—true or not—it is refreshing. And frustrating." She raised her brows and gave him a half smile.

"Sorry. This is a small town and news travels fast, as you've noticed. I've learned over the years to share what is mine to share and to try to not say anything I mind others knowing."

"Isn't it okay to share your opinion? As long as you're honest?"

It was his turn to bounce his feet. "Granny always says, 'If you don't have anything nice to say, don't say anything at all.'"

Raven lifted her chin and appeared to be searching the stars. "I'm not sure I agree. At least not for everything." She shifted her gaze to the ground. "Maybe if someone had given their opinion about my mother's drug problem when she was younger, before she got into the heavy stuff, I wouldn't have missed twenty-one years of my life here."

"Yeah." He took a deep breath and exhaled. He sent a prayer for wisdom. "Can I give my opinion?"

She smiled, then made eye contact. Her smile faded. "Maybe."

He lifted his brows.

"Okay, go for it."

"I can't imagine the suffering you endured. Being separated from your sister, your grandmother, your father."

She looked away, then pulled the handkerchief from her sleeve and wiped her eyes.

He laid his hand on hers. "Still, had you not gone through all those difficult challenges, you would never have met your foster parents. You would never have attended the prestigious pastry school. And, you would never have met Will, your best friend."

A sob escaped her.

Oh, no. I went too far. He grabbed her hand. "I'm sorry."

She sniffed. "I asked for it, didn't I?" She blew her nose. "This hankie thing sure came in handy." She blew her nose again. "We got distracted. How about we get back to Sarah—and what's his name."

He chuckled.

They spent time talking about the engagement and Sarah moving away.

Oh. Did that inner nudge mean what he thought it did? *Are you sure, Lord?*

Yup. He was. "May I give another opinion?"

Raven grimaced. "Will it sting like the last one?"

"Sorry."

She patted his knee. A lightning bolt shot through his body. He swallowed with difficulty.

"No, I needed to hear a different perspective. I will be chewing on it for some time. Go ahead."

He cleared his throat. "You seem to have clear intuitions about Drew. I don't know if I agree or disagree, but I see your logic. What if you prayed?"

"Prayed?"

"Yes." He stood. "Want to walk?"

She joined him. "Don't I have to believe in God to pray?"

"Nah. He's not intimidated by your disbelief."

She punched him in the ribs. He felt it through his coat. *Strong little thing.*

"Sorry. I promised myself to not hit people anymore." She stuck her hands in the pockets. "What do I pray?"

"Pray for wisdom. I always start there. And discernment. You know, making sure what you're sensing is real. Is it coming from God or from you merely not liking Drew? Or are you looking for reasons to keep Sarah here?"

"Whoa. You don't mess around with this opinion stuff."

"This was more like advice."

"I will think about it," she said.

They walked to the EE lot where their vehicles were. "Here we are, where we started. Ready to head home?"

Raven looked over her shoulder, then up at him. "There's something else I need to talk about. Unless you need to go."

Asher's heart warmed. He could stay with her forever. "No, I don't need to go."

Raven closed the front door. Even though it was after midnight and her body would pay for the lack of sleep tomorrow, the peace was worth it.

After hanging her jacket, she rubbed the circulation back in her arms. She had returned Asher's coat, and the drive wasn't long enough for the car to warm up.

She had an urge to write down her thoughts. The last time she had journaled was when she was in elementary school.

Her teacher had given her a journal—only to her, no one else in the class. The book had a cloth cover with pink and yellow and blue flowers. Over the weeks, she had written page after page. About living in a condemned building. About the men who came in and out of her mother's room. Of hiding in the basement behind old crates when it got loud or people knocked things around.

Raven walked into the kitchen and peeked inside the fridge. A mason jar of Sarah's leftover homemade beef and barley soup beckoned to her. Her attempt to pull out a saucepan quietly failed. She stepped into the living room to see if she'd woken Sarah. No lights. No sound.

As the soup heated, she continued her memory. She had always been careful to hide her journal, but one day one of her mother's "friends" went through her backpack and found it.

She shook her head. Thinking about it now, what she had thought were her own thoughts and experiences to write were pretty incriminating evidence about drug dealers and her mother. Scarface had beat her until Lizzy intervened.

Raven couldn't convince him no one else had read the diary. He almost kept her home from school—permanently. He burned her journal.

Once her teacher spotted the bruises and black eye, she sent Raven to the nurse's office. She and her mom had to sneak away and move to another town.

Raven had loved her teacher, but she never let anyone get close again. The people her mother associated with didn't fool around. Kid or adult, they would do bad things to those who got in their way.

She stirred the soup, tiny bubbles telling her it would be ready soon. Raven loved Sarah's soups. The girl had a way with seasoning that rivaled anything Raven had ever tasted.

Maybe she should buy a journal and write down her thoughts, her memories—the good and the bad. She needed perspective. Sometimes her mind was like a washer on spin cycle, with the occasional monkey wrench thrown in.

Asher's revelation about how even her crappy life had purpose, as though there was a divine hand moving people around in her life, was a different way of looking at things.

When she asked him about the offer from YBN, he was excited for her, but refused to offer his opinion. Which drove her nuts. The only advice he gave was what he said about Drew—pray for wisdom.

She had begged him to tell her what to do. Instead, he asked her what she wanted out of life.

A week ago, she would have said fame and fortune in the baking world—maybe her own show and bakery. Now, she wanted family, a home, and the ability to improve her craft—to stay fresh in her creativity. The long conversation hadn't produced an answer for her as she drove home.

As frustrating as that was, she admired Asher. He respected *her* enough to let her make her own decisions, and he sincerely wanted to know what was important to her.

Even Will wasn't able to give her the space to make her own decision. He seemed afraid she would move on and leave him in Missouri.

She stirred the soup. Guess she wasn't the only one who feared being left behind.

Yeah. She needed to start writing her thoughts.

The soup was ready. She turned off the burner, grabbed a bowl from the cabinet and ladled a generous portion, then placed it on the island. Once she settled on the stool, she took a deep whiff of the deliciousness. The first bite warmed her throat and traveled to her cold tired body.

She had nearly finished the bowl when her eyes drooped.

Releasing a contented moan, she pushed the bowl from her and laid her head in her arms. Only for a moment. Then she'd go to ...

Chapter 29

Sarah opened her eyes to Raven's made bed. She listened for the shower or movement in the house. Nothing. Did Raven come home? Did something happen to her?

She threw back the covers, slipped her feet into her slippers, and scuffed out of the bedroom and down the stairs.

The kitchen light was on. *Oh, thank You, God.* She stood at the doorway. There was her sister, still dressed, asleep on the counter. Snoring. A near-empty bowl of soup precariously perched on the edge of the counter. She couldn't help a soft giggle.

Quietly she cleaned the kitchen, made coffee, and headed upstairs to shower. Her sinuses were full—a hot shower should the relieve pressure.

By the time Sarah had dressed, Raven walked into the bedroom looking like her teddy, Henry—bedraggled.

"Good morning, beautiful."

Raven managed a goofy smile. "'Morning."

"Got in late, I take it?"

The pattern of Raven's sweater was imprinted on her cheek. Sarah turned before she burst out laughing.

"Do I smell coffee?"

"Yup. You were sleeping in front of it. I see you finished off the beef and barley soup."

She rubbed her face. "It was good. You should open a restaurant." Raven stumbled toward the bathroom but looked over her shoulder. "I'll be ready quick as a—a—"

"Rabbit?"

Raven's eyes softened. "Yeah."

Who is *this person?* Sarah liked this version of Raven. Cute, funny, vulnerable.

She went into the kitchen and withdrew two frozen Sweet's croissants from a Zip-lock bag and popped them into the toaster oven. She pulled out a selection of Granny's homemade jams—apple butter, pear, and strawberry preserves. No butter needed—there was enough butter in the lamination process.

By the time Raven entered the kitchen, she was awake and ready to go. She smiled. "You made breakfast for us?"

Sarah pushed out the empty stool with her foot. Once her sister settled, Sarah bowed her head and thanked the Lord for the food. They dug in, sending flaky crumbs everywhere.

"Are you getting a cold or something?"

Sarah sniffled. "I hope not. The last thing we need is missing staff." She placed her hand on Raven's. "Thanks for filling in while I was gone Monday and out-of-it mentally yesterday."

Raven shrugged. They ate a few bites in silence.

"What do you think about selling coffee at the bakery?" Raven took another bite.

Sarah chewed her bite and the idea. "Are you talking about a pseudo-Starbucks, or what?"

"I thought to begin simple. Brewed coffee, but not brands from the distributor. Something locally roasted? Is there a roaster around here?"

"Not in Minersville. There is a roaster and café in Eureka."

Raven tapped her chin her eyes enlarging. "Fun! A café with a roaster and—"

"Yes! I could make soups and have fresh crusty breads, and of course, amazing desserts by Raven." The ideas tumbled into her brain faster than Sarah could speak.

"Yeah!" Raven raised her fist for a bump. She stopped, then lowered her hand. "I guess when you move to St. Louis, you'll do all these things." She pushed the plate away. "You'll be brilliant, Sarah."

How could she forget she was getting married and moving away—maybe to Germany? Drew received the call last night that Untergarten scheduled his flight for Sunday.

"You forgot, didn't you?"

Sarah swallowed around her raw throat. She sneezed. Her cold chose that moment to come on full force.

Drew warned her that if it did, they couldn't see one another until after he came back from Europe. Maybe Sarah would feel better once they could see one another. He complained again she wasn't supporting him.

"You okay?" Raven pushed away a strand of hair from Sarah's forehead. "You look like you have the weight of the world on your shoulders. My foster, Mandie, used to say that to me. I never got what having the world on my shoulders looked like."

"Until looking at me?" What could she share with her sister? Moving to Germany? How could she *think* about leaving Raven, much less talk about it?

"You don't feel safe talking with me, do you?" Raven lowered her eyes. "I haven't been supportive. I can understand why you don't trust me. Will says I'm too reactive."

Oh, how I want to, Raven. For twenty-one years she had prayed for her sister to confide in. She reached for Raven's hand and cupped it in hers. "I know you love me."

Raven's chin and lips trembled. She bobbed her head.

"I know you want the best for me. Like I want for you." They stared at each other. Blue eyes to blue eyes. Similar, yet different. "Can't that be enough for now?"

"Sure," Raven whispered. "Maybe you could talk to Asher. He was good at helping me see different perspectives."

Raven squeezed Sarah's hand and held tight.

"He might be brilliant—like Dr.-Phil-genius, Sarah. You know he asked me what *I* was passionate about. What was *my* dream? It helped me refocus. Maybe you can ask yourself that? You probably already know Drew's dreams. What do *you* want?"

Nope. Not going there. "What *are* your dreams?"

Raven shook her finger back and forth. "Nope. Not until I know yours." She looked toward the stove. "Geez, look at the time. The boys will beat us to the bakery."

"Let's get going."

Sarah grabbed her coat but couldn't forget Raven's question. What *was* her passion? Shouldn't she be focused more on Drew's dreams and not be selfish?

Lord?

Will pulled a large tray of ciabattas from the oven. He was digging bread making. His biceps were sore, but it was better than any workout at the gym.

The climate in the bakery had improved over the previous day. Less friction. More productivity. Ash loaded the truck for the deliveries. The sisters finished the baked produce. In the natural choreography of experience and cooperation, they were accomplishing amazing things.

If only life could be that way. He sighed. Then maybe his heart wouldn't be like the crumbs he swept up at the end of the day.

He inadvertently tipped the tray and one of the rolls fell.

"Got it!" Sarah made a perfect catch before it hit the tile.

"Well done," Will said.

Hours later after the first rush, Sarah, Raven, and Will discussed adding the sale of coffee to the bakery. The consensus was it would be extra work, but the return on investment would occur quickly.

Sarah had calculated the numbers. It was the first time Will saw her glow in days—even before the engagement.

His phone rang. He pulled his cell from the apron pocket. The caller ID read *HOLLYWOOD*.

"Rave." Will held it up.

She leaned in and grimaced. "I guess it's time."

Sarah rested against the display case. "Time for what?"

"Quit."

"Resign."

Raven and Will spoke together.

"You sure?" Will studied her.

She gave a half-smile. Good enough for him.

Thumbing Elton's speed dial, they waited.

"It's about time, William," their soon-to-be ex-boss said.

Will placed the call on speaker.

The conversation was brief and ended surprisingly well ... for Raven. Her decision to stay in Missouri given the circumstances of being reunited with her long-lost grandmother and twin sister were understandable. Although Elton sure didn't like losing his baking celebrity.

Will deciding to stay, however, was met with questions he didn't want to answer in present company. Frazzled from the heated portion of the conversation directed at him, he stepped outside into the sunshine. He yanked off the hairnet and lifted his face toward the sky.

He knew the answers to Elton's questions. They were simple but bizarre—at least they would be to his now-former boss. Returning to Los Angeles could—no, *would*—jeopardize his new life in Jesus. Too many temptations.

And it would mean leaving behind his best friend, new friend, and the woman he loved. Who was engaged to someone els—

Hold on. What did he just admit?

Yes, I love Sarah.

A steady stream of cars drove by. People walked in and out of the local shops. They weren't acting normal. They were normal. Living their lives.

He walked down the sidewalk, his heart dragging behind him.

A spinning red and white barber pole caught his eye. Printed on the front window—*Sal's Barber Shop*. Before he could talk himself out of it, he walked inside.

The place was empty except for a rotund guy with a shiny bald head reading a newspaper. He looked up then went back to reading. "You lost?"

"You Sal?" Will asked.

"Guilty."

Will plopped into the other chair. It squeaked and rotated on its own. "I need a trim."

"Try Shear Elegance across the street." Sal turned a page and resumed reading.

"I need a haircut."

Sal peered over the newspaper. "That right?" He inspected Will as he folded the paper and set it on his chair. "Let's see if we can get you sorted out."

Will reentered the city foot traffic, fifty pounds lighter. He ran his hands through his freshly shorn hair. Strange to not tangle his fingers in long locks. He looked different, to be sure, but he felt freer. Not because he would no longer have all the hair maintenance, but because he didn't have to focus on his appearance. Something he had done a lot of in the past.

Too much.

Sal was fascinating. The guy had served in the Air Force during Vietnam. He had signed on as a barber but helped the medical personnel. Will was sure he was a hero. You never knew about people.

He liked this small-town life. The pace was slow enough you could get to know people.

Sal gave him a bear hug before he left. "Anyone who would drop everything to help Hope is okay in my book."

Of course, the haircut facilitated Sal's good opinion of Will too.

He opened Sweet's door and walked in. Sarah and Raven assisted a few customers. Sarah looked up. She tilted her head, her brows wrinkling. Then she held his gaze.

Her brow relaxed and a bright Sarah-smile appeared.

"Why would he chop off his hair?" Raven paced Sweet's back parking lot. Alone. Will's hair was part of who he was. Was he changing that much?

This Jesus thing had gone too far.

Was he morphing into a small-town Hoosier? Next thing she knew he would wear Levi's and flannel shirts.

The door opened. Will stuck his head out. "Mad at me?"

She kicked at a piece of litter, then bent and picked it up. "No. But I'm freaked out." She opened the dumpster and threw in the bit of trash. The lid crashed shut and made her jump.

"Because I look more handsome? More like a troll?" He stepped outside and shut the door.

She chuckled. "Too early to tell."

He stood looking down at her, his green eyes sparkling. *Are his eyes brighter? Clearer?*

"It's still me, Rave."

"Are you? I mean, are you the same?"

He gave her a crooked smile. "Good point. I guess I have changed." He ran his hand behind his head, then pulled it away. "Wow. I have to get used to nothing being back there."

Raven pursed her lips. Honestly, she had always thought Will spent an inordinate amount of attention on his hair. He enjoyed girls going crazy over it. Depending upon his mood, he took advantage of it too.

"Wait. Is this about Sarah?"

His cheeks pinked.

"William Durning, are you blushing?"

The pink darkened. "Shut up." He turned around.

She grabbed his arm and tried turning him around, but he wouldn't budge. "It's adorable."

"Adorable? Yeah. Right."

No doubt, he didn't want Sarah to marry Drew. Maybe they could put their heads together and find a way to talk her out of it. Having her sister marry her best friend would be the greatest thing ever!

"Listen. We have to do something about this engagement." She looked around to make sure no one was around to overhear them.

Will turned toward her. "There's nothing we can do. Should do. They love each other and want to be together."

"You honestly believe they love each other?"

"Who wouldn't love Sarah? She's amazing. Intelligent. Beautiful. Talented. The way her eyes brighten when she's excited. The way—" He grimaced as though someone had slapped him. "We need to get back to work." He strode back to the bakery. "Raven, please don't tell anyone. I need to hand this over to God. Ash says it's in His hands anyway."

What? How ridiculous.

Maybe Asher wasn't as brilliant as she thought.

Will disappeared into the bakery.

In fact, what a thing to tell someone whose heart was breaking. *"Hand it over to God?"* What did that mean?

Should she rethink the whole praying thing? Because Will needed to fight for her sister, not give up.

Sarah's cold had gone into high gear. Her bed awaited, but she hadn't been able to move from the living room couch since Raven dropped her off after work.

With her nose plugged up, pressure had mounted in her head. Her body was like over-kneaded dough. She coughed into her elbow. *Ouch.*

Since she was a kid, she'd suffered from chronic bronchitis that developed into bronchial infections. Enough of the symptoms of bronchitis were there that she had already called Doc Holloway. He said he would phone in an antibiotic to the pharmacy.

She couldn't keep her eyes open. *Maybe, I'll rest them for a few seconds.*

"Sarah?" Raven squatted in front of her. "Why don't you go to bed?"

She tried speaking, but a froggy croak came out. She tried to clear her throat and contorted over the pain. Someone had used a trowel and hollowed out her esophagus.

Raven tugged Sarah onto her feet.

"Come on. Let's get you to bed." Raven helped Sarah to their bedroom and assisted her out of her clothes and into her nightgown.

"I picked up supplies. My fosters have tried and true remedies for colds."

Tucked into bed, her teddy bear Hank in her arms—which Raven insisted was part of the cure—and a dose of a nasty-tasting *blue stuff* as Raven called it, Sarah was already better. At least more comfortable.

She heard banging in the kitchen, but then she dozed.

"Sarah—" Raven was whispering at her. "I have chicken soup for you. Jewish penicillin."

Sarah opened one eye. Raven held a tray.

"You didn't have to do this."

Raven shrugged. "Come on, sit up, or you'll wear this soup."

Sarah rearranged the pillows, then sat back. Raven carefully set the tray on Sarah's lap. What remained of her olfactory senses appreciated the aroma.

"It's not as good as you would make, but the deli guy said it'll do the trick." She ladled soup onto the spoon and tried to feed Sarah.

"Let me, Sis." They smiled toward each other. Raven handed Sarah the spoon and moved over to her bed and sat.

At least Sarah thought she could do it. She spilt a few drops on Hank. "Oops."

Raven grabbed the bear. "I'll clean him up." She took Hank and left the bedroom.

Sarah glanced at Raven's matching bear, Henry. They looked even more different than Sarah and Raven did. Life had altered their once sameness.

She continued to eat her soup and Raven returned, a cleaned-up Hank in her palm. "Your bear *is* much lighter than mine." She went to her bed and picked up Henry. "A lot lighter."

Raven massaged her bear, her brow furrowed. She looked at Sarah. "There's something in here."

"Maybe it's matted stuffing. Or maybe mom used different material when she mended it." Dread soured her stomach.

Raven left the room. Sarah could hear her in Granny's office, then she came back holding a pair of scissors.

"It's probably nothing." Raven snipped the seams in the center of the stomach. Like a surgeon she opened the bear, then removed cotton-ball-sized pieces of stuffing.

Raven gasped.

Sarah moved the tray aside. "Raven?"

Her twin stuck her fingers deeper into Henry and pulled out a plastic bag.

What on earth? "What is it?"

Raven lifted the baggie—filled with a white substance. "Cocaine."

Sarah jumped up, then dizziness sent her back to the bed. "No." She struggled to breathe. "Did our mother put that—that *garbage* in your bear? A child's toy?"

"I remember Scarface accusing her of stealing from him. He tore apart the place where we lived looking for it. I was hiding downstairs with Henry." Raven poked around inside the bear, then pulled another, smaller bag.

Sarah cringed. The dream Sarah had held onto all her life—of a confused mother who loved her kids, who wanted them, but needed help—was dying before her eyes. She looked at Raven with new understanding. "Oh, Raven."

Raven didn't respond. Instead, she inspected the interior of the bear. She pulled out stuffing from the arms, the legs, the head. She yanked it out until the bear was nothing but a floppy shell, then threw it across the room.

"Raven." Sarah managed to move to her sister's bed and wrapped her arms around her. Raven was as hard as the oak tree in the backyard.

Father, please, we need your peace. Wrap your arms around us.

She hummed and rocked her sister like Granny had done for her when a nightmare frightened her. Raven had *lived* a nightmare most of her life, and for the first time, Sarah was beginning to comprehend how bad it was.

They swayed. Eventually, they snuggled together in Raven's bed, as only sisters can do, and fell asleep.

Sarah dreamed of a faceless evil chasing her and Raven. They ran to the light and the open, strong arms of someone waiting for them. She pulled Raven along.

Evil ran from the light.

They were safe.

For now.

Chapter 30

Raven wolfed down several thousand milligrams of vitamin C, then took another bite of her raisin toast. Sarah still slept. The two of them had slumbered peacefully in Raven's twin bed. The peace was short lived, though. Gone the minute Raven opened her eyes.

Waking up to her sister's sinus snoring wasn't bad. A few cricks in her neck weren't bad.

Waking up to two bags of drugs? Devastating.

And there they sat on her grandmother's shiny granite countertop.

She took a sip of coffee. What should she do?

She thought about flushing them down the toilet, until she remembered a news show about how eighty percent of the rivers and lakes were contaminated with prescription drugs. Sewage systems couldn't filter these drugs and now fish and other aquatic animals were showing adverse effects. If prescription medications had such ill effects, imagine what cocaine would do?

No. She needed to dispose of it elsewhere.

She sighed and ran her hands through her hair. If she wanted to get to work early to make up for Sarah's absence, she needed to leave now. She jumped off the kitchen stool, grabbed the baggies, and threw them into the freezer.

Once things calmed down at Sweet's, she would call and let Sarah know.

She walked out of the kitchen, then spun around. *What if Sarah happened to open the freezer? She might freak out.*

Opening the junk drawer—as Sarah called it—she grabbed a pad of paper and pen. After quickly jotting a short note, she laid it on the counter.

S. Hope you're feeling better. Put drugs in freezer. Will deal later. R

Drew had a million errands to run before his trip—he stared at the pharmacy clock—and where was he? Picking up a prescription for his girlfriend? Fiancée? *Whatever.*

The line snaked around the pharmacy counter. *Great.* People coughed all around him. He tugged his T-shirt collar over his nose. He would drop the medicine off at the Sweetings' and leave. The last thing he needed was to get sick before his trip to Germany.

Once he bought the antibiotic, he sped to Sarah's house. The front door was unlocked, as Sarah had texted. He thought about throwing the bag on the floor, then changed his mind.

"Sarah! I have your medicine." No response. Was that the shower?

He walked into the kitchen and set the bag on the counter. There was a note. He picked it up.

Drugs? *In the freezer. Deal later?*

There were drugs in the freezer? He opened the freezer door. Two clear bags lay across a pack of frozen peas. He poked the bags with his cell, then slammed the freezer door.

He knew it.

Raven was selling drugs. He knew she was up to no good.

His Sarah couldn't know anything about this, could she? It didn't matter. He would vouch for her when he called the police.

He scruffed his hair. Should he call the police?

He rubbed the back of his neck. Untergarten might frown on any controversy. This might look bad for him. Especially since they knew he had proposed to Sarah. The drug dealer's sister.

Maybe he should wait. At least until after the interview. And he should talk with Sarah. He glanced at the oven clock.

His class was in fifteen minutes, followed by his advisor's meeting, and then a tutoring job.

It would have to wait.

In the meantime, he'd take the note and hold it as evidence.

Raven waited while the producer wrapped her brain around what Raven had just laid on her. The traffic on Main Street flowed as she sat on Sweet's narrow window ledge.

"So, let me get this straight," Sunny's excitement vibrated through the fiber optics. "Because you appeared on *Cupcake Rivalry, our show,* your identical twin sister found you and you were reunited with her and your grandmother after *how* many years?"

"Over twenty years," Raven said. "With Granny in the hospital and the bakery short-staffed, it doesn't seem fair to be gone at this time."

"Wait, wait, wait. Are you telling me they *all* work at a bakery?" The producer kept covering the phone and yelling at someone.

"Granny owns Sweet's Bakery. Sarah grew up baking." Sunny's voice muffled.

"Hello?"

"I'm sorry," Sunny said. "I was talking with my assistant. Raven, I totally understand. Can I get back with you?"

"Ms. Lofgren, like I said, it is inconvenient at this time."

More muffled conversation between Sunny and someone on her end. "I hear you. I hope your grandmother is better soon. Can we keep in touch?"

"Of course. Is it possible you might still consider me for an episode in the future?"

"I can guarantee that."

They ended the call. Raven closed her eyes and soaked in the moment. She opened them to a magnificent sunset.

She'd done the right thing saying no. She knew it.

Asher switched off the neon *open* sign and gave her a tight smile. Why be mean to such a nice guy? She waved. He waved back, his smile broadening.

Is being nice so difficult, Raven?

Walking back inside, Will looked up, his eyebrows raised.

"Yes, it was Sunny Lofgren from YBN."

"What did you decide?" Will rested his elbows on the counter.

"I told her it wasn't a good time." From her peripheral vision, she noted Asher's nod. "I told her I was interested, and she indicated she would consider me in the future."

"Cool," Asher said.

Raven turned toward him. "Thanks."

"Yeah, great." Will pounded the door to the kitchen as he left.

"What's with him?"

Asher looked away. "You and your friend need to talk."

Sometimes Asher's integrity annoyed the heck out her. If her best friend was working to emulate him, would he still be the same fun Will?

"After I check in with Sarah, I'll head to the hospital." Asher said. "See you tomorrow."

She nodded. With the decision about the television show behind her, she could redirect her attention to the bags of contraband in her grandmother's fridge. Will's issues would have to wait. Lizzy's unwelcomed "gift" was enough for her.

Would the fallout of Lizzy's messed-up life ever end?

Will accompanied Asher to see Sarah. Asher knocked on the door. No one answered.

Asher tried the door. It was unlocked.

Will shook his head. People were way too trusting out here.

Asher stuck his head inside. "Sarah! You awake?" No answer. Someone coughed in the distance.

Asher looked relieved. "She must be sleeping. I'll drop off today's paperwork and the thumb drive."

Will nodded. Good thing Raven would be home soon. She would keep an eye on her sister.

They went back to Ash's truck and drove to the hospital, riding in silence. Theirs was a peaceful quiet. Will was learning to appreciate his friend's mild manner. His uncomplicated nature.

Ash wasn't simple—the man was brilliant—but he appreciated real conversation. Not small talk.

In the quiet, Will also observed the splendor of the world around him. The beautiful sky. The stately trees.

He could hear those thoughts he never gave time to. Important thoughts about life—like faith. Who knew his life had been so noisy?

He and Raven were doing it. Making Missouri—this tiny town, and its people—their home.

He needed to tell his parents. Move his stuff. Find a more permanent home. Maybe Asher could be his roommate.

The hospital was ahead. He looked forward to seeing Granny. Allowing her to love on him like an old-fashioned grandmother could.

They parked next to his rental car. Raven had beat them there.

He would need to get rid of his BMW Z4.

Maybe he'd buy a truck. Hmm. Maybe a black SUV with tinted windows. And a great sound system.

God didn't expect him to change overnight, did he?

Drew couldn't keep his mind on his student's questions. Raven keeping drugs in his girlfriend's house was beyond belief! He knew from the moment he had met her she would cause trouble. And according to a few of the locals, she came by it naturally, what with her mother being a drug addict.

Had he not needed the money, he would have cancelled the tutoring session. But if he didn't earn the extra cash, he'd be hard pressed to make his excursion into Switzerland.

And he *had* to do that.

The sooner he got Sarah out of this town, the better.

"Mr. Collar," Drew's student said. "I still don't get this equation."

Drew tried not to roll his eyes. How did this kid get into an engineering college?

"Let's review the equation, line by line." Good thing he was paid by the hour. He looked at his watch.

At seven, he was out of here. He had to figure out how to get Sarah away from Raven.

Whatever it took.

Chapter 31

Raven scrolled through the website article on her phone. Sarah slept upstairs, sounding better than she had that morning, but she was a long way from being well.

The article described how to dispose of prescription drugs. They should be able to adapt the instructions for the cocaine.

According to the article, she could double-bag the baggies and add water to it. Then seal it with duct tape and place it in a "durable packaging that does not show what's inside." The photo of the box made her think of a coffin.

She set down her phone. *A coffin. Death.*

Memories flooded of her mother's funeral. It wasn't much. To this day she wasn't sure who had paid for Elizabeth Anna Sweeting's cremation and interment. The attendees were the funeral-home guy, her foster parents, and herself. The short, stubby funeral guy had short, cropped gray hair like a miniature drill sergeant. His squeaky voice had made her laugh. Which frustrated him and the Gillians.

She cringed. What if they thought she was laughing at her mother's death? At the time she didn't care what anyone thought—she was fourteen and had watched her mother die—in her arms. Who wouldn't be traumatized and act out? At least, that's what the gracious Gillians had told her.

Did she know anything respectful to say about her mother even today?

Flipping over her cell, she looked again at the photo of the prescription medication tucked inside a dark blue cardboard box.

Oh.

She took the stairs two at a time and entered Granny's office—the room she was told had once been her mother's bedroom. She opened the closet and searched for anything of her mother's she might use.

Deep in the closet she found a cardboard box marked, "Lizzy." She pulled it to the center of the room and sat next to it.

Inside were journals, photos, yearbooks, and—

She gasped.

She lifted a square, bejeweled wooden box, roughly the size of her hand. A few of the rhinestones were missing, but she recognized her mother's handiwork. The tiny hinges squeaked as she opened it.

She moaned.

Inside were tiny baby bracelets made of white beads with black lettering.

One said *Sarah Hope*. One said *Rachel Raven*.

She held them in her palm. So small and delicate. Had Lizzy made these?

Also in the box were three hospital bracelets, two for twin girls, and one for the mother. At the bottom were two tiny plastic zip lock bags. One baggie contained strands of snow-white hair. The other, strands of curly brown.

Lizzy had kept all this in a treasure box. Raven laid the bracelets back into the box and closed it.

"Hey."

Raven jumped. Sarah leaned against the doorway in her pajamas and fluffy robe, her blonde hair in a messy ponytail. "Sorry. Didn't mean to startle you."

"Look what I found."

Sarah sniffed and joined her on the carpet. "Ah. Mom's treasure box."

Raven handed it to her. Sarah held it for a moment then opened it. She sighed. "I haven't looked at these in years."

"Lizzy wasn't sentimental when we were together." Raven drew up her knees and held them. "This is sweet. A side of her I wish I'd known."

"Me, too."

Sarah shut the box. "It was this mother I had always dreamed would return. The mother who was clean and sober and loved her children. The mommy who treasured the memories of our birth."

Sarah laid her head on Raven's shoulder. "But, that mother—"

"Died long before she overdosed." Raven wrapped her arms around her sister. How she wished she could give Sarah something she could hold onto. She sighed. The cruel reality was Lizzy never said a word about her sister.

"Sarah, I know how to get rid of the drugs."

Later, the contents of the treasure box safely in their room, they set about ruining the drugs. Sarah had the brilliant idea of adding bleach to the contamination— instead of plain water.

Following the article's instructions, they double wrapped the drugs in baggies and shoved it into the treasure box. Raven failed to convince Sarah to stay inside, so they both went outside to bury the box.

My sister is as stubborn as I am.

Bundled up, they went to the backyard and stood under the old oak tree. Looking at the clear, starry night, there was a sense of bigness. Maybe even that what they were doing had significance in the universe.

Burying the past. The treasure box of their mom's one-time innocence now shrouded the sad outcome of foolish and selfish choices.

Raven sighed and gripped the shovel she had found in the garage. She dug a hole while Sarah hugged her waist and sniffed, then blew her nose.

Finally, the hole was large enough. Sarah tenderly laid the box in the ground. They wrapped their arms around each other and stared at the tiny grave.

"Father," Sarah whispered. "We don't know where our mother is. Is she with You?" Sarah took a shaky breath.

Raven had never thought of her mother's eternal home. If there was such a thing. She shuddered at the possibility her mother could be in a horrible place.

"I guess," Sarah continued. "We have to leave her in Your hands. Your loving, merciful hands." Sarah wept.

"Mom," Raven looked at what remained of her mom's memories. "You messed up bad. I don't want to end up like you. Alone. Full of regrets."

"Father—" Sarah's voice clotted with emotion—"I'm praying You give my sister something to hold onto about our mother that isn't about pain and sorrow. A memory. Something we both can hold onto."

Sarah's prayer was impossible. Still, it was a nice sentiment.

Raven shoveled dirt over the box. Sarah took the shovel and did the same until it was covered. Without a word, they both knelt and patted the dirt.

"Goodbye, Mom." They said it together.

Raven's arms tingled.

Sarah sneezed.

"Get back into bed. I'll be there soon." Raven helped her sister to her feet, then watched her go inside.

Raven leaned on the shovel and regarded the "grave," then looked at the sky. She'd never seen so many stars. Their beauty argued the possibility of a grand designer.

If that was the case, then He sure blew it with her family.

A branch cracked. Raven jumped, then surveyed the fenced backyard. It was too dark to see anyone. Was someone spying from behind the fence?

Her warning system was usually accurate, but no other sounds came ... only a barking dog in the distance.

Maybe it was nothing. This wasn't a big, scary city after all.

She carried the shovel to the garage and placed it on its holder, then entered the laundry room and made her way through the dining room to the kitchen. Sarah set two cups of something sweet and fragrant on the counter.

The warmth she needed was waiting for her.

She smiled at her sister.

Drew sprinted back to his car. What was Raven burying, and where was Sarah?

Did Raven bury the drugs? Why? Maybe she had to hide them until she found a place to sell them. Based on the white stuff he'd seen in the freezer and after a quick Google search, the bags appeared to contain cocaine.

I don't need this now.

Once he returned from Germany, he could focus on how to handle Raven.

He'd been concerned any payback he leveled at Raven might upset Sarah—they were sisters, after all. Nevertheless, Sarah knew what was right and what was wrong. Drugs were wrong. Her faith was strong enough to handle her sister's arrest.

Yes. He started his car.

When he returned, he'd set everything in motion.

Sarah's alarm buzzed. She stretched and yawned ... and breathed through her nose for the first time in days. *Wow, thanks, Lord!*

She turned toward Raven's bed. Her sister's black hair peeked over the top of her blanket. Even with the emotional sendoff of their mother last night and being outside in the cold, Sarah was rested and content. She swallowed.

No pain.

Lord, I know this is you. I'm not sure what it means, but I am grateful.

She peeled off her covers and slipped her feet into her slippers. A cup of coffee sounded awful good.

While the coffee dripped, trying to be as quiet as possible, she showered and dressed for work. Even if she didn't go in, at least she wasn't wearing her pajamas.

Opening the fridge, she bent to search for something she could make. Eggs sounded good. She opened the egg carton—only two. Rats. She set the meager offering on the counter.

All the bags of groceries Raven brought home, and she forgot the eggs. Sarah chuckled.

The breadbasket held a fresh loaf of sourdough. Raven must have brought it home from the bakery. She smiled.

How about a nice hug?

Minutes later, she dropped an egg into the hole of each slice of bread.

"Morning." Raven stretched like a lazy cat. "You look great."

"I feel great. I'm going to work."

Raven stared at Sarah from the tops of her eyeballs. "I don't think so."

"We'll see." Sarah gently turned the slices of bread.

Her sister helped herself to coffee and sat at the counter. "What are you making? It's smells toasty and buttery."

"Egg-in-a-hole."

Raven set down her cup. "Mom made egg-in-a-hole for me once."

Wow. Had she ever heard that wistful, soft tone in Raven's voice before?

Sarah turned off the burner, then leaned on the island. "Tell me."

"It was a few days before she—you know. I came home from school, and she greeted me at the door. We lived in a condemned apartment building. There were no facilities, but she had a conduction hot plate."

Raven took a sip of her coffee. Sarah made herself breathe.

"Anyway, I came home from school, and I was angry at her because ... well, I was fourteen and always angry at her. She was making the egg-in-a-hole. Even in the stale and musty environment, I could smell the butter and toasted bread."

Sarah didn't have to imagine the aroma—the scent was with them now.

Raven chuckled. "The bouquet of the butter and toast cooking made my mouth water, but I wasn't about to tell her that. Anyway, she met me at the door, smiling. She'd lost teeth over the years and was self-conscious, so she rarely smiled."

Sarah cringed. She didn't want to picture her mother with missing teeth. She bit her lip.

"'I made you a hug,' she said."

"She said 'hug'?" All the years Granny had said to her, "You want a hug for breakfast." Did her mother remember that from her childhood?

"Yes. Why?"

Sarah waved her hands. "I'm sorry to interrupt. Please."

"So, I said something rude and stormed off to my room." She chuckled. "It wasn't long before the aromas filled the place. I couldn't resist and went into the kitchen area. She'd set up a makeshift table and chairs out of crates. The meal was on paper plates with plastic forks and paper towels."

Raven's eyes moistened. As much as Sarah wanted to comfort her sister, she knew Raven needed to feel this as much as Sarah needed to hear it.

"We sat in silence and tried to eat the eggs and toast. The flimsy forks couldn't cut through the bread. Finally—"

Raven giggled. "Finally, Lizzy picked up the bread and shoved the whole thing in her mouth." Raven wiggled her fingers over her lips and chin. "Yolk ran down her chin and got on her fingers and the front of her shirt. I started laughing, then shoved mine into my mouth. Which was equally as messy."

Raven held her cup against her cheek. A tear ran down her cheek, but she smiled. "We—we laughed so hard. After, she and I talked about school. I guess it was me doing all the talking. She sat there watching me as though I was the most interesting thing on earth."

Raven set down the cup, folded her hands, and raised them to her forehead. She shook her head. "Eventually, her new dealer came—I don't remember his name. Which meant I had to hide. There was a lot of yelling and things being tossed around. Mom had a few bruises. A few days later ..."

Sarah strode toward her sister and took her hand. "This is the first memory you've shared that has given me hope about our mother."

Raven tugged her hand away. "Hope? She's dead, Sarah."

"I know. I mean, that deep inside she loved us—loved *you*." Sarah swallowed around her sadness. *Focus on Raven. This is important.* "Even though the drugs tried to strangle the life out of her and her love for you, she fought to keep you as safe as she could."

"I guess," Raven said. "But the drugs beat her, and we lost."

Did our mother lose, Lord?

Sarah went back to the stove. She dished the eggs onto plates. After setting them on the counter she went to the fridge and grabbed a selection of Granny's preserves then set them in front of the plates.

An idea blossomed.

She found plastic forks and tore off two paper towels. She handed them to Raven. Understanding shone in her sister's crystal eyes. Raven folded the towels and placed a flimsy white fork on each one.

Sarah sat next to her. "Lord, thank You for this memory. Thank You for showing us something good from our mother's heart. Thank You for this hug."

They said "amen" together.

Lord, You know my longing and how I'm struggling with envying my sister's time with our mother, even though it was mostly horrible. Help me not mess up our relationship for something that can never be.

As they made a mess of their eggs and their faces, they laughed and cried.

The *hug* Granny had made for Sarah all her life never tasted better.

Will helped Asher load the delivery van. This was a great morning. He finished his bread orders for today. Who knew he would enjoy making bread? It was rather therapeutic. Slapping the dough on the stainless table gave him a visceral release. And all the kneading had strengthened his bicep muscles.

"Thanks for standing in the bread gap, Will," Asher said. "I had to pull another all-nighter to catch up preparing my dissertation."

Will gave Asher a brotherly pound on the back. "No problem. I'll be able to take over the bread baking and delivery. Once you get your PhD and become a professor, no more four o'clock in the morning baking."

Asher climbed into the delivery truck. "I don't know. I like doing this. Maybe not every day, but I'd miss everyone."

"And there's nothing like the aroma of baking bread in the morning." Will waved, then entered the kitchen. Raven looked up from crumb-coating another vegan cake. This one had three layers. The chocolate ganache was smooth and shiny.

"Are you working on the Wilson birthday cake?" he asked.

"Um-hmm."

Raven had been distracted since she arrived.

He went over to the order clipboards and produce schedule for the day. "Is Sarah better?" He spoke without looking at his friend.

"She is. It's weird how much better she is. But I bullied her into staying home one more day to be sure." She kneaded white fondant.

She had something more to say, so until she was ready, he prepared his *mise en place* for six dozen of Raven's now-famous oatmeal-raisin-dark-chocolate-pecan cookies. Three Bible studies had ordered two-dozen cookies each.

"Sarah made us breakfast this morning."

"Nice." He weighed and measured the dry ingredients.

The fondant now pliable, Raven sprinkled cornstarch on the sheeter and ran it through several times. Once it was the proper thinness, she brushed off the excess cornstarch with the pastry brush, then lifted it with her forearms and covered the cake with it.

"She made egg-in-a-hole." Raven smoothed the fondant.

"Never heard of it." He beat the butter and eggs and sugar.

She described it as though it were a magical potion.

"Sounds pretty good," he said.

"Yeah."

What was she not telling him? They worked in silence until his cookies were baking and she put the finishing touches on a Captain America cake. Truly, a work of art.

Once the cake was safe in a Sweet's Bakery box and in the display fridge out front, Raven pulled out her cell. She thumbed through her pictures, then held the phone for him to see. There was a selfie of Raven and Sarah caught in mid-laughter, both covered in what he assumed was egg yolks.

Did they have a food fight? Even with egg yolks, Sarah looked beau—

"You two are nuts."

She pulled the phone back and smiled. "Yeah."

"It was a good breakfast?"

Still looking at the photo, she smiled. "The best ever."

Drew didn't expect Sarah to answer the phone on the first ring. "Hey, you sound better."

"I am. Raven kept me from work, though." Sarah giggled. "It's kind of a miracle."

Miracle or not, he wasn't taking any chances. "Untergarten called with the flight information. I'll be leaving on Sunday afternoon at one forty-five."

"Oh."

"What do you mean, *oh?*" *Unsupportive. Again.*

"I'm sorry, Drew. What time will you arrive?"

"About nine in the morning on Monday. They want to make a decision earlier rather than later." His heart thumped like he'd played a game of one-on-one with Big Lewis.

"I'm happy for you."

Not convincing. "Yeah. It's exciting. Are you okay?"

"Yes. Maybe, I'm more tired than I thought. Can I help you get ready?"

"No. No, thanks." *No germs.* "You get well. And when I get back, we'll be able to celebrate." *And maybe you can finally tell your grandmother and sister we are moving to Germany.*

He *was* moving there. He knew it. And Sarah would be grateful to him when she was finally reunited with her father.

Raven drove Sarah's car back home. Another great day at the bakery. Even being shorthanded, they managed to keep up with the baked items and deliveries. Still, she, Will, and Mabel had to eat cookies on the fly for their lunch.

When Sarah married and moved to St. Louis, they would need to hire someone fulltime. At least until they knew what condition Granny would be in long-term.

Her cell rang. She was about to let it go to voicemail but noticed the caller ID. *YBN NTWK*. What now? It had taken all she had to tell Sunny she couldn't do the show.

She pulled into a gas station and answered.

"Raven, Sunny here." The woman sounded breathless.

"Hey. Everything okay?"

"It's only amazing!" Sunny yelled.

Raven pulled the phone from her ear.

"I shared the story about you and your sister finding each other because of our *Cupcake Rivalry Show* with the network honchos, and they went crazy. They want *both* of you for the first episode of *Sweet Rivalry*."

"*What?*"

"Yes. And there's more. They will fly you two first-class and get you in and out of here in a few days. But they want to interview you and your sister for the website and call a press conference when you're both out here."

Raven covered her mouth to keep the squeal from escaping. This was incredible.

"Hello? Raven what do you think?"

"This is—I can't even begin to thank you for this opportunity. I can't answer for Sarah. She just got engaged. But Granny's due out of the hospital any day and she'll need at-home care. I don't know. This would be complicated to pull it off."

"You'll try, though, right?"

You bet I'll try!

"When do we have to be there?"

Sunny filled her in with the details, then they ended the call.

"Woo-hoo!" She pounded her palms on the steering wheel. "Thank you. Thank you." She pulled back onto the street. Only a few minutes to home, so she'd wait to call Sarah.

After the longest three blocks in history, Raven pulled into the driveway and slammed the gearshift into park. She ran toward the front door, stumbled, but somehow managed to keep herself from falling.

She opened the door. "Sarah!" She strode to the kitchen. "Where are you?"

"I'm right behind you."

Raven grabbed Sarah and hugged her.

Sarah *oof*ed. "What is it?"

Raven held her sister at arm's length. "The producer from YBN wants you and me on their new series! *And* they want to interview us for their web vlogs. *And* they want us at a press conference!" Raven gasped for air.

Sarah resembled an anime character—her eyes large and round. "Me? They want me too?"

"Of course. I told them about how you found me—I told them the whole thing. Not everything, but all the good stuff. And they were so jazzed they want us there to celebrate and tell our story."

Sarah stood, her mouth open.

"I mean, it's a scheduling nightmare, but they want us on the first episode of the new series *Sweet Rivalry.*" Raven stepped away and ran her fingers through her hair. "It's crazy to even consider doing this right now, isn't it?"

"Crazy," Sarah whispered, her eyes glittering.

"It's an unbelievable opportunity."

"Unbelievable."

Raven paced the living room. "I mean, we're shorthanded at the bakery. Granny's coming home—"

"No. Nurse Alma just called. Granny has a blood clot; they're keeping her a few more days."

"Oh, no." Raven sat on the arm of the sofa. "People die from that, don't they?"

Sarah laid her hand on her shoulder. "Yes, it's serious. But because she was already in the hospital, they were able to diagnose the clot immediately and have begun treatment. If Granny had been home, they might not have caught it as quickly as they did."

Raven exhaled. "Thank God."

Sarah raised her brows. "Yes, thank God."

"Then we shouldn't go. I mean they're saying they will fly us out early on Sunday for the whole meet and greet, interviews. Filming all day Monday—it's too much." Raven slipped from the arm to the seat of the sofa.

Sarah twisted her hair into a ponytail, then released it. "Before we go and make any decisions, we need to pray about it."

Raven shrugged. Great. Why did she have to go and get all spiritual? "You can."

"I will. In the meantime, when do they need to know?"

"Saturday." Raven flopped onto her back and covered her eyes. *No way!* "Tomorrow. It's impossible."

Sarah squatted next to Raven. "We need to call in reinforcements."

"Who are you calling?"

Sarah laughed. "Asher and Will."

"Great idea." Was Raven going to mention Sarah had forgotten her fiancé?

Nope.

Sarah took her antibiotic, then arranged the peanut-butter-chocolate-chip cookies on Granny's floral serving platter. The guys would be there any minute.

Raven brought in a tray of cups and the teapot. She shrugged, trying to send her usual message of distaste for this "religious stuff", although she was more graphic in her terminology.

Yet Sarah couldn't deny the sparkle in her sister's eyes. Did her sister remember God's gift to them that very morning? The hug from the past—the hug that connected them with their mother—and Him.

She straightened and sighed.

The more she thought about this opportunity, the more she marveled at the impossible timing and the undeniable sense of calling. It was such a perfect opportunity to share how God did a miraculous work and yet, how could they leave their responsibilities?

It was an event they would share as sisters.

Asher and Will arrived. The guys each took one of the comfortable armchairs. Sarah and Raven sat on the couch. Raven curled up like a roly-poly bug in one corner.

"Can someone fill us in on the details," Asher said. He leaned forward, resting his elbows on his knees.

Since Raven received the phone call, she relayed the information. Initially her voice was measured and her description objective, but as she went on the excitement took control. She sat at the edge of the cushion, her arms a blur of movement.

Sarah managed to hide her chuckle.

"So, what I'm hearing is," Asher rubbed his chin, "they want you to fly out on Sunday, film on Monday. Interviews on Tuesday, then fly you back Tuesday night?"

Will caught Sarah's eye. Was he upset?

"That's three days away," Will cleared his throat. "And one of those days the bakery is closed. Guys, from a logistical perspective, it's doable. We can gather the part-timers. Prebake a couple days' worth of produce tomorrow." He sat back and waved a hand. "It's doable on our end. Right, Ash?"

"Absolutely. Then there's Granny."

"Yes," Raven said. "Which is the most important part."

Yes, Raven. Sarah grinned.

"Sarah." Asher picked at a thread on the chair. "Have you spoken with Drew? He's flying to Germany for his interview on Sunday too."

"Germany?" Raven turned toward Sarah. "What does Asher mean?"

Sarah's stomach sank to her toes. She stared daggers at Asher. His face paled.

She turned to Raven. "I-I didn't want to say anything until he knew whether or not they offered him a job."

"Germany? Does Granny know?" Raven's hand tugged at her hair. "Sarah, you can't let him do this to you! Take you away from your home and family."

"Granny doesn't know yet." *And it's my decision, not yours.* She pressed her fingertips to her lips. "He may not even get the job."

"I was getting used to the idea of you moving to St. Louis. But this—this—" She pounded a cushion.

Asher stood. "Maybe Will and I need to leave and give you guys some privacy."

"No!"

"Don't go!"

Sarah and Raven said together.

He sat.

Sarah glanced at Will. He sat staring at the floor. "Will, are you okay?"

He took a deep breath and exhaled. "No." He lifted his green eyes, clouded with sadness. "Here's the deal. We can't be distracted by the job interview."

"Distracted!" Raven sprang from the couch.

"Raven, cool it. Don't borrow trouble." Will looked at Sarah. "Not that the interview is trouble. God has given you both an incredible opportunity. And yes, I believe this is from God. If I'm wrong and it's not from Him, then he'll close—what do you say, Ash?"

"The door."

"Right. Then God will close the door. We should pray." Will looked intently at Raven. "And you will join us, my friend. This is too important."

Sarah's heart and cheeks warmed. If she'd had any doubts about Will's commitment to God and about living his faith in Him, they had crumbled.

Who was *this guy?* Raven couldn't stop staring at Will. His eyes closed, he prayed like he expected an answer. Like right away. She'd never seen this side of him. Compassionate. Focused.

The funny, never-take-life-seriously attitude was gone. In its place was—what was the word she was looking for?

Connected. He was connected to the universe. Or to God? After what happened between her and Sarah, she had to admit the egg-in-a-hole *hug* seemed more than a coincidence.

Her body shivered. All this was getting strange.

"Father," Asher was praying now. "We know You see our lives. All of this is much more than coincidences."

Raven's arms prickled.

"What we don't know precisely is what to do next, except—" He paused.

She knew. With absolute certainty. "Talk to Granny." The prickling went up and over Raven's shoulders.

The other three responded with amens. Bobbing their chins, eyes still closed.

What on earth? Raven wanted to run. Yet she wanted to stay to see what might happen next.

"So, Father," Asher said. "We will now go through the next door and speak with Granny. We accept Your will and not our own."

Sarah prayed a few more things, but Raven was too distracted to listen.

Her chest heated and her heart picked up its pace. This praying thing was real! She would be interested to see what

this God—this Father they talked to—would do next.
Very interested.

Chapter 32

Hope spied the clear night's first star. It wouldn't have long to wait for its friends. She tried to appreciate the moment. To be grateful. To put a lid on the pity stewing inside her.

She was tired of the setbacks. Tired of missing out on getting reacquainted with her granddaughter. Tired of being a burden and irrelevant.

"Father, I don't want to be a complainer. I don't want to be useless—and old and fragile. Can't I be Your servant and help others, even when I'm relegated to this bed?"

She clutched at her blankets, willing herself not to yell, "It's not fair!" Hot tears betrayed her resolution.

"Granny."

"Granny."

Sarah and Raven stood together at the doorway. Raven entered carrying a platter of something. Their smiles and sweet voices pushed the gloom from her thoughts.

Hope wiped away any evidence of her pity party and allowed the genuine happiness to surface. Opening her arms, she welcomed them.

Raven ran—plate and all—into her embrace. A pile of cookies tumbled into Hope's lap.

They laughed while cleaning the mess.

"My darling Sarah, why are you hanging about in the hall?"

She pouted. "I'm sick—or I was. Nurse Alma said I had to keep away from you. Raven convinced her to let me social distance."

Raven scooted a chair across the floor to Sarah. "There, more than enough distance."

They all chuckled.

Hope took a nibble of one of the larger crumbs scattered around her blanket. The bite sent a flavor delight to her taste buds.

"Oh my! This is delicious!" She savored the taste. "I'm getting peanut butter, chocolate, and—" she held the bite then swallowed— "am I tasting coffee?"

Raven sat in the chair next to her bed, her feet propped on the mattress. She beamed. Hope had no doubt from the pride on her features who created this delicious morsel.

Sarah crossed her legs and hugged her knee. "You should see all the new creations Raven has introduced to our Sweet's customers."

So why had Sarah's usual radiant smile lost its luster?

"I look forward to sampling them all." Hope snuck another bite. "Although the doctors may disagree."

The girls squirmed in their chairs like two-year olds. If Hope didn't know better, she would say they had done something they were trying to hide. "Okay girls. What's going on?"

"Granny, you won't believe what happened," Sarah began.

"It is amazing. The problem is, we don't know if it's the right thing to do." Raven looked at her sister, but Sarah's focus was on Hope.

"Don't leave me in suspense," Hope said.

"Raven, you got the call. You tell her."

And tell her Raven did.

Hope sat in awe. She could see God's loving hand. How He was even now, softening Raven's heart. And Sarah, well she had not seen her this excited about baking in years.

Remembering when they were toddlers looking up at her—covered in mud or flour or chocolate and always swathed in a generous coating of happiness—overwhelmed her.

The image of sisters in love with the world and each other had been an everyday miracle for the Sweeting household back then. It didn't matter what they did, as long as they did it together, they were content.

She sighed, allowing the tears to tumble.

"Oh, Granny—" Sarah reached toward her. "I'm sorry. We shouldn't have burdened you."

"We will tell them no." Raven held Hope's hand.

Hope shook her head. "You will do no such thing, young ladies."

Their beautiful half-moon eyes rounded.

"You will call that young woman and tell her you *will* be there and *will* make your grandmother proud."

Hope longed to gather them both in her lap as she did when they were babies. Instead, she wanted to learn how to better revel in their womanhood and watch in awe as they moved forward in their gifts and passions.

Thank You, Lord. It's all so perfect!

Chapter 33

Drew repacked his suitcase for the third time. By himself. Just when his future shone bright—an exciting life in Germany with his new job and wife—Raven went and spoiled it all.

He threw his suit across the room, then ran to retrieve it.

Sarah in Hollywood with Raven. She was leaving a few hours before him. How could Sarah be well enough to go? And how could she, in good conscience, not drive him to the airport?

He laid the good suit his parents had bought him into the travel bag, smoothed the wrinkles, then zipped the bag. He would show them all! He would get this job. And he'd reunite Sarah with her father.

Then she would shake the dust from her shoes and never return.

Chapter 34

Sarah watched Raven as she finished the conversation with Sunny. Even though Raven had placed the cell on speaker, and Sunny knew Sarah was present, she didn't seem important to the conversation.

Once finished, Raven grabbed Sarah's hands and the two of them danced around the living room. They threw themselves on the couch and laughed. Once the giggling subsided, Sarah stared off at the family photos. All those moments Raven, their mother, and their father missed.

She pulled out her cell and snuggled close to Raven.

"What are you doing?" Raven knit her expressive brows together.

"Capturing another moment." Sarah held up the phone and centered the shot. "One without egg plastered all over us."

Raven moved her head next to Sarah's and grinned. "I liked the egg pics."

After a few moments of silly snaps, they both yawned.

"I guess we should get some sleep." Raven stood and extended her hand to Sarah and pulled her up.

"We'll need to. Tomorrow will be a busy day. We'll need to figure out all the pre-bakes and get those done. Then see if all the part-timers can work the shifts. Oh, and we'll need to write our bios for Sunny and—*mphf!*"

Raven had covered Sarah's mouth with her hand. "You flipped on your brain, didn't you? We'll never get to sleep now."

Sarah smiled beneath her sister's palm. She was right, of course. Her brain had kicked in. "Should I fix coffee or cocoa?"

Raven gave her the top-of-the-eyeballs look.

"Cocoa, it is."

Somewhere around two in the morning, Sarah looked over at her sister. She sat there, forehead on the counter, arms dangling at her side, her now-familiar gentle snore sounding. Would she ever get used to the wonder of her sister being with her? She hoped not.

Sarah gave a quiet chuckle and reviewed their list one more time. She spied her antibiotics next to the coffeemaker—and gasped.

Her symptoms were gone. Not even a sniffle or sneeze. From a fever, horrendous sore throat to all the symptoms of her recurring bronchitis to ... nothing.

God had healed her! She closed her eyes and thanked Him. Lifting her arms, she worshiped Him.

Raven muttered in her sleep. Sarah leaned closer and smiled at the gibberish.

"Again, thanks Lord for everything."

"Yes," Raven whispered.

What? Goosebumps! She leaned closer. Was Raven awake?

No. Still sleeping

She grinned. "*Yes*, Lord."

Will loaded three boxes of cookies into Wilma Hornsby's SUV. This morning had been frantic. Waving goodbye, he headed back to Sweet's and Attila-the-Sweet-Bun—as he had dubbed Sarah. He had never seen this side of the sweet, good-natured Sarah.

He liked her feistiness.

He chuckled as he entered the bakery and made his way through the crowd. Somehow word had hit the Minersville grapevine, the sisters were going to Hollywood—at least to the Your Baking Network's Burbank studios. Sarah, Raven, Asher, Mabel, and even the part-timers CeeCee and Ashley were all working.

"Will," Mabel's voice rose above the noise. "Someone from the *Minersville Journal* is asking for the girls."

Will took the phone. "This is Will, the sisters are swamped, could they return your call?"

Sarah rested her hand on his arm. "It's okay. I'll take it."

Ever the gracious one, Sarah rested the phone on her shoulder, grabbed an empty tray, and walked backward through the swinging door. The smile never leaving her beautiful face.

And the ache in his heart grew.

Raven rolled up her underwear and shoved them deep into her knapsack. Sarah packed her rolling bag.

Saturday evening was here! Ninety percent of their to-do list was accomplished. Asher and Will assured them they could finish the remaining tasks.

It seemed the impossible happened.

In a few hours, they would drive to the airport. The flock of butterflies in Raven's gut had moved to her chest and threatened to clog her esophagus.

Sarah was folding another flowy dress and placing it in her suitcase.

What would *she* wear for the interviews and press conference? Not that Raven would be caught dead in a flowy dress, but it would be nice to have something other than her jeans and black T-shirt, or her white baker's uniform.

What did she expect? She was the poor, unwashed kid with the druggie mom. Would she disappoint YBN, her family? What if she had a full-fledged panic attack? *During* the press conference?

She grabbed a pair of black socks.

"Raven?" Sarah tilted her head.

"What?"

"You okay?"

"Yeah." Raven wadded the socks and threw them into the sack.

"Uh huh." Sarah turned Raven toward her. "Are you upset Drew is coming over?"

"I wasn't, but now ... "

Sarah rolled her eyes. "Come on. What is it?"

Raven sighed and grabbed another pair of socks and rolled them. "I guess I'm anxious."

"You?" Sarah sat on her bed. "I'm the one who has never been on television. I've never flown anywhere. Are you worried about something in particular?"

Raven nodded.

Sarah studied her, then took her hand and tugged Raven next to her. "Are you apprehensive about the interviews? Talking about why we've been separated for over twenty years?"

Raven rested her head on Sarah's shoulder. "Yeah. Partly." She sniffed. "I mean, what do we say? How can we explain without dissing our mom?"

"We don't have to talk about the drugs. Couldn't we say she was troubled?"

That was certainly the truth. "Would you do the talking? You can put a nicer spin on the whole thing than I can."

"Spin?" Sarah wrinkled a brow and tugged her ear.

"You know what I mean. I can talk about my time on the Cupcake Rivalry show and stuff, but can you handle the family situation?"

"I guess so. I'll do my best."

Someone knocked on the front door. "Hello!"

Drew.

Raven cringed. She wouldn't antagonize Andrew. If he stayed downstairs and she upstairs there was a fighting chance for success. Otherwise, she might have to lock herself in the bathroom.

"I'll be right down, hon." Sarah gave Raven a hard stare.

Raven carried a few zipper bags to the bathroom to load her makeup and toiletries. She caught a glimpse of Drew from the top of the stairs. She smiled—trying to make it look sincere—then closed the door.

Sarah and Drew's voices wavered in and out of her hearing. Something about Sarah not being supportive. Not taking him to the airport.

Oh, brother!

Raven opened the door and moved closer to the landing. The discussion became more heated. Raven was about to charge out of her sanctuary to intervene when the voices quieted. She leaned forward but only made out traces of the conversation.

She returned to thrusting her make up into the baggies.

Don't interfere. Remember how that went before.

If she thought any more about Germany, it would strangle her.

What did Will say? "Don't borrow trouble"?

Okay, God.

Was she really doing this?

I do not want to borrow trouble, God, but I don't know how to fix this. Can You help me?

Something Raven couldn't describe—something warm and bright, electric—filled the tiny space.

Fear not.

Raven swiveled around. "Who—?" She clutched the sink and stared at her reflection, half-expecting to see an apparition reflected there. "Get a grip."

Okay. All the stress *had* gotten to her. She was hearing voices. Now was not the time to go crazy.

She worked to control her breathing. The electric sensation was gone, but the warmth and brightness remained. It wasn't an unpleasant sensation—perhaps strange because it was new.

"Raven." Sarah knocked on the door. "You can come out now."

She took one last look in the mirror. *What if I tell Sarah about this thing—this whatever just happened?*

Wait. Won't she get angry because I was talking about her and Drew to God. Going over their heads, so to speak?

She shook her head. What was she thinking?

Asher.

She would ask him about it.

Asher yawned as Raven hitched up her heavy backpack, ready to enter the terminal. She gave him a weak smile. The whole drive to the airport he'd sensed she wanted to talk.

There was no private time, but the two-hour-plus drive went fast as they sang old 1980s songs. The sisters sounded good together. He and Will couldn't carry tunes if their lives depended upon it.

What he and Will seemed to excel in was praying. While Asher had peace about the girls taking the opportunity, Will sensed there were real battles ahead—for both sisters. Perhaps Raven was concerned about this, or maybe about her sister's possible move to Europe. If only they'd had time to talk.

Will lifted Sarah's suitcase from his trunk. His growth in the Lord was impressive. Asher didn't know if he could have as much self-control. Will loved Sarah, but his willingness to stand back and let God direct these circumstances was more than Asher could have handled.

Which was why he would never allow himself to fall in love without the certainty of reciprocation.

Chapter 35

Sarah glanced at Raven. Wrapped in the airline blanket, her head resting against the window, she resembled a swaddled baby.

Sarah's first flight was amazing. Other than a few minutes of turbulence here and there, riding in first-class was nothing short of luxurious.

In an hour, they would be in Los Angeles to whatever awaited them. It would be a whirlwind.

Father, thank You again for this opportunity. Please, let me be Your vessel and fill me with Your wisdom.

"Do I smell coffee?" Raven stretched and yawned.

"Yes. We can catch the flight attendant on her way back."

Raven nodded and yawned again. "What time is it?"

Sarah checked her watch. "It's five after seven. The time differences have me turned around."

"We're due to arrive around eight Pacific Time." Raven reached down to pull her purse from under the seat in front of her. "I'd like to freshen up before we land."

"Great idea."

By the time the plane landed, they were ready to meet whoever was picking them up. Sunny would probably send one of her "people," as she called them.

She and Raven gathered their carry-ons, then exited and followed the crowd to the luggage carousel to retrieve her checked bag.

They had found the designated carousel when someone shouted, "There they are! The Cupcake Twins!"

Within seconds, they were surrounded by lights and cameras and people calling out questions. Raven cursed and covered her face.

"Is it true you've been separated for over twenty years?" A blonde, tanned woman who could have been a movie star held a microphone in Raven's face.

Oh, no. Don't do that, lady.

Sarah placed her arm around Raven's shoulder. "Yes." Sarah smiled as best she could with her heart lodged under her tongue. "It is quite the story. A miracle."

"There will be plenty of time and opportunity for Sarah and Raven to answer your questions." A petite brunette with large brown eyes had positioned herself in front of them like a mini security guard.

Raven sighed. "Sunny. Thanks." She shifted her knapsack and shook the woman's hand. "Sarah, this is Sunny Lofgren."

Oh, thank God! Sarah hugged the woman. "Thank you."

"Listen, you did great. Things will be better at the press conference. More orderly." She tried to take Raven's duffle, then dropped it. "Whoa! This thing weighs as much as my Volvo e-tron. Let's get Milo over here."

She stretched her arm and waved at someone. A tall, dark, and handsome man dressed in black trousers and a tight black T-shirt approached them.

"Ladies, this is our driver, Milo."

Milo dipped his chin and proceeded to relieve them of their burdens as though they were bags of feathers.

Goodness. Was everyone in California gorgeous?

Once ensconced in a block-long limo, they traveled at lightning speed down a palm-lined street.

The three of them sat on the back seat, Sunny in the center.

She handed Sarah and Raven portfolios with the YBN logo. "Okay, ladies, we have to make the most of these couple of days. How is your grandmother, by the way?" Sunny spoke faster than anyone Sarah had ever met.

"She's doing much better, but still has a few hurdles before she can come home." Sarah said as she opened her portfolio.

"We'll think good thoughts. In the meantime, here's your itinerary, various iterations of the YBN press releases, etc., etc., etc." Sunny held a computer tablet for herself. She laid it on her lap and scrolled back and forth. "Where do we begin? Here. Let's talk about the new series."

Sarah and Raven exchanged excited looks. No way Raven was more excited than she was.

"The new show is called *Sweet Rivalry.*" Sunny grabbed their hands. "How perfect is this? Sweet's Bakery. *Sweet Rivalry.* I had to get you on the show. Had to."

Sarah grabbed her stomach. It tumbled faster than the words coming from Sunny's mouth.

"The concept is similar to *Cupcake Rivalry*—which of course, Raven, you know all about." Sunny winked at Raven. "Except it's not about cupcakes. It's all manner of sweet baked goods—cakes, cookies, pies, streusels, candies, you know, anything sweet."

Maybe I can handle this. Except there would be cameras and bright lights and millions of people watching her. Sarah bit her lip. *What am I doing here?*

"Also, no teams. It's *mano e mano*—one on one."

I'm competing against my professionally trained, newly-discovered sister?

Sarah gulped through a glued-on smile.

"So, we're calling the first episode, *Sibling Rivalry.* Get it?" Sunny shoved their knees. "We have two other contestants who are siblings. It will be perfect."

Sarah's heart dove to her feet. They're capitalizing on my insecurities? On national television?

She looked at her shoes, then worked to keep the smile on her face before catching Raven's eye.

Raven's brows knit. Sarah blinked, then gave Raven a side-nod and weak smile.

"Wait. Are you two doing twin-speak?" Sunny's head flipped from side to side as though watching a tennis match. "You know, how twins have their own language? What did you say?" Sunny covered her mouth. "Oh, right. It's secret for a reason. You don't want me to know."

Sarah had to laugh. Raven joined her. As intimidating as this woman was, she was entertaining. It was like watching a squirrel. On three double-espressos. "I'm sorry, Sunny. I'm out of my element, and Raven wanted to be sure I was okay."

Sunny swiveled back and forth, her shiny, glossed lips shaped like an *O*. "Without ever saying a word. Wow. I'll bet one of you two wins."

Sarah sighed. *I have no doubt it will be Raven.*

No doubt it will be Sarah. She knows how to captivate people.

Raven shifted in her seat, contemplating moving to one of the side-bucket seats.

Drop her into any kitchen, and she could whip up something new and decadent and delicious. It didn't matter if there were cameras or bright lights or millions of people watching her. But make her communicate and be charming? That turned her into an ugly toad hopping around to avoid being stepped on.

Who thought this was a good idea? Her eyes darted to the car door. Could she make a getaway? Something tapped her on the shoulder. Raven jumped. *Good grief, it's Sarah, not the boogieman.*

"Sunny," Sarah said. "Could we switch places? It's difficult to—as you say—twin-speak when we don't have eye contact."

Sunny was petite enough she stood to let them switch places. "By all means. And I'll try not to stare." She was practically giddy.

Sarah snuggled next to Raven and took her hand. Wow. She hadn't realized how tense she was until her muscles relaxed. Wasn't *she* supposed to be helping Sarah through these strange waters?

Sunny continued briefing them on the show. It was straightforward. Four contestants. Three competition vignettes. The third being the final competition. The winner got the $25,000 prize.

Raven's heart burned. Pitting siblings against each other? Somehow, she had understood it would be like *Cupcake Rivalry* where she and Sarah would be a team. The most uncomfortable part would have been which of them would take lead. But competing against each other?

I don't like it.

Sunny pointed their attention to their schedules.

"You'll have an hour at the hotel to rest up. Then Milo will bring you to the YBN studios where we'll have our first press conference, then meet with the network execs for lunch. I would eat a bite before. My assistant dropped off a basket of goodies to your room."

She stopped and gave a long, head-to-toe look at Sarah, then Raven. "Don't worry about hair, make-up, or wardrobe. Our team will take care of it." She focused back on her tablet.

No doubts Sunny's comments were meant for the inappropriately attired sister—herself. She swallowed back her retort to the offense.

"Monday, we film the show. Then, depending upon the outcome, we may have another press conference." She winked at them again. "Tuesday, there might be a few early-morning televised interviews, but we'll see. At ten, we'll shuttle you to the airport and off you go back to Missouri." Sunny fanned herself with her tablet. "Whew! That's a lot, even for me!"

She leaned across Sarah and looked at Raven. "You two will do great. You'll be the darlings of YBN, whatever happens on Monday."

Yeah, right. When had she ever been anyone's darling?

Chapter 36

Me? Wearing pink?

Raven stared at her reflection in the full-length mirror. A scruffy, light-pink corduroy jacket, to be precise. Over a black knit tank and black skinny jeans. But it was cool.

Sunny walked into the greenroom scrutinizing her tablet. "We have four minutes until the photo shoot, then on to the press conference." She looked up and whistled. "You both look great!"

Sarah twirled in her 1940s blue-and-white polka-dot swing dress, complete with crinoline.

They had spent an hour in hair and make-up, and then another hour with a scary-intense stylist. Raven had to admit, they all knew what they were doing.

Sunny applauded, then changed her expression back to business. "Let's go, sisters. Hold on." The hyper producer turned her back and whispered into her headset.

"Are you ready for all this, Sis?" Raven waved her arms around.

"As much as you."

"Uh-oh."

Raven wrote a group text.

NEED U 2 TO DO THAT THING U GUYS DO.

"Texting the guys?"

Raven nodded.

"Could you ask them to step up the praying?"

"I just did."

Sarah's phone chimed. She viewed the text.

"'That thing you do?'" She laughed.

Their cells chimed again.

Will had sent several laughing emojis.

ASHER: WILL DO

Raven exhaled.

Sunny cleared her throat. "Let's head to the conference room. Reporters showed up early. The word got out there was food." Sunny embraced her tablet and squinted an eye. "There may not be a large turnout because this was last minute—and it's a Sunday. But if we had waited until Monday, the attendance wouldn't have been as good either. We'll have to cross our fingers."

Okay, boo on her for just telling us this now. Then again ... Raven exhaled. Less pressure for her. Less of an opportunity for her to mess things up.

As for the finger crossing thing—she trusted the guys doing *their* thing more.

Sunny steered them through a hallway.

What was that noise? Sounded like angry bees.

Before them was a closed door. Sunny placed her hand on the knob.

"Ready?" She blinked a few times. "You both look marvelous. You'll be great."

The door opened to reveal the bees. Lights flashed and voices called out.

Only a few people? The room was packed!

Raven's breath retreated. She wanted to follow it.

Sarah gripped Raven's hand and tugged her into the room.

A rectangular table covered with a blue and white checked cloth, and three microphones and three chairs were a few steps from them. Sunny took the first chair and stood beside it.

Sarah's brows lifted. Raven didn't know what to do.

"Go ahead and sit." Sunny pointed to the chairs.

A large screen behind the table flashed various photos of Raven on *Cupcake Rivalry* and some from the recent photo shoot.

Sarah pulled out her chair, then Raven's, before sitting. Still holding her hand, Sarah pulled until Raven placed her behind onto the metal folding chair.

"If I can have your attention." Sunny raised her arms and the room silenced. "What a great turnout. Thank you. How was lunch and dessert?"

The crowd cheered.

"By the way, the cupcakes were all Raven's recipes from her time on *Cupcake Rivalry*."

Raven chanced a glance at the crowd. Every chair was occupied. Several video cameras were behind the last row. *Great.*

"Inside your press kits is a thumb drive with the photos shown here," Sunny swiveled toward the flashing screen behind them. "There are hard copies of various press releases, bios of Sarah and Raven, headshots, and information about our newest show, *Sweet Rivalry*.

"These ladies will be contestants on the first episode." She regarded the two of them, fondness in her eyes—at least, it *seemed* sincere. "Without further ado, Your Baking Network is proud to introduce the Cupcake Twins."

The tepid round of applause made Raven want to crawl under her chair.

"Ms. Sweeting? Sarah?" A woman dressed casually, holding a small camera stood. "Alison Caruso, *Sunnyview Times.*"

Sarah squeezed Raven's hand. Raven swore she heard Sarah's heart pounding like a jackhammer. Raven squeezed back. *Be strong, Sarah.*

"Alison, your question?" Sunny announced.

Alison lifted her chin. "Is it true that until you watched your sister on the show a few weeks ago, you didn't know where she had been for over twenty years?"

Sarah let go of Raven's hand and moved the microphone closer, then repositioned her trembling hands to her lap.

"Yes, Ms. Caruso." Sarah shifted her gaze to Raven and gave a quivering smile. "Our mother took Raven from our grandmother's home when we were three."

"Your mother left *you* behind?" Alison's brows knitted together.

Sarah's posture sank.

Oh, no, you don't, lady. Raven moved her mic closer.

"Yes." Raven answered, then grasped Sarah's hand. "Our mother was very troubled. Which is evident by the fact that she chose the rowdy kid as opposed to the sweet-natured one."

The room erupted in laughter.

"Not true." Sarah gazed at Raven, her eyes moist. Flashes went off. "Our mother wasn't thinking rationally, or she wouldn't have left at all."

"Ms. Sweeting!"

"Ms. Souwer!"

Hands shot up all over the room.

Sunny pointed toward the back. "Ernesto Machado of the *Baking Times.*"

An older Hispanic gentleman stood, holding a legal pad. He removed his black-rimmed glasses and gave what appeared to be a genuine smile. "Senoritas, your mama, she is happy you found each other, yes?"

Who would answer *this* question? Raven's throat had tightened.

They exchanged a quick glance. Sarah nodded. "Senor Machado, our mother is no longer with us. She passed on around ten years ago."

A murmur rose in the room.

"Our grandmother is still with us and is a magnificent woman of God who happens to own the most successful bakery in Minersville." Sarah winked. "Well, the *only* bakery in Minersville."

Relieved laughter replaced the uncomfortable murmurs.

The questions were lively and allowed Raven and Sarah to talk about the craft of baking. Raven shared about hers and Will's experience on *Cupcake Rivalry* and her education at the Art Institute. It was as if something carried her ... like wings of peace supported her.

"One more question, ladies and gentlemen. I want to be sensitive to your schedules and deadlines." Sunny's smile lived up to her name.

She's happy. Good.

Sunny pointed to a rather shapely woman in the front row.

"Audrey Anderson, of the *Bakersville Sentinel*." Audrey stood and brushed a few crumbs from her blue slacks. "Delicious cupcakes, by the way." She pulled a sheet of paper from the press kit. "YBN's newest show, *Sweet Rivalry*, sounds like a fun offering." Placing a finger on the page she continued, "It says here this first episode is entitled, *Sibling Rivalry*." She looked up, eyebrows raised. "Is there a little sibling rivalry between you two since you've been reunited?"

Raven scooted back in her chair. Her fists tightened. How *dare* this woman!

"This is entertainment, Ms. Anderson." Sunny gave a nervous chuckle. "It's all in good fun."

The reporter dipped her chin and pursed her lips. "Come on, Ms. Lofgren. Conflict and drama are the stuff of great ratings. And isn't YBN struggling?"

Sunny took a step back. "I—"

"Ms. Anderson?" Sarah's sweet voice interrupted. "While my sister and I can't speak to YBN's ratings, I can say most of *my* favorite shows are on this network. How about you, Sis?"

"Yes." Raven squeaked. "Yes." She said more clearly.

"And, for certain, I am blessed they featured Raven on one of their most popular programs, because, as everyone in this room knows, our lives were forever changed." Sarah took Raven's other hand and held it.

Ms. Anderson sat her considerable behind on the chair, her shoulders stiff.

"As to your question about sibling rivalry." Sarah sighed and looked at the woman. Her features held no malice or anger. Only kindness.

How did she *do* that?

"Raven and I are only beginning to learn about each other. You can imagine after over twenty years of lost history, the frustration and tension and amazement this has caused."

Some laughter and nods.

"Being part of this show is an incredible opportunity to demonstrate the gifts God has given us. It's also an opportunity to get to know each other even better."

Sarah turned to Sunny and reached for her hand. "We're grateful to Sunny and YBN for inviting us."

Raven exhaled. When did she start holding that breath? And when did Sarah develop such depth of grace and wisdom?

"On that note, everyone—" Sunny raised her arms as though ready to embrace the whole room once again—"we close this press conference. There's a step and repeat in the lobby, and if we ask the ladies nicely, you can get photos with them."

Sarah leaned toward Raven. "What is a step and repeat?"

Raven smiled. She was just glad there would be no repeat of this afternoon.

Chapter 37

Sarah kicked off her heels. "My feet!"

Raven flopped onto the hotel bed. "My body! All I want to do is get into my nightgown and veg in front of the television."

Sarah peeked through the curtain. What if she spotted a few celebrities? "Was this the most incredible day of your life?" Sarah laid on her bed and kicked her legs and squealed. She had even lost some of her intimidation about tomorrow's filming.

Raven rolled to her side chuckling.

They might be identical twins, but there was no question they were the opposites when it came to personality.

Where Sarah was energized by the press conference, photo shoots with various reporters—including the no-longer snippy Ms. Audrey Anderson—and the second lunch with the YBN executives, Raven seemed to have been wrung out like a dishtowel.

"Raven, wasn't it?"

Raven rested her head on her palm. "Not even close."

Sarah sat up. "No?"

Raven grinned. "The best day was when I met my sister and my grandmother."

"Aww. Oh no!" Sarah looked for her phone. "We forgot to call Granny and the guys!"

Raven lay on her stomach as Sarah scrolled through her cell. Several texts waited for her.

WITH GRANNY. CALL US! TELL US!

The reprimand came from Will.

Sarah gasped. And she hadn't *once* thought of Drew. He must have had his interview by now.

Raven looked up. "What? What's wrong?"

As great as they were getting along, mentioning Drew would spoil the mood. Later she would call him. "Let's call Granny and the guys!"

Sarah clicked on Will's number and put the phone on speaker.

"There you girls are!" Will tried to sound cross but didn't succeed. "You're on speaker, by the way."

"So are you."

"My sweet babies! How did it go?" Granny sounded good. Her voice was strong.

Raven's eyes glowed. "It went great, Granny. Sarah is a natural. The press loved her. How are you doing today?"

"Happy because I hear your voices. And we can talk about my health later. There are two young men here who have been praying up a storm with me."

"It's working," Raven whispered.

Amen to that.

"We can attest to the Lord answering those prayers. We had a measure of conflict, but all went well." Sarah swallowed. It was time. "Granny, could you and I talk privately?"

Raven tilted her head, then comprehension darkened her eyes. She left her bed and sat next to Sarah. The gesture gave Sarah courage to continue.

"Okay, sweetie, I'm alone. What's on your mind?"

Sarah patted Raven's hand, then thumbed off the speaker. She stood. "Granny, I know about Mom."

Granny gasped. "I'm so sorry, Sarah. I'm—"

Raven gave her a thumbs-up, gathered her shoes and purse, then left the room. Twin-speak was working overtime.

"I know you were trying to protect me all these years."

"How did you find out? Did Raven tell you?"

Should she cover for Drew? No, these secrets had to stop. "Drew found out and told me."

"He had *no* right!" Her grandmother was talking and crying and making it difficult for Sarah to understand her.

"Granny. Stop, Granny. I know you love me and wanted me to have the best possible childhood." She didn't fight her own tears. "You should have told me. Helped me to understand."

"How could I help you understand when I didn't? I couldn't fix my own daughter."

That was fair. Who could explain why a mother would separate her children and take one from a loving home? She grabbed a pillow and hugged it to herself.

"Isn't that the problem?" Exhaling, Sarah stood and went to the bathroom, to grab a handful of tissues. "We keep trying to fix what only God can."

Wasn't she doing the same by not telling Granny about Drew's possible job in Germany?

Father? Is that what I'm doing? Do I even want *to move to Germany?*

Do I want to marry Drew?

Chapter 38

Raven opened her eyes to Sarah sitting in one of the overstuffed chairs reading. She was certain it was Sarah's Bible.

"Good morning. You're up at the crack of early."

Sarah moved her gaze toward Raven and smiled. "I'm still on Midwest time." She put her book down. "Did you have a good sleep?"

"You don't have to stop reading." Raven rolled the covers back and stretched. "And, yes, I slept well. How about you? You had a pretty emotional end of the day."

Granny and Sarah finally had the inevitable conversation about their mother. No surprises, but necessary. Meanwhile Raven had filled Asher and Will in on their conversation while sitting in the lobby.

Later, she and Sarah talked into the night, ordering room service instead of exploring the city, which was fine with Raven.

Sarah pulled her knees to her chest and rested her cheek on them. "I slept well, too. It's like a great load lifted off my shoulders." She drew a deep breath through her nose. "I hadn't realized knowing bits and pieces about our mother—those intentional and unintentional words spoken to me over the years—had made me a part of the secrets too."

"Granny meant well."

"She did. And like you said last night, there was no way to explain why our mother did what she did."

"I don't know about you." Raven stood. "But I need coffee."

Sarah lifted a paper cup. "I made the room stuff. It's not bad."

"If you're desperate." Raven glanced at the clock on the nightstand. "It's four-thirty. We have an hour to eat and shower before Milo picks us up."

"And more hair and make-up." Sarah stood and placed her hands on her hips. "Something you love, right?"

Having showered and polished off the last of the goodie basket YBN had given them, they made their way to the lobby carrying their portfolios as Milo pulled under the impressive stone veranda.

In the drama of the previous night, neither of them had spent much time being nervous about the show or reviewing the particulars. All that changed the moment they set their behinds on the leather seats.

Milo held the door a moment. "Ms. Lofgren sends her apologies for not joining you on the ride. Several emergencies came up. She also wanted to remind you to study the show synopsis."

Sarah and Raven swapped wrinkled foreheads.

"No need to be concerned, she said to be sure to tell you." He gave a five-hundred-watt smile and shut the door.

"You know, when Will and I filmed the *Cupcake Rivalry* show, Sunny was nothing but a blur running around handling things. Milo's right. There's nothing to be concerned about." At least, she *hoped* that was true.

"It's not her emergencies that concerns me, it's studying the stuff about the show." Sarah already had her nose in the folder. Her eyes raised and her lips formed an upside-down U. "Did you see who is hosting?"

Raven searched the form. "Sasha Harmony? Who is that?"

"Are you kidding? Sasha? From the musical group Sons of Harmony?" Sarah squeezed Raven's forearm.

"I'm gathering you like them."

"They haven't recorded anything in years. They were popular when I was in junior high." Sarah settled down and went back to reading. "Anyway, Sasha was my favorite."

Ah. Raven would have to remember that. Sounded like intel she could use on her later. She chuckled to herself and continued her look through the brief.

"Did you see who the judges were?" Sarah held the three pages of judges' photos and bios.

Raven had seen and her stomach went queasy around the apple she had eaten earlier. Their challenges would be based on the expertise of each judge.

"Amber Williams was one of our judges on *Cupcake*." Raven had had the distinct impression the woman hated her and was the reason she and Will didn't win.

"I remember now." Sarah patted Raven on the knee. "Won't knowing her give you an edge?"

Raven blew air through her lips. "Nope."

Sarah's brows squished together.

"Remember, her saying—often—I hadn't respected the ingredients."

"Oh." She pouted, then flipped a bio toward Raven. "Who is Petra Klug?"

"She is an amazing chocolatier." Raven scanned the woman's bio. "Petra has won a bunch of European competitions for candies and sculptures. I was obsessed with watching her YouTube channel. Chef Garniere was Will's and my instructor at AI, and he said she is the most underrated genius in—"

"Raven, I can't do any of those things. I've made chocolate peanut balls! Sculptures?" She winced as she read further. "Don't you have to know how to temper chocolate and a lot of other stuff?"

Scooching closer to Sarah, she tried to think of something encouraging to say. "Listen, all they want is to challenge us to try something new. If you try one new thing—not everything—you'll do fine. What do they always say on these shows? 'If you do simple, do it perfectly.'" Raven squeezed her sister's hand. "Do what you do, and the love will shine through."

Sarah laid her head on Raven's shoulder. Raven patted her cheek and held the bio of the third judge.

"Okay, Jean Paul Levesque, pastry chef at Coronado Hotel. He's been a judge on a lot of YBN shows. He was a guest lecturer at AI and a nice person."

Sarah pushed herself away from Raven's shoulder. "We're here."

Milo opened the door and extended his hand to help them exit.

God? My sister is such an amazing person and baker. Let everyone else see that too.

God? What am I doing here?

Sarah sat in the familiar swivel chair as YBN's make-up people performed their duties. At least they weren't as heavy handed as they were for the press conference.

Raven reached over to clasp Sarah's arm. Her sister's warmth comforted Sarah.

"Good morning, ladies." Sunny glanced at them before refocusing on her tablet. She spoke into a headset and finished instructing someone "to get them into make-up now."

She emitted an unladylike grunt. "We almost lost our other two contestants. Literally. The Morose brothers arrived early from Chicago to go sightseeing in the San Bernardino Mountains and had trouble finding their way back." She scrolled her screen a few times and blew air from her full lips. "From now on, we'll have to insist that contestants play tourist *after* filming."

If Granny weren't in the hospital, it would have been nice to have Raven show her around. Maybe next time. Sarah's stomach sank. Who knew when she would be back? She could be in Europe before next year. Married. To Drew.

Who, by the way, hadn't returned any of her messages.

"Okay." Sunny hugged her iPad. "First we'll record your intros in front of a green screen."

"Intros?" Sarah turned to Raven.

"It's the written bios you sent us. You'll film them—with attitude and personality."

"You'll be great, Sarah." Raven stood as the hair and make-up people unsnapped her plastic cape.

"Listen to your sister. You were great during the press conference. The intros are a lot like interviews. Someone will ask you the questions." She waved her hand as though waving away an annoying gnat. "Besides, everyone was delirious about you. Oh, and you too, Raven. Since you both were last-minute, we don't have the backstory footage. You'll have to film those and get them to us as soon as you get home."

Maybe Raven would translate what that meant later.

Sunny gave a Cheshire-cat smile. "Which reminds me, we have you both booked on three local morning shows before you fly out tomorrow."

Sarah took deep breaths. Raven strode over and situated herself next to Sarah, forcing a make-up person to move.

"What? Is something wrong?" Sunny wrinkled her brow.

"No. No. It's a surprise," Sarah said.

"What Sarah means to say is, this is a lot." Raven folded her arms across her chest.

Sunny plopped into the chair Raven had vacated. She stretched her legs and sank deeper into the seat. "I know it is. And I almost—almost—told them you couldn't. But trust me on this, please, this is not only publicity for YBN and the show, but also for you."

Raven lowered her chin. "Why do *we* need local publicity?"

Sunny bit her lip. "Like I said. Please trust me on this."

Sarah studied Raven's expression. She recognized the default distrust, then curiosity, then acquiescence. A slight shrug of a shoulder told Sarah what she needed to answer.

Sarah nodded. "Okay."

Sunny gave a controlled squeal. "Oh, you did it again. Twin-speak!" She pushed herself out of the chair. "We begin filming the intros in fifteen minutes. Then the show begins! Oh, and you'll have voice-overs after the show."

Their producer glided from the room, barking orders into the headset.

"All done." One of the hair guys removed the cape. Sarah stared at her reflection. They had listened to her. A functional bun, a pink fabric headband above her forehead, and minimal make-up compared to yesterday. All good, given she would sweat up a storm.

"Thank you so much, everyone," Sarah said.

As the crew reloaded for the Morose brothers, Sarah and Raven ran into a young man also wearing a headset, who guided them to the greenroom. A beverage-and-snack area had been added. Their guide pointed to the couch and explained the network didn't want the contestants to see the set until they were filming, so the reaction was real.

Oh, her reactions would be real.

Butterflies had mounted an attacked in Sarah's gut. Yet she was excited too. She sat on the couch facing the door. Raven joined her and took her hand. Raven dipped her chin and looked intently at Sarah.

"I'm okay." It was a lot like the first time she rode the crazy rollercoaster at Six Flags in Eureka. Once they had strapped her in, there was no going back. Sitting there waiting for it to begin was more terrifying than the actual ride. When it was over, she wobbled off, ready to go again.

They were strapped in—time for the ride of her life.

Chapter 39

Raven shook Shawn Morose's hand. Sarah performed the same deed with his brother Robert. Then they swapped. The guys looked like they lifted weights. Muscles bulged like the mountains they couldn't find their way out of.

Raven couldn't help staring. They looked like Jersey Shore boys. Sarah elbowed her in the side.

"Quit smirking," Sarah whispered.

They each wore a bib apron stitched with *Sweet Rivalry*'s new logo—a lime-green silhouette of two bakers arguing over a three-layer cake in a circular white background.

Sarah's apron was pink, hers lime green. Shawn's was indigo blue, and Robert's lemon-yellow.

Her sister looked so cute in her pink apron and headband. She had folded her hands and pressed them against her lips. No doubt praying.

Go for it, Sarah.

"Sure glad you have different hair colors," Shawn rested his hands on his hips. "When they said you were identical, I figured we wouldn't be able to tell you two apart." His tall, muscular frame vibrated with laughter. His brother followed.

"Thank goodness you guys found your way back from the mountains or we wouldn't have had a show." Raven knew what Morose was doing. Trying to psych them out.

Sarah touched Raven's shoulder. "We're glad you arrived safely. It must have been a harrowing experience."

Her sister then redirected the conversation to the weather. Small talk was not Raven's forte, but the innocuous discussion sure defused Raven's assault.

Sunny's assistant came behind them. "Walk on." He herded them behind the stages until they arrived at a large doorway covered by a curtain. "Sunny will call you in off-camera." He pointed to Sarah, then Raven. "You two go first. Then the brothers."

He circled his finger around his mouth. "Big smiles." He touched the headset and said something. "Wait for Sunny." He grimaced.

"Did I tell you this show is scheduled to air in the Spring?"

All the bakers answered, "No."

He shrugged. "Right, you've been officially told." He pressed a finger to the earphone. "Ready?"

A voice from the set yelled, "Bakers! Now!"

Raven grabbed Sarah's hand. They didn't skip exactly, but it was a lively stride as they entered the competition arena. Rather than scoping out the beautifully designed set containing every ingredient, tool, and appliance they would need, Raven watched the wonder waltz across her sister's features.

A sandblaster could not have wiped Raven's own wide smile off her face. But one cruel remark from the judges would.

Please don't let there be any!

Thank heaven Raven held her hand, otherwise Sarah might float away in pure ecstasy. "Oh, look at all the colors! Look at the logo on the stations! We have our own stoves. And look, the mixers match the color of our station—oh. *and* they match our aprons!"

Were it not for the camera sentinels, she would have thought she was in kitchen heaven. She might need an eternity to explore all the appliances, ingredients—everything a baker needed.

A handsome gentleman in his forties made an entrance.

"Bakers! I am Sasha Harmony. Welcome to the first episode of *Sweet Rivalry*!"

It's him. It's him. Sarah pumped Raven's arm until Raven had to release her hand.

"We have two sets of siblings competing. We're calling this episode, *Sibling Rivalry*. Let's meet our bakers!" Sasha's voice had more inflection and range of tones than a flock of myna birds.

"First, two sisters who are identical twins separated as toddlers, but baking brought them back together after twenty years! Raven Souwer and Sarah Sweeting!"

And just like that …

Sarah's brain turned to mush.

Chapter 40

Drew shoved back the heavy curtains. The sun pierced his retina. He promptly closed them. Even as an Alpha brother, he could count on one hand the number of mornings he regretted overindulging. He and his frat brothers might have exceeded his beer limit from time-to-time, but not wine.

Germans loved their wine—and in some locations more than beer. Whatever his hosts had poured, he drank. He hadn't wanted to appear the rude American.

He checked his cell. *Ach.* He had wanted to be on the road by now. At least Herr Oscar was still at his office.

Scrolling through his messages he noticed several from Sarah and his parents. He grabbed his head and pressed. Maybe a shower would help this horrific pain. Maybe he was dehydrated.

The shower took the edge off. He sat on the bed a towel around his waist, another around his neck. He drank as much water as his stomach allowed, then flopped back, his legs dangling.

I'll close my eyes ...

Drew shot from the bed. It was two hours later! Grabbing the clothes laid out the previous day, he hastily dressed.

He'd missed his window of opportunity for his morning strategy. Now he would have to wait until Herr Oscar came home from work. Which meant he would have to drive back to Freiburg at night.

He slipped on his good loafers and checked himself in the dresser mirror.

Unless Mr. Oscar invited Drew to stay the night.

The face in the mirror brightened. *Yes.* He might be asked to stay for dinner. Meet the whole family. Drew could show Herr Oscar photos of his beautiful daughter.

He saluted the future son-in-law of Herr Howard Oscar and left his room.

The next step in his plan was one-hundred-and-eighty kilometers away.

Chapter 41

"The baker not moving on to the next challenge is ..."

The long dramatic pause had Sarah cutting off the circulation of Raven's arm. She wished she could comfort her sister, but she was just as nervous.

"Robert Morose." Sasha folded his hands and gave a sympathetic nod. "The judges said your flavors were delicious, but you ran out of time for the diplomatic cream and gelato to set."

Robert waved to the judges, shook his brother's hand, whispered something to him, and thanked everyone for the opportunity as he walked off set.

Raven looked at Sarah.

They were moving on to the next challenge!

Before Sarah could process that she was moving forward, Sasha gave instructions for the next challenge.

One of the stagehands rolled out a cart. A pink cloth hid their next challenge. Sasha strode to the cart and lifted the cloth with a flourish.

"It's our chocolate challenge!"

Sarah's heart sank. The samples on the cart were elaborate free-standing sculptures. She had no idea how to fabricate one. A rotating globe. A large woven basket filled with what appeared to be life-size marzipan fruit.

"Bakers, you have three hours to create chocolate candies to share and a complementary themed sculpture. Your time begins…" Sasha raised his arm.

Leave your arm there, Sasha, until I can think of what to make.

Down went his arm. "Now!"

The three remaining bakers scurried back to their stations. Raven ran toward one of the supply shelves. She jumped, trying to see the top shelf better. Sasha stood by her, doing the interactive MC thing. As they spoke to each other, he reached up and grabbed a large block of something and handed it to Raven.

What can I make? What if she made the chocolate-coated peanut-butter balls?

No, too simple. The judges dinged her on her first offering of the angel food cake. She placed her palms on the stainless counter and leaned forward. *Lord?*

Raven carried a block of something pink.

Sarah studied it. "Is that white chocolate?"

"Even better." Raven smiled. "It's ruby chocolate and very rare." She laid it on her counter, alongside various sized plastic molds, then began pulling utensils from under her station. "Do you know what you want to make?"

"I have no idea." Sarah glanced toward Robert's station. A double boiler was already melting chocolate. No doubt he would craft something amazing.

"Sarah." Using a large knife, Raven chopped chunks of the pink chocolate. "You are an artist. I've seen your work at Sweet's." She gave a closed mouth smile and winked. "Remember, there are all sorts of fondant and modeling chocolate."

Modeling chocolate? Peanut-butter balls. *When I think of peanuts, I think of—*

Elephants. Elephants like peanuts.

Dumbo! One of her favorite Disney characters. The outcast who had a secret talent—he could fly.

The scene appeared in her mind. Dumbo wearing his clown hat and collar, holding a feather in his trunk. Now the peanut-butter balls had meaning.

She grabbed a shopping basket and ran to the supplies. Placing the basket on the floor, she found a large mound of modeling chocolate, a large block of puffed rice cereal, edible paints, peanut butter, corn flakes, semi-sweet chocolate and dark chocolate, vegetable oil, and the list went on.

What about mocha truffles and peanut butter and banana balls?

She added the ingredients for these variations.

How she was remembering these components was nothing short of miraculous. She muttered her gratitude as she deposited each item into the growing mountain of materials.

Once the basket was full, she delivered it to her station, then headed to the refrigerator to get the dairy items.

As much as she wanted to work on the sculpture, she knew the truffles and peanut butter interiors had to chill first.

The producers were helpful enough to have a boiling pot on the stove. She could begin melting the milk chocolate in the double boiler, but she needed another pot boiling for the dark chocolate.

Once all the truffle insides were made, she popped them into the blast chiller, then ran back to her station. Pulling a pair of gloves from the box under her station, she slipped them on and thought back to her art classes. She shaved the puffed rice treats into the body of Dumbo, sitting. The treats were pliable as she formed the legs and head.

The large ears and trunk would need to be supported somehow. Wire. She yanked off the gloves and searched the shelf.

She called out, "Did anyone see modeling wire?"

Shawn looked at her, then went back to his work. No help there.

"Check by the tools," Raven said.

She ran to the shelf containing sculpting tools. Yes! Several rolls of various gauges. A wire cutter too.

Once the wires were covered in the puffed rice, she pulled a hunk of chocolate and began kneading it.

"Sarah." Sasha appeared at her side, causing her to jump. "I see you're about to make something here. Is it your complementary free-standing sculpture?"

Sarah nodded, working to calm her heart. "Yes." She cleared her throat. "I'm making my favorite Disney character."

"And who is this character? Can I have a hint?"

The chocolate was a perfect texture, so she applied it to the body. "I'm making peanut-butter balls covered in chocolate."

His elbow resting on his arm, as he held his chin, he shrugged. "I haven't a clue."

Sarah smiled. "How about coming back around in a few minutes." Golly, he was handsome. Her face heated. Was she flirting?

"I will be back." He smiled, bright white teeth blinding her, then he called out, "Two hours remaining." He walked to Robert's station.

Would she finish in time? She needed at least thirty minutes to dip the chocolate. The sculpture for the elephant could take two hours alone, much less the painting.

And how to display the candy?

Dumbo performed at the circus. How about a popcorn box?

Leaving her sculpture, she ran to the shelves and searched.

"What are you looking for, Sarah?"

She looked over her shoulder. Raven was painting chocolate flowers on molds. "I'm looking for popcorn boxes."

Raven inspected her mold, a brush stuck in her mouth. "I saw some by the blast chiller."

Sarah sprinted across the room. *There.* Adorable boxes for popcorn. *Oh!* Right behind them, there were peanut bags! Even better!

Thank You, Lord!

She grabbed the stack and sprinted back to her station.

Raven chewed her lip as Sarah zipped by her, again. She needed to warn Sarah to pace herself. There was still the big challenge in a few hours—if they survived this one. Based on the adorable elephant figure her sister had created, she would move to the next round.

"Ninety minutes, bakers!" Sasha warned them.

She refocused on her project. The candy centers were chilling in the fridge. The purple, pink, and lavender chocolate petunias she had painted inside the large egg molds were hardened enough to pour the ruby chocolate. The nesting chicken mold had its first coating of white chocolate. The ruby chocolate—pink and creamy—was ready in the double boiler.

Now, to temper it so the beautiful pink would be shiny and have that snap when bitten into—as opposed to the mealy, dull non-tempered chocolate.

The large marble slab was stored under the counter. She lifted it with a grunt and set it down. Pouring two-thirds of the melted chocolate, she took her trowel and offset spatula and began spreading it out, then scooping it back to the middle.

Tempering relaxed her. The smooth motions centered her. The beautiful fragrance of the chocolate made her smile. She admired the glossiness.

The thickness indicated it had cooled, she grabbed the thermometer to confirm its readiness. Eighty-four degrees. Perfect.

She transferred the tempered chocolate back into the bowl and mixed it in the untempered batch. Once the full batch was at ninety degrees, she was ready to mold.

On the counter to her left were three sheet pans, each holding four large egg molds. Each egg would be eight by six inches, and once put together, five inches in diameter. The candies would be inside. When the judges cracked open the egg, candies would tumble out.

With the sour, fruity notes of this unique chocolate, the fruit gummies would be a delicious complement to the dark chocolate strawberry and blueberry creams. All shaped like flowers.

She poured the tempered chocolate into the molds. Enough to cover the bottom and sides. Each mold coated, she dumped the excess into the bowl and inverted them to dry. She breathed a sigh of relief. The painted flowers were still intact.

What if she also covered the creams in the ruby? She smiled as she finished pouring. While she waited for the chocolate to harden, she would apply the second coat to the creams, then pour the second layer of the chicken mold in white chocolate.

"Raven, the light pink of the ruby chocolate is exquisite." Sarah laid her arm across Raven's shoulders.

Raven smiled and looked toward her sister's station. The most adorable elephant sat on the counter. Its trunk lifted. She stepped over to get a closer look. The elephant's ears drooped to the counter. She turned toward Sarah. "Aren't the ears too big?"

"It's Dumbo." Her brows lifted, her smile toothy.

"Who's Dumbo?"

Sarah's eyes rounded. "You know, the Disney character? People made fun of him because his ears were too big, but those ears helped him to fly."

Raven knew there was Disneyland, which she had never been to, despite living ten miles away. She knew there were

Disney movies. She'd seen one on television, but this elephant character, she knew nothing about. "I feel pretty stupid."

"Please don't." Sarah rubbed Raven's back. "Up until the live-action movie, most people didn't remember him."

A live-action movie? Another part of a normal life she missed.

Shake it off, Raven.

Raven returned to her station and checked her molds. Time for the second coat for the eggs. She repeated the process, then strode to the refrigerator to retrieve her candies. A quick tap on several samples of each variety, revealed they were ready.

Shawn assembled his structure. It was a series of delicately thin hollow chocolate balls. Each ball had different sized holes. They hung on chocolate tree branches.

"How beautiful, Shawn."

He regarded Raven over his shoulder. "Thanks." His response was the antithesis of his elegant craftsmanship.

She assembled her station to give her goodies a chocolate bath.

Can't be bothered by his tepid reply. Can't.

"Five minutes, bakers!" Sasha's voice carried the intensity of the atmosphere.

Sarah took a sharp intake of breath. Her hand shook as she touched up the clown collar with the fine brush.

The chocolate creature before her looked like Dumbo. The coated candies were tucked into four peanut bags. One for each of the judges and one for display. Each bag lay on its own red-and-white striped plate in a semi-circle around Dumbo. At the last minute she had added real peanuts. They were scattered inside the bag and here and there on the plate.

Is it too simple?

She brought her fingertips to her lips and fought the urge to bite her nails. She bit her lip instead.

The display board was covered in graham cracker "sand." She was glad one of the crew would transfer it to the display table, it was too heavy for her.

Raven's display was like a scene from a Beatrix Potter illustration. A colorful chicken nested on a basket. Sarah marveled at Raven's skill. The chocolate now gave the impression of porcelain. The eggs nestled in green dyed coconut flakes.

Shawn's offering looked like a sculpture on display in a museum. Each judge received a single, large chocolate ball resting on a raspberry cream swoosh. Through various sized cutouts a smaller sparkling gold ball was visible.

Sarah sighed. *Mine is too simple. Again.*

"Four, three, two, one! Time is up!" Sasha shouted.

Time was up for her too.

Raven stood with her hands behind her back—her heart scurrying like a hamster on a wheel—as the judges tapped on their large ruby-pink chocolate eggs. An assortment of candies poured out.

Chef Petra sat straight and grinned as she investigated the raspberry-flavored pink gummy flower. She popped it in her mouth and closed her eyes.

Yes. The nod.

Chef Jean Paul sampled one of the eggshells. "Is this the ruby chocolate?"

Raven smiled. "Yes, Chef."

Chef Amber's poker face gave Raven nothing. Raven inhaled and held her breath.

Chef Petra took a sip of water.

Sasha leaned against the judges' gallery. "Well, judges, what do you think of Raven's offering?"

"Ah," Chef Jean Paul leaned forward. "I do not know about the ladies, but I found Raven's work masterful. Beautiful molding and painting. My favorite was the blueberry cream covered in the ruby chocolate." He pointed toward the hen. "Is there another blueberry cream?"

Raven giggled and turned to pick the candy from the display. "Yes, Chef." She walked it over to him.

He ate it in one bite.

"Hey!" Sasha said. "You took my piece!"

Everyone laughed.

Chef Amber folded her hands. "Chef Raven, I must admit, your chocolate work is beautiful. Often, the work is better than the taste." She gave a knowing glance to the other judges. They bobbed their heads.

Raven swallowed. *Here it comes.*

"However, your taste equaled and, in some cases, as with the dark-chocolate strawberry creams, exceeded." She sat back. "Well done."

Chef Amber cracked a smile—almost.

Raven expelled the breath she'd been holding. "Thank you!"

Chef Petra's critique barely penetrated her brain before they excused her to the greenroom.

Sarah ran toward her. "How did it go?" Her sister was still glowing from her judging.

"I guess I'm next." Dread oozed off Robert. like tree sap.

Her sister, ever the compassionate one, placed her hand on one of those bulky arms. "Shawn, your work is gorgeous. I don't envy the judges trying to make a decision. I'd love to learn your techniques."

He chewed his upper lip, where perspiration had formed. "Thanks." Without a backward glance, he exited the room.

Sarah's brows raised. Resting her elbow on her arm, she placed her middle fingers on her lips.

A picture flashed in Raven's mind. She stepped back. "Whoa!"

"What?"

Raven placed her arms on her head. "Did you used to suck your thumb?" Raven shook her head. "Not your thumb. Your middle fingers?"

Sarah's mouth opened. She gripped Raven's arm. "Did you remember something?"

"I think so." Raven turned away and plopped on the couch. "It was a flicker of you as a baby. A moment ago, when you put your fingers on your lips, it triggered the— whatever it was."

"The memory." Sarah sat next to her and took her hand. "Yes, I used to suck on my middle two fingers." She sighed. "After our mother kidnapped you, I resumed the habit for almost a year."

Raven swiveled her body. "What does this mean?"

"I don't know. Except—" Sarah's eyes moistened. "You had an early memory."

"Yeah." Raven looked at her lap. "I don't know if I want to remember all my childhood. After Lizzy took me, things weren't so great."

Sarah nodded. "I'm praying whatever memories surface will be part of your healing. We are made up of the good and bad experiences."

"What if *I* don't have faith?" Raven withdrew her hands and stood. "I don't believe in a Supreme Being who cares about me, like you and Asher do."

"And Granny. And—" Sarah stood, "Will."

Raven exhaled. "I gotta tell you, Will's a shocker." She looked intently at Sarah. "I mean I know some of the wild stuff he did."

Girls. Parties. Clubs. Drugs. Things Sarah would be shocked to know.

"Do you trust his sincerity?"

Sarah's question carried more weight than the words she was asking.

298

"Do you mean, is Will the real deal?"

Sarah looked away, but not before Raven noticed the pink rise on her cheeks. The wanting in her eyes.

Raven smiled and laid her hands on her sister's shoulders. "Yes, Sarah. I've never seen my best friend more at peace."

Her sister ran her fingers across her lips.

"And when will admit you love Will?"

Chapter 42

Drew pulled off the street. The other side was Howard Oscar's residence.

The entire side of the street.

Drew had gotten lost three times thanks to not understanding Swiss German. Him being fluent in High German only frustrated the various people he sought for help.

He put the Fiat Mini in park and set the brake, then rested his chin on the steering wheel and studied the chalet. The sun had set. Home and streetlights illuminated the development nestled in the mountains.

Maybe he should have called ahead. Or emailed. Something.

Or maybe he should drive back to his hotel.

He groaned. The idea of driving another three hours revived his headache.

One of the garage doors lifted. A young woman wearing a colorful ski parka exited, following behind appeared to be a small horse. *Is that a dog?*

He stretched to the passenger window crank and rolled it down. "*Entschuldigen Sie mich, Fräulein?*"

The dog barked and charged—its mouth large enough for Drew's head to fit inside.

Drew worked his elbows to rolled up the window.

"Sebastian! *Nein*! No!" The young woman yanked on a leash attempting to keep the beast from him.

"*Sprechen Sie Deutsch*? English?" He yelled.

She walked toward his car. Or maybe the dog dragged her. He couldn't tell. The animal placed his paws on the roof of the Mini, presenting evidence of his gender. The young woman peered into the passenger window.

"Are you American?" Her English was clear, only a hint of an accent. Her blue eyes reminded him of Sarah's. Same shape. Brown hair like her father's. A teenager, perhaps fifteen or sixteen, and already taller than Sarah.

Still the resemblance made him swallow. They could be sisters. Half-sisters.

"*Ja*. Yes." He had to be careful he didn't reveal too much to her. "I interviewed with Untergarten and I attend your dad's alma mater."

"In Missouri? Untergarten is where mein Vater works. How did you find our house?" She stood and pulled out her cell.

"Yes, Missouri. I was hoping to meet him, but I got lost." Did she hear him with the barking? Was she calling the police?

He sank lower in the seat. The last thing he wanted was to spend the night in jail. It would not look good on his resume. Had he jeopardized his dream job?

A figure appeared in front of his car. He didn't look happy, but he did look like Howard Oscar.

He shone a flashlight in Drew's face, blinding him.

"I'm—my name is Andrew Collar. I attend the University of Missouri in Minersville. I interviewed with Herr Luecker at Untergarten. I—"

The blinding light turned away. "Sebastian, *halt!*"

The beast silenced and whined.

"Come!"

Was Mr. Oscar commanding him or Sebastian? The dog released the Mini, causing the vehicle to rock.

Drew exhaled. "Thanks so much—*vielen Dank.*"

"Fabienne, *geh ins Haus.*" Mr. Oscar took reign of Sebastian.

"*Vatti*," Fabienne grumbled.

"Now." He pointed. She stomped away but gave a brief glance over her shoulder.

Howard Oscar stood next to the driver's side door. He inspected the interior of the car, as if looking for something.

Drew lifted his hands. "I'm unarmed."

Mr. Oscar lifted a corner of his lips and rested his forehead on the Mini's roof. "That is good, because I would have to give you to Sebastian for a snack. Why have you arrived unannounced to my home, Andrew Collar?" Although Mr. Oscar was born in St. Louis, after twenty years in Europe, he had developed a slight accent.

Okay. How do I do this? "I interviewed—"

"*Mit* Heinz Luecker, as you said. Why are you here?"

Drew shrugged and rubbed his hands on the steering wheel. "You've been my idol since undergrad."

"Have you been stalking me?" He pulled Sebastian toward the window. The animal fogged the glass. "Why are you here?"

"No. Nein. No, sir!" Drew's heart was about to hurtle out of his chest like a speeding comet. If he hadn't already given his and Herr Luecker's names, he'd peel out of there.

"I'm waiting!"

"I'm engaged to Sarah Sweeting." *Oh. He hadn't meant to say that!*

Howard's body straightened. He cursed as he walked away. A woman appeared behind the beam of another flashlight. She glanced toward Drew then moved toward Howard. "*Was ist los, darling?*"

Drew couldn't hear their conversation. The woman must be his wife. She covered her mouth with a gloved hand a few times. Finally, she walked to the car and knocked on the window. "Good evening, I am Howard's wife, Laraina."

"Good evening, ma'am. I'm Andrew Collar." *Why* did he think this was a good idea? "I'm sorry to interrupt your family's evening."

"It is perhaps too late for that." She opened his door and extended her right hand.

He shook it. "I can leave and y'all can go back to your family." Great. Now his southern drawl decided to show up. "Please, forget I was here."

"Too late for that as well."

Mr. Oscar, his back turned, rubbed his salt and pepper hair. Sebastian sat looking at Drew, then Mrs. Oscar.

She followed Drew's gaze to her husband. "Ah. My husband has worries about our children. Too late for him as well." She stared intently at him. "You are the fiancée? Which twin?"

"Sarah, ma'am."

She folded her arms across her chest and looked over her shoulder at her husband. "Come here, Howard. Do not leave me alone to manage your secrets."

Howard shook his head.

"If I may, ma'am, Sarah is the most kind, beautiful, compassionate, intelligent woman I've ever met. Mr. Oscar would be proud—"

She closed her eyes and held up her hand.

"*Mutti!* We have twin sisters?" Fabienne stood up from the front of the car like a jack-in-the-box and rushed to her mother. "Are they on Instagram?" She clutched Drew's arm. "Do you have photos of them?"

Drew was about to grab his cell when Mr. Oscar strode toward them. "Fabienne, go to the house now!"

"But—"

"Listen to your Vater." Mrs. Oscar's voice was soft and gentle. She cupped her daughter's cheek in her hand. "We will talk later. Please say nothing to your sister and brother. Wait until we come in."

Fabienne hung her head and walked away. She paused to look at Drew. "Wiedersehen."

"Wiedersehen, Fräulein."

Too bad Mr. Oscar didn't have Fabienne's enthusiasm. Hope Sweeting wasn't the only one who kept secrets.

Howard Oscar marched toward Drew. "Why are you here? Do you want money? Did Hope send you?" Each question brought Oscar's face closer to his, until Oscar's heavy breath made Drew's eyes flutter.

"Stop!" Laraina shoved her husband aside.

He growled like Sebastian.

"Ma'am, I didn't come for money. Ms. Sweeting doesn't know I'm here. She's in the hospital after having a heart attack and—"

"Do the girls know you are here?" Howard stepped closer. Mrs. Oscar extended her arm to keep him back.

"No. Neither of them knows about you, as far as I know." Despite the cold, he rubbed his sweaty hands on his slacks. "Ms. Sweeting doesn't know I'm here."

"Who? Who told you?" He pointed toward Drew. "It was the Wests, yes? They never respected—"

"Stop, Howard. It matters not. He knows. Now our Fabienne knows." She groaned. "Andrew, our family must discuss these things privately."

"Yes, ma'am."

"May we depend on you to not say anything to anyone, including to the people at Untergarten?"

"Of course." He tried not to show his relief. "No one has to know anything. Ever."

She held up her hand. "People will know, but we desire to be the ones to reveal this information. Beginning with our children." Her dark blue eyes lasered his.

"Yes, ma'am." He wanted to keep apologizing, but his survival instinct said to run. He climbed into his Mini and was about to close the door when Howard grabbed it, then clutched Drew's jacket sleeve.

"You think this is over? You tell Hope she is not getting anything from me."

"Howard! Do not make a scene! Our children!" Laraina pulled on her husband trying to yank him away. "Let him go!" She wrestled her husband away and hugged him. "Let him go, my love."

Drew started the engine and raced away, the door slamming closed on its own. Drew glanced in the rearview mirror. His idol stood alone in the road, watching him.

"What have I done?"

Chapter 43

Asher chuckled at another of Will's wild stories. Granny wiped a tear from laughing.

"Dear boy—" she gasped. "I don't know when I've laughed so hard."

His friend had lived an interesting life in Los Angeles. Would Minersville be enough for him?

The hospital room phone rang. "Oh, do you think it's the girls?" Granny asked.

Asher looked at his watch. "It's still early there. Unless—"

"Unless they were already voted off." Will raised his brows.

Hope answered the phone.

"Hello." She gasped. "Don't use that language!"

Asher could only hear muffled shouting.

"Who *is* this?" Granny's face paled. *"Howard?"* Her lips trembled.

Asher leaned toward Will. "It's Sarah and Raven's father."

Will stood next to Granny and took her hand.

"No, Howard. I would never—I—no—" Granny shed more tears, but these were not brought on by funny stories.

Asher stood, ready to snatch the phone and end the offensive call.

"I didn't know. The girls don't even know where you live—no. They're in Los Angeles, filming a television show."

She shook her head. "No, not about you. They're both bakers and—"

Asher had had enough. He grabbed the phone. "Mr. Oscar, this is Asher West. I must end this conversation as Granny had a heart attack a week ago and, as you apparently know, is still in the hospital."

"Did you have anything to do with sending Andrew Collar to my home? My *home!* Now my children know the sordid details of my past!"

Sordid? "Sarah and Raven are about as sordid as a spring rain. And I had nothing to do with Drew. I thought he was in Germany."

"Laraine, I had to. Don't you see?" Howard's conversation had diverted to someone else. "West, did you say? Young Asher West? Son of Arlin and Linda?"

"Yes." And then Asher remembered. *Oh no.* His parents had told Drew.

"Your parents put him up to this. It's their fault. I am calling my lawyer! I'm—" Noise came from the other end, as if Howard had dropped the phone.

"Granny?" Will bent over Granny. "Are you okay?"

She did not look okay. At all. Her breathing came in spurts. She clutched the front of her gown. Asher looked at Will. "Go get a nurse."

Will ran from the room.

"Hallo. This is Laraine Oscar, Howard's wife." A woman, with an accent. German? "I apologize for my husband's behavior."

"Ma'am, I have to end this call. Hope may be having another heart attack."

Several nurses ran into the room, "Mrs. Sweeting, are you in pain?"

Granny nodded.

"Please, Mrs. Oscar, Drew's visit was all his own doing."

"Ja, yes, it is as I suspected. I am sorry. Please, I hope Mrs. Sweeting will be okay."

"Thank you." Asher hung up and got out of the way of the growing number of medical personnel.

Please, dear Father, let Granny be okay.

Chapter 44

Arms interwoven, Raven and Sarah held their hands together. Shawn stood, feet apart, hands behind his back, like a gladiator.

Which of the three of them would be voted off.

Please, don't let it be Sarah.

Sasha had given the judges' critique summaries for Raven and Sarah. He was beginning Robert's summary. "Shawn, the judges loved your artistic abilities. Your chocolate sculpture could have been displayed in a museum."

Uh oh. Raven bit her lip.

"However, the judges were disappointed that the all-important taste factor was missing. Giving them only one type of candy and not tempering your chocolate took away from your enchanting confection."

Sarah decreased the circulation in Raven's arm, again.

Sasha tilted his head and gave a sad smile. "I'm sorry, Shawn you will not continue on in *Sweet Rivalry*."

What? Raven stepped back as though someone had shoved her.

Sarah turned toward Shawn. "I'm sorry."

The judges said something about him being talented and it was close. Which was vaguely familiar. Hadn't they said the same thing to her and Will in the cupcake episode?

Shawn nodded once. "It's been an honor. These ladies are talented."

Raven and Sarah moved to console him, but he backed away, then turned and strode to the door. One wave and he was gone.

"Raven and Sarah! You are the finalists for the first *Sweet Rivalry Baking Competition!*"

"Cut!"

"What happened?" Sarah's eyes had enlarged to the size of cinnamon buns.

Raven was so proud of her sister.

Sasha approached them. "Congratulations, ladies. Well done!" He shook their hands. "We need to clear the set. The designers need to get in here to prepare for the last vignette."

A half-dozen or so men and women had already begun to replenish supplies, then rolled in a cart covered with a red-and-white checked tablecloth.

Sasha's strong arms ushered Raven and Sarah to the exit. "Come on, girls. No peeking."

Sarah giggled. Raven loved that sound.

Sunny emerged amidst the activity—iPad smoking. She stopped and looked up. "Sarah! Raven! I *knew* you two would be the finalists!"

She pushed away the headset mic and leaned toward them. "I'm not supposed to say this, but you both were so much more creative than the brothers."

Sarah's spine straightened.

Uh-oh.

"There's food in the green room." Sunny fluttered away, barking orders. Sasha looked at his watch and marched in the opposite direction.

"You didn't like what Sunny said?"

Sarah shrugged. "I'm wondering ..."

"What?"

Her sister sighed. "It's probably nothing."

"Sarah, what?"

They stood in the hallway between sets, while YBN staff scurried about. Sarah folded an arm across her abdomen, then propped her elbow there. Fingers to her lips.

Uh-oh. She's upset.

"Tell me."

Sarah lifted her fingers to speak. "Is the network setting us up to win for … for … I don't know, for publicity?"

"Whoa. You think we didn't deserve the win?" Raven ran her hand through her hair, her stomach dropping to her toes.

Sarah glanced around. "Maybe Robert needed to be eliminated, but Shawn's sculpture was amazing. How could Dumbo beat his work of art?"

A mental image of the adorable elephant stomping floating chocolate balls materialized. A chuckled bubbled inside Raven. She tried to keep it in, but it only grew into laughter.

"It's not funny, Raven." Sarah's pinched expression made Raven laugh harder.

She wrapped an arm around her sister and tugged her into the greenroom, then shut the door.

It didn't matter who won *Sweet Rivalry*. Raven had already won. She had a family. A sister. She couldn't wait to see Granny and Will.

Raven's cheeks warmed.

And Asher.

Chapter 45

Will never wanted to go through that again. He sniffed and swiped at a stray tear. A leftover from the drama played out a half-hour ago.

Granny slept. They gave her something to help her relax, which was good because the doctor was adamant about keeping her calm.

Thank the good Lord, it wasn't an infarction. According to the cardiologist, she had had a panic attack. Except the guy used a scientific term.

These things could mimic a heart attack and were caused in part by stress. It was no wonder. The last few weeks was more than most people could handle.

The arrival of her long-lost granddaughter. The news of her daughter's death. The heart attack itself. The sisters competing in a televised baking show. Sarah marrying Drew and possibly moving to Germany. And then the idiot father's phone call.

His own heart thumped thinking about it all—especially Sarah's engagement.

Asher slipped on his jacket. Will patted Granny's hand, then retrieved his coat from the back of his chair.

This evening's revelations about Drew were disturbing ... and validating. Would Sarah come to Drew's defense about *this*?

They walked to the elevators.

"When is Drew returning?" *Never would be nice.* Will sighed. *Sorry, Lord.*

Asher pressed the down arrow. "I'm not sure. Thursday?"

The elevator arrived and opened. Will pressed the lobby button. "And Sarah and Raven will return tomorrow night."

"Right."

They rode in silence. Will, however, bit his tongue trying to keep from asking the question. He cleared his throat several times. The elevator dinged.

"What, Will?"

"Okay, who's telling Sarah?"

Asher shook his head. "Buddy, you're too much."

They walked through the automatic doors. A brisk wind sprayed them with dried leaves. Asher pulled up his collar. Will did the same. He always thought upturned collars looked cool in photographs, who knew it had a practical use.

"So, Ash—" Will chose to not look at his friend "Who will tell Sarah what Drew did?"

"Not us."

They climbed into Asher's truck.

As Asher cranked the engine and turned up the heat, Will had a few moments to think. "It needs to be Granny, right?"

Asher blew into his hands. "Or Drew."

Will whipped his head toward his friend. *"Drew?"*

Putting the car in reverse, Asher backed out of the parking spot. "Yep." He glanced at Will. "Where to for dinner?"

"Need you ask?"

Chapter 46

Drew dragged himself into his fraternity room and kicked his luggage toward the closet. It was two-something in the morning. He still wasn't sure how he had made it home in one piece and two days early.

He checked his phone for messages. Would Mr. Oscar call Herr Luecker to tell him Drew was not Untergarten material?

Three messages. He sat on the bed and played the first one. Sarah. He hit forward. Second message, his parents, forward. The third message, Sarah's voice for a second before he hung up. He laid back and thanked God for mercy.

Drew had made a good impression on both Herr Luecker and his wife. Frau Luecker was excited to meet Sarah. Over dinner he had shared photos and told them all about her competition in Hollywood.

He snarled as he pulled the bedding back, then flopped on top—without removing his clothes.

Was Sarah still filming? Only if she was good enough to move forward.

Maybe Raven was voted off with the first round. *Yeah.* She could come back to Minersville a loser and then be arrested on drug charges.

He would talk to Lewis about the best way to handle this—or he would talk with Lewis's cop brother. He yawned. But not now. Jet lag had the better of him. He'd call.

Later.

Chapter 41

In hindsight, Sarah and Raven should have taken a quick nap before the last vignette. As they stood outside the entrance to the set waiting to be called in, they both yawned. Sarah attempted to hide her yawn. Raven allowed the yawn full reign.

Sarah giggled.

"And here come our finalists, Sarah and Raven!" Sasha announced.

She took Raven's hand and they walked onto the set. They both gasped.

It had been transformed into a 1950s kitchen. Black-and-white checked tile. Old style ovens and refrigerators in cherry red. One of the stage designers handed them new aprons—pink ruffles for her, and lime-green gingham for Raven.

They changed into the new aprons and stood before the judges.

"You ladies, look great!" Sasha said. "Ready for our last competition's brief?"

Sarah and Raven answered in the affirmative. With lots of energy, as instructed by Sunny.

"Chef Amber, what is our finalists' last challenge?"

Raven's jaw tightened. Sarah squeezed her sister's hand.

"We're asking you both to step back into time and make an old-fashioned apple dessert. It can be a pie, strudel, cobbler, whatever family recipe or a new riff on it." Her smile looked sweet, but mischief danced in her eyes. "You have one hour and thirty minutes. Time starts, now!"

There was no way Sarah could do a strudel in an hour and a half. She stood before the stocked shelves. Not a true strudel.

What to do?

I need flour. Hefting the large glass canister, she half-walked, half-ran back to her station. Leaning on the counter, she exhaled loudly. *Father help me to focus on You. It's not like we're solving world peace, but ...*

"Great-great-grandmother's caramel apple pie."

"What?" Raven looked up from a cloud of flour coming from a bowl.

"I remembered our great-great-granny's World Peace Caramel Apple Pie."

"World Peace Caramel—"

Raven's pursed lips and scrunched brows made Sarah giggle.

"Apple Pie. Yes. Our great-great-poppi said if we sat warring leaders around a slice, they would all be buddies by the last bite."

Raven closed her eyes and shook her head. "You'll have to tell me more. Later."

Was it too simple? Sarah didn't care. She gathered the ingredients to make her crust. God had shown her what to bake. Win or lose, her last confection would be a tribute to their family.

As she cut the cold butter into the flour with her fingertips, she reminisced of her childhood Thanksgiving meals. Students unable to go home for the holidays filled their table, year after year.

Did Granny need to fill the table to make up for their missing family?

The flour's texture was ready for the remaining ingredients.

She separated an egg and added the yolk to another egg, a tablespoon of vinegar, then enough ice-cold water into the mixture until the dough was firm enough to make into ball.

She could hear Granny's warning: *Handle with care, dear one.*

Lord, please take care of Granny.

After wrapping the dough in plastic wrap, she ran it to the fridge. Several cartons of heavy cream sat on the top shelf.

Yes, she'd need cream for the caramel. And what else?

This Thanksgiving would be bittersweet. The sweetness of Raven's homecoming, mixed with the bitterness of their mother's death.

Traditionally, a giant scoop of homemade vanilla ice-cream was served over the warm pie. What if she made a more savory ice cream? She bundled several cartons of cream in her arms and scurried back.

Setting the cream on the counter, she shot another prayer about the ice cream.

Think, Sarah. What's on the menu for Thanksgiving, or Christmas? Turkey, stuffing, cra—cranberries!

Tart, sweet, refreshing. Spot-on.

Another trip to the produce supply, she found fresh cranberries, lemons, and oranges.

Raven ran past her with an armful of ingredients. A sheen of perspiration on her forehead, veins protruding in her neck and forehead.

Lord, please help my sister.

It was always the simple recipes that stumped chefs. Raven leaned her palms on the counter and looked at the mess. Apple and pear peelings, flour, sugar, cinnamon. Her puff pastry was in the refrigerator on its second lamination. The timing would be tight, even with the quick recipe.

Her plan was a French Apple Caramel Tarte Tatin. The saucepan held the apples and pears, simmering in the caramel sauce. Once the pastry was ready, she would lay it over the top and bake.

Was it enough? She rested her chin on her shoulder and watched Sarah. Her sister had made short work of peeling her apples and was making a caramel sauce. She'd also made a cranberry puree and seemed to have the ingredients for ice cream.

Raven bit her lip, then stopped before she drew blood. Would the judges grumble that their desserts both contained caramel? She had wanted to make a salted caramel ice cream, but maybe that wasn't a good idea.

"Raven," Sarah called out to her. "Just *do* it!" She dipped her chin and mouthed, "Make the ice cream."

Yes. She'd make the ice cream, which would make this the best apple tart she'd ever made.

"Bakers, forty-five minutes remaining." Sasha announced. "I'm getting whiffs of deliciousness."

Then she had better hurry.

Sarah stood next to Raven on their marks. Sasha stared off into the distance. The judges arranged their clothing or smoothed their hair. Two display cabinets on wheels were behind the sisters.

The first one held Raven's elegant apple tart.

On the second cabinet, her rustic, homey pie.

Rather than individual baker's tasting and judging, the powers-that-be decided she and Raven would bear witness to the success or failure of their offerings.

Sarah tried catching Raven's eye, but her sister was more interested in studying her shoes. It was as if her sister had rebuilt the wall around her heart.

"We're ready in three—" One of the camera guys yelled as he held up three fingers, then two, and then, he mouthed, *one*. He pointed to Sasha.

"We're back!" Sasha reanimated and swept his hand toward the panel of judges. "Judges, for this competition both bakers will receive their critiques."

Sarah worked a smile on her face as best she could. Raven showed no emotion.

"I'll tell you, judges—" using his cue cards, Sasha fanned himself. "The aromas for the last two hours have made me drool. Are you ready?"

The chefs affirmed.

"Then let's begin with Raven."

One of the stagehands rolled in Raven's display table. The aroma made Sarah's mouth water.

"Raven, what have you prepared?"

"Chefs, I have prepared a French Caramel Apple-and-Pear Tarte Tatin." She cut slices for four plates, winked toward Sasha, and scooped a generous ball of ice cream. "The final touch, homemade salted-caramel ice cream."

Raven stepped back as the customary silence ensued. The judges took their first bite. Chef Jean Paul poked at the puff pastry with his fork. "*Ees* this the quick pastry recipe?"

"Yes, Chef," Raven said. "Due to the time allotment, I couldn't make the traditional recipe."

He took another bite. "In any case, Raven, well done. I like the pairing of pears and apples. The salted caramel ice cream is—" He kissed his fingertips.— "*magnifique!*"

Sarah reached for Raven and squeezed her forearm. Part of Raven's upper lip lifted, then went back into neutral.

Sasha leaned on the judges' table. "Chef Amber, I have to say, I would never play poker with you. I can't read you at all."

Raven refrained from nodding. *Neither can I.*

Chef Amber's last critique had been glowing compared to Raven's previous encounters. But who knew what awaited her now?

"Well," Chef Amber began. "The Tarte Tatin was perfectly executed given the puff pastry wasn't traditional."

Raven bit her tongue. *And why was it impossible to execute a traditional pastry? Right. You only gave us ninety minutes.*

Chef Amber shrugged. "I mean, it was good. I'd order it again in any restaurant. It—" She waved her hand in the air, then looked toward the ceiling as if expecting angelic intervention. A condescending sigh and a lift of a shoulder, then, "It was good."

Great. Why not say you hated it? This tepid evaluation was like a slap in the face. No valuable takeaway. Nothing.

"O-o-kay." Sasha stood back and shrugged in Raven's direction. He pursed his lips and lifted his brows. "Chef Petra, what did *you* think of Raven's apple-and-caramel Tarte Tatin?"

"I have not had a Tarte Tatin as delicious as this in—oh, not since *Bistrot Paul Bert* in Paris." She gave a side-glance to Amber. "And I loved the ice cream, yes? Its savory notes, perfection to the sweetness of the tarte." She took another bite and moaned.

Raven's shoulders and stomach relaxed. She hadn't realized she was tense. "Thank you, Chef."

"When we come back," Sasha spoke to the camera. "Our judges will taste Sarah's confection. And we'll announce who is the Sweetest Rival!"

"Cut!"

Sunny stepped onto the set. "Don't move, folks. We're changing around the props and cart."

"You okay?" Sarah stepped into Raven's vision.

"Glad it's over." Raven exhaled. "Are you ready?"

Sarah moved closer and attempted to block the judges' view. "What's with Chef Amber?"

Raven moved her head to see if the chef in question watched them. "We have history from *Cupcake Rivalry*." Raven lifted a shoulder. "It is what it is."

"The other judges loved your tarte."

"Seemed to." Raven hugged her sister. The judges had better be kind to her sister, or Raven might have to knock a few heads together.

"Okay, places everyone." Sunny shouted. "Oh, Raven and Sarah, please change spots. It's easier for the camera guys. Thanks ever so."

The judges' table was cleared and ready for Sarah's desserts.

Please God, don't let them beat her up.

Sarah couldn't swallow. Her throat was as dry as week-old bread.

Sasha's lips moved, but a high-pitched ringing in her ears made it difficult to hear.

"Tell us about your apple dessert, Sarah."

Okay, I heard that.

Sarah cleared her throat. "I have prepared for you our family's World Peace Apple-and-Caramel Pie with fresh cranberry ice cream."

The judges laughed.

"World Peace?" Chef Jean Paul chuckled. "What does this mean?"

"My great-great-poppi said great-great-granny's pie was so good, if the world leaders sat down for a slice, they would all walk away friends." Sarah turned toward Raven and took her hand. "It's our great-great-grandmother's recipe, but Poppi was the one who named it." Raven squeezed back.

"Presumptuous perhaps?" Chef Amber's eyebrows raised—her lips now pursed.

"The proof will be on the plate, judges," Sasha said.

Sarah served four portions and scooped the cranberry ice cream next to the pie. She set a plate before each judge. The fourth plate was for the camera—eventually someone would polish it off like Raven's fourth plate during the break.

The judges examined the crust. From where she stood, it appeared flakey, but was it enough for them? One by one they ran their fork through the ice cream, then through the pie and into their mouths.

They chewed. Chefs Petra and Jean Paul closed their eyes and sighed. Chef Jean Paul took another bite of the pie.

"My goodness." Chef Petra laid her hand over her heart. "I'm back in my grandmother's kitchen and—" She waved her hand next to her now-moist eyes.

Sasha handed her an extra napkin. "Feeling sentimental, Chef Petra?"

"Oh my." She cleared her throat a few times, as she dabbed her eyes. "Jean Paul, please, you go."

Sarah's eyes teared. "I'm sorry, Chef."

All three judges and Sasha said, "No! Don't be sorry!"

"It's a good memory, Chef Sarah." The emotional judge leaned forward. "I loved my grandmother." She gestured toward both Sarah and Raven. "As you both love your grandmother, yes?"

Sarah laid her head on Raven's shoulder. Raven kissed the top of Sarah's head. They answered together, "Yes."

"Chef Jean Paul, what are your thoughts?" Sasha attempted to bring everyone back to the task at hand.

"The crust was delightfully flaky. What type of apple did you use?"

"Granny Smith and gala."

"Ah, good. The gala gave us a sweetness and blended well with the tangy Granny Smith." He smiled. "Was the Granny Smith choice also to commemorate your grandmother?"

Sarah giggled. "No. It's what we've always used as the base. Each of us have had our own preference for the sweet apple. Oh. And our great-great-grandparents had an orchard of Granny Smith."

"Delightful. Just delightful." He took another bite of the ice cream. "And the cranberry, do I taste orange juice?"

"Yes. Fresh squeezed."

"Perfect."

Sasha dipped his chin and winked at Chef Petra. "Was there anything else you wanted to add before we move on?"

She covered her mouth and finished her chewing. "It was as Chef Jean Paul said, 'Delightful.'"

Sarah focused on Chef Amber.

Sasha was right. No emotion could be read—good or bad. Her stomach churned. No doubt, the surly chef was ready to blast her.

Okay, Lord. Don't let me cry in front of America.

Please don't let me ugly cry.

Raven struggled to keep the tears at bay.

Hearing all the stories about Sarah's family—*her* family—played havoc with her mental state. She kept swiping errant tears.

Mercifully, because she and Sarah had switched places, she wasn't in the camera's direct line of sight.

Her nemesis, Chef Amber tapped a blood-red fingernail on the plate holding Sarah's dessert. If she said one hurtful thing to her sister, Raven would—*hmph*, the prissy chef wouldn't look so prim and proper with a plate of pie in her lap.

"Sarah, thank you—" Chef Amber began.

Sarah opened her mouth, then shut it. Raven's remained open.

"Thank you, Chef Sarah. You've baked a flavorful dessert using skilled techniques. However, what I'm most grateful for is you did it all with love."

Who are *you? And where are you hiding Chef Amber?*

"When you told your story—it is a true story, isn't it?"

"Yes." Sarah's brows raised. "Of course."

"You can't be so sure around here. Especially when the cameras are rolling." Chef Amber rested her elbows on the table and folded her hands. "You have given us a dessert which carries both history and innovation."

She turned toward Raven, her well-plucked eyebrows meeting. Chef Amber's disapproval balled its fist, ready for a fight. At least it was aimed at her and not Sarah.

"Too often chefs forget why we bake. It's not all about technique and expensive schools and awards and—"

"Wait a minute!" Sarah took a step forward, hands on her hips.

Sarah?

"Are you criticizing my sister because she worked hard to pull herself off the streets? Are you criticizing my sister because she doesn't have childhood memories to pull from because she was raised in crack houses? Yet somehow she was an *honor student* with a full scholarship to IA?"

Sarah took another step forward hands fisted. Raven tugged her back.

"Sarah, no."

Raven stroked her sister's back. Sarah's eyes popped open, as though she had awoken from a trance.

"I'm sorry." Sarah covered her lips with her hand. "Please forgive me."

"Cut!"

Raven rubbed Sarah's back as they sat on the greenroom couch. Sarah's head hung low.

"God forgive me," Sarah kept repeating. She raised her head and grabbed Raven's arms. "I'm so sorry I shared intimate details of your life. I had no right. Will they edit it out?"

Raven doubted it. It was way too juicy.

Did she want the world knowing her shame? No. But she couldn't deny her sister loved her and had her back. And she would give her life for Sarah.

Goosebumps raised on her arms.

The door to the greenroom opened, Sunny poked her head in. Lips pressed tight. Eyebrows uneven. "Is it safe to come in?"

"Sunny, please forgive me." Sarah stood. "Is the show ruined? Am I disqualified? Raven should win."

"Whoa, girlfriend." Sunny joined Sarah and Raven. "Let's sit down."

The three sat together. Sarah tucked herself against Raven. Raven laid a protective arm around her.

"I asked you to sit—especially you, Raven—because—" Sunny's brown eyes moistened— "Amber is in the other room, crying."

Raven's first reaction: No way.

"I need to go to her and apologize." Sarah attempted to stand. Sunny pushed her back.

"Ladies." Sunny looked intently at Raven. "Amber wants to apologize to both of you. Especially you, Raven, now that she knows your background."

"There *is* a God," Raven whispered, then inhaled sharply. "I'm sorry."

"No problem. This *is* kind of like a miracle." Sunny took Sarah's hand. "How about we give the poor woman a break and let her clear her conscience?"

Sarah pivoted toward Raven. "You okay with this? I'll forgive her no matter what, but you don't have to if you don't want to."

One week ago, Raven would have reveled in Amber's suffering. Today?

She was wrapped in a cocoon-like sensation of astonishment and compassion. It was weird and exciting.

"Yeah. Sure."

"Good—" Sunny stood and walked to the door. "She's waiting." Sunny opened the door.

I think I can, I think I can.

Chef Amber leaned around the doorway. The chef searched Raven's face—her lips trembling. "I'm so sorry, Raven. I had no idea."

Raven strode toward her, arms open. They hugged hard, nearly knocking the wind from each other. "I know. It's okay."

Sarah joined the huddle and more apologies followed.

It wasn't long before the other chefs and Sunny joined in—one big ball of crying and apologizing.

Raven couldn't help giggling. It wasn't long before the rest of the group were chuckling as well.

Okay. This is beyond weird. Did You do this, God?

Sarah squeezed Raven's hand. They stood on their marks for the last time. The poor make-up and hair people had to work overtime to clean up all the emotion from both bakers and judges.

A quick side-glance toward her sister, she wanted to tell Raven—for the thousandth time—she was proud of her. Her twin had been gracious and forgiving to Amber. The caustic chef wept in Raven's arms. Then the whole group had merged into a group hug.

Yet now they were poised and professional.

Sasha spoke to the lit camera. "Welcome back! What a judging, folks, but it's time to announce our first *Sweet Rivalry* winner!"

Raven whispered something Sarah couldn't hear.

"Please God, let it be Sarah."

"And the winner is ..."

Raven hated this forced suspense. It was so—

"Sarah Sweeting!"

Her sister froze, eyes bulged, mouth open.

Raven pulled Sarah into a hug. Her sister's arms came to life and wrapped tight around Raven.

"Me?"

But Raven couldn't answer, as her laughter and crying kept her from uttering a word.

Overhead a shower of confetti and balloons fell on them. Sasha was signing off. The judges once again joined the twins' huddle.

"Cut! That's a wrap!"

They weren't finished, they still had post-production interviews and several local morning shows interviews. But for now?

Raven was with her sister, celebrating a victory that had nothing to do with baking.

"I knew it! Congratulations!" Sunny jumped into the merriment. Briefly. She then checked her computer. "Don't forget dinner with the execs in a few."

Raven laughed. That was so Sunny.

Chapter 48

Drew's phone woke him.

He rubbed his eyes. Where *was* his phone? Oh yeah, still in his trouser pocket.

He checked caller ID. Untergarten. He shot from the bed, then looked again. The area code was 314. Why would the St. Louis office be calling? Were they assigned to let him down easy?

"This is Andrew Collar." Was his greeting professional enough to hide his fear?

"Mr. Collar, please hold for Ms. Lugar." Drew recognized the voice of Daphne's assistant, Erik.

"Of course." Drew slid to the floor. This was it.

"Gutten tag, Andrew!" She didn't sound upset.

"Gutten tag."

"Herr Luecker was impressed with you. Which, for me, I am disappointed."

"Disappointed?" *Uh-oh. Here it comes.*

"I had planned to offer you a position in our sales department here. However, it appears Germany may be offering you something in R&D. Still, I would like you to consider our offer." She continued discussing all the advantages of working in St. Louis and then made the salary offer.

Whoa! He grabbed a pen and wrote down the stock options, 401K, and other benefits on his palm. If his dream job weren't still possible, this was worth consideration.

No. He couldn't be distracted.

Still, don't burn any bridges.

"Thank you—" Drew stood and placed a hand on his hip. "I will consider this generous offer."

Not.

Chapter 49

Raven speed-dialed Granny's hospital room. She and Sarah sat, legs stretched, in the uncomfortable chairs at their gate. Their plane was delayed. They had a few precious minutes to give Granny the good news. Once it started ringing, Raven put the call on speaker.

"My sweet Raven! I've been trying to reach you and Sarah."

"Hey, Granny!" Sarah called out.

Raven grimaced. "Sorry. They've had us running from morning show to morning show."

"Oh my! How exciting!"

Sarah and Raven giggled. How long could they tease Granny?

"Girls! Now, stop! Did one of you win?"

They leaned closer to the phone. No sense in the whole airport knowing the secret.

"Sarah won, Granny."

"Oh, my goodness! Sarah?"

"Granny! You didn't think I could win?" Sarah stuck out her lower lip, then winked at Raven.

"You *both* should win! How about you, Raven?"

This is what it's like to have a grandmother? I like it.

"I came in second. It was the Sweeting twins in the finals."

They chatted about the show and Granny's health until they were called to board.

"We can't wait to see you." Sarah wheeled her suitcase toward the gate.

"I can't wait to hug my girls!"

"See you soon!" Raven pulled the telescope handle of her new rolling bag—which contained all the outfits and shoes she had worn—a gift from the producers of *Sweet Rivalry*.

Sarah was given hers as well. Somehow Raven didn't think her sister would be wearing them much.

"Love you, my sweet girls!"

"Love you, Granny," Raven and Sarah responded together.

They seemed to be doing that a lot lately. Saying the same thing at the same time.

Sarah walked ahead of her sister to the plane. How was this all possible? The best of her past had merged into the most impossible dream of a future.

She and Sarah settled into the plane's roomy leather seats.

Did all this good stuff have to do with the God who Asher and Sarah, and now Will, thought was so glorious?

She looked out the portal window as the plane taxied the runway. Was it all luck? Or was there a Father who loved her? Cared about her? Saw her among the billions of people on this earth?

Maybe it was time to investigate this further.

Her feet bounced as she sat on her shaking hands. How did she begin? She stared at Sarah, willing her sister to read her mind.

Sarah crossed her arms. "What's going on in that noggin of yours?"

"You'll never guess."

But maybe she wasn't ready just yet.

Asher pointed to a parking spot. Will pulled in and shut off the engine. They hadn't spoken most of the trip, unusual for Will.

Will palmed his keys and stared ahead.

"You okay?" Was Will still irritated with Asher?

"I've been thinking about what you said." Will kept his focus out the window. "We can't be the ones to tell Sarah about what Drew did."

Asher's stomach clenched. Were they about to argue again? "Yeah?"

"You're right." Will glanced at him. Asher could see the pain in his friend's eyes.

"But how are we gonna *not* say anything when we'll all be together, in close quarters, for over two hours?"

Lord, I need wisdom … Asher shifted in the cramped car until he was facing Will. "Please understand, it's difficult for me too. I've known Sarah practically my whole life. She's like my sister. But—"

"But it's not our place to tell her."

"Right."

"I don't know if I can keep my mouth shut." Will grunted. "It would take a miracle."

Asher chuckled. "Is your mouth more powerful than the Creator of the Universe?"

Will's arm flew out and nailed Asher on the stomach. "Oof!" He bent forward. "Okay, I deserved that."

"Sorry, buddy. I didn't mean to do that. I've picked up a few of Raven's bad habits."

They laughed as they headed to the terminal.

Lord, Will isn't wrong. We need a miracle to do what's right.

There she was. Will sighed like a schoolboy.

Sarah.

He bounced from foot to foot, trying to get a better view of her, willing the other people to get out of the way.

When she spotted him. Her eyes lit as she waved. "Will!" Then she waved in another direction. "Ash!"

Once Will spied Raven, she winked and raised her chin in greeting.

After the side hugs, Will and Asher took the ladies' rolling carry-on bags.

"Wait." Will halted. "Since when do you have fancy luggage? And a designer label to boot?"

Raven shrugged. "The show's producers gave it to me as a gift."

"And her bag is stuffed with designer clothes." Sarah wrapped her arm through Raven's.

Raven bumped against her sister. "Wait until you see Sarah's Barbie-doll wardrobe."

I would love *to see that. Stop it, Durning.*

The sisters laughed. A stereo of melodic tones Will could listen to forever.

Because of the additional luggage, he and Asher accompanied the weary travelers to baggage claim. As they all waited for the carousel to begin its rotation, Raven sidled next to him and laid her head on his arm.

This is new.

He lifted his arm and wrapped it around her. "What's up?"

She didn't look at him. "Can I sit up front with you? I need—I'd like to—I have questions."

What was this about? "Of course."

The buzzer sounded. The great metal belt stirred to life. Will watched Raven. She seemed—vulnerable.

After collecting the bags, they all headed to the car. The girls chatted about their flight and what they ate. Once Will squeezed the extra luggage into the trunk—reminding himself to never get a subcompact again—Sarah and Asher climbed in back.

"You guys want to stop for a bite before we get on the road?" Will spoke over his shoulder. "We won't get to Minersville until around midnight."

"Sure," came the replies from the backseat.

"Rave?" Will looked at his friend.

"Could we go to Steak 'N Shake?"

Asher Googled and found a Steak 'N Shake close to the airport. They placed their order and drove to the pickup window.

"Will, you certain you don't want to eat inside? You'll have to juggle your food." Sarah leaned against the back of his seat. He closed his eyes as the flowery scent of her hair wafted over him.

"Will?"

Raven pushed his arm. "Sarah's talking to you."

"No, I'm fine." He coughed. "I want to get on the road."

He passed the bag of food to Raven, who doled out the fries and burgers. The drink carrier he set on his lap and distributed sodas—and one Butterfinger shake to Raven. Will wolfed his burger down while waiting in the long line to exit the restaurant. He yawned as he pulled onto Lindbergh Boulevard and headed for the interstate. How would he stay awake?

His Dr. Pepper in his cup holder, he shoved a handful of fries into his mouth. Hot, salty, and crispy. He took a sip of his soda.

"How's your shake?" He worked to return his drink to the cup holder. Raven directed it in.

"It's great." She sipped and then held it. "I remember the first time I had this."

"A milkshake?" Sarah giggled.

"A Butterfinger shake." She ran her fingers through her hair. "My mother bought it for me when she took me away from Sarah."

Oh, man.

"What? Raven, what did you say?" Sarah leaned forward.

Will watched Sarah from the rearview mirror. Hunger for more details was written all over her beautiful face.

Raven fiddled with her straw, then took a sip. "I was crying because she took me and Henry away from you and Granny. And she left Henry's red sweater in your crib." She pivoted in her seat toward Sarah. "I remember waking in the backseat, scared. All I wanted was to go home."

Sarah stretched to reach for Raven's hand.

Oh, man. Breathe, Durning.

"She yelled at me. Then she pulled over, got out of the car, and screamed, 'Shut up!' She terrified me enough I stopped crying. She stayed out there for a while. Maybe she was using—or drinking. I don't know. She said I wasn't Rachel anymore."

"Rave." Will gripped the steering wheel, the burger he wolfed down threatening to come up.

Raven took another sip, rattled the cup, then put it in the cup holder. "We stopped in Eureka, and she bought the shake. By then she was nice and called me *honey* and *baby*. The shake was my breakfast and lunch." Raven turned toward the front.

Sarah still sat forward as far as her seatbelt allowed.

"I called out for you for days." Raven inhaled, then exhaled. "At one-point Lizzy began slapping me across the cheek anytime I mentioned your name or Granny's. At some point, she said she would come back for you, Sarah."

Sarah gasped. Will still felt like barfing.

Wait. He needed to pray. Right now. What his friend was revealing—remembering—was heartbreaking. How would she ever believe there was a loving Father still watching out for her? If he'd been through what she had, he didn't know if he could.

As Will prayed, he spotted Asher in the mirror, lips moving. He caught Will's eye and nodded.

Good.

"Our mother was a *horrible* person."

Sarah, no. Lord, protect Sarah's heart too.

Raven turned back toward her sister. "Oh, Sarah, don't." She reached to her. "What you said before made sense to me. Our mother was troubled. She was an addict. Somewhere deep inside, she wanted to be a good mother."

Raven sniffed, then wiped her nose on her sleeve. "Remember the egg-in-the-hole memory? Maybe there are more moments and memories like that for both of us."

"I hope so." Sarah's voice sounded like a lost little girl's.

It took all his inner strength to not pull the car over and hug her. Let her know how amazing she was.

How much he loved her.

No, son. Wait on me.

Lord?

Raven settled back into her seat. Sarah did the same.

In the rearview mirror, Asher caught Will's eye and mouthed, "*Keep praying.*"

God was doing something here. No stopping now.

Silence had filled the car for a while. Raven glanced toward the backseat. Her sister's head rested on the window, her eyes closed. The familiar soft snore drifted to Raven. Asher's head leaned back. His mouth open.

Adorable.

"Looks like they're sleeping."

Will squinted at the mirror and smiled. "Ash will sound like a hibernating bear if he doesn't close his mouth soon."

Raven chuckled.

"I'm sorry your memory was painful." Will patted her knee then grabbed his soda.

"It's okay. It was an important one."

"What triggered it?" He glanced at her, then set the cup back.

"When I handed Sarah her food. I remembered our mother passing me the shake."

"Wow."

"Yeah." She glanced back at Sarah. "I can't tell you what a relief it is to know I grieved being ripped from Sarah and Granny. There was a reason I had to eliminate them from my memory."

"Yet they were there the whole time. Safely tucked away until—maybe until you were ready to remember."

Will squeezed the steering wheel.

"You think God kept this memory for me? He decided this was the right time?" Raven observed her friend. He was so ... calm.

"Yes."

A simple answer from her once-complicated friend. Not sure what to think about that.

"I can't deny there have been some pretty strange things—like miracles—that have happened since we arrived. Sarah seeing us on *Cupcake Rivalry*, me loving to bake, and the Amber thing."

"What happened with Amber?"

Raven chuckled. "That's a whole other bizarre tale for another time."

"All I know, Will, is these memories have, like, a buffer around them. Other than the nightmare about Scarface, they've been easy to absorb."

"Which is good, right?"

"It's weird, but, yeah, it's good." She picked at her new jeans. "So, you believe this God has been there all this time?"

He exhaled. "Maybe it didn't seem so with everything you've been through, but yes, I do. There are too many good things interwoven into the bad to be coincidences. How could a kid raised in crack houses be such a good student? How did your foster parents know to take you for cooking and baking classes? Why were you passionate about baking?"

"Okay. I get what you're saying. But there were bad things that happened to me. There were—" Was she really talking about this?

She looked out her passenger window. They were in the middle of nowhere. Above them were millions of stars. The thumbnail of the moon. She cracked the window and inhaled the brisk, forest-scented air. Everything seemed so clean. Not like her.

"I did bad things, Will. I went to juvie for possession of drugs. I stole school supplies and food from stores." She took another deep breath. "If this God is so powerful, wouldn't He know what a mess I am?"

"Rave—" he stared at her until he had to concentrate on the road— "I was no boy scout. There were women. A *lot* of women." His cheeks turned bright red.

He was ashamed? Will?

"When I first met you at AI, I had plans to nail you. You're gorgeous and vulnerable and scrappy. But I couldn't. It was like my heart wouldn't let me—God kept me from taking advantage of you."

He had wanted to—

"Eww." She covered her mouth. She checked on Sarah and Asher. Other than Asher's head, which was now resting on the other window, they were still sleeping.

"What? You didn't think I was dreamy?"

Raven snickered. "I thought you were too pretty. Besides, I wasn't interested in anyone romantically. Until ..."

"Until the big man in the backseat?"

Raven slapped her hand over Will's mouth. "Stop it!"

"Okay. Okay." His voice muffled through her fingers. She pulled her hand away and wiped it on her thigh.

"How can God forgive me for all the stuff I've done?"

Will fidgeted in his seat. "Have you heard of Jesus?"

"I'm not stupid, Will. I've heard of Him. And not just as cuss words. The Gillians talked about Him and tried to get me to pray."

"Hold on. The Gillians are Christians?"

Oh. Raven's spine straightened. "That couldn't be a coincidence, right?"

"Asher says there are no coincidences."

Asher would know.

Raven laid her palm on Will's arm. "Tell me more about this Jesus."

Sarah let the tears flow. Her sister's hunger for the heavenly Father's love and acceptance was obvious.

Please, dear Father, get through to her. She needs You, like we all do.

Will's simple explanation of a Father willing to do anything for His children, even sacrifice His precious Son, was perfect. She couldn't have described it any better. The reality of the Son of almighty God, who was willing to leave His home and come to earth as a helpless baby, was making it difficult to not blubber out loud.

She longed to be the one to share the Good News with Raven, but in His infinite wisdom, God had selected her sister's best friend. The first person she had opened her heart to.

Yes. Will was the right one.

Gooseflesh prickled Sarah's arms, legs, neck. *Will was the right one.*

Was Will the one? For her?

The answer rose like a guiding light in the dark sky.

Yes, he was. Her cheeks warmed. Was her sister right after all? She was in love with Will?

Chapter 50

It was well past visiting hours—so what? They had to be at the bakery in a few hours, but Raven couldn't sleep if she tried. She wanted to see Granny.

Needed to see her.

"Slow down, Rave." Will and Asher, and Sarah were no match for her speed-walking.

She passed the nurses' station. Several looked up and were about to stop her when recognition flashed. They smiled and raised their collective thumbs.

Raven chuckled. Asher was right, living in a small town had its benefits.

Granny's room was the last on the right. As Raven approached, she noticed the lights were on. She knocked on the doorjamb. "Granny?"

Her grandmother squealed and reached for her. Raven ran into her arms and snuggled next to Granny.

"My sweet, sweet girl." Granny kissed the top of her head and held her.

A memory floated in like a fluffy, cotton-candy cloud.

Rachel was crying. Her knee was skinned. It hurted bad. Sarah had tried kissing the boo-boo, but it didn't work this time. She ran into the kitchen.

Granny turned from the stove. "What happened, my sweet girl?"

Between sobs, "I," Sniff. "Fell on the tree legs."

Granny knelt next to her. Pushing Rachel's curly bangs out of her eyes. "The tree legs?"

Rachel nodded.

Granny lifted her with a grunt and walked into the living room. They sat together on the rocking chair. Granny hummed and rocked and held her tight.

Sarah entered the living room, crying. "Is my Rachel okay? I couldn't fix her boo-boo, Ganny."

Granny reached out to Sarah. She snuggled on the other side of their grandmother's lap.

Rocking. Humming. Kissing.

All better now.

Was that real? Raven could almost feel the gentle rocking. She sniffed.

"I just had a memory." Raven said, not moving from the warmth of her grandmother's breast.

"Was it a good memory?" Sarah asked.

Raven stretched out her hand and clutched Sarah's, tugging her onto the bed. After an adjustment, they snuggled together.

Granny laughed. "You girls are getting too big to sit in my lap." The three giggled.

"What was the memory?" Sarah yawned.

"It was about the tree legs."

Granny gasped.

Raven lifted her head. "What?"

"Oh, dear Lord." Granny's heart beat rapidly through her thin gown.

"Granny?" Raven sat up.

Their grandmother took a deep breath, then exhaled. "Girls, you need to hear all of that memory."

Raven and Sarah both bit their upper lips.

"Raven, you came into the kitchen crying."

"Yes. You were at the stove, and I showed you my boo-boo."

Another deep breath and exhale. "You didn't see your mother sitting at the kitchen table, did you?"

What? "No, only you."

Granny shook her head. "You walked right past her. She wanted to comfort you. Stood to go to you." Granny caressed Raven's head. "But I was angry. She had come in late the previous night. Drunk.

"Father, forgive me, I didn't believe Lizzy deserved to comfort you—to be a mother to you."

"Oh, Granny." Raven was a kid—a toddler—at the time. But what child doesn't run to her mother first?

"Granny," Sarah sat up— "was mother still in the kitchen when I walked in? Because I didn't notice her either."

Granny's eyes closed. Her lips trembled.

Raven patted her grandmother's hand, then held it to her heart. "It's okay. We don't have to talk about this."

She shuddered. "No. God brought this up for a reason. Details are falling into place." She opened her eyes, determination pressed through. "Your mother wasn't in the kitchen by then. She had moved to the dining room. Sarah, you walked by her when you joined Raven and me in the rocking chair."

Sarah's brows scrunched. Her chin wobbled. "I did?"

"Yes." Granny's brows wrinkled and a vein on her forehead appeared. "I am ashamed to say I took a lot of satisfaction in that. I wanted to—I don't know—*guilt* her into changing."

"It didn't work." Raven covered her mouth with her hand. What Granny did seemed so cruel.

"No. It didn't. In fact, it had a terrible effect. Dear Lord, please forgive me."

Granny's face paled. Raven's heart raced and she moved toward Sarah.

Did they want to know? The sisters linked arms, waiting.

"Granny," Raven whispered. "You don't have—"

"Raven, your mother left with you that night."

Chapter 51

The bakery had been swamped with customers. Will recognized the regulars, but there were a lot of new faces. Once the news about Sarah and Raven returning hit the streets of Minersville, a line of people formed from the moment the bakery opened.

He yawned as he cleaned the display case for the night. They were all exhausted.

The sisters had fielded all the questions. Amazing what an expert Sarah had become at deflecting the question they all wanted answered: Who won *Sweet Rivalry*?

Will, Asher, and Granny were sworn to secrecy. Will supposed Sarah planned to announce the news to Drew later.

But Granny said nothing to the girls about their father's call, or Drew's role in the affair.

Drew had called Sarah. He was home with "wonderful news!" The jerk must have gotten his dream job.

Had Drew told Sarah what he'd done? Of course not.

Which meant the plan for him and Sarah to move to Germany was in play.

Will crushed the rag in his hand and gave it a pound on the shelf.

Sarah counted the cash. Will was not his usual chipper self. She had wanted to talk with him, but it had been crazy since they stepped through Sweet's doors at four o'clock that morning.

She recounted the ones for the third time—having come up with different totals each time.

Her ring finger was naked. Drew's engagement ring sat on her dresser. She dropped the money.

Focus, Sarah.

Raven swept by, moving a pile of crumbs. She stopped and kissed Sarah on the cheek, then nodded her head toward Will.

I know, Sis, I'll talk with him.

Her sister wiggled her brows and moved on.

Will looked up from his task. Those beautiful green eyes drawing her. What was she waiting for?

"Will?" She stuffed the cash back into the register and closed the drawer. "Will, can we talk?"

His head lifted. He searched her face. A smile formed.

The bakery phone rang. "Don't answer it!" He ran toward Sarah.

Raven looked up from sweeping. "It's okay, I'll get it. You two talk."

"Thank you, for letting us know." Raven slammed down the phone. "This will devastate Granny. We have to go home, Sarah!"

Sarah grabbed Raven's arm. "Why? What happened?"

"That was the journalist we spoke to last week. She said the police are at our house looking for drugs!"

Sarah stood with Raven, Asher, and Will—and the rest of the neighborhood—in front of their home. Flashing blue, red, and white lights everywhere. The front door was open and askew. Police officers entered and exited.

Will's arm held her. She leaned against his firm chest, his heartbeat grounding her in the midst of this madness.

Officer Sue from church caught Sarah's eye then looked down. She paused to talk to another cop then made her way to Sarah.

Sarah extended her hand, then retrieved it. "Sue, can you tell us anything?"

The officer rested her chin on her shoulder looking behind her, then grimaced. "Someone called in a tip about drugs on the premises."

"What! What a pile of—!" Will shivered.

Who would do something so hateful?

Raven tugged on Sarah's jacket and pulled her aside. "Could someone know about mom's stuff? Maybe someone spotted the note I wrote."

Sarah's stomach clenched like a pack of rats invading a bakery. Oh, no.

A tap on her shoulder made Sarah jump. She turned to Officer Sue.

"Sarah, I have to get back. If I'm allowed to share anything, I'll let you know."

"Thanks." Sarah stepped closer to Raven, her heart rising to her throat. "*What* note? Did you put it in the box we buried?"

Raven's hands went to her mouth. "Remember, I put the bags in the freezer until I could come home and figure out what to do?"

Sarah had been sick, she barely recalled anything. "All I remember is you and I putting bleach in the baggie and burying it in the box mom made. Under the tree."

Raven dragged her fingers through her hair. "I left a note saying the drugs were in the freezer. And something else—"

Raven crossed her arms over her head. "I wrote something like I'd deal with them later."

"I never saw a note, Raven." *Where could it have gone?*

Raven paced in circles. Her arms still crossed over her head. She stopped. "It wasn't there when we were in the kitchen, was it? I would have remembered."

"Who would have taken it? No one else was there—"

Sarah gasped. No, that wasn't true. Someone else was there. Someone she'd called and asked to come.

Drew.

Drew mingled in the crowd of bystanders. He held his cell above people's heads, recording the events. Maybe he could sneak into the backyard for a closer look.

This was rich! Raven getting her just desserts. The perfect icing on the cake of his success. Sarah's worried expression was necessary—for now. But the front door? He hadn't expected the cops to damage Granny's property.

Why were they searching the whole house? The tip he gave to Lewis's cop brother was that Raven buried the drugs in the backyard, under the tree.

Just then, someone yelled over the fence. "We found something!"

At last. He chuckled.

He looked toward Raven. Asher had his arm around her—and she looked good and scared.

Sarah—

What?

Will had Sarah locked into an embrace. Did he just kiss the top of her head?

No, he didn't!

Drew shoved his way through the crowd. His eyes fixed on Will, his mind imagining how he would hurt him.

Two police officers approached Sarah and Raven. He couldn't see the sisters' faces, but the officers escorted them away.

No! This wasn't supposed to happen! Not to Sarah!

Chapter 52

Raven and Sarah sat arm-in-arm at the police station's interrogation table. The two-way glass facing them. What anonymous person watched them? Judged them?

Four other empty chairs sat around the table.

Poor Sarah shook as though she sat on an iceberg. Raven, unfortunately, had had experience with all this.

Still, she could think of twelve million other places she'd rather be.

Of course, the police had found the box, and of course there were no other drugs in the house. Of course, it wouldn't matter.

Not for her. Because of her record.

The door opened and a guy in an expensive suit, carrying a briefcase, entered. Raven rolled her eyes. A lawyer. *Will, what did you do?*

"I'm Philip Auner, your attorney." He dragged one of the chairs next to Sarah. "Have you said anything to the police?" He unbuttoned his jacket, set his case on the table, then sat.

"Did Will hire you?" Raven eyed him. She'd never trusted these guys.

He needlessly adjusted his red tie. "Mr. Durning has retained my services for your defense, that would be correct."

"Right. Couldn't you have simply said yes?"

Sarah swiped at Raven's hand. "Behave. I'm glad he's here."

Raven patted Sarah's arm. Her sister needed to leave this to her.

"Listen, I know you're merely doing your job, but let's not make this more complicated than it is."

He raised one plucked brow and pushed out his jaw. "And what is uncomplicated about the raid on your grandmother's home and the police taking as evidence a box containing suspicious substances?"

Raven flopped back against her chair. Okay. There was that.

The door opened again. An older plain-clothes officer entered, holding a clipboard. "Ladies, I'm Lieutenant Billy Sawyer, and I'm sorry for this mess."

He lifted his brows toward the lawyer, "Auner."

Thank You, God. Raven had never meant anything more in her life. Sarah hugged Raven's arm.

Lt. Sawyer dropped his clipboard on the table with a clatter and massaged his temples. "We received a not-so-anonymous tip that there were drugs buried in your backyard." He flipped a small piece of paper clipped to the board back and forth.

My note! She glanced at Sarah. Sarah mouthed, "Your note?" Raven nodded.

"This little guy was what prompted a more thorough search. That, and you, young lady—" He gave Raven the cop look. "And your time in juvie."

She swallowed. "But no convictions."

He pinched the bridge of his nose. "Right. No convictions. On the surface, it ticked all the boxes." His one cheek dimpled. "Listen, I read the full reports on you. What you endured at the hands of your mother—" He looked away. "Lizzy wasn't always like that."

Raven stared at her hands, willing herself not to cry. *Did* everyone *know?*

"You and Mom went to high school together, right, Lt. Sawyer?" Sarah tightened her hold on Raven's arm. Sarah's fear had vanished, in its place, something—

Auner cleared his throat. "How about releasing these ladies, Lieutenant."

Lt. Sawyer raised his hand to silence the lawyer. Raven was beginning to like this guy.

"I have one question, why the box? You destroyed the drugs—decimated them. Which was well done, by the way. Why bury it and not throw it in a dumpster somewhere?"

Auner leaned toward Raven. "You don't have to answer."

"Chill." Raven turned to Sarah, let her gaze ask if she could explain. Sarah nodded, her gentle smile encouraging her.

"Our memories of our mother are not the best, Lt. Sawyer." Raven shifted her gaze to the cracked and chipped Formica table. "A few have surfaced that have helped us forgive her, like the box. She made it."

Raven glanced at Sarah. Her sister lifted one side of her rosebud lips. "Originally the box held baby bracelets she had made for us when we were born, as well as locks of our hair." Raven touched her hair, then attempted to clear the emotion from her throat. "Anyway, things a mother who loved her kids would hold on to."

Sarah's face was now covered in tears, but peace shone in her blue eyes. If ever there was a representation of the love of this Jesus, it radiated from her sister.

Jesus. He was here, wasn't He? The same warmth she felt that night she prayed in the bathroom was here. Her heart skipped.

"Sarah didn't get to say goodbye to Mom. Lizzy died—*Mom* died in my arms, but I was in shock and angry and didn't understand she was only human. A person who had lost her way. And we hope—you know, Sarah and I hope on that day ten years ago ..."

Raven closed her eyes and took a shaky breath, then exhaled.

She could tell them her mother had hid the drugs in her cherished teddy bear. She could share all the sordid details of her mom's poor decisions, but she wouldn't. Out of respect for Elizabeth Anna Sweeting.

The warmth grew within her.

"Sarah and I hope and pray that on that day, our mother finally found her way. So, we destroyed the symbol of her past, and buried it in the reminder of her love."

Was her explanation enough? She opened her eyes.

Sarah pulled Raven into an embrace. "Jesus loves You so much, Sissy."

Raven squeezed her sister. "I know." And she was beginning to think she loved Him too.

Raven chanced a look at the officer. He rubbed his eyes with his forearm. Auner pulled a handkerchief from his pocket and blew his nose.

"You both have been through enough unhappiness for a lifetime." He reached across the table and shook their hands. "It's a privilege to meet you."

The lieutenant shook the lawyer's hand. "Auner, these remarkable young women may have enough evidence to sue the pants off that not-so-anonymous tipper."

Auner's eyes lit like a Christmas tree.

Asher! Raven ran past Sarah and Will as they descended the stairs of the Minersville Police station. Past the annoying reporters calling out questions. Past the onlookers and straight into Asher's open arms.

He lifted and spun her, laughing and thanking God until she couldn't catch her breath. She held tight, marveling how their hearts beat in unison.

"Asher." Her voice muffled against his leather jacket. He set her down, his brown eyes exploring hers.

"I'm free."

"I heard. We've been pray—"

She placed her fingers over his full lips, feeling the rough stubble of his unshaven face. "No, Asher—" she cupped her hand around his cheek. "I'm *free.*"

His brows pinched together, then understanding shown bright. "Because of Him?"

She nodded.

He lifted her and spun her again. She held on tight.

Holding tight to Asher. Yes, I might just do that for the rest of my life.

Sarah held Will's arm as she descended the stairs of Minersville Police station. A bevy of reporters called out to them as they walked toward the parking lot. Mr. Auner had said it was best to not say anything—he'd manage things now.

She was happy to oblige.

She spotted Raven and Asher. He spun her in circles. She could hear her sister's laughter from several rows of cars away.

Thank You, Lord. My sister is free!

Before they left the interrogation room, Sarah prayed with her twin to ask Jesus into her heart. No fancy words. Just, "I'm Yours. We'll figure out the rest as we go along."

Her sister was so brave. Sarah couldn't wait to learn from her—here, in Minersville.

Will opened the passenger-side door, his hand resting on the small of her back.

Sarah hesitated. *Will is the one.* "Will?"

Be brave like Raven.

He turned toward her, those emerald eyes sparkling, even in the harsh parking lot lights. "Hmm?"

She wrapped her arms around his neck and drew his handsome face to hers. Her lips found his and lingered against his warmth. His arms encircled her waist and pulled her closer.

When they finally broke away, they were breathless.

"Woo-hoo! It's about time!"

Sarah would recognize that voice anywhere. She and Will laughed and waved at Raven and Asher as she climbed into Asher's truck.

"Sarah?"

She turned.

Drew stood a few feet from her and Will. "What is *this?*"

Mr. Auner had discovered who the anonymous tipper was and told her and Raven. If Sarah were honest with herself—and she promised from this day forward she would be—she knew Mr. Andrew Collar was the tipper.

Drew stepped toward her. Sarah held up her palm. He stopped and studied her. His lip curled, and his brows pressed together. There was no remorse in his countenance for the pain he caused.

If she weren't so relieved by the outcome, she might have been angrier.

She stared at him until his fair complexion reddened and his eyes turned away.

Will helped her into the car.

Together, they left the chaos behind and drove to the hospital to tell Granny all was well.

Epilogue

Sarah sat next to Will with Asher next to Raven as they waited for the first episode of *Sweet Rivalry* to air on YBN. Two teddy bears sat between her and her sister. Henry, Raven's bear, was restuffed. A gift from the local seamstress Sarah had taken him to. Reunited with his bright red sweater, Henry looked mighty dapper.

Granny, healthy and enjoying her semi-retirement, sat on a new recliner, her feet up.

A large basket of cookie flowers from YBN sat on the coffee table—several already missing. It had arrived accompanying the contract for a new reality series featuring Sarah and Raven and Sweet's Bakery.

Hit or not, it sounded like fun to Sarah and Raven.

Sunny had called them every day to make sure they hadn't changed their minds. And to ask questions about their faith.

The oven timer buzzed. Raven jumped up. "My pie!"

Asher followed her into the kitchen. A few seconds later, he whistled. "That is, no question, the best-looking World Peace Apple-and-Caramel Pie."

Sarah called out, "*Award-winning* World Peace Apple and Caramel pie."

They all laughed.

Sarah folded her hands in her lap. Will took one hand and brought it to his lips. "Nervous?"

"Of course. You may have second thoughts about being my partner at the café after watching my televised fit."

He kissed her hand again. "I am confident of being your partner in any and every endeavor." He waggled his brows. "And I love it when you're feisty."

Her face heated as she returned the kiss.

"Okay, you love birds." Asher and Raven returned to the couch. "Pay attention, two of the most gorgeous women in the world are about to be seen on the screen."

"Oh, I like the theme music," Granny said.

"Awk, look how short my hair is!" Raven curled her now shoulder-length light brown hair behind her ear.

Asher kissed the top of her head. "You're beautiful no matter what length your hair." He cleared his throat. "Or color." Raven tenderly elbowed him.

An hour later, the group alternately wiped their tears and laughed as they headed to the kitchen for pie. Raven arrived first.

Did she do a good job on the family recipe—which had no written recipe? It was Granny and Sarah showing her how to make the pie—until she could do it in her sleep.

Granny had helped her learn the feel of the dough. Would she be as good as Sarah one day? It didn't matter, as long as it tasted good.

"Raven, the crust is perfect!" Sarah said as she cut into the pie.

Raven's face heated, the smile pushing tears into the corners of her eyes. "Shall I make coffee?" Raven opened the cabinet over the coffeemaker. She was about to reach for the bakery's newest roast—*Sweet Sunshine*.

Everyone called out, "Decaf!"

Raven pulled the other bag of beans labeled, *Good Night, Sweets.*

The house phone rang.

"Who would call at this hour?" Granny punched the speaker button, then opened the freezer to pull out the freshly churned salted-caramel ice cream. "Hello."

"Hello?" The voice sounded like it came from a trashcan. "Hello? Is this Mrs. Hope Sweeting's home?"

Raven turned from making coffee. "Yes, who is this?"

"Is this Sarah or Raven?"

Will leaned toward the phone. "Who wants to know?"

Sarah shushed Will.

Several voices whispered from the other end.

"Hello?" Sarah placed a slice of pie on a plate.

Granny scooped ice cream. "Probably one of the kids from church."

"Sarah and Raven?" The voice was breathless. "We are your sisters and brother. Your half-sisters and half-brother."

Raven dropped the bag of coffee, scattering shiny beans everywhere.

"What?" Sarah grabbed Raven's wrist.

"Our father is Howard Oscar too. My name is Fabienne, I'm sixteen. We live in Bern, Switzerland."

Sarah gasped.

Raven moved closer to the phone. Was it possible?

"We're here, Fabienne." Raven didn't know what else to say.

"My name is Seraina, I will be thirteen in two months." Seraina's sweet voice had a beautiful accent.

"*Und* I am your brother!" A young male voice shouted. Feminine voices whispered. "Ja, *mein*—my name *ist* Leinhard! I am seven!"

The kitchen broke out in laughter.

Two sisters and a little brother? Raven couldn't speak around a dinner roll-sized ball of emotion.

"Fabienne, Seraina, and Leinhard, we're so excited to meet you," Sarah said. "Is—is your father there?"

Raven glanced at Sarah. Did he know his children were making this call?

"This is Fabienne. Ja. Our father is here." A pause. More whispering. "Yes, he said he cannot talk right now. I am sorry."

Raven and Sarah exchanged sad looks. Raven understood not being ready.

Raven reached for Sarah and wrapped her arm around her waist. "It's okay. Don't worry, Fabienne. Are you in high school?" Raven pulled her sister to the kitchen stools.

One by one, everyone left Raven and Sarah to chat with their newly discovered family.

The four sisters spoke long into the night, Leinhard having grown tired of "too much girl things."

The younger sisters wanted to know about the show—they had watched the first episode too. What was it like to meet Chef Petra—one of their local favorites. They were proud of Sarah for standing up for her sister.

Raven wanted to record every moment of the conversation. Another life-altering moment.

One never knew when God would bring a blessing—even from another country.

They wanted to know about the horrible man who had come to their house and who had accused Raven and Sarah of horrible things. Sarah assured them Drew was out of the picture.

Once they had exchanged cell numbers and friended each other on social media, Sarah and Raven planned to fly out to Switzerland in the summer.

Perhaps their father would be ready to meet by then.

"Mutti says we must say *auf weidersein* for now." Fabienne sniffed.

"We'll talk again soon, dear sisters." Raven blew her nose.

"We love you. Please give Leinhard a hug from us too." Sarah grabbed a handful of tissues from the box Will had set on the counter for them.

"We will, dear sisters," Seraina said.

"We love you," Raven managed to choke out.

"Oh! Yes! We love you too! *Ciao!*" Fabienne cried.

Sarah walked toward the phone and reached out to disconnect the call.

"I look forward to meeting you."

A mature male voice.

Raven held her breath. *Our father?*

Sarah's hand shook.

"Father?" Raven said.

Silence. Sarah turned to Raven. Raven could see the longing in her sister's eyes. And she knew it was in hers as well. *Please, God, give him courage.*

"Yes." He cleared his throat. "I will see you soon, yes?"

The twins nodded first to each other, then together they said, "Yes, Father."

Sweet Rivalry
Questions for Discussion (Spoiler Alert)

1. Sarah and Raven are very different. Discuss how they are different.

2. Yet the sisters are similar in many ways. Discuss those similarities.

3. Sarah's childhood was filled with love and warmth and acceptance. Granny loved her and raised her in a Christian household. Yet, Sarah felt rejected her whole life. Why do you think that is? Have you felt like Sarah?

4. Lizzy chose to kidnap Raven. Why do you think she didn't take both sisters? Why choose Raven? Discuss.

5. Both sisters had "brother" figures in their life. Raven had Will. Sarah had Asher. Have you had brother or sister figures in your life? Or perhaps mother or father figures? Did they help or hinder you? How?

6. We know Sarah struggled with rejection. How did that affect her behavior? Especially in her relationships?

7. Raven struggled with trusting people. How did that affect her behavior?

8. Drew, Sarah's boyfriend had exciting plans for them. Several things were missing from those plans. Discuss.

9. Raven did not trust Drew almost immediately. Why do you think she deemed him untrustworthy, even before the bad blood developed between them?

10. There were many emotional scenes in *Sweet Rivalry*. One of the most emotional scenes I wrote was the "burial" scene when Raven and Sarah symbolically said their final good-byes to their mother. How did that scene affect you? Why?

11. Another emotional scene was the scene, when Raven discovered the drugs that her mother had hidden inside her teddy bear. How did it affect Raven? How did it affect Sarah?

12. There are many reasons why the teddy bear is so important to Raven. Discuss the ones most obvious to you.

13. Granny is a Godly woman. She loves the Lord and her granddaughter. But Granny had many secrets. How did those secrets affect Sarah? Raven? Lizzy?

14. Have you ever kept a secret—thinking it was protecting a loved one—but it had the opposite effect? How did that play out? What did you learn?

15. I debated how and when and with whom Will would accept Jesus as his Messiah and Savior. I finally decided that the unconventional Will would have a very conventional experience. What did you think of that scene?

16. Despite that decision with Will, I did want Raven to have an unconventional conversion. What did you think of that scene?

17. Before Raven's conversion, Will shared the Good News in a very Will way. Discuss how it was different than the pastor's message. Discuss how it was the same.

18. Lizzy had an addiction to drugs and alcohol. Do you know someone with an addictions problem?[1] Did you know there are support programs for loved ones who have an addict in their life?[2]

19. Another bittersweet scene between Raven and Sarah was the morning of the breakfast "hug." How did you feel about Lizzy's "hug" with Raven?

20. Drew's trip to Europe was quite eventful. Why do you suppose Drew thought he would receive a warm welcome from the sisters' biological father, Howard?

21. When the sisters are invited to compete on the new baking show *Sweet Rivalry*, the producers wanted to pit the twins against each other. Discuss why they may have done that?

22. What was the outcome of the network's attempts to create rivalry?

23. In the epilogue, the sisters receive a surprise phone call. What were your feelings about that call?

24. What was your favorite scene?

25. Who was your favorite character?

26. Other than Drew, which character bothered you the most?

---

1   Alcoholics Anonymous (AA) is an international fellowship requiring no membership dues or fees dedicated to helping alcoholics peer to peer in sobriety through its spiritually inclined Twelve Steps program.[1][2][3] Non-professional, non-denominational, self-supporting and apolitical, an avowed desire to stop drinking is its sole requirement for membership. www.aa.org

2   Al-Anon's primary purpose is to help families and friends of alcoholics, rather than stopping alcoholism in others or assisting with interventions. https://al-anon.org/

27. Which recipe from the book would you like to try? (There are a few in the back pages.)

28. Which sister do you think will get married first? Why?

29. What is your takeaway from *Sweet Rivalry*?

30. How would you see the sisters in five years?

Have any questions?

Have a book club, I'd love to "visit" in person or via zoom.

Feel free to email me at terri@terrigillespie.com

About the Author

An award-winning author and beloved speaker, Terri Gillespie writes stories of faith and redemption to nurture women's souls. Her novels, devotionals, and blogs have drawn readers to hunger for a deeper relationship with their Heavenly Father.

Life is a journey. Terri lived in fear most of her life. Stories helped her see life through the lens of adventure and God's abiding love. Those stories changed her life. They empowered her to be brave. She hopes hers will do the same for you.

She is the author of critically-acclaimed *Making Eye Contact with God*, award-winning *She Does Good Hair, CUT IT OUT!, Really Bad Hair Day*, and award-winning, *Sweet Rivalry*.

Terri loves to keep in touch with her readers and has special goodies for her subscribers.

- Her newsletters: https://authorterrigillespie.com/
- BookBub: https://www.bookbub.com/authors/terri-gillespie-03735cb1-12a1-470f-8caa-467d4113919d

- Her YouTube Channel gives insights into new books and interviews with bestselling and award-winning authors—who give books away!: https://www.youtube.com/channel/UC2iMKu7zt6wB4vmPKqsM7EA
- Facebook:https://www.facebook.com/AuthorTerriGillespie
- Twitter: https://twitter.com/TerriGMavens
- Pinterest: https://www.pinterest.com/terrilgillespie
- Goodreads: https://www.goodreads.com/author/show/2775460.Terri_Gillespie
- MeWe: https://mewe.com/i/terrigillespie

Sweet Rivalry Recipes

The Recipe That Almost Won the *Cupcake Rivalry* competition for Raven and Will.

RAVEN'S CHOCOLATE DR PEPPER CUPCAKES

INGREDIENTS:

- 2 cups all-purpose flour
- 1 tsp baking soda
- ¼ cup unsweetened cocoa powder
- 1 cup unsalted butter softened
- 1 cup granulated sugar
- ½ cup brown sugar packed
- 2 eggs room temperature
- 2 tsp vanilla extract
- 1 cup Dr Pepper
- ½ cup buttermilk

WILL'S FRITOS CREAM CHEESE FROSTING

- 4 cup powdered sugar
- ½ cup unsalted butter softened
- 6 oz cream cheese softened
- 4 T Dr Pepper to taste

Original, Regular flavor Fritos (up to 1 cup)—Don't use the scoop type

INSTRUCTIONS:

1. Preheat the oven to 350° F. Prepare 2-12 count muffin tins with cupcake cup liners (22-24 total).
2. In a medium bowl, sift together flour, baking soda, and cocoa powder. Set aside.
3. Using a stand mixer (or a hand mixer and large bowl), add in butter, granulated and brown sugars, eggs, and vanilla. Beat on low until fluffy, about 2-3 minutes.
4. Keeping mixer speed on low, add half of the dry ingredients to the wet ingredients. Mix in the Dr Pepper.
5. Add the other half of the dry ingredients as well as the buttermilk. Mix until just combined—do not overmix. Batter should be thick and fluffy.
6. Pour cupcake batter into prepared muffin tin, filling cups 2/3 full. Tap the tin on the counter a few times to level the batter.
7. Bake cupcakes one batch at a time for 18-20 minutes, or until a toothpick comes out clean.
8. Place muffin tin on a wire cooling rack to cool for 5-10 minutes, then remove cupcakes and allow to finish cooling on wire rack.
9. Wait until cupcakes are completely cooled before applying the frosting.

WILL'S FRITOS CREAM CHEESE FROSTING

1. Use a clean stand mixer (or a hand-mixer & large bowl) on high speed beat the softened butter until smooth and creamy, roughly 2 minutes.
2. Drop speed to low and slowly add the powdered sugar. May be clumpy at this stage—don't worry.
3. Keeping speed on low, slowly beat in softened cream cheese. Will recommends cutting the cream cheese into 4-5 pieces and mixing in one piece at a time.
4. Finally, add in the Dr Pepper. Now if you want more Dr

Pepper flavor, you can add more, and you can add up to a cup more of powdered sugar, but after that, you lose the great cream cheese flavor.

5. Finely ground ½ cup of Fritos. Almost as fine as coffee grounds. Fold in by hand into frosting.
6. Frost the cupcakes.
7. Remaining Fritos you can either roughly ground and sprinkle on top, or Will likes to leave one Frito curl nestled on top, right before serving.
8. Eat immediately—I mean, who would wait?

RAVEN'S VEGAN, SOY-FREE, NUT-FREE FUDGE, MINT AND RASPBERRY CUPCAKES

These mini-cupcakes flew off the shelf at Sweet's Bakery.

CUPCAKES:

- 1 cup coconut milk
- 1 Tablespoon white vinegar
- 1 cup gluten-free all-purpose baking flour
- ½ cup unsweetened cocoa powder
- ¾ teaspoon baking soda
- ½ teaspoon double-acting baking powder
- ¼ teaspoon plus 1/8 teaspoon xanthan gum
- ¼ teaspoon salt
- ¾ cup sugar
- 1/3 cup vegetable oil
- 1-1/2 teaspoon pure vanilla extract
- Mint Frosting [add bullets]
- ½ cup vegan butter
- 3 cups confectioners' sugar
- 2 Tablespoons coconut milk
- 2 teaspoons mint extract
- ½ teaspoon vanilla bean paste
- ¼ teaspoon salt

RASPBERRY COMPOTE

- 1 cup fresh raspberries
- 1 Tablespoon sugar
- Chocolate Ganache [add bullet]
- 1 cup vegan chocolate chips

DIRECTIONS:

For the cupcakes:

1. Preheat oven to 350° F. Line a 12-cupcake pan with cupcake liners.
2. Combine coconut milk and vinegar and set aside. In a separate bowl, sift together baking flour, cocoa powder, baking soda, baking powder, xanthan gum, and salt.
3. In a large bowl combine the sugar, oil, and vanilla extract with the milk and vinegar mixture and beat with electric mixer for 1 minute. Add the dry ingredients to the wet ingredients and mix thoroughly.
4. Fill cupcake liners ¾ full of batter, tap the pan on counter to level batter. Bake until tops spring back when touched, about 22 minutes.
5. Cool cupcakes completely.
6. Once cool, remove cupcakes from paper liners and cut horizontally in half creating two pieces—like a sandwich.

For the Frosting:

1. Whip butter until it is white and creamy, about 3 minutes.
2. Add confectioners' sugar 1 cup at a time until thoroughly combined.
3. Add coconut milk, mint extract, vanilla bean paste, and salt. Mix until smooth.
4. Put frosting in a piping back (or use a zip lock bag) and cut ½ inch off the tip.

For the Compote:

1. Combine raspberries and sugar in small skillet and cook over low heat for 10 minutes, stirring occasionally. Remove from heat and let cool.
2. For the Ganache
3. In a small saucepan, melt the chocolate chips over low heat, stirring frequently. Remove from heat and let cool until it is still warm and easy to spread.

To Assemble:

1. Lift top off a cupcake and generously frost the bottom with mint frosting.
2. Drizzle with raspberry compote and replace top.
3. Spread approximately 1-1/2 Tablespoons of ganache on top.

OPTIONAL

If you're not concerned with glutton issues, take thin mints Girl Scout cookies and crush into crumbles. Sprinkle on top.

EGG-IN-A-HOLE
ALSO KNOWN AS GRANNY'S AND LIZZY'S HUG

The breakfast that was a breakthrough for Raven—both with Lizzy and Sarah.

For each serving:

- 1 fresh egg (room temperature)
- 1 slice of bread (a large slice, ½" thick of sourdough is awesome—that's what Sarah used)
- Butter (softened)
- Round biscuit or cookie cutter

Directions:

1. Tablespoon Butter in an iron skillet and melt on medium.
2. In the meantime, crack an egg into a small bowl.
3. Using a biscuit or round cookie cutter, cut a hole in the center of the bread. (Be careful to not get too close to the edges of the bread).
4. Butter both sides of the bread, including the piece from the "hole."
5. Place the bread and hole piece in the skillet—be sure the pan is hot, and the butter melted.
6. Add a pat of butter into the hole and let it melt.
7. Carefully place the egg in the hole.
8. Cook until the yolk is white, but the yolk is still runny, then gently flip over. Flip over the little round hole piece, too. (The little hole piece is a great way to check to see if the bread has browned enough, but it does take a bit of finesse)
9. Cook only a minute or two on this side.
10. Remove from pan and enjoy!

If you want to enjoy like Raven and Sarah, utensils optional. However, I recommend utensils.

Our family saves the little round hole piece as "dessert." Place a dollop of jam or jelly and enjoy the extra goodness. Apple butter is the best!

More delicious recipes on www.authorterrigillespie. com/bonusfeatures